# Assassination in Al-Qahirah

## The Third Book of Talon

# Assassination in Al-Qahirah

## The Third Book of Talon
## By James Boschert

www.Penmorepress.com

**Assassination in Al-Qahirah** -By James Boschert

Copyright © 2011 by James Boschert



Edition 2 - 2013   420p

ISBN: 978-1-942756-163  Paperback
ISBN: 978-1-942756-17-0  Ebook

BISAC Subject Headings:

FICTION / Action & Adventure
FICTION / Historical
FICTION / Thrillers

*Address all correspondence to:*

Michael James
920 N Javalina PL
Tucson, AZ 85748
mjames@penmorepress.com

1.0

# Contents

# Glossary

Al Andalucia: Arab Spain

Al Qahirah: Cairo city

Al Iskandrîyah: Alexandria city

Annessa: Miss

Batinis: One of many names for the Hashashini Ismaili

Berber: Tribal people of North Africa. Fanatical Islamists

Bezat: Byzantine Gold coin (devalued)

Bir: Water well

Dinar: Gold coin of the Egyptian and Arab world

Dirham: Small copper coin

Dronan: One- or two-masted war galley with either one or two rows of oars. Originally designed by the Byzantines, it was copied by the Arabs for their navies.

Emir: Prince

Baklava: Light pastry

Hadith: Statements regarded by traditional Islamic schools as important tools for understanding the Quran.

Hashashini: Ismaili followers of Hassan E Sabah in Persia and Sinan Rashid in Lebanon

Kafeya: Linen or cotton cloth wound around the head and lower face to protect from the sun and sand

Kharagi: Foreigner

Mamelukes: Slave warrior, mostly recruited from Turkish tribes but also from Northern peoples and other slave boys.

Nubian: People from the south of Egypt (Nubia); their land started at the first cataract of the Nile river and extended south.

Oustez: Mister

Ramadan: Month of fasting

Syce: Horse groom

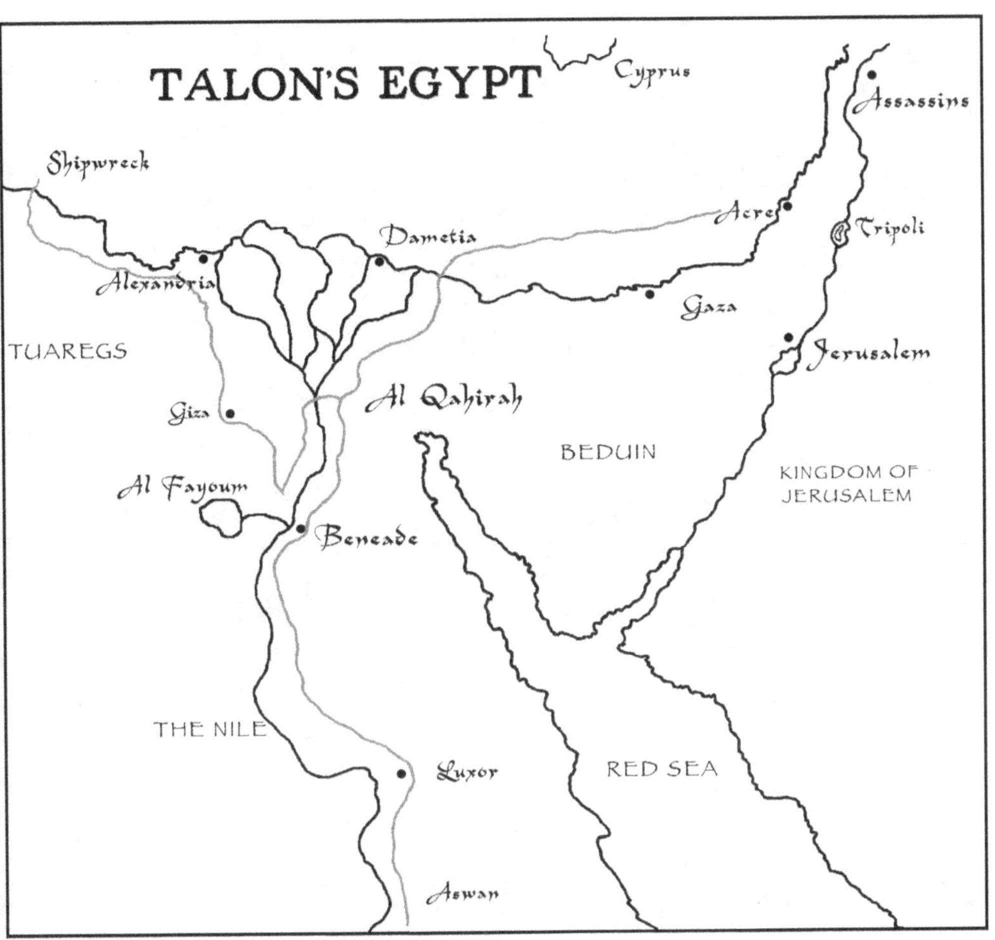

TALON'S EGYPT
Cyprus
Assassins
Shipwreck
Acre
Tripoli
Dametia
Alexandria
Gaza
TUAREGS
Jerusalem
Al Qahirah
Giza
BEDUIN
KINGDOM OF
JERUSALEM
Al Fayoum
Beneade
THE NILE
Luxor
RED SEA
Aswan

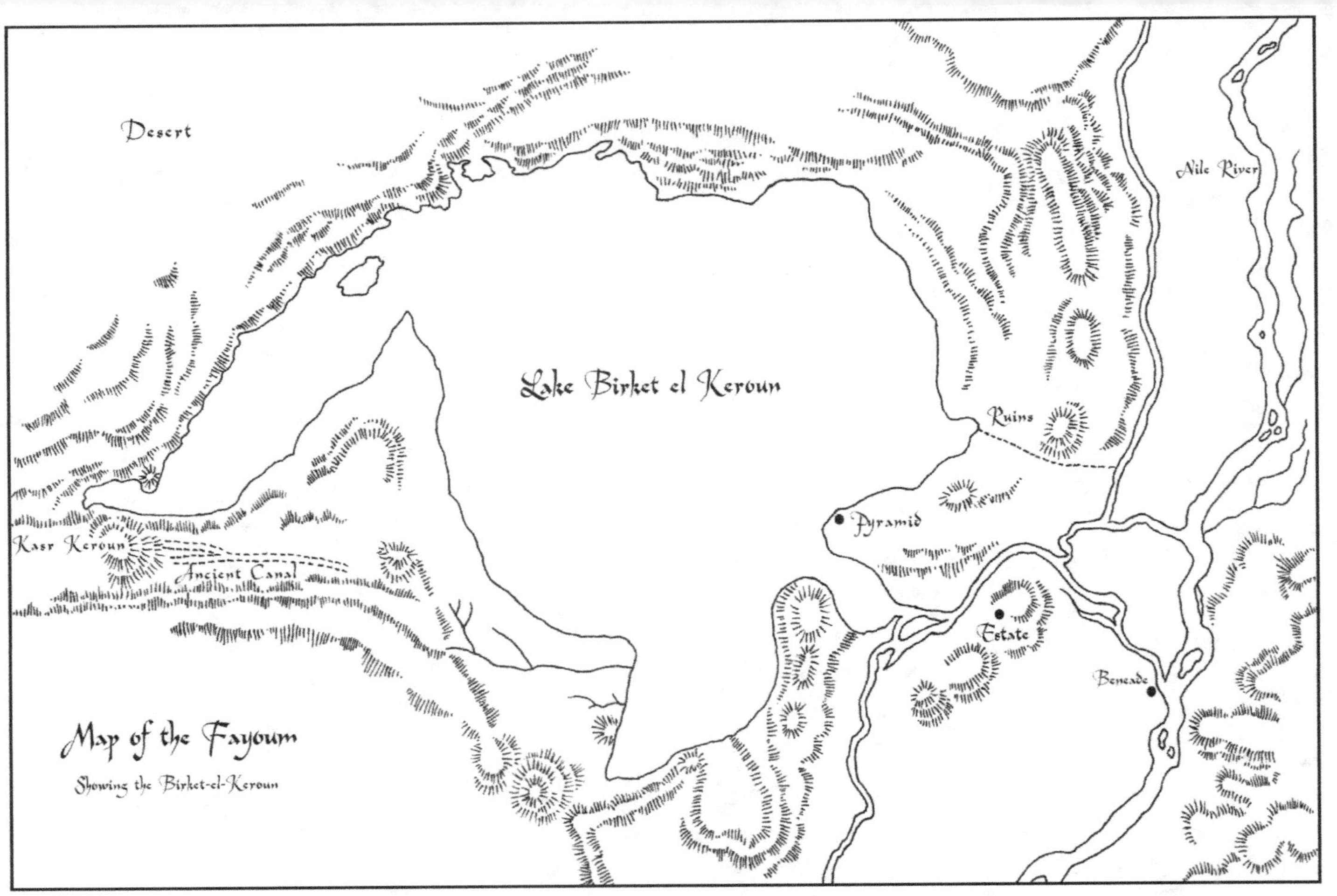

Desert
Nile River
Lake Birket el Keroun
Ruins
Kasr Keroun
Ancient Canal
Pyramid
Estate
Beneade
Map of the Fayoum
Showing the Birket-el-Keroun

# Chapter 1

# The Storm

Talon woke with an uneasy feeling that all was not well. It was their fourteenth day at sea and he had become used to the rise and fall of the ship as it ploughed its way eastward. Now there was an ominous feel to the vessel, and its timbers were groaning and creaking in a manner that was distinctly different from their customary noises.

He sat up in the dark on his pallet of old straw and canvas and tried to understand the meaning of the distant shouts and the harsh rattle of tackle being moved down to the waist of the ship. The rolling and pitching became such that the equipment stacked in the corners now slid noisily across the long cabin where he lay, and things were falling about with every pitch and roll. Men began to wake up cursing. Saddles and other hardware were falling off their pegs onto them.

There was a distant outcry, and the ship seemed to slow, but then the rhythm of rolling and pitching began again, followed by more shouting. By this time, others of the group of men who had been sleeping in the cramped quarters of the cabin were rousing themselves and calling out in the darkness.

"What is happening?" It sounded like Max.

"God's mercy! The ship is filling with water!" someone else shouted.

Indeed, water was sloshing about the floor, dripping down from the seams of the deck above and washing in through the open ports on the side. Men got to their feet in a hurry.

"Is there a candle? Light a lamp, someone. I cannot see in this infernal darkness!"

"God have mercy on our souls, this ship is in trouble!" another voice cried in the darkness.

Someone began retching, and the crowded cabin grew more unpleasant from the stink of vomit mingled with the other fetid smells of unwashed bodies and cordage.

There was a brief flash of light, followed by the crash of thunder almost overhead. Talon decided it was time to get onto the deck above and learn what was happening. He fumbled in the dark for his cloak, wrapped it round his shoulders, then brushed past his comrades and forced the door open. The wind was driving against it with such force that it resisted at first, but by leaning hard into it he finally managed to push it open. Staggering out onto the short balcony of the deck in front, he made a grab for the railing just as the sea swept across the lower main deck. The wind-driven spray from the crested waves struck his face, stinging and cold. It was a stormy, gray, early dawn and there was barely light to see by.

Within minutes, despite his cloak, his clothing was soaked. Lightning flashed in a jagged line in the distance, followed by another crash of thunder as he peered out at the turbulent sea. He saw mountainous waves and the spume off their tops flying in the wind, mixing with the driving rain. His heart quailed. Each time a wave washed past, it left an ominous dark hollow that appeared to be about to suck the ship into it. He shivered, not only from the cold, but with fear.

Water streamed from the side of the ship and she tried to right herself from being canted over to starboard. The crewmen down in the waist were trying to control the huge spar that held the sail, hauling on the halyards with all their might but to little avail. Despite their efforts and the shouts from the captain, they could not turn the spar to where he wanted it.

Another wave swept over the deck and three men who were down in the waist were swept off their feet and into the scuppers of the other side. The straining ship groaned as she slowly righted herself and began to roll in the opposite direction, water now pouring off her sides with floating pieces of wood washing to and fro. One heavy wooden grating that was placed over the hold broke loose and followed the tide as it crossed to the port side. It crashed into one of the helpless men in the scuppers, crushing him to death. His scream of agony was cut off by the rushing waters that covered him.

Talon glanced up. There were dense clouds overhead and flashes of lightning that flickered across the sky, illuminating a scene from hell. The ship was turned into the sea now, with the wind on its port quarter. Waves smashed against its bows and sometimes carried right over the fore deck when the boat dipped into a hollow.

The sail above them snapped with a loud retort and began to flap with wild abandon. It shredded within a minute, while one of the ropes holding its bottom corner broke, either because it was rotten or simply from the strain.

Talon, watching the sail reduced to rags in front of him, felt a leaden feeling in his stomach. He realized that they were now at the mercy of the wind and sea, unless somehow they could salvage this sail or raise another and regain control of the ship. He looked up at the mast and saw that the huge lugsail that had originally been there was also gone, the remnants flapping like so many gray pendants, useless for sailing by.

He was aware that Max had joined him on the short deck and he tried to speak to him, but the keening of the wind blew his words away. Instead, Talon pointed to the deck above and began to make his slow way up the steps to the quarterdeck. Max elected to stay where he was. The wind was even worse on the steps, for there was no shelter. It tore at Talon with a fury, as though trying to tear him from his hold and cast him into the foaming water. Below at least, he had been able to take some shelter from the rise of the deck and the mast.

Talon had to crawl up the steep steps, hanging onto the ropes that led along either side, buffeted and shaken by the gusting winds and wondering if at any minute a wave would come and sweep him away. At the top he managed, despite the howling, tugging wind, to stand up and stagger over to the mast where he hung on grimly; from there he stared back at two steering men who were trying to control the bucking and swinging rudder bar. It was throwing them about like dolls. Even in this dim light he could see there was a look of exhaustion and terror on their bearded faces.

The captain was nearby, leaning over the front rail which he gripped with white knuckles. "Get that God-smitten spar down and get the useless rags off it," he bellowed. "Bend another sail onto it for your lives, or we are drowned."

His voice boomed above the storm, and the crew ran to comply despite the heaving and rolling deck. They knew their lives depended upon getting the sail replaced, or the ship might go sideways into the sea and roll over.

Talon held onto the ropes around the mast at the front of the quarterdeck in an effort to get his bearings. He realized that the ship was now pointing south, as there was a glimmer of light showing through the clouds off the port bow that indicated the beginning of dawn.

He could not tell if there were any other ships nearby, but they too would be concentrating on survival and could not come to their aid, even if they had so wanted. He looked back down into the waist of the ship and wondered how the horses were faring. The grating had been torn off one of the holds and he was sure the ship was taking seawater. That meant the horses would be knee deep in water and terrified for their lives. It would be pandemonium down below.

His companions were either at the front of the ship, in which case they were completely water logged by now, or in the space reserved for knights below the quarterdeck cabins, which were beneath his feet.

Other than Max, no one else had followed him out, and Talon caught a glimpse of Max being violently sick by the masthead. The top of the mast and spars moved in a huge arc from side to side that made him dizzy if he looked up. The ship's motion took the hull over so hard that the sea was almost level with the top of its sides.

He clung with all his strength to the ropes and began to pray.

The men down in the waist of the ship were frantically trying to bend another sail to the spar that was lying across the ship's sides, and they were making good progress despite being hampered by the wind and horizontal rain. Anyone could be swept overboard or smashed to death by some of the large objects that had broken loose. There was a shout from a steersman. Talon's head whipped round and he saw one of the sodden men pointing ahead.

"Laaand! Dear Lord save us, it's land!" he screamed, but it was not with relief. Talon could clearly hear the panic in his shout.

He strained his eyes against the gloom and the hissing rain to make out what the man was pointing at.

Another flash of lightning helped to illuminate a dark, ominous mass looming low out of the gray horizon. Sure enough it was land, and his heart sank. His eyes swiveled wildly down into the waist again, to the crew. The captain was leaning over the rail screaming at the men to hurry or they were wrecked.

The ship now wallowed so deep in the water that it was rolling less. Talon heard the screams of the panicked horses below. His blood went cold when he knew he could do absolutely nothing for them, including Jabbar, his old friend. Even if he could release his Jabbar he could not get him out of the hold. Despite the wind tearing at his face, Talon felt tears flowing and the horizon ahead of him blurred.

But he was quickly made to realize that his own life was going to be in question and very soon.

A shriek of alarm from the front of the ship; there was no mistaking the terror of the scarecrow figure pointing forward. Talon crossed himself.

"Rocks ahead, only half a mile!" The wind carried the rest of the words away.

The steersmen fell to the deck and began to cry and pray. The captain, however, was a doughty man who was not ready to give up. He left the rail, kicked the two men to their feet and forced them back to the tiller, screaming abuse at them as he did so. Then he returned to encourage the crew, who had now bent the sail onto a spar and were rushing in two lines to haul the sail aloft.

Talon felt a flicker of hope as the sail bellied almost immediately, making it difficult to hoist; with a last, desperate effort the men managed to haul it up and into place, and the ship took on a life of its own again. From being nothing more than a wallowing log in the water she gained direction, whereupon the captain rushed to the tiller and with his two men began to haul and push against the long bar to turn the ship out to sea.

The men in the waist were still making the lines fast and there were now people coming out of the cabins to cluster on the short decks at the back of the ship and in the poop. He saw Montague and Jeffrey come to join Max.

The knights and their sergeant were utterly dependent upon the skill of the crew, unable to help but not willing to go below and feel trapped. So instead they watched in fearful fascination as the crew and the ship battled for all their lives against the storm and the sea.

But the sail had gone up too late. The ship lurched and there was a rending crash from below. The mast whipped forward and then back, the shocking blow dislodging the spar. The sail began to fall.

The cries of fear from the sailors as they realized what had happened were carried to the knights and Max. The ship had not been able to avoid the rocks and had cut herself open on their razor-sharp points. As the stricken ship reared up, its bow torn apart by the rocks just below the surface of the sea, the men on the poop deck were tossed in all directions like rag dolls. Many went straight into the sea and disappeared from sight in the raging waters. Others managed to hang onto something, and Talon could hear their cries over the howling of the wind and rain.

He himself was nearly shaken off his hold, and he watched in horror as the main mast now split and tipped forward to fall in a tangle of canvas and rigging onto the front of the boat.

Talon called, "Max, where are you?"

"I'm here, Talon!"

"The ship is doomed, and so are we if we stay here. It will sink quickly!" Talon called out as he dove for the stairs leading down to where Max was clinging to railings. He glanced around, looking for something to hold onto, and his eye landed on the grating that had only a short while earlier killed a seaman. He wondered what had happened to the ship's boat but realized it had probably been torn free of its lashings and washed overboard as matchwood long ago.

As he landed on the deck where Max, Montague, and Jeffrey were gathered with the others, he saw men on their knees praying, while others gripped onto some handhold for a feeling of safety; but other than Max and his two companions, no one seemed to know what to do, and they looked to Talon for some form of leadership.

The ship groaned and tipped at a steeper angle as water flooded into the bows. The kicking and screaming of horses trapped below was a cruel sound and Talon wished he could block it from his ears, as he knew that they were to soon die.

There was no sign of the captain or the two steersmen. Most of the men were frozen with fear because they could not swim. Others were crawling about in a wild panic.

"Quickly! We must take that grating or we are lost!" Talon shouted. Indeed, as he spoke the grating broke loose and began to drift away.

Talon grabbed Max by the arm and dragged him to the steps leading down to the sloshing water on the deck; reaching it, he pulled Max in with him. Although he was already soaked, the cold of the water still made him gasp. He saw a rope that hung off the grating and grabbed it.

"Max, Montague, Jeffrey, get on the grating, unless you want to drown with the others!" he shouted.

They did not need further persuasion. They dove for the grating and pulled themselves onto it. Just as they did so another wave curled over the waist and tore the grating away from Talon, ripping the rope from his grasp. He made a desperate lunge for their outstretched arms but fell into the water and was carried off the ship. He went under for a moment but then struggled to the surface, gasping and choking, in time to see the grating flipped over by yet another huge wave that tossed two of his companions into the sea.

They went under, and the back surge brought the grating closer to where Talon was trying to keep afloat. Somehow Montague had managed to hang on. Talon made a desperate lunge to reach his only means of salvation. He grasped wood and hung on grimly. At first Montague was not aware that he was there until Talon shouted for help. Then the burly man turned and threw a hand out to grab Talon by the shoulder. Montague heaved Talon onto the wooden raft where he lay gasping, trying to find his breath. Then he looked around.

"Montague, where is Max? Max! Jeffrey!" he called. "Where are you? I am here! I am here! Can you hear me? Dear God, please save them, they should not die like this!" he cried.

Montague added to the shouts, but the shrieking wind tore their words away. In the distance they heard a faint call came back to them, but even with the help of a gray light of dawn, Talon could see nothing, and only when the waves lifted his raft up high could he catch a glimpse of the stricken ship. What he could see through the lashing rain and spray was that she was now down at the aft section, which had almost disappeared, leaving only the remains of the bow and the shattered mast pointing into the sky.

He could see nothing of the crew and passengers. He guessed that some of the remaining survivors might be clinging to the mast and bows but they would be few, and their time nearly done. At one time he thought he saw a person struggling in the water a hundred yards away, but there was no way he could affect the direction the raft was drifting. In his despair he called on God many times to be merciful and spare others. But although the storm was clearly abating and the rain had eased, the waves were still high, with windblown spray sweeping across them.

He was soaked; his teeth began to chatter and his body shook with cold. Then a hand came out of the water as though a body was beckoning him to the depths. He started back in fright, but he recognized the sleeve and snatched at it and hung on. Montague had seen as well, and he reached out and seized the extended arm in a vise-like grip.

Max's head surfaced and he blew a huge spray of water out of his mouth, gasping for air with his mouth wide open. Talon and Montague continued to pull on Max's arm, and then Max recovered enough to seize hold of the grating edge and support himself long enough to take more breaths. He looked up at them and bared his teeth in a grimace; then, with their help, he scrambled onto the grating where he lay flat, pressed against Talon.

"Dear Lord, have mercy on us," he groaned as he looked about him.

"The ship is finished. I do not see Jeffrey anywhere or anyone else. God be kind to their souls!" Talon shouted, pointing with his chin at the dark silhouette of the doomed ship. There was a distant cry, and then the wind and the roar of the seas prevented them from hearing anything more. The ship slipped under the waves. Talon wept for Jabbar as he watched.

The three men remained gripping the sparse handholds of the grating with fingers locked, while the waves continued to wash over them and the sea drew them farther and farther away from the scene of the wreck. They called out until they were hoarse, but there was no response from anyone. Talon prayed that they would not end up being drawn out to sea; none of them could survive for very long in this condition. Yet he was equally afraid of being dashed to death on the rocks of the hostile coastline their ship had foundered upon.

Talon beat his head on the wood and wept. "What is to become of us?" he cried. "Thank God we are saved together, but we will die from this freezing cold, if we are not soon dashed upon the rocks." His arms and fingers ached and he kept his eyes mostly shut against the stinging salt and constantly splashing water.

He must have lost consciousness through exhaustion. Later he lifted his head and looked around with bleary eyes. It was well past sunrise, and his fingers and arms were locked in a cramped grip on their wooden platform. Max was still beside him, but he was either asleep or unconscious, and Montague was lying still as a corpse, although Talon could tell with relief that his companion was breathing.

Looking up, he saw low clouds scudding by, but there was now a glimpse of blue above as well. All the same, it was a cold, gray morning that greeted him. He turned his head painfully to the left and right to try and find out where they might be.

Then his heart lifted. Ahead, about two hundred yards away, was a short beach upon which breakers were crashing. On either side of the sandy stretch were black, wet rocks and cliffs. The rocks seemed menacing, despite the fact it was at least land. The breakers marched in ranks to crash against the rocks and toss spray high into the air. He saw that their raft had drifted into a narrow cove, framed with low cliffs on either side of a short beach. But they were headed toward the rocks and that was death, so he unlocked his cramped fingers from their hold and pushed at Montague and Max until they awoke and then showed them the danger. They needed no other persuasion and began to paddle as hard as their exhausted limbs could move to try to guide the unstable raft toward the thin strip of beach. They were still too far away to risk swimming; in his present frozen and depleted state, Talon knew that he would not survive and doubted that either of his companions was in any better condition.

They managed to change the direction of the grating sufficiently to feel that the rollers were now going to take it onto the beach, so Talon paused for a moment and took stock of their surroundings. Montague and Max, heads down, continued to paddle weakly.

The realization came to Talon that they were quite alone; there were no others from the ship that he could see. Still, there was a lot of flotsam accompanying the raft toward the beach. Many objects that had floated off the ship were bobbing alongside, including, he realized with a start of horror, some bodies of their former companions and crew, luckless people who could not swim and had not found a means to survive.

He stared in dismay at the several bodies that were nearest to them. One of the closest was that of the former crewman. Face down in the water, his body was limp and drifted loosely as the swell pulled it this way and that.

Talon whispered a prayer for the dead man then turned his attention toward the shore. As the grating came into more shallow water, it was seized by a wave and driven forward toward the beach on a long swell. It struck the sand, tossing the three men into the surf. Rolling in the water, Max seized Talon by the collar and held onto him. They crawled out of the retreating wave onto the dry sand, where they lay inert for long minutes, gasping for breath. Eventuall, Talon lifted himself off the wet sand on hands and knees, and gave thanks to God for his deliverance. He looked at Montague and then over at Max. His companions were lying on the sand, their chests heaving, too exhausted to move.

Talon felt deadly tired; his bones ached, and he was again feeling the cold from a wind that was blowing ashore. There was no shelter on the open sand. The wind whipped the spray from a crashing wave so that it stung his face.

Max sat up. "We have to find a cover or we will perish in this wind," he said.

Montague pushed himself up onto his hands and knees; then staggered to his feet.

"You are right, Max, but where?" he grunted.

Talon got slowly to his feet, too tired to say anything. All three stared wordlessly out at the calmer sea of the inlet, amazed that they had survived.

"There is no shelter on the beach. We must go inland." Max pointed weakly up the slope.

They tottered up the low rise of the sandy beach to see what lay beyond and saw what appeared to be the remains of a boat lying on its back, partially buried. Talon tripped and fell to his hands and knees in the soft sand. He felt weak and close to fainting. He lifted his head and saw a dense copse of low trees about a half mile ahead. Closer, he saw that a small stream emptied into the little bay, which explained the cloudy currenthe had vaguely noticed while still in the water as their raft pushed to land.

"There, that boat, we can find shelter under it," Montague gasped.

Talon looked in the direction Montague was pointing. He noticed that the boat was not seaworthy; its underside was stove in. Right now he did not care; it provided them with the only shelter available from the cold wind, and they needed cover urgently. They dragged themselves through the narrow gap of one side. The other side was buried in the sand. It smelled of old fish, but he did not care. Talon pushed deeper into the underside to get fully out of the wind, then he and his companions curled up together for warmth, and the three of them fell immediately into an exhausted slumber.

# Chapter 2

# The Caravan

The line of camels plodded slowly along the almost trackless desert, heading towards the distant palm trees on the eastern horizon. Their heads were tilted back against the curve of their long necks and their eyes mere slits in their puffy lids. The sun was well past the mid-afternoon peak, and although much lower in the sky, it was still burning the sand, the backs of the men, and the rears of the camels. They moved as though sleepwalking through the shimmering haze towards the promised water and shelter of the oasis.

There were about thirty camels in all. Their shadows reached ahead of them: distorted silhouettes projected on the myriad of rock-strewn sand dunes, almost as though the camels were accompanied by elongated phantoms. It had been a long, hot day for the men and animals; the late spring sun already threw out its scorching heat after the cool of winter.

Haidara Abdul 'Ikrimah, the owner and master of the caravan, was seated upon the swaying back of one of the lead camels. He wiped his brow with his *kafeya,* a loose cotton rag he used to cover his lower face; he was a portly man who sweated profusely from the afternoon heat. He glanced nervously back at the train, shading his eyes, to check that there were no stragglers. Haidara hated to have the caravan spread out over half the desert in its virtually unprotected state.

His drovers, men and a few boys, were hardened people of the desert, but he was only too aware that they lacked the soldiering skills to resist a determined attack from robbers, especially the fierce Tuareg, who were known to come out of the deep desert without warning to kill the riders and loot caravans such as his. It had been many weeks since they had left the safety of Barqa, and longer still since they had left the region of Magrib, that last promontory of North Africa from where the land known as Al Andalucía could be seen across the narrow strip of sea. This had meant many sleepless nights and long days of trying to stay awake when what he wanted most was to sleep. He could have paid for an armed escort, but he was a miserly person, and besides, those particular trained men, the Berbers, were more trouble than the dubious protection they were supposed to offer.

His precious cargo of minerals, hides, and wool bales was destined for Al Iskandrîyah, the royal city of Egypt. His caravan had left the south coast opposite the Iberian Peninsula some two months previously. Some of the silver had come from the sultanate of Granada, as had the pelts of wild animals. Other goods were from the fabled city of Cordova. He even carried books that he knew would fetch a high price in the literary quarters of the city. There was an almost insatiable need for books of the kind that came from Al Andalucía these days, as the supply from other libraries was drying up—for reasons he did not care to investigate.

Weeks before setting out, he had made the journey across the sea to Granada in southern Al Andalucía, where he had bargained for fine cloths, as well as bear and wolf skins. He had obtained amber and silver from the cold northern lands of the infidels, brought south by some of the more adventurous Jewish merchants. Now he was making his annual pilgrimage to Al Iskandrîyah to sell his wares. He prayed every evening that the prices were as good as last year, when he had made a killing.

He observed the trees ahead with some relief. As they approached the dense clump of palms clustered around the *bir*, or waterhole, still a mile away, he became aware of the sound of the sea to his left. The faint booming of the surf told him that he had less than a week more of travel following along the coast line, and then he would be in the great city. He would have a bath and then a woman and then a hot meal. Perhaps he would have all three at once! Then he would enjoy a bed that did not consist of sand. He smiled to himself.

He knew this area they were crossing had once been inhabited by pirates who preyed upon defenseless merchants, both on land

and sea. They had been cleaned out of the bay some time ago by the troops of the new young Sultan in Egypt, Salah al Din. Haidara muttered a prayer of thanks to Allah for having provided the young man with the courage and will to take care of these vermin. It saved him an extra month of travel, as he would otherwise have had to make in a wide detour to avoid the place.

When they were still a half mile from the trees, Haidara, ever cautious, beckoned to one of the riders behind him. It was difficult to make out the boy's features, as his face was swathed in what had once been a white linen *kafeya*, now turned brown like the sand, leaving only his eyes and the bridge of his nose open to the harsh climate. But Haidara knew which one he was.

"Dhakiy, go forward with 'Utbah and check that no one has taken our camp for the night. If you see anything, get back here as fast as you can. There will be no one else there, *Insha'Allah*."

"I go, master!" the boy called back.

With a shout to his companion, he maneuvered his camel adroitly past the lead animals and slapped it with his stick to get it to lumber into a heavy trot, while the other boy shouted with excitement and beat his camel, kicking its hump with his heels and whacking its furry neck to get it to catch up.

Haidara raised his hand and called back to the men behind him to stop. They slowly bunched up and then, without being told, they formed a half circle and squatted on the sand in the shade of their patient camels to await the return of the boys. Some fingered their bows and checked on their arrows.

"We are about three days, maybe a week out from the city, and *Insha'Allah* we will arrive with no unwelcome interruptions," Haidara commented to no one in particular. He waved his fly whisk idly in front of his face, peering towards the distant trees through the shimmering heat.

It did not take long for the boys to do a cursory inspection of the clump of trees clustered around a small spring of sweet water. It was a very cursory inspection. To their untrained eyes there was no one there and had not been for some time. They did find the remains of a fire, but it was cold. There were no other signs of recent human visitation that they could detect.

They trotted their clumsy charges back to the waiting caravan and shouted that all was safe. The caravan moved in noisily; the scent of fresh water energized everyone. The camels and men followed the well-worn routine for setting up camp. The snarling, roaring camels were forced to their knees. The more recalcitrant ones were hauled down painfully by a string attached to their noses, protesting loudly, while the favorites were gentled down by their drovers. They were relieved of their loads, hobbled by their front legs, and taken to be watered downstream from the oasis. Later they were fed from the fodder carried by other camels.

Only then were the fires lit, and the meager fare, consisting of dates, thin strips of dried goat's meat, and a creamy mixture of camel's milk and crushed grain, was laid out on hastily thrown mats.

Now, however, it was time for prayers, led by Haidara, who always assumed the lead place for his men. He had performed his ablutions dutifully with the available water in the tiny stream. Hitherto they had been forced to perform their ablutions with sand, as there had been no water available. God gave dispensation to those in hard desert conditions, but now there was the luxury of water and they were all content.

After the meal, and with the sun a great red orb on the edge of the burnt western horizon, the two boys Dhakiy and 'Utbah were allowed to explore. They decided to go the short distance to the bay about a half mile away. They followed a path, excitedly looking for a sight of the sea, which they had not seen since they left the coastal city of Barqa two weeks before. Neither noticed that the track was well-worn and had been in use very recently. Nor were they aware that they were observed as they came near the beach. It was only when they breasted the sand bank where the track ended and the beach of loose sand began that they realized they were in trouble. With a shout of surprise Dhakiy slapped 'Utbah's shoulder and pointed. There, in front of them, was a construction that could only just be called a hut. They stared at it in silence for a moment, trying to grasp its meaning.

But their pause cost them. A man jumped up a few feet in front of them and grimaced horribly in silence. Both boys were frozen in terror for a second, which was enough. Hard hands seized them from behind and pinned them, helpless to move. Then, just as quickly, hands were clapped over their mouths before they could scream. The man who had jumped out in front of them now shambled towards them.

He spoke a strange language and looked terrifying. His beard was very long, and he had a tangled mass of filthy red hair sprouting out of his head. His eyes, terrifying blue bulging eyes, glared at the boys, who were just getting over their shock and trying to cry out in alarm. Dhakiy was so frightened that he wet himself.

"Do not make a sound and we will not harm you," one of the people said in a low voice.

Dhakiy twisted his head and gazed up at another wild looking man in similar garb.

The man, still holding him firmly in a vice-like grip said again, "Be quiet, both of you, we mean you no harm. But if you scream we will have to kill you."

The same man addressed the other two in a strange language, and they all turned their eyes over their shoulders at the distant trees as though expecting to see other curious visitors. The man holding Dhakiy said something briefly to his companions, whereupon the boys were marched down the beach, well out of sight of the oasis. The boys' legs and hands were tied with some old rope. The men dumped them without ceremony on the sand and then squatted, facing them.

"Where have you come from? Where are you going?" the man who spoke their language asked. He was burnt a golden brown from the sun, his wild, knotted hair was light brown, and he had disturbingly intense green eyes. He spoke the language hesitantly but well, with a slight accent as though he had not used it for a while and was just getting used to its flavor again.

"We...we are with a caravan. We are going to Al Iskandrîyah," Dhakiy said shakily. He was terrified, but the men did not behave threateningly, even though they did look wild and unkempt. Burned by the sun and with rags as clothing, they nevertheless smiled reassuringly at the two frightened boys.

"Our master is Haidara Abdul 'Ikrimah. He is a great warrior and will come and cut off your heads if you do not let us go!" 'Utbah squeaked. His teeth were chattering.

"I am sure he is a great warrior and we are much afraid," the one with the green eyes and a scar on his jaw said. He smiled, but neither boy was reassured.

"How many men does he have, this great warrior chief of yours?" he asked them quietly.

"We are two hundred men and all warriors. You will not stand a chance against us."

"I counted nearly thirty camels, so perhaps you are lying?" he replied in a soft voice, but his eyes became cold. Then he said with a menacing tone, "If you do not stop saying stupid things to us I will throw you into the sea and you can swim to Al Iskandrîyah. And you know very well the sea monsters will eat you before you get anywhere."

"There are twenty of us all together," 'Utbah muttered. He shivered at the prospect of encountering sea monsters.

"How far is Iskandrîyah? Tell me the truth, because if you do not, you will be cut into little pieces and we will eat you. We have not eaten meat for a very long time," the green-eyed man told them, making big eyes at them; they believed him.

"We are maybe three days, maybe a week from the city, perhaps a little more," Dhakiy whimpered.

The man turned to his two companions and spoke in a low voice. They nodded, whereupon they picked up the boys and carried them towards the ramshackle shelter they had first seen.

The sun had set by now, leaving only a strip of red glowing on the distant horizon, and darkness was sweeping in from the east. Dhakiy gave a whimper of fear as they were dumped on the sand inside the shelter. 'Utbah muttered scornfully at him. "Why are you so afraid of them? We shall escape, and then they will be in trouble."

"*Insha'Allah.* You should just be patient, my young warrior. We will come back for you later. Now be quiet and do not upset this man," the man who spoke their language said, pointing to the hairy one in front of them. "He likes to eat children, especially boys, and he has not eaten one for a long time, so he is very hungry."

"We are not children!" spat 'Utbah. "We are men."

"Ah, I forgot. Pardon me, little warrior."

The man's teeth flashed in the gathering dusk and he was gone; the big man who was squatting in front of them was looking them over balefully. Dhakiy shivered and wriggled closer to 'Utbah, who was trembling himself. They were silent.

* * * * *

Now that the sun had gone down, Haidara felt at ease. There was fresh water and no one to share it with, so he could spread out and enjoy the cool side of the oasis when morning came. Had there been others, he would have found himself and his caravan on the outside perimeter of the place for later arrivals, and the early comers would have had the benefit of the shade of the date trees the next day and not him.

The group of men had enjoyed a leisurely, if meager, dinner; and then, having posted two guards, the rest had sat around a fire to enjoy the precious dark coffee beans brewed over the embers of the fire in small, slim brass containers with long handles. The aroma of the brewing black liquid permeated the small oasis. Haidara intended to buy another sack of coffee while in Iskandrîyah; his present hoard was almost finished.

Haidara noticed that the boys were missing, but assumed they were still down by the water and would be back soon. In any case, he knew this area and there was unlikely to be any danger from other people this far into the desert, especially since it had been cleaned out of pirates. Any threat would be in the form of another caravan, and he was quite sure they were alone.

So he relaxed with his men, and the murmured conversation continued until the sky was ablaze with stars from one end to the other. There was no moon, but the light from the stars, which seemed to be almost within reach, was enough to throw the distant ridge of mountains to the south and west into dark relief, while the sand and rocks in the middle distance became large black shapes on the pale desert floor.

Nearer at hand, the palms rustled under the light cool breeze wafting from the sea that caressed their fronds. It brightened the glow of the embers of the dying fire, causing the flickering flames to throw up men's shadows that danced among the tree trunks, creating a crowd of dark phantoms which shared the camp with the living.

Long before midnight, everyone was wrapped in his cloak and asleep on the ground or among the baggage piles, except for Haidara, asleep in his tent, and the two sentries. These two men were leaning against trees at opposite ends of the camp, staring outwards, one to the dark eastern horizon and the other one back along the track from the west where they had come from. They were barely awake themselves.

The first hint either had that there was danger about was when a knife slid around the first man's throat, and a vice-like grip came down on his right wrist. A voice whispered,"Do not move. Do not shout, or you will be sent on your way to account for your sins to Allah. Nod if you understand."

The sentry gingerly nodded against the blade of the knife that dug into his trembling throat. He was forced down onto his knees and then bound. His head covering was conveniently used to blindfold him, and then he was gagged. The rough hands sat him down and propped his back against the tree trunk. He was admonished not to move or he would die.

The trembling man did exactly that: he sat as still as a log.

* * * * *

The next morning, Haidara was awoken just before dawn by an agitated drover who pleaded with him to wake up and come outside. The camp had woken up to find that many things had happened during the night.

He roused himself, and, rubbing his eyes, he followed his man out of the tent. The top of the sun was appearing in the east and he knew that by noon it would be a large white orb that threatened to bake the desert to a cinder. There, before his tent, he found that most of the men had already gathered, and as soon as they saw him they all began to shout at once. He hushed them and asked one man to speak.

During the night they had been visited by someone or something from the desert. The sentries were missing, as were the two boys who had not been seen all night. Worse than that, four camels were missing. They had disappeared, as though taken by magical Djins. Haidara raised his hands to calm the men, who babbled with fear at the word 'Djins'. Another man said that, to make matters worse, many of the men's weapons were gone: swords, bows and spears. They had had few enough weapons to start with, but now they had almost nothing. A plump man added that food had been taken, as well as some of the leather water sacks. They all voiced their concerns and their fears in a noisy tumult.

Haidara was astounded by what his men told him. He tried to collect his wits, but the shouting distracted his thinking. "By the ears of the Prophet, will you bunch of chattering jackals shut up and let me think!" Haidara yelled back at them.

He composed himself, but he was frightened all the same. How could men, if they were indeed men, come and take what they wanted without making a noise, or disturbing a single person? How could it be that no one heard the camels, which always made a noise when getting to their feet?

No one was hurt or dead, other than maybe the sentries. He shivered involuntarily.

"First we must find the men who are missing and then the boys. Perhaps they are already dead," he said, trying to appear calm. "Have you looked everywhere?"

They chorused that they had. He told them to look again. After wasting an hour tracking around the trees and further out into the desert, someone mentioned that the boys had taken the road to the beach the previous evening and might still be there. *Insha'Allah!*

With dread in his heart, Haidara led the way towards the sound of the distant surf. The booming of the surf grew louder as he puffed his way through the soft sand of the dunes and stared about him at the sea. He saw something strange erected on the beach; it looked like a makeshift shelter of some kind.

Nervously drawing his sword and ordering the men with some kind of weapons to be alert and to stay with him, he walked slowly down the slope towards the jumble of drift wood, followed by his men in a tight group behind him. The sight that greeted him when he arrived at the opening to the shelter left him speechless. There on the sand, side by side, where the two boys and the two sentries. They were bound hand and foot and gagged.

It took a moment for Haidara to regain his composure, upon which he shouted to his men to come and release the prisoners. The boys and sentries spluttered their indignation as their gags were removed, and all four began to talk loudly at the same time.

Haidara felt that he was getting a headache from the din, and shouted at them to shut up and tell him, one at a time, what in the Prophet's good name had happened.

"They were Djins!"

"They were wild looking men from the sea!"

"One had huge blue eyes…like a fish from the sea!" Dhakiy stammered.

"They had hair down to their waists and wanted to eat us!" 'Utbah blubbered.

"How did you get captured?" Haidara yelled at one of the sentries, his patience finally running out.

"I did not hear anything! Nothing at all, Master. Before Allah, I heard nothing, but then there was a knife at my throat and next thing I knew I was bound and gagged and blindfolded. There were many, many of them. They carried me here!" Gam stammered. He was one of Haidara's least reliable drovers.

"That happened to me as well! On my soul before Allah, I did not hear a thing before I was overcome and brought here with the others," Hazim said.

Haidara stared skeptically at Hazim.

"How many were there, Hazim? I want to know the truth, not the babbling of a couple of idiots who cannot be trusted to stay awake on guard."

He whirled upon the boys. "Did you see how many?" He demanded. In his agitation he didn't realize that he was mining his nose with his little finger.

"I think there were three of them," 'Ubah squeaked nervously.

"Three! How in the name of the Prophet could three men do this?" Haidara shouted, anger replacing his fear.

He considered this for a moment, and then realized that he had lost precious time looking for the boys and men while the perpetrators of this crime were gone.

"Get up and come with me! We have to find which way they went," he shouted and led the way, his voluminous garments billowing in the light breeze from the sea as he went. He didn't wait to see if the other men had freed the prisoners.

Haidara arrived back in the encampment to find that nothing had happened since he left. No one had thought to break camp and load the camels. An awful thought occurred to him. He rushed off to his own baggage where he kept his coins. To his horror, two of the small bags of silver were missing. He raised his arms in the air, his fists clenched, and screamed his rage and frustration.

"As God is my witness, what did I do to deserve this outrage? May pestilence and disease strike these people who have pillaged my caravan and slay them slowly! May they burn in Hell, forever!"

His rage increased to the point where he grew apoplectic. He laid about him with a stick at any of his men and camels that got in his way as he ran about distractedly screaming at them to get ready to leave.

Then another unpleasant discovery was made. Most, but not all of the bindings of the packs had been cut, as were most of the water skins. They had to make repairs before they could leave the oasis. The ropes could be knotted together, but they could not depart without water.

At this point, Haidara became ill and was forced to retire to his tent to rest and let the men concentrate upon the necessary repairs. It would take hours before they would be ready, and he was exhausted.

* * * * *

Many miles away, following the faint track that led along the coast line, four camels trotted at a quick pace, heading east.

Talon de Gilles looked back for the hundredth time to see if there might be any pursuit, and then at his two companions, Max von Bauersdorf and Montague. Neither had ridden a camel before. They were hanging on nervously to the high saddle-like contraptions, clutching the single cord that led from the camel's nose in one hand and a spear in the other.

Talon grinned. All three of them had looked like scarecrows with their unkempt and wild hair and bearded faces, but now all this was hidden under the layers of cloth that Talon had stolen the night before for this purpose. Now they looked more like Bedouin, he thought, although he supposed they were known by some other name here in Africa.

After his talk with the boys, he had reasoned that they were probably in the country of Egypt, and although it was a gamble stealing from the caravan to continue their journey, it was really the only way out of their predicament. He let his camel slow down, allowing the other two to catch up with him.

"How long before we can expect them to give chase?" Max asked, his voice slightly muffled by the cloth covering the lower part of his face.

"They will be held up until noon, I hope, if they are to repair the skins and ropes," Talon responded.

"I still find it hard to believe that no one saw nor heard us leave!" Montague exclaimed.

"I told you that Talon learned skills in the east that we will never know the full account of," Max said.

"That caravan was our last chance. I contemplated asking if they would take us with them, but there is no mistaking either of you two for Franks. They might have taken us prisoner and sold us, or betrayed us when we got to the city. I could not take that chance," Talon said.

"By God, I think that you made the right decision, Talon. But you frighten me some times with your skills," Max said. "I, for one, am glad that we are on our way...even if it is to go deeper into the Saracen country," he added.

"I agree. I was heartily sick to death of shellfish, crabs, and what fish we could find in the bay. I have not eaten a piece of dried meat that tasted so good!" Montague was chewing on some of the food that Talon had purloined.

"I told the boys, to keep them quiet, that you ate children, and that you were so hungry you might eat one of them anyway."

Montague gave a bark of laughter. "I might have ...I have been hungry since we were ship-wrecked, what must be months ago."

"God's mercy, but I shall never forget that storm! How we survived can only be due to his mercy!" Max said fervently. "I wonder if any other ships were lost that night??" he asked ruminatively.

"I am not sure of His mercy sometimes," Talon said. "We lost all we possess and many friends, may he be merciful to their souls...including my Jabbar. I still miss him sorely; he was not only my horse, but my friend. We shared much together."

"Well, now the church will think that you have died and it will not continue to pursue you anymore, Talon," Max offered, trying to lift their mood.

"I think that the Order of Templars will be able to deflect that priest's requests. He trumped up the charges of witchcraft, as all know, just to get rid of me. Well, he succeeded, and now I am on the other side of the world...unable to do him any harm."

"Talon, do we keep this speed until we come to the city?" Max asked plaintively. The camel's gait was unlike anything he had ever experienced.

"We have to put many miles ahead of the caravan, Max. I doubt if they will send men after us, as they do not have very many to spare, and I think that their loads are more important to them. We have robbed them, but they still have their lives and camels and most of their goods. The master of the caravan might just consider that he got off lightly and not chase us. Besides," Talon laughed, "I only took half of the silver he keeps near his sleeping mat. His snores were moving the tent walls!" They chuckled at that.

"All the same, we must keep this pace and put many miles between us, because we could not fight twenty men, even if they are not as well armed as we now find ourselves."

"Will these camels last the pace?" Montague asked.

"If we do not push them too hard; I picked out the ones I thought might be in good condition, but it was difficult to see in the dark which were the best."

They continued in silence, each getting accustomed to the swaying motion of their camels, each immersed in his private thoughts.

Talon's mind went back to France, which he had left under difficult circumstances. After helping his father to keep the fortress bequeathed to his wife by her father and winning a small castle as the spoils of war, he, Talon, had found himself accused of witchcraft. The priest from Albi had come to the fort, accused him, then arrested him, and would have taken him to the prison in Albi to face trial. That had failed thanks to his friends, the Welsh archers, who had ambushed the party and slain all but the priest and one other who escaped. Talon had been freed by his Welsh companions, who had then slipped off into the forest to make their way back home to Wales, from where they had been gone for two years or more on crusade.

Talon and Max had made their way to the Templar stronghold, Mas Dieu, where Talon had been inducted partially into the Order of the Templars. With an experienced Sergeant of the Templars like Max to help him, Talon had quickly learned the ways and discipline of the order. Montague had also been there as a new recruit, and the three had sailed for the Kingdom of Jerusalem, along with a fleet of other ships from Aigues Mortes, the royal port.

The shipwreck had presented them with a harsh change to their plans, but now they might just be able to reach their destination after months of surviving on the beach.

Talon doubted that there would be a hot pursuit, but he did not want to take any chances, so he pushed them on for the rest of the day, stopping only once before nightfall to allow the camels to take a little rest and water from their meager supply. They went on through the night, the camels tied together in line, following one another while the men on their backs slept.

He hoped there would be another oasis along the route, but as he did not know the way he could only hope.

* * * * *

It was nearly a week later when they sighted human habitation and cultivated fields. They were again starving and very nearly out of water, although they had stumbled onto two small watering holes. The camels were in a pitiable condition, having had almost no food along the way. One had died a day earlier leaving them with only one mount each.

Talon stopped his mount and squinted over the shimmering ground at the palm trees in the distance.

Max and Montague brought their camels alongside Talon's.

"Why have you stopped, Talon?" Max asked.

"I think we are close to the city of Al Iskandrîyah. We Franks know it as Alexandria. There are many more palm trees than there would be for a simple oasis, and I see other signs of habitation. We must proceed very carefully now, as we have still a formidable barrier to cross: the great river. It is called the Nile, and I do not know it."

Late that night, once they were camped and had hobbled the camels, they discussed their options. Talon stared towards the east and thought he saw a dim light reflected against the sky and drew his companions' attention to it.

They stood and stared at a glow that seemed to wax and wane, to brighten and to dim again, but in the complete silence of the desert they had no clue and could not discern what it might be. They slept until the early hours of dawn and then continued east, still following the coastline within a few miles.

It was around noon that they began to encounter farms and irrigation ditches full of muddy water, and the country gradually transformed itself from bleak desert into green swathes of cultivated land. Palm trees and other vegetation became plentiful.

"I think we have arrived at Alexandria," Talon said.

*Ivory palaces built on earth*
*And mansions lined with galleries-*
*With marble columns on inlaid floors*
*In spacious halls that filled with parties:*
*In a flash I saw them all as rubble*
*And weathered ruins without a soul*
*— Moshe Ibn Ezra*

# Chapter 3

# Al Iskandriyah
# (Alexandria)

The city of Al Iskandrîyah was now in sight. They rode their tired camels along a wide spit of land that held the sea to their left, while to their right there was a huge lake bordered by irrigated fields and orchards. They stared around in wonder at the abrupt change of scenery.

From the high vantage point of their mounts, they could see out to the calm blue sea where there were many kinds of boats: large galleys anchored, sleek sailing ships that danced lightly on the swell, and fishing boats clustered around a few ungainly hulls that wallowed rhythmically to the rise and fall of the surf.

They filled their lungs with the salty air that came their way with the light breeze from the sea. Their tiredness lifted at the soothing sight of the well-tended green fields and the lush orchards neatly set along the lake side of the dusty road. Everything indicated that they had arrived at an impressive city. As they ambled towards the city walls, they passed by a cluster of small dwellings.

Talon told his friends that it looked to him like a burial ground where poor people had built shelters to live among the tombs. An old, almost toothless man perched on the back of a sleepy looking donkey that was trotting the other way confirmed that it was the city of the dead.

"I shall be there soon, waiting for you!" he called with a toothless cackle, and he waved his stick at them.

They had little difficulty in gaining access to the city itself. Its high walls were well maintained and the gates were manned by soldiers who watched the constant stream of people entering and leaving. It was obvious they were bored, but all the same Talon tossed them a coin, and it was all that was needed to get past. After a few enquiries, Talon discovered modest lodgings for himself and his companions at a rented room that was a short walk from the main port of the city. He admonished his friends not to speak one word to anyone and to keep quiet when within ear shot of passersby. The man who rented to him wanted money up front, and clearly mistrusted the looks of these ragged scarecrows. Talon tipped a couple of small silver coins into the man's grubby hand whilst giving him a warning glare that told their new host to mind his own business.

As it turned out, Talon's concerns about mingling with the crowds on the streets had little foundation; they passed unnoticed, even though they still wore their dusty stolen desert clothes wrapped about them. Their faces were covered almost completely, but so too were many others on the crowded streets.

It seemed a little odd to Talon that no one remarked on the blue eyes of his two companions, but when he passed some other desert people at the bazaar, he realized why. They, too, had blue or gray eyes.

However, encounters could not be avoided for long, and the first was very nearly a disaster. One look-alike desert dweller, recognizing something about the way they dressed, accosted Montague and wanted to talk; Talon hastily intervened and said his companion was dumb and they must hasten to prayers which were conveniently being called just at that time from the minarets of the mosque nearby. They hurried away, leaving the puzzled man staring after them.

Talon sold the camels to a drover at the first opportunity. He did not want to have them in his possession and be accused of theft should the caravan they had stolen from make its way into the city and raise an alarm and a search. After some haggling with the skinny man, who wanted to pay a fraction of what the animals were worth, he managed to walk off with a few silver coins to add to his pouch. He intended that they should find a passage out of the city as soon as possible, by boat. This idea had come to mind as he watched the extent of the shipping in the harbors.

One evening, when they were preparing to go to sleep, Montague whispered, "I have never been near the people of the Islamic east like this. It makes me uneasy and I feel threatened.

"The crowded streets of the city do not help. I do not know whether I should draw my sword and set about me, or behave like a mouse and do nothing!" he complained. Talon snorted a suppressed laugh at his friend's obvious unease.

Max was more relaxed, having spent many years in the Kingdom of Jerusalem.

"You must learn that you will rub shoulders with our enemies as much as you fight them," he admonished Montague. "Even now you live in another world that is confusing with regard to friend and foe. There are Bedouin who are Moslem and live in the deserts to the south of the kingdom of Jerusalem, near Ascalon, which is where Sir Phillip and I met, and they are our friends. They do not like the sultans nor their Turkish mercenaries any more than we do."

"God's truth, but I am a fighter, and I like to be clear who my enemies are," Montague growled. He gave a ferocious look at his friends that made Talon and Max grin at him.

"All the same, I find this city of Al Iskandrîyah huge and magnificent, Talon," Max remarked.

Talon nodded agreement. "Max is right. We are not in a world where everything is clear. There are many eddies and currents here that are not easy to see, but a man must learn to swim in them to survive. This is an ancient city, but I don't know much about it, my friends. We must be careful."

Talon observed that there were many wealthy residences; this was a rich city. Some were huge buildings that seemed more like fortresses, he noted. The one edifice that most awed them was the tall construction situated on the end of a sand bar on the other side of the harbor. It seemed like a fortress at its base but the tower was taller than any other building in the city. At its summit there seemed to be a fire tower. To the three men, it did not seem to be a palace, nor to have much of a function.

They remarked, on the nights when they went up on the flat roof of their accommodation to enjoy the cool of the evening, that a great light came from it, and it shone primarily out to sea. It perplexed them, until Talon had the opportunity to finally ask one of the people in the street what it was.

The answer was contemptuous. "You are not from here, are you? Where do you come from that you do not know of the great Lighthouse of Al Iskandrîyah on the island of Pharos? Great fires are kept alight on the very top and reflected by mirrors; it is for the ships at sea so they can see at night when they are on course for the city. You are ignorant desert folk; it is easy to tell by your weird blue eyes and filthy clothes! By the Prophet, but you stink!" The local man stalked off sniffing and theatrically waving his hand about his nose. They watched him go in puzzlement.

Talon had not fully understood the explanation, but he translated what he heard for his companions.

"He called it a light tower. There is some kind of a fire house on top of the tower and the flame guides ships at sea to find their way into the city harbor."

"That makes some sense," Max reflected. "It is so flat around here a ship would be half way across the desert before its captain knew he had made land, if they did not have some such to warn them off."

The others snickered.

They could not stay here any longer, as their supply of money was fast disappearing and they had to find a way to continue eastward. They needed to gain passage on a boat to Jerusalem, or at the least, out of Egypt to somewhere north in that direction.

They were strolling in the back streets of the harbor and Talon thought he saw an inn. It was a miserable affair but he guessed that it was a place where a ship's master might hang out.

He pointed it out and they wove their way along the crowded, noisy passage to a door of what could be a tavern. Avoiding the filth, the scuttling rats and the beggars, they ducked under a leather curtain. It took a second or two for Talon's eyes to become accustomed to the dimly lit room, and then for his nose to adjust to the lack of air. The fetid atmosphere assailed his nostrils, while the shouts of drunken men pounded his ears. He pulled his *kafeya* over his nose to block out some of the stench. He noticed two scruffy looking men seated in a corner, one of whom, by the look of his dress and his wide seamed and bearded face, had to be a seaman from the north. He decided to ask them first. He made his way across the room, closely followed by Max and Montague, their hands on their sword handles.

He realized that there were many men in the inn who looked like seamen and who had found their way to this filthy drinking hole. The sale of wine was forbidden in public, which explained why this hovel was well hidden. He supposed that the authorities turned a blind eye to this kind of place that was patronized by the Greeks, Genoese and Venetians who brought the town their valuable cargoes. It was best to know where they were entertained in this otherwise austere city of Islam.

They were accosted twice while moving through the crowded room by painted whores who offered their services for almost nothing, baring their breasts and wriggling their hips suggestively. Shrugging them aside, Talon approached the two men, who were obviously in their cups. He tossed a small silver coin onto the rough stained table top to get their attention.

It was clear the larger man was not an Arab, although his scrawny companion could have come from any country along the northern seaboard of Africa. The wide faced man looked up at the three ruffians standing in front of him and leaned back on his stool. He wore a greasy leather jerkin over equally well used canvas cloth shirt and breeches. Talon noted that the other man's hand slid towards his belt, where he probably kept a knife.

The big man frowned and asked in bad Arabic, "What do you want?"

"*Salaam Aliekom.* We are looking for a ship's master."

"I am a shipmaster; what is it to you?"

"We want passage to Cyprus. Do you know of anyone going there from this city?" Talon asked politely.

The man looked him over and then turned his gaze upon his two silent companions.

"Where are you from?" he asked in a truculent tone.

"That is our business. Can you take us to Cyprus?"

"I can, but it will cost you. What do three Tuareg want to go to Cyprus for, in any case?"

"How much?

"Four gold Beziers.

"That is far too much. I have silver to pay with." Talon almost had to shout over the noise of the room. "I can pay you twenty pieces like the one on the table."

They haggled over the price, with Talon agreeing to work their passage to help offset the full price the man wanted. The man gave his name as Caravello; he was from Venice. Wine was delivered to their table by a servant Caravello had beckoned over from the other end of the crowded room.

Talon begged off the drink, saying that they were good Moslems and would not sin. Caravello shrugged and took a swig of his wine.

Then his skinny companion tried to get Montague and Max to talk. Talon intervened each time, warding off inquisitive questions, but the man persisted for some reason, and suddenly said in a sure tone, "You don't look like a Tuareg. You are too light skinned for that, although your eyes are blue. Where are you really from? " He addressed his question directly at Montague, who looked blankly at him.

"I am tired of your inquisition. If you don't want a knife in your ribs, you will be silent, now!" Talon said with a fierce look on his face.

He turned on the captain. "Is our deal good or not? I do not want to stay in this filthy hole any longer than I have to."

"You pay me half now, and half when we leave the port," the captain said.

Talon spilled the silver onto the table and stood.

"Where do we meet you?"

"On the water's edge, to the east quay where there is a galley, the biggest in the harbor this day. I am the Master. You will be expected; we leave tonight. I shall not be taking any livestock, so leave your stinking camels in the desert!" Caravello gave a bark of laughter, scooped the silver off the table into a small leather bag, and returned to his drinking.

Talon shouldered his way out of the crowded room and into the side street, followed by his two companions. He breathed in the cleaner air of the street and then exclaimed, "By God, even the air out here in this stinking street is less foul than that of the pig sty in there!"

Montague grunted acknowledgement. "I nearly passed out when the skinny one breathed on me. I thought I smelt a rotten whiff of sulphur!"

Max spoke next, "That man is dangerous, and I trust neither him nor the captain of the ship we are to take. Do you think we can trust them, Talon?"

"I trust neither of them, but they are all we have. I cannot take you clear across Egypt as we are. Each day we risk exposure and prison, or worse. We barely have money to pay for our fare. I never thought a place could be so expensive!" He scowled at the sight of how little silver remained in his palm.

"Come on friends, we have to get what remains of our equipment, and find our way back again before dark. Besides, I am hungry," he said, leading the way to their refuge.

Dusk drew in and the hubbub of the city stilled somewhat, to be replaced with the call from the minarets across the darkening horizon. Talon was reminded of another time when he listened with a sense of calm to the call of the mullah as he recited the prayers to God. "*Aaallah-Ackbar! God is great!*"

They had dined frugally upon some stale unleavened bread and anchovies with a half a fig thrown in for good measure; it had done little to still Talon's growling stomach. He had been frugal with the money he had stolen, knowing they would need it to bribe inquisitive officials, and others, and to pay for the boat. The price for the passage was too high, but he did not think they had much choice at this point.

Montague came and stood next to the open window and listened with him.

"I hate that sound," he muttered. "I so much prefer the sound of the bells calling us to church. I miss that, Talon, do you not?"

"I have spent most of my life in this part of the world. I spent four years staying alive in the world of Islam and grew to like much of it. While I do not agree with their faith, they have much knowledge that we could learn from."

Montague coughed and spoke in an uneasy tone, "Isn't that heresy, Talon? Are we not dedicated to fighting everything they stand for?"

"You should listen to Talon, Montague," Max said. He joined them at the window to watch the red orb of the sun as it dipped below the level of the roofs and the distant palm trees. He continued while they watched the sunset.

"He has lived not only in the Kingdom of Jerusalem, but in Persia, too. He has told me wondrous things about their way of life, and for the life of me, I am quite envious of them in part." Then he added hastily, "But I would not give up my faith for it."

"Of what do you talk, Max?" Montague asked. "They are heathen, and followers of a pretender! What can they offer us in exchange for our faith?"

"There is much, Montague, especially here; the civilization of the Egyptians far outruns that of the Islamic faith, which is new, as history goes," Max replied.

"The people of these eastern countries were conquered in the name of Allah, but their skills and sciences were begun long before the conquest by Islam, and now they thrive under its mantle. It is of these that I have spoken to Max. It is these things we, from our northern Christian fastness, should learn," Talon said.

"You should remember that their doctors make our leeches look and smell like butchers!" Max added with a chuckle.

Talon glanced at the last rays of sun that gleamed though the distant trees.

"Come, it is time we left. I pray God that we will be in Cyprus two days hence, and back with our own people soon after."

They slipped out of their chambers without being accosted by their landlord. Talon had paid him well enough so that, although their absence would be noticed in the morning, there would be no outcry.

They walked unobtrusively along the darkened streets towards the harbor, watchful for anyone who might be acting suspiciously. This was the time when thieves and whores came out of the shadows to accost the unwary or those looking for the pleasures of the flesh. The crowds had thinned considerably as darkness descended upon the city.

The evening meal was being prepared in many courtyards, and the wafting scents of chicken, goat's meat or fish being grilled on fires and made Talon realize that he was still hungry. He would obtain some food to take with them on the trip, he decided.

They could see the masts of the ships in the harbor several streets away, and the cry of those few sea gulls that were still searching for food was indication enough that they were nearing the dirty harbor water. Talon picked up the pace and, with his companions in tow, strode onto the stone quayside that ran the length of the harbor. There was more traffic here than in the city, as the port never seemed to sleep.

Ships were preparing to leave on the tide and give way to others which had been waiting their turn. The merchants were impatient to lead their camel trains onto the quays and to unload their cargo. The camels already there were squatting patiently, waiting for crews to take their wares off their back and load the ships. Talon noticed many long white ingots, one on either side of some of the camels, and curiously touched one as they walked by. Its grainy surface was slick. He touched his fingers to his tongue after first sniffing his fingers. It was salt. He did not think he had seen so much in one place. The lighthouse on Pharos Island threw a blaze of light across the dark oily waters of the inner port.

None of them noticed the soldiers on the quay side until it was too late. Talon saw enough in the descending dusk to realize that they might be heading into a trap, and turned away hurriedly.

"I think they are waiting for us, my friends, we may have been betrayed," he muttered. He had just glimpsed the thin man from the inn with the soldiers. He must have seen them as they turned away, because he pointed toward them and yelled excitedly at the leader of the soldiers.

"There...there they are! Look, you! Those three men over there! They are *Kharagi*. Those are your quarry, quickly, catch them!"

The soldiers saw Talon and his companions escaping through the tangle of cordage and cargo, dodging between the laden camels which were everywhere. Their shouts as they gave chase added to the already noisy roadway.

Running was to no avail, as others among the crowd pointed at them and tried to obstruct them as they ran. It was only when Talon and his friends drew their swords and waved them menacingly that the drovers and others backed out of the way, falling into each other to avoid getting cut by a blade.

But the crowd had slowed the three men enough for a spear to clatter to the stones near their feet, and then some arrows whispered by, thudding into bales beside them. Men shouted and dove for cover. Talon turned to his friends.

"I shall delay them, but you must escape!"

He had absolutely no idea how his companions would manage that, as neither was equipped to survive in the city without him, but he knew he had to attempt something. His heart was pounding and his breath short with the anticipation of having to fight for their lives.

Montague, red in the face with rage, pushed him aside and growled, "No, you escape. I shall stay and fight them, Talon. It is time I stopped skulking around in disguise and fight as I am meant to. Go you with God, and say a prayer for me!"

He threw off his over robes and, brandishing his sword high, he let out a roar and charged the soldiers. He so intimidated them, that an archer, who could have shot Montague point blank, weakly let his bow wobble and his arrow flew off harmlessly into the harbor. It was the last thing the man did as Montague decapitated him then and there. The body stood bolt upright for a moment before falling over backwards, spraying his fellow soldiers with blood. The head bounced onto the stones.

Montague paid it no heed. He dove in among the shocked soldiers and hacked and stabbed with a fury. Talon and Max, after the slightest hesitation, ran to join him.

"If it is our fate to die here, Talon, then so be God's will!" Max yelled over his shoulder as he parried a spear and hacked a man's arm off with his sword. The man shrieked and fell to the stones, writhing and clutching at the stump of his arm.

Talon followed. He had a sick feeling in his stomach because he knew they could never hold off this many men and survive, but his companions had committed themselves to the fight, and so now must he.

He parried a slashing sword, stabbed a man in the face and then whirled and caught a thrust spear just in time to slide his sword up and take the spearman's fingers off at the hand. The screams of the injured men and the bellows of Montague combined with the yells of Talon and Max so surprised the soldiers that they fell back in confusion.

There was a brief pause before an officer screamed at the soldiers to attack and take them prisoners. Talon, meanwhile, saw their betrayer just behind the nervous soldiers, urging them on.

Pointing at Talon, he yelled, "There, that man, he speaks Arabic! He is for sure a spy! Kill them..."

His words were choked off as the spear Talon grabbed from the ground and hurled in one fluid motion pierced the betrayer's chest. The man stood transfixed against a huge bale, his arms flapping feebly at the shaft, his life's blood pouring onto the slippery ground. The soldiers looked at him with shock and fear, but their officer slapped at them with the flat of his sword and shouted that they must take the fugitives prisoner.

Then there was a pounding of feet, and more soldiers came from behind. Talon and his companions became aware of this when an arrow pierced Montague in the back. He stood in the middle of a pile of corpses, himself already covered in gore. But the arrow from the soldier was true and Montague fell onto his knees, dropping his sword with a gasp of agony, trying to reach the shaft protruding from his back. His face was a mask of anguish.

"Talon, Max, I am done! Pray for me...my... Lord, receive me!" He fell forward onto his face, dead.

Talon and Max had no time to even say a prayer. They were surrounded by a horde of angry soldiers who prodded them hard with points of their spears and shouted at them to lay down their weapons.

They looked at one another, both realizing there was no purpose in fighting on, other than to die. Their weapons clattered to the stones and they stood still. The angry and frightened soldiers proceeded to beat them and punch them to their knees.

Oblivious of the rough handling, Talon gazed down at Montague and murmured the prayer for the Knights. Max was doing the same, even as he was struck on the head and face by angry men who shouted abuse at them. Leaving the body of their companion behind in a pool of his and others' blood, the two were hauled to their feet and hustled off.

As they were shoved along the quay near the side of the galley they were to have sailed on, Talon saw the Master lean over the hand rail. The man was watching him and gave a wry shake of the head and a shrug, as though to say, "I could do nothing about this."

It was little comfort to Talon, who was trying to pay attention to their surroundings and to where they were being taken. His despair at having lost his companion and the desperate future they faced left him feeling numb. He barely noticed the buffeting they were receiving from their captors. Their arms had been bound painfully behind them, making it difficult to stay upright against the blows they were receiving from all sides. He realized that blood was running down his front from a blow to his face and nose, but he was too numb to feel the pain.

By the time they arrived at the gates of a large fortification, both of them were bruised and bleeding and could barely stay on their feet. They were followed by a curious and boisterous crowd of onlookers, who described the fight to one another, exaggerating the story of the battle more and more as they repeated it to passersby.

The officer in charge banged on large wood doors with the haft of his sword, shouting for entrance. Rough hands shoved them inside the courtyard. The massive doors were slammed shut in the faces of the excited people outside, and the bars dropped with a thud. The noise of the crowd abated somewhat, but their captors continued shouting at one another, still excited by the engagement and their catch.

A man in fine clothes approached their group, and after a brief talk with the commander of the soldiers he waved the guards aside and approached Talon and Max, who stood shakily waiting.

He looked them over. "Who are you, and why were you trying to escape on the ship?'

Through bruised and cut lips, Talon tried to bluff it out. "We are merchants from Cyprus, my lord. The man who betrayed us owed me money and lied to these men. We were not trying to escape!"

"So...you speak Arabic. Where did you learn our language this well?"

"My lord, I am a merchant from Armenia. I have travelled over many lands and learned the languages of many places. This man is one of my companions, as was the other who has been murdered wrongly by these soldiers. They do not speak your language. But merchants like me have to know the language of the countries we trade with, to ensure we are not cheated."

"Then why did you not tell the captain of my soldiers these things? Instead you fought them and killed many. That is not the behavior of a merchant. I think it is you who lies, and by the Prophet I shall find out in due course."

The officer who had been with the soldiers interjected, "He killed one of the men from the ship, my lord, the very man who informed us about him. I saw him do it. No merchant could throw a spear the way this man did, my lord."

"Take them to the prison. I shall find out what they were doing before too long and then they can go in front of the Emir before they are sent to the executioner."

Without further ado, the two prisoners were hurried over to a large mud and stone building with slits in the walls for windows. A door opened and they were forced up worn stone stairs and down a long corridor with doors on either side. One was opened and they were flung into a small stone cell.

The door slammed shut and the soldiers tramped away. There was silence in the cell, except for the labored breathing of the two men lying on the floor. Their captors had not bothered to release their tied arms.

Talon lay where he had fallen, breathing through his mouth because his nose was full of blood. He did a mental inventory of his injuries. Some of the blows had been very hard, and at one time the shaft of a spear had been rammed into his ribs. They hurt badly, but he could still breathe, so he did not think they were broken.

He rolled onto his back and whispered, "Max?"

Max stirred. "Talon," Max grunted.

"I am sorry, Max...so sorry."

"Don't be, Talon. This was bad fate. We were betrayed...by that scum, the Master of the ship and his weasel. At least you killed him...that was a good throw. He can enjoy his Judas money in Hell now."

"Max...do you remember when we were ambushed in France?"

There was a silence, then a sigh. "Move over and I shall see if I can get to it."

Max wiggled along the floor by scooting his knees and elbows until he reached the knife that Talon always kept in his boot and gingerly began to cut Talon's bonds. Finally they both sat against the wall in the darkness and rubbed their wrists in an attempt to restore the circulation of blood. Talon asked, "How badly did they beat you, Max?"

"I can still breathe, and my legs and arms work, sore as hell though they be. I think I have three black eyes instead of two, because they hit me twice on the same eye. Bastards!"

Talon chuckled...then groaned from the pain. He was relieved that Max was alive, and where there was humor there was a chance. Max was not giving up yet.

"I shall miss Montague...he was a great warrior. We needed men like him in the Holy Land. God bless his soul," Max muttered. His voice was low and full of regret.

"I agree, Max. I too will miss him. God receive his soul...but he died the way he wanted to, as a warrior, and God will receive him kindly, of that I am sure. I shall pray for him at the church of the Holy Sepulcher when we arrive there."

"Do you think we will, young Master?" Max asked tentatively.

"I am sure of it, Max," Talon lied. "But first we have to get out of here, change our plans and find our way across the great river, the one they call the Nile. I have heard a lot about it but have never seen it. They say it is vast."

They talked for about an hour of their chances, and although both of them tried to sound optimistic, neither felt any confidence in their future at all.

Finally Max said, "For now, I think we must rest and then plan on getting out of here tomorrow, as there will be no time to waste. Get some rest while you can, Talon."

Talon heard his friend shuffle next to him and then Max lay quietly. Talon did the same, but his mind would not stop worrying. He relived the incidents of the day, trying to think of what they might have done if they had had more warning. He finally slept a fitful and uncomfortable sleep, plagued by ghosts and demons, tossing restlessly on the cold stone floor.

The last sound he heard was that of squeaking rats somewhere in the dark cell.

# Chapter 4

# Prison

Talon and Max spent a bad night in their prison cell. The walls were made of thick sandstone which cut them off from all sound from the outside other than what they could hear through the cracks of the thick wooden door. These sounds were mainly from other prisoners, who cried their despair to the indifferent walls. There were no windows in their cell, which made the air stifling, and it was difficult to know what time of the day or night it might be.

Even in the darkness one could tell that the cell was filthy as though it had never been cleaned. There were small bones, picked clean, rags and other objects that the previous prisoners had left behind, strewn over the eight foot by six foot area of the floor space. Chains hung from the walls where other luckless creatures might have hung; they did not bear closer inspection, as there were strips of something hanging off the shackles. The stink of the place was enough to make Talon gag and there were rats competing with an army of cockroaches and other biting insects for whatever was left over. They all somehow came and went as they pleased.

The first thing Talon did upon waking was to scratch himself vigorously, as did Max. Talon's eyes were barely used to the dark; he could just make out his friend's pale features. Max's face was swollen and cut, and his eyes were puffed from the blows he received the previous evening.

"How are you today, Talon?" Max asked, licking his parched lips with a dry tongue. They had received neither water nor food during the night, and both were ravenously hungry and thirsty to the point of desperation.

"I am as well as can be expected, Max, but we must think of how we are to escape, because to stay here is to surely die."

Max nodded somberly. "I think I am going to envy our dear companion Montague before very long," he grunted. "I am sure that he would have had something to say about this lousy accommodation. I preferred the seaside with all its hardships, to this!" He scratched himself again. "I am already covered in fleas!"

They heard noises in the corridor, which appeared to signal the day had commenced, but no one came their way. In the distance they did hear high pitched screams and shouting.

The noise died down and they were left alone for many hours, still without food or water. They wiled away the time planning how they might escape.

"If we can get out at night, we might have a chance. If we attempted to escape during the day, the whole city would join in to chase us and there would be nowhere to hide. But we must find a way to get out of here, and as soon as possible," Talon stated more firmly than he felt.

Max nodded grimly. "I shall follow your lead, young master."

Talon shook his head in distress. He simply did not know what was to become of them, and he had a deep sinking feeling in his stomach about their future. While they waited, he honed the blade of his knife on the stone of the wall one more time and then hid it under the filth in the cell, as there was a fair chance that their gaolers would remember to come and search them sooner or later. After the excitement of the battle, their captors had thrown them straight into jail without searching them. They were careless, and Talon counted on the security to be lax enough to provide a way out, when the moment presented itself.

It seemed like many hours later that they heard footsteps, and the door to their cell slammed open. Several well armed men crowded the doorway. The leader, who carried a sword at the ready, shouted at the two prisoners to get up and come out. Pretending to be injured, Talon struggled to his feet and limped, seemingly painfully, towards the men. They grasped his arms and tied his wrists behind his back. They did the same with Max and then jostled and pushed them down the dark corridor, towards another opening where they could see daylight flooding in. The guards clearly did not remember that they had tossed the prisoners into the cell with their hands bound the night before.

Talon blinked in the harsh sunlight as they exited the prison and were pushed down the stone steps. He stumbled, limping in an exaggerated manner.

"Water! For the love of Allah, water, I beg of you!" he cried, pretending to be near fainting. Max, whether from real or feigned exhaustion, fell to his knees, signaling he wanted water as well.

The leader of the group exclaimed, "You speak our language, *Kharagi* scum? You will have to wait for the water. Our noble lord wants to see you and it is now."

At least when they passed a trough, he had one of the men dash water into their faces. The cool water on Talon's face was a real relief and he licked all he could that came to his lips.

Talon knew better than to push his luck by asking for more and kept quiet as they were hurried across the interior maidan of the fortress to another entrance, and then to a hallway where the rough stone of the fort walls was replaced with finely painted tiles and the floor was laid with wide flag stones. The party stopped and the guards made obeisance to a group of richly dressed men standing near to a fountain.

He felt dizzy from lack of sustenance and the sound of the water rushing made him feel faint. One of the well-dressed men noticed the soldiers, waved them over and then walked towards Max and Talon, stopping about ten feet away. The others of his group followed at a respectful distance. Forced to their knees by an iron fist and held by their necks, Talon and Max waited while the man spoke to the leader of the soldiers.

"Are these the people I have heard about?"

"They are indeed the fugitives we caught in the fight on the harbor, lord. They were trying to buy their way out of the country, but a man told us of them. They killed many of our men before Allah intervened on our behalf and we could subdue them. They fought like lions, my Gracious Lord. This one," he kicked Talon in the ribs, "claims he is a merchant, but our officer says that if that were so, why did he fight?"

"I see. They look like wild Bedouin and they stink," said the man, upon approaching the prisoners.

Just as he said this while twitching his nose, a young boy came up and stood behind him. Peering past the finely dressed man, he asked, "What are these men doing here, father?"

"They are brought to answer for their crime before men, and in the name of Allah the Almighty. You may stay, but do not say anything. Watch and learn."

"You," he then said loudly, addressing Talon.

Talon looked up from his forced contemplation of the tiles.

"Me, *Osstez*? Oh Lord of many Provinces." He looked into the man's eyes. They were intelligent eyes that shrewdly assessed him. The man was older than Talon. He also held the power of life and death over them, so Talon was careful not to cause offense. The man stared in silence down at him for a few long moments. Finally he said, "Yes, you! Where are you from? You do not look like any Egyptian."

Still looking the man directly in his eyes, Talon responded, "My lord, as Allah is my witness, I am originally from Armenia within the lands of the Byzantium Empire. I am a simple merchant and have been trading in this land as well as the lands to the east and west of this fair city."

"My men tell me that you fought like warriors. Are merchant men warriors too, these days?" His tone expressed the disdain that a noble would have for a mere trader.

"My lord, I was trained in the art of defense by my uncle in Isfahan who is ...was, a trader and doctor. He also taught me medicine and the healing crafts at the hospital. He believed that a man who travelled the dangerous roads of today needs to know how to defend himself."

Talon wanted the man to know that he was no mere trader but had other capabilities as well, which might sway him in their favor.

The elegantly dressed man seemed to think about this for a moment. His fine, dark-featured face, aquiline nose and well trimmed beard and moustache denoted a man of nobility, and judging from his clothing and the rings on his fingers, he was wealthy. However, Talon could see strong wrists and scars on the man's forearms and a lean body, all of which told him that this man was a warrior, and not to be trifled with.

"Are you then a physician, as well as a trader...and warrior?" The man asked, sounding skeptical and amused.

"*Insha'Allah,* I shall one day be qualified to sit in the shadow of Abū 'l-Walīd Muḥammad and heal the sick using the skills Allah might see fit to provide me, My lord."

"You do not seem old enough to know these things you speak of. You use the name of our God, as though you were a believer. Are you, then, one of the faithful?" The man looked at Talon keenly, as though defying him to lie.

"I was raised in Persia, My lord. I am of the Shia' faith," he stated simply, and without adornment.

"I was told that you were Christian spies, seeking to escape. Instead I find a heretic at my feet...you are no better than the rest of the Shia' scum. Our Lord and master the Sultan has sworn to the Caliph in Baghdad that he will eradicate the Shia' and Ismaili from this country!"

"My lord, as I kneel before you and Allah himself, the man who betrayed us to the soldiers was a thief and a liar. May his soul rot in Jehannum. He was one of the people I dealt with over some merchandise and we had a disagreement about payment. I gave him and his master passage money, but he sought to make more from *Kharagi* in a foreign land."

Talon tried to sound convincing. He knew his lie was flimsy, but one of the men who might dispute it was dead, while the other was presumably at sea.

"He killed the man he is talking about, Oh Gracious Lord," volunteered the leader of the soldiers. "He made a very good throw with a spear!"

"How convenient! It would seem that you have helped keep the crime in this fair city of ours down. Not only that, you have gained the admiration of my men!" said the man in front of Talon dryly, but with a glare at the soldier for his impertinence. The man cringed in response.

He looked at Talon and at the kneeling Max, speculatively.

"I am still not sure I believe all you have said. But the fact remains that you killed some of my men and that merits death as punishment. A mere merchant would have tried to explain himself before he attacked an armed detachment of soldiers who were just doing their duty. Not only that, you are heretics as well. The Sultan, may Allah protect him and provide him with great wisdom, has pronounced the Shia' as deviants along with the Ismaili."

"My lord, I cannot contradict you on my faith. But all men of the faith are the same under God, are they not? It does not mean that we could not also be the faithful servants of the Sultan, may Allah protect him.

"On the other issue I swear on the name of the Prophet that we were taken by surprise. My men are also warriors and they sincerely believed that we were under attack, without provocation. The one that is dead reacted foolishly, and without my permission, but by that time we were beset on all sides, and did not know what to do, other than to defend ourselves."

Talon knew he was being unkind to Montague and gave a small prayer to his erstwhile companion to forgive him. Max did not understand the foreign words, so he could not react.

"What is your name?" The man in front of him asked, sharply.

"My given name is Suleiman ibn Mahmud Omar, which name my uncle gave to me when I came to him in Isfahan Persia as a very small boy, my lord," said Talon with deference. "May I enquire, most respectfully, who it is that condescends to question me?" he asked.

Before one of the soldiers could kick him for his impertinence, the man raised his hand to stop him and said, "My name is Emir Abbas Abdur Rahman ibn Athir Faysal. I am descended from the faithful followers of the Prophet who left Medina four hundred years before this time. You should count yourself very lucky that merciful Allah is smiling upon you this day, as I have decided not to have you executed in the *maidan*. I shall think on what to do with you shortly. In the meantime, you are prisoners, and shall remain so at my pleasure. Take them away."

He turned and left them, taking his boy with him, talking quietly to him as they went. Talon stared after him. He did not have much time to reflect on their fate, for the soldiers seized him and Max and hustled them back to the prison cell.

On the way, Talon again begged the leader of the soldiers for water and food.

"You must have found our Lord in a fine mood today, *Kharagi*. He gave you back your worthless lives; that in itself is very unusual. I shall get water and food to you, although I should slip a sword into you for killing my companions," he added bitterly.

"May Allah be kind to their souls, Your Honor, but I was defending myself; and what would you have a warrior merchant do? Grovel like a worm, or fight like a man?"

The soldier, a tough looking infantryman, who by his scars had clearly seen his share of fights, nodded reluctantly and grudgingly acknowledged Talon's comment.

"You are right, it is better. I shall see to it," he said briefly.

Talon discouraged any comment from the hitherto silent Max until they were back in the cell. The soldier released them from their bonds, which were beginning to hurt, and gave them both a cursory check over to see if there were any weapons concealed on their persons. He did find a few of the silver coins Talon had kept on his person for just such an eventuality. These were confiscated with the laconic comment, "You won't need coins in this place."

"I hope that it buys you much. Consider it a present from me, *Oustez*," murmured Talon, politely.

They were left alone in the gloomy cell. Max rubbed his wrists to get the circulation back and then stood saying, "I did not understand a word of what went on there, Talon. For the love of God, now tell me, are we to die? What is to become of us?"

Talon was in the same discomfort as Max, as he leaned against the filth-encrusted wall of their cell and thought about what had transpired.

"We live...for the time being, Max. The man we were talking to is a noble man with a long name who is in charge of this prison. That puts him high in rank, but at what level I do not know. Perhaps this man is a relative of the Sultan; it is a fair bet that he might be. In any case he decided, thank God, not to have us executed on the spot, saying he wants to think on what to do with us."

"Does that mean that we might be able to escape, Talon?"

"I think that, God willing, we should try. He might change his mind, and I would hate to think that we sat on our arses doing nothing when we might have tried," Talon said. "Let's see what develops, as now we have seen the outside surroundings and have a little time to plan more carefully."

The hours passed until they heard the clamor of men moving along the corridor again, and guessed that they might be seeing food and water. Sure enough, the door slammed open and a pitcher of water was placed inside, along with some stale flat bread and a bowl of stewed vegetables and lentils. The soldiers told them to eat and drink and that this was their lot for the day and night.

"You are lucky to have anything at all," they were told, "as Ramadan has started and we are yet to go to our own food. Prisoners should be made to fast for the whole month; it would cost us less!"

Both men grabbed for the water and had to restrain themselves from drinking it all in one go. Max insisted that they ration it carefully, because, as they both knew, they would not see any until well into the next day. Having slaked their thirst, they then deliberately ate the food provided. Having lived for months on the barest of scraps from the seashore this was not such a hardship for them, although it was so foul that ordinarily they would have gagged on it.

They laid back against the wall, oblivious to its filth, and talked. Not for the first time Talon, to divert his somber thoughts, quizzed Max on his background. Max was willing enough to tell him.

"I have already told you that I grew up in the mountains of the land north of the great mountains, the Alps," he said, as he scratched his arms again.

"Yes, Max, they sound like real mountains, they must be like the ones I lived among in Persia. Those were very high, and in winter all was covered in snow and ice. I never liked it, but I got used to it."

"I grew up in a tiny town that was deep in a forested valley of the mountains. Life was very hard. Each winter we had to kill much of our livestock because there was not enough food to keep them alive for the entire winter. It is fortunate that we were not so far from the salt mines, as that is what preserved our meat for a long time. But we also kept our remaining cows and sheep on the ground enclosure beneath the houses and this kept us warm. I shall never forget the sweet smell of cows!" He leaned back and sighed. "I do not like the stink of camels or that of goats, although I know they are useful creatures; there is something I just don't like about them." He slapped at a whining mosquito. "We did not have these pests in the mountains either," he remarked.

Talon agreed that he found the whining insects most annoying. They swarmed in the night, despite the seeming lack of openings in the cell walls, and made sleep difficult.

"In the winter, I could hunt deer high in the mountains with my father and brothers. We would cross the snow on boards tied to our feet which made it possible to cross great distances without being buried. We did not always bring home game, sometimes only a couple of rabbits. Ah me, but I remember the rabbits in wine and herbs. And I remember your mother's cooking, Talon. How I miss that home of yours."

They fell to reminiscing about their time in the household of Sir Hughes, which brought the Welsh archers to mind, and they too came up in the discussion.

"Good fighters one and all. I mourn Anwl; he never made it home, but the others did...at least, I pray to God that they did," Talon said crossing himself. Max did the same automatically.

"Do you remember that Devonalt, the big one? The girls never seemed to have enough of him," chuckled Max.

"I know. Gareth and I caught him at it once, and I had to tell Gareth that unless it stopped, then Devonalt would be staying in Albi!" They laughed and it helped to calm their fears. They talked long into the night about their friends and the good times in Albi, nestled in the foothills of the Languedoc.

They watched the goings on and the routine of the prison, then waited through the ensuing week, trying to work out who did what work in the prison. They were never let out, not even to wash or defecate outside of their cell. As time went by, their condition became worse and the stink of their cell more noisome. At least they were not chained, and they received food and water twice a day, although neither was very palatable. They watched the gaolors for opportunities and the pattern of their work day, as far as they were able to verify it.

Their meals came late in the morning and often very late in the evening, if at all; but they had no idea as to how close to sunset the day had come, and they could not even hear the call to prayers in the city, the walls were so thick. It would have helped to know the time of day. Talon was growing desperate to make a move, as he feared that they might still go to an execution. He feared that he might have made a serious mistake by confessing the fact that he was Shia'. The reaction had been chilling. But he recalled his education at the hands of his mentor, Dr. Far'jan, who had told him that Egypt was the center of the Shia' faith. The disputes the doctor had talked of were the differences between the Ismaili and the Sunni, not the Sunni and the Shia, which seemed to be the case here today. What could have changed, he wondered?

He had found out from their gaolers that the name of the sultan of the country was Salah Ed Din, a Kurd, not even a true descendent of the Prophet's followers, but the nephew of Nur Ed Din, the Sultan who ruled Damascus. Beyond that they knew little.

As they estimated the evening of the seventh day approaching, they heard once again the tramp of men marching towards their door. Talon hastily retrieved the knife and hid it in the folds of his tunic. The door banged open, and a soldier stood at the entrance. He beckoned to Talon. "You are to come with us," he ordered. "Our Lord wishes to see you. Your fate has been decided."

"What fate would that be?" Talon demanded, his heart pumping.

"The Master has left for the south where our overlord Salah Ed Din's brother is fighting the invaders. I have been commanded to bring you before his administrator, who will sentence you today."

"What will become of us, *Oustez*?" Talon asked, faking a whining, servile tone.

"He will probably sentence you to slavery. He likes to make life a torment, before his slaves die."

Talon did not like what he heard. He tensed. "We can always wait for your Lord to return," he said, ingratiatingly.

"You are to go to work on the Great Light building, because you are a heretic and he is an unbeliever," the soldier pointed at Max. "You will become slaves," he sneered, "as good a fate as any for the deaths you caused our friends."

Talon saw only three men in the corridor and none of them had his weapon at the ready. It was dark in the corridor behind the men, their one torch held high by the second man, so he guessed that it was past sunset.

He said in a low voice to Max, "It is now or never. They intend to make us slaves. Be quick about it, when I make my move."

Although tired and undernourished, Talon still had speed on his side. He slipped in very close to the soldier who had spoken. His knife came out and he plunged it into the first man's throat, dragging the sharp blade around and down hard, opening the man's throat almost from ear to ear before either of the other two could react. Blood spurted in all directions, splashing his face and clothing. The man jerked back convulsively with a choked gargle, clutching his open throat in a feeble attempt to stop his life blood from flowing away.

The knife came out of the man's neck and sped into the midriff of the next guard, with an audible thump. The man gasped and would have screamed but for Talon's hand over his mouth. Max lunged forward and seized the third man by the arm and hauled him into the cell. The man gave a yelp of surprise and fear, but Max rammed him head first into the stone wall. There was a sickening crack, and the man fell backwards into Max's waiting arms. Max seized the guard around his throat and began to strangle what life was left out of him.

Talon, meanwhile, had finished off the second man. He turned and buried his knife in the back of the third. It was all over within seconds. The torch was now on the floor and beginning to go out. Talon retrieved it and held its sputtering flame high, the better to see their handiwork. He took a swift look out of the open doorway, but the corridor was dark, and apart from the occasional groan behind one or two of the cell doors, all was quiet.

"We must escape quickly. They will be expecting these men to come out soon." His hoarse whisper sounded loud in the chamber. The blood was beginning to puddle beneath the bodies of the dead men.

Max retrieved the soldiers' weapons and passed a sword to Talon.

"You search them while I stand guard," he whispered.

Talon only wanted to know what the men possessed that he would need. There was a large set of keys which he took and tied to his belt, and then he took their turban cloths and threw one at Max, who wound it around his head. It had the effect of changing Max into an unidentifiable man from anywhere in the region. With his luxuriant, albeit filthy, beard, he could pass in the dark for a beggar or laborer.

"We need to find some charcoal for your hair later," Talon muttered, eyeing him critically in the light of the torch.

He did the same for himself and then retrieved some metal discs from the necks of the corpses. He thought these might be useful as identification. The soldiers had carried a few coins between them and he took these also. Now they were ready.

They locked the door behind them, then Talon had an idea. He knew there were cells above them, so he told Max to stay near the main door and keep watch.

"What are you going to do?" Max asked, "Let's get out of here while we can."

"I want to create a diversion. Wait here," Talon commanded.

Leaving a very nervous Max hiding in the dark shadows clutching a spear and watching for danger, Talon skipped up the flight of stairs until he came to the top landing. He ran to the end of the corridor and began to unlock doors. He did not open them until he had reached the last, then he called into the darkness, "Everyone out, there is a fire!" He heard stirring sounds from the cells, but he did not pause. Then he risked the same for the corridor where they had been incarcerated. He then tossed the torch onto a pile of old sacking, wood and other leavings in a corner. Before long the flames licked hungrily at the material and some wood had caught. There was a lot of smoke and the stink was nauseous.

"Max, let's go," he shouted.

"It's about time. I was wondering what you were up to," Max said nervously, from near the entrance door.

They slipped out of the door and shut it quietly and heard the first of the prisoners panicking as the smoke infiltrated their cells. It would not be long now, Talon thought to himself. He hoped they had enough time to reach the gate and make an exit while the prison riot ensued.

They moved forward across the maidan without being challenged, towards the far wall where the main gate was located, and slipped into the deep shadows nearby to await events. Before long the main door of the prison swung open with a crash, and a yelling mob of ragged prisoners poured out then rushed down the steps. Talon and Max could see the red glow of the fire as it spread, and they heard the screams from those who had been too slow to escape.

Suddenly the men of the fortress realized what was happening and began to shout and raise the alarm. Some rushed out of a door in the main building to try and stop the prisoners, while others ran to try and find water. If the fire became widespread it could engulf the rest of the fort. They were too few and too slow to react.

The men who tried to stop the prisoners were no match for the crazed scarecrows who leapt upon them and killed them with their bare hands. Snatching up the fallen guards' weapons, the prisoners rushed for the gate and butchered the guards who tried to stop them. The huge bar was lifted by many hands and under the determined weight of the maddened men, the great wooden gates opened ponderously, to crash against the walls outside. Talon glanced at Max in the firelight and they knew it was their opportunity to join the escaping prisoners as they poured onto the street in an excited mob, yelling and brandishing their new weapons. They were out for blood this night.

Talon had no idea where they might be going, but decided that running deeper into the town after the maddened men was not a good idea. He glanced up and saw to the north there was a glow, and he assumed it to be the great light on the Pharos point shining by the entrance to the harbor. Using this as his compass, he set out in a westerly direction towards what he remembered as the graveyard city. He surmised that they might be able to hide there from the inevitable hue and cry that would soon ensue.

He wanted to get them a horse or a camel and he kept his eyes open while they ran through the darkened streets. The rest of the prisoners had charged off to loot and steal what they could find and would be easy prey for the soldiers when they came looking for them the next morning. None accompanied Talon and Max as they ran into the darkness trying to put as much distance between themselves and the prison.

Due to their enforced idleness and lack of proper nutrition, it was not long before the two men were winded and tired, but Talon kept urging Max on, saying that they had to keep going till they found a safe place to hide. Unfortunately, the options were sparse, as they could not see for any distance, and all around them the buildings were dark and unwelcoming. A light cool wind was beginning to come in off the sea. They felt it close, may be less than a mile to their north, but to the fugitives in their underfed condition, it meant hardship from the cold.

Fate was kind to them this night. On the outskirts of the main city where the houses had thinned out, they came across a cluster of buildings set in among a large grove of Cyprus trees and palms that swayed in the night breeze and rustled in the dark. They paused to watch for any danger of running into people on the road, but the buildings were just far enough away for them to be indistinguishable from the darkness to anyone watching from the houses.

Then Talon stiffened and touched Max's arm. "Look, Max, I see horses...we might be able to take one or two of them."

Max grunted in the dark. Like Talon, he was exhausted from the privations of the prison and the lack of exercise, combined with the recent excitement and now this long walk. He peered towards where Talon was pointing then whispered, "I see the horses, but how do we take them?"

"With care," his companion whispered back.

Talon began to move towards the shadows, closer to where the horses were hitched. It soon became clear from sounds of carefree laughter and loud talk that there was a party going on within the courtyard of the large block of buildings. Although he could not see the activity, there was a bright glow from many oil lamps. He heard reedy music, accompanied by the tapping of a small drum and the clapping of hands.

Peering through the main entrance, which was open, he guessed that it might be a marriage celebration. His eyes by now were well used to the dark, and he noticed that while there were guards on the walls, their attention was focused on the events taking place inside rather than on the restive animals outside. He leaned towards Max, who was deep in the shadow of the bushes near him.

"The horses might be guarded, Max. I shall go and get them. You keep watch."

There was a slight rustle in the bush in acknowledgement and then Talon moved towards the animals. There were several of them grouped around a structure that looked like a well. They were still saddled, and ready to leave at any time. His suspicions proved to be correct: a guard was slumped against a cypress tree; but the snore Talon heard was clue enough to how alert the guard would be. He walked slowly towards the animals. He did not creep towards them, as he did not want to startle the horses. He found the guard was fast asleep; the smell on his clothing and breath told Talon he was happily drunk and unlikely to waken any time soon. Talon inspected the horses and found to his delight that they were prime animals.

They were Arab desert war-horses and well accoutered. He untied the reins of two of them, whispering gently to them as he did so. The animals had watched him come, so they were not surprised. Their ears were cocked and their noses pushed forward to be touched and to take the scent of a new person, and if they were lucky, to beg for a treat. He had nothing to give them, but he stroked their noses, and then led them slowly away so that their hooves would not make noise. He moved deeper into the shadows away from the celebrations. As he came to the dark of the cluster of trees, he was startled at the sound of a voice behind him calling, "Where are you going with those horses? Who are you?"

"I am Ahmad and I have been told by my master to walk his horses. He is going to be late and did not want his precious beasts to be tired from standing so long. He is soft on his lovely ponies. Your friend is drunk, by the way."

A man walked out from where he had been relieving himself in the bushes with a laugh. It sounded as though he too had been drinking. Talon had to stop and get his breath; it could so easily have gone badly, and he did not want to leave bodies all over the place.

He stroked the muzzles of both horses, and got a curious nudge in return. It comforted him to have their sharp smell in his nostrils and to feel their warm breath after the filth of the previous months and weeks. Max materialized out of the dark and took one of the horses from Talon.

"That sounded close, Talon. What did he want?"

"To know what I was doing. I told him I was the syce and walking the horses. He was taking a piss!"

They walked alongside the horses for another hundred yards and then quietly mounted and walked them for a half mile more until they knew they could not be heard, and only then touched the sides of the animals and moved into a canter.

"We cannot go back the way we came, Max, and the man back there knows we headed west. The sea is to our north so our only way is to the south. Once we are past the end of the lake we'll veer south. That is the way we must go, and very fast."

Max felt his saddle bags. "I think there are coins in these bags, Talon."

Talon reached behind him and felt the bags on his own saddle. They chinked. "Yes, Max, it appears we are blessed with coin for our escape!"

They set their mounts to a long gallop. For the first time in months, Talon felt the wind in his face and the pleasure of a good mount beneath him, and began to think that they were at last free.

# Chapter 5

# Highwaymen

Talon and Max sat upon their stolen horses on the slope of a low hill and stared down at the road below that ran alongside a narrow river. This river meandered from the plain to the east which was obscured by the heat haze. It flowed into the west towards what looked like a large lake. They were, as ever, cautious about revealing themselves when near human habitation or on roads; and while they were mounted they stayed hidden among the scrub trees and rocks of the hillside looking down on the activity along the river banks.

They were still filthy but had managed, with the help of a few coins, to purchase new clothes and bathe in a ditch some way back. Although their clothes were more or less the same as any other traveler's on these roads, stained and dusty, neither had trimmed their beards, so while they might have smelled a little better, they still looked like a pair of wild-eyed scarecrows.

Anyone who looked close could see that they were astride a couple of magnificent war horses, worth a lot more than the two ragged men should be able to afford. Talon leaned down over his mount's neck and stroked its sweaty flank. His mount was a compact dark bay beauty with a short back and slim legs; the one Max rode matched it perfectly. His horse shook its magnificent head and snorted impatiently through flared nostrils. Talon brushed away the flies that were bothering the animal, a gelding.

Talon wished that it had been entire, but he knew that stallions of this breed were prone to erratic behavior when their absolute obedience in battle was needed, which was why they were gelded.

"I shall name you Rakhsh, because you are fleet of foot," he told his mount. He received a rolled eye and a stamp of impatience for an answer.

"Patience, my beauty, we will be down by the water soon," Talon said with a chuckle.

The road more or less followed the bends of the meandering river on its south side. However, to Talon's eyes, it was not quite a natural course of running water. Peering through the heat haze, he could see beyond this first one another huge river, perhaps two miles away to the east.

He realized that river had to be the Nile. Shading his eyes from the glare of the sun he could distinguish boats of many kinds on its vast expanse of water. The most common were the quick, slim falukahs with their lateen sails that made easy headway driving upstream and had great speed sailing downstream with the wind and the current behind them. His eyes traced back from the Nile to the flowing water below them. It had to have been modified by man, he thought; its banks did not look natural enough, they were bright green with papyrus clumps interspersed with tall reeds, and even taller cane brakes, while in other places trees had grown up into small dense copses that provided welcome shade to travelers.

He and Max were four days into their journey south. This unexpected barrier gave Talon cause for concern. This strip of water winding through the valley, narrow though it was, would require a boat to cross, of that he was sure; and he could not guess what lay further south. Perhaps they should turn east.

He was not certain if they had avoided a city known as Al Qahirah, which he knew existed somewhere over to the east; he wanted to avoid it at all costs. During their stay in Al Iskandrîyah he had heard people in the souk talk about the city called Al Qahirah [Cairo] with envy and with some scorn, as it was the new city of the sultans.

They, the people of Alexandria, wondered why their city, one of the fairest in the world, was being slighted for a city that lay in the swamps of the Nile delta. Talon only wanted to avoid it as he knew it would be swarming with soldiers, and hence could be a trap.

"I think it is time to turn eastward and take our chances with that big river over there." He pointed to the east. "If we can steal a boat, we can cross over, and then head north towards the Kingdom of Jerusalem. I see no purpose in continuing south anymore."

Max nodded, "I agree, and if we have avoided that place you call Kwiro? We should be going east by now."

"Cairo." Talon corrected him. "The Arab people call it Al Qahirah. In truth, my friend, I do not know where we are right now; but we must not lose sight of that huge river, for then we are truly lost." He pointed to the east again.

"Indeed, it seems vast, Talon," Max said, sounding bemused, peering at the mighty river in the distance.

"But we cannot do anything until they leave," Talon said, pointing with his chin to a group of people.

The sun was still in the eastern quadrant of the sky. Its rays reflected off the water, creating a glare that blinded and made it hard to distinguish the size of the few boats on the water of this man-made channel. None appeared to be interested in landing nearby, despite the fact that there were people resting by the banks, under the shade of a small but dense plantation of palm trees and shrubs. There was the usual collection of camels and donkeys standing in the shade that denoted a traveling caravan.

It was the presence of the people on the roadside that had arrested their journey. They were now waiting to see when the travelers would leave, allowing them to go down to the water unnoticed. Both they and the horses were thirsty. The horses were restless, reacting to the scent of water below.

Talon placed his hand on the neck of his fine mount to calm its straining and to brush off flies that appeared in swarms no matter where they stopped, if even for a moment. The horse responded by pawing at the ground as though to say, *"Why are we not flying like the wind instead of being tormented by these flies?"*

Talon smiled and patted its neck reassuringly.

He wiped his face with the tail of his turban. It seemed hotter than usual; the humidity was rising, which made him sweat profusely, and he wondered if he might have a fever. For some days now, he had not felt very well. The sun was hot and the heat haze that was forming on the water and on the land partially hid the distant buildings from view.

"I would like to go down to the water and bathe, Talon. I have not washed for so long I have forgotten the pleasure of it. I am also sick of the fleas in my clothing and wish to wash my garments before I am eaten alive by the vermin," Max moaned as he scratched at himself for the hundredth time that morning.

Talon nodded and grinned ruefully. "I agree it is a distinctly unpleasant thing to be downwind of you."

Max grinned. "So now you know why I am upwind of you."

Talon grinned.

They had been avoiding villages and any other form of human habitation as much as possible; there had not been that many so far away from the great river. This had meant hovering on the edge of the desert where the land was barren and often not easy to travel along.

One remarkable night they had ridden past some huge angular mountains which Talon was sure had been built by men, their lines were so sharp. These had been on their horizon for two days and a night. Their surprise had been complete soon after when they rode past a monstrous head that stuck out of the sand. It looked like some ancient deity that the kings of long ago might have worshipped.

Neither Max nor Talon could explain these wondrous sights that were illuminated by the light of the moon and stars. The great silence that had surrounded these marvels had further awed them, and they had made the mistake of drifting further eastward to see more.

They were rudely awakened by the sudden sighting of villages and human habitation, something they had wanted to avoid. Dogs had barked and men had called out. Silently they had reined up and slowly retraced their path back into the desert's edge, to where they were now.

"Look," Max said.

He pointed to a small caravan in the distance, making its way towards them along the road below. It was indistinct in the heat, so Talon did not pay it much attention at first, other than to imagine that it might be just another merchant on his way to a market somewhere. But even at this distance he noticed that there was a palanquin being carried on the shoulders of some stout looking men, which indicated that this was a more important caravan than he had supposed at first.

As the group approached, it became easier to distinguish the individuals. There were two outriders on good horses, well forward of the main party, armed with lances. The main party was similarly armed, their lance blades glinting in the sunlight, while the riders were in a protective ring around the palanquin. Trailing along behind the armed group walked a line of camels and donkeys heavily laden, their drovers walking, or in some cases seated high on the swaying backs of the camels. Talon touched Max on the arm.

"We should not be seen by those people, Max. We need to get well out of sight."

Max nodded and slowly they eased their horses further back off the crest of the hill, till all that might have been seen of them from the road was their heads. "I count about six or eight men at arms and two scouts out at the front," Max said.

"I agree, but look over there. Those other people have disappeared. I wonder where they went and why?" He pointed to the grove of trees where they had seen people seemingly resting in the shade. The grove was now still, with no sign of life, where formerly there had been much activity. From their vantage point of just under half a mile, the two men had had a clear view of the people in the grove and had supposed them to be fellow travelers, but now all of them were gone, including their baggage animals. There was something very odd about their sudden disappearance. Talon's eyes flicked from the clump of trees to the caravan and back.

"No they have not gone, Talon. Look," Max said, pointing, "they're hiding behind trees. I can see them."

"Do you think they are afraid to be seen...like us, Max?"

"I do not know, but I think we are about to find out."

The caravan, its pace dictated by the strides of the men carrying the palanquin – Talon assumed they were slaves – slowly approached the trees. The two front riders arrived and stopped in the shade. Suddenly, just as they were beginning to dismount, the people hidden among the trees ran out to surround them. To Talon and Max's utter surprise, they dragged the riders off their frightened horses, threw the men on the ground and began stabbing them.

It was unclear exactly was going on, but neither Max nor Talon doubted that the attackers were about to ambush the small caravan. He could not hear any shouts, which made Talon think that there had been no time for the two scouts to do so. He watched in grim silence as the murders took place before them. Max, a hardened warrior, grunted in disgust.

The killers hurriedly dragged the dead bodies out of sight and led the horses into the cover of the trees. Again the small copse seemed bereft of life, and the caravan, oblivious of the danger, continued to approach.

Talon looked at Max. "I know it is not our quarrel, Max, but someone innocent is about to be murdered by that band of thieves. What should we do?"

"I was thinking the same, Talon. Do you remember why the Templars came into being?"

"Was it not for the protection of the pilgrim along the path to Jerusalem, Max?"

"Indeed it was, young Master, and here we are, two Templars, watching an offense against God taking place right under our noses. It might not be the road to Jerusalem; but by God's good graces we need to at least warn them."

"Max, you are a wonderful man and I agree whole heartedly with you. We should go down there and warn them of the danger and then leave. Come, my friend. We will do this in the service of God this day."

Excited now, they kicked their eager horses into action. The two Arab horses needed no persuasion. This was the direction of the water, and they were thirsty. They leapt over the rocks and onto the crest of the hill. But Talon could see that they might even now be too late. He drew his battered sword, as did Max, and they shouted as they galloped their sure-footed steeds down the hill, waving their swords in the air, yelling and pointing.

But the caravan had already stopped. The guards, seeing the ambushers rushing at them from the woods, tried to defend themselves as well as the occupants of the palanquin, but they were quickly surrounded and a fierce fight broke out. The shouts and clash of steel upon steel came clearly to his ears and Talon hoped the guards could hold their own. But there were at least twenty men with spears among the attackers, while the men of the caravan had to control their frightened animals and defend the palanquin. Men began to fall, despite giving a good account of themselves. It became a melee of shouts and screams, flashing knives, stabbing spears and hacking swords.

"We cannot let this happen, Talon," Max said as he stared at the fight going on a few hundred yards away. "We must help them."

"I would rather we did not have to, as we are without shield or mail and our steel is not of the best, but you are right. Come, we fight!"

Together they rode knee to knee, and shouting the words "Deus Lo Volte!" they charged recklessly into the rear of the melee.

Talon drove his animal directly into the backs of several men on foot who were trying to take down a large man in chain armor who was wounded, blood pouring off his right shoulder and down his fine mail shirt, but he continued to hack bravely at them with his wounded arm.

With a straight thrust, Talon ran one of the attackers through the back and let the shocked man fall off, and then with a ferocious back hand, he slashed at the neck of another who disappeared into the dust of the road. The third was caught between Talon and a rider who leaned over and stabbed the cringing man in his exposed neck.

After a quick look of gratitude the horseman glanced around and exclaimed, "They are at the palanquin and my Lady and my lord, her son, are in danger! May Allah bless you, Sir, but I need to go to them."

He tried to turn his horse but was weak from loss of blood and too slow. Talon instantly understood and danced his mount forward to the palanquin, striking an armed footman as he rode.

He heard Max's roar as he shouted his war cry and saw a decapitated head bounce on the road. Despite their peril, Talon laughed out loud with the exhilaration. He need not worry about Max. Instead, he concentrated on saving the people in the Palanquin.

He noted that the slaves had vanished, but there were men on foot struggling to protect the palanquin which now rested on the ground in disarray. The curtains were torn and there were screams from within. A large man dressed in a filthy abaya was leaning inside and poking with his sword at someone. Two others were yelling their approval and laughing as they looked on and tore at the remaining fabric surrounding the palanquin. Talon kicked his horse through the struggling footmen and brought his sword's edge down as hard as he could onto the large man's back.

With a roar of pain he staggered back, trying to reach the gaping wound, but Talon leaned down and skewered him through the chest. The body fell backwards without another sound, spurting blood everywhere. His two supporting accomplices witnessed this ferocious attack from behind and scrambled out of the way, shouting with fear. Talon spun his mount on his quarters and knocked one over with the shoulder of his horse and then pierced the other before he could turn away. Quieting his now excited horse, Talon danced it back to the palanquin. Leaning over the disordered conveyance, Talon had a glimpse of a disheveled young woman kneeling with a knife in her hand that she held high in defiance. Next to her, a young boy, also kneeling, held a long knife up like a sword. Behind the two of them was a teenage girl huddled against the back frame, her knees drawn up, crying hysterically, her hands to her mouth and her eyes huge with fear.

Talon's eyes met those of the young woman, but nothing was said. He nodded, and she lowered the knife a little in acknowledgement. Their eyes held, he grinned, and then he glanced around to make sure they were all relatively safe. He turned his attention to the fight still going on nearby.

Three of the horsemen were down and there were still attackers darting about from the trees, but fewer now, and Talon sensed that they were disheartened by the unexpected attack from the rear. Some were even beginning to run away. He spurred his horse over towards Max, and on the way slashed down a man who was about to spear another horseman engaged with two men on his other side. Talon's victim fell away with a scream. He saw Max lean over his horse and deliver a mighty blow to one of the ruffians who was trying to stab up at him: the man lost an arm and fell away with a shriek, but another with a spear came from behind and drove it into Max's back.

Talon gasped with horror and drove his horse alongside his friend, dispatching the spearman as he went, but it was too late. The tip of the spear had penetrated right through and the point broke the skin on his front. Max was staring down at it in disbelief.

"My God, but I am killed, Talon," he gasped, his face suddenly gray. Then he slowly fell from the back of his excited mount and landed with a thump in the dust.

Without thinking, Talon leapt off his horse and ran to his friend. Max was arching his back in agony. Talon knew what he had to do but he felt more like vomiting. With trembling hands he grasped the haft of the spear and pulled hard. The head of the spear came out of Max's shoulder where it had penetrated high up under the shoulder blade. It came out with a sucking sound and then a rush of blood. Throwing the spear away Talon lifted his friend's head from the dust. There was blood on Max's lips, but Talon could not tell if it was from within. Max's eyes were glazed with the pain but he recognized Talon.

"I am gone, my young Master Talon. I beg of you to say the prayers for the Templar for me, although I am not a knight."

"To me you are a Knight Templar, my dear friend. Oh God!" he cried, "What have we done to deserve this?" He wept while he held his friend close. He seemed to be going fast. Talon repeated the prayer for the dead, oblivious of the noise around him, as the battle came to a close.

He was bent over Max reciting the prayers when a blow to his head knocked him forward and he landed atop his dying companion. He knew only blackness.

* * * * *

Talon awoke in darkness and groaned. His head hurt at the back and he had a pounding headache. His body felt like it was burning up. Then it all came back in a painful rush. He groaned again, as much from the pain in his head as the anguish he felt. He tried to sit up.

A hand held his shoulder and forced him back onto the bed. A cool damp cloth was placed upon his forehead, while a gruff but somehow calming voice spoke out of the darkness.

"Be still. You received a nasty blow from Jalal before I could stop him. He regrets his mistake but he thought you were one of our enemies. You were lucky he did not take your head, he was so angry."

"My ...my friend, where is he? What have you done with his body?"

"Your friend is very badly wounded but he might survive if Allah so wills it," responded the distant voice.

Talon jerked almost upright with the news, but then fell back, while tears coursed down his face. "Do you...is he? You said he lived?" he croaked incredulously, as he thought of the cruel fate Max had come to. If only they had not come down from the hills in their madness to help the caravan, his friend would not be wounded and they would be well on their way.

"You weep for your friend," said the voice. "That is good in the eyes of Allah. Friendship and a warrior do not always mix well. But he lives yet, and we are taking care of him. Is he your servant or a companion?"

Such was Talon's relief that he forgot himself and said, "He is my Sergeant and...and my companion. I must see him. Where is he...where are we?"

The firm hand came back and pushed him down, as he again tried to sit up.

"Drink this, it will ease the pain and let you sleep," he was commanded. A shallow bowl was placed in front of his lips. He sipped some bitter tea which soon made him feel drowsy.

"We shall talk more of this in the morning. We owe both you and your friend a debt of gratitude for what you did, and this we shall discuss when you are better rested. What is your name?"

"Suleiman," Talon whispered as he fell asleep.

He did not wake up the next day. Some kind of fever had struck him and he was unable to rise from his bed. The fever kept him in a stupor for many days, during which time he had nightmares.

He even found himself fighting lions again, which seemed to be very real, and he sat up in the bed sweating profusely and shouting, as he tried to get away from them. On another occasion, the terror was so stark, although he could not define it, that he was frozen in place, paralyzed and unable to move a limb to protect himself while terror moved closer and closer.

In other, calmer moments, he thought he might be in some kind of litter, going somewhere, but he knew not where. Then he would come out of his delirium and all was still. He dreamt that a beautiful woman was talking to him and bathing his face and forehead with cool water. He thought he had died and that Rav'an had come to him, and he wept with happiness, calling her name. But then he would fall into blackness, as the fevers gripped him and the image faded away. During one of his more lucid moments, he found a man leaning over him who told him his name.

"I am Malek, and I am the servant of Emir Abbas Abdur Rahman ibn Athir Faysal, a nobleman who is in the south, fighting alongside our Sultan's brother against the Nubians." Talon barely registered the words, and soon fell back into his torpor.

When he did finally wake up from the nightmares and free of the fever, he found himself on a bed in a sunlit room, with rich furnishings both on the low sleeping platform and on the floor all about him. The floor was decorated with many colored tiles forming intricate patterns. There were fine carpets of red and black designs in profusion on either side, while the covers of the bed itself were of silk and finely woven linen. He thought he recognized the patterns on one of the carpets; it might have been from somewhere in Persia. This was a rich man's house. He briefly wondered if he had finally gone to the Paradise that had been promised to him many years ago in Alamut castle, that wondrous first night.

He fingered the sheets as he contemplated his situation, and realized that he had been very sick. He felt exhausted, but no longer feverish. The sunlight was welcome and he could hear activity outside, including a squabble going on between a young boy and someone female not far from his window.

"I want to go fishing today. Why can I not?" The boy demanded truculently. Talon smiled, he could almost see the boy's pouting face.

"Because Malek is away, and it is dangerous for you to go outside our compound or even to the gardens, until he or another is with you," a female voice stated firmly. "Come and read to me instead. Your sister and I enjoy it when you do." The voice was gentle but assured, and Talon was intrigued by its quiet melody.

At this point, a slave woman, as he could tell by her dress, came slip-slapping on bare feet into the room where Talon lay. She looked over at him, and then gave a short gasp when she saw that his eyes were open. She ran out of the room.

"He is awake...he is awake, my Lady!" There was an exclamation and then hurried steps. He could not hear the words exchanged after that, but within a few minutes there was a light step outside his open doorway.

A woman walked into the room followed by a young boy. Despite the fact that she was veiled Talon had no trouble recognizing her and her son. They were the two he had seen in the palanquin the terrible day of Max's injury. He tried to rise in deference to her presence but she raised her hand indicating he should lay back. She was beautiful, and it was hard not to stare.

He opened his mouth to say something, but only choked. Clearing his throat he tried again.

*"Salaam Aliekom...* My lady, what am I doing here? And forgive me for being disrespectful, but who are you?"

She took a little time to answer, as though unsure as to what she should say. But before she could speak the boy spoke up.

*"Salaam,* Sir. You saved our lives, my sister, my mother and me. Suleiman? Is that your name? Malek told us that it was, when we arrived here. You had the fever. Are you better now? I am sorry about your brave companion and his terrible wound. You are both great warriors. They still talk about you!"

"Kazim," the woman spoke sharply, "where are your manners?" "We must not tax the man with silly questions; he is still recovering from the fever. Sir, I am glad that the fever seems to have abated. Malek tells us that you had the river sickness. Have you been traveling long on this road?"

Just as she finished speaking, there was the patter of small feet and another child arrived breathless at the door.

"Mother, is he awake at last?" a breathless young girl enquired.

"Yes, my dearest...our visitor is awake, at last. Now, be silent both of you, I want to hear what he has to say."

She repeated her question. "Have you been traveling long, Sir?"

"No... my Lady," Talon answered. "I...we have come from the north near Alexandria."

"It does not matter ...you are better, and we, my children and I, are grateful to you for what you did. Allah be praised that he placed you nearby when we were attacked by our enemies. We owe you a great debt that will not easily be repaid."

Talon shook his head, "It was nothing, my Lady. We could see you were in distress. What else could we have done?"

Her veil slipped and he could now see her fine features, light translucent olive skin and huge amber-brown eyes.

"Sir, you could have left us to our fate, but you did not. You have paid a terrible price with the wound to your friend. This I... we shall not forget. Please rest until Malek comes to talk to you. He will return this evening. Come, Kazim, Jasmine, we must leave now."

"Madame...I must know. Will my companion live? Where is he that I can see him?"

"He is in the servants' quarters but in good care. His wound was terrible, but with Allah's help and the good physician, he will live. I shall ask Malek when it would be good for you to see him. In the meantime you must rest."

She pulled her veil back into place and turned away, holding out a slim hand for the young boy to grasp. They walked out of the room, and the boy looked over his shoulder, smiled and waved. Jasmine, the young girl, her veil carelessly dropped onto her shoulder, looked back at him too, but with large curious eyes that were solemn. Watching them leave it seemed to Talon a part of the sunlight had gone with them. But a faint scent of sandalwood and of rose attar remained.

He lay back feeling empty and tired. He must have slept. A serving woman woke him to give him some delicious stew of lentil and cabbage with meat scraps which might be chicken or pigeon. It was growing dark outside, and with the darkness came quiet in the rest of the house.

As he ate he took stock of himself. He had been bathed, and no longer felt filthy, which was a relief. His hair and beard had also been trimmed. He presumed that slaves had taken care of him. He still wanted to bathe himself. The hot water of a bathing pool would clean more than his body.

He lay in the bed with a prayer on his lips, reliving the terrible moments when Max had been wounded. His concern for his friend denied him much appetite.

Later that evening, just after sunset, he heard people calling to one another. Then he heard heavy wood doors thump open against the walls and the sound of horses' hooves on hard packed ground. There was the jingle of harnesses, and he saw the flicker of flaming torches sending shadows dancing across walls. More voices and then the stamping of boots on the steps outside, as a man walked towards his bedroom. Talon sat up further and prepared himself to meet the visitor.

A tall, well-built man, with a thick neck that seemed to make his head seem small, paused at the doorway. He possessed a large nose on a slightly fleshy face. Talon thought he recognized the man; perhaps he had talked to him at the beginning of his illness.

The man wore his hair in two long braids that fell down his back. He was well-dressed, clearly for war, wearing a fine chain mail vest and thigh mail as well as greaves for his shins over well made riding boots. He contemplated Talon as he removed his gloves and walked to the bed and gave a short bow. His beard was well trimmed and his hands wore several rings. He gazed at Talon with dark, slightly protuberant eyes that assessed him shrewdly.

Looking down at Talon, he said, "*Salaam Aliekom.* Peace be with you. You seem to have recovered, Suleiman...if that is your name. How do you feel today?"

"*As-Salamu Aliekom.* Peace be with you, my lord. Allah be praised, I am better," responded Talon.

"Hmm, that is good, because I have some questions. There is a puzzle surrounding you that has not been dispelled by your illness."

"I hope to be able to answer some of your questions, Sir. Please, tell me your name."

"It is Malek ibn Nidh'aal al Misre...I am the steward of the estates here in the Fayoum, for our Lord and master, may Allah grant him long life and much wisdom, Emir Abbas Abdul Rahman ibn Athir Faysal, who is descended of the 'Alā'-ad-din. He is a commander in the army of Salah-Ed Din. I want to thank you on behalf of both myself and my lord's family for your timely arrival at the scene of the ambush, a week ago."

Talon gasped. "I have been with the fever that long?"

"Indeed you have. You had the river sickness, although it is out of season and few get it at this time of the year. Sometimes the sickness comes to the country and then moves north to the delta.

"Where did you come from that day, Suleiman? You appeared like a pair of devils and saved the life of my brother, who is one of my lieutenants, not to mention my Lady and her son and daughter, my lord Kazim and Jasmine. My brother saw what you both did when you arrived and saved him from three men who were attacking him. He nearly died from loss of blood, his shoulder wound was deep. I, too, witnessed your deeds, and those of your companion as well."

"I pray to Allah that your brother lives now, my lord," Talon said, trying to delay the moment when he would have to invent another lie.

"He will live; it will take more than a couple of slashes with a knife to kill that man. Tough as a crocodile is my brother," Malek said with a smile. He stroked his moustache.

Talon had no idea what a crocodile was but he said, "I am told that my companion lives, when I was sure he died in my arms, my lord. I must see him."

"So you shall, so you shall, but there is time. He is not in as good condition as you are, but he is slowly pulling out of the fevers induced by the wound. The physician has high hopes for him and we all call upon Allah in our prayers to aid him," Malek said. "So, Suleiman," he continued, "where did you come from, and where were you going, when you decided to come to our rescue?"

"My companion and I were in the hills watching the men in the trees because we did not quite trust their actions. It never hurts to be cautious, Sir."

Malek nodded in thoughtful agreement.

"But we could not know that they were planning an ambush for you," Talon stated, skirting the question.

"Oh yes. May Allah strike them *all* dead and then cast them into Hell for eternity. They were waiting for us, Suleiman, of that you can be sure."

Talon's face betrayed his surprise. "Might I ask why, my lord?"

"You may call me Malek; I am not your lord. My lord is a man of the highest station; very close to our Sultan, may Allah protect him. Therefore, he has many enemies, and this time they nearly succeeded in either murdering or kidnapping his son and his daughter...and second wife."

Talon was shocked. "But who would do such a thing...Malek? Also why did you not go by boat? Would it not have been safer?"

"We had taken the boat south on the great river from Al Qahirah, but that would have meant disembarking at Beneade, and since we had been warned that they might be waiting for us there, we disembarked before that town, and then took the road... thinking we might outmaneuver our enemies.

"Wisely or unwisely, it was by then in the hands of Allah, all praise to him, that my mistress decided to take a chance and come here by road. I, too, mistakenly thought we might have enough men to ward off any attack. It seems that both of us were mistaken, and I have written to my master to tell him of the event. I do not know at this time, Suleiman, if I will keep my head when he gets back here. I do know that he will be raging, and once he knows who it was, then we can expect a fight, this time to the finish."

He yawned. "I am tired, and while I still have questions for you they can wait, as I have to go to our mistress and report on the grain count before I go to my bed."

He stood over Talon and said, "You and your companion fought like lions on the road and we have seen your scars. My men and I heard you laughing as you killed. I don't doubt that you are a warrior, and you have told me of your companion being a Sergeant...what is a sergeant? Now there is a riddle you must answer soon. I bid you goodnight, Suleiman."

"Go in peace. May Allah grant you a restful night, Malek," Talon intoned politely.

He tossed and turned that night. He had much to think about, and he wondered where they were and what the lay of the land was. But he was elated, too, that Max had thus far survived. He said a prayer for him, hoping that it would be heard.

He pondered Malek's statements. There seemed to be a feud going on between some nobles and the family with whom he was staying, and they were in danger. Then he wondered how he would fare in the face of persistent questions as to his origins and those of Max. Talon wondered what Max might have told them. He wanted to fabricate a plausible story about where they came from, who they were. Talon said a small prayer for their lost companion Montague, then slept.

The next morning a middle aged man came to see him, and after the usual elaborate greetings he said, "I am the family physician."

After an inspection, during which he laid his hand on Talon's forehead for a moment and told him to put out his tongue, he stared at his eyes after lifting his lids with long slim finger tips. Then he listened to Talon's breathing by placing his ear on his chest, after which he said, "I think the fever is now gone and you have recovered enough to go out into the courtyard and the garden."

After the physician had left, he was visited by Malek. "Take your ease in peace, Suleiman. I have to go away to supervise our harvests, but I shall be back this evening to talk to you. Do not go outside the compound, as I cannot guarantee your safety outside these walls. Our enemies are everywhere. This evening you can go and see your companion. He is very weak, and you should not tire him."

Talon nodded. He was relieved that the moment of truth had been postponed for the time being. He was ravenous and devoured his breakfast of nan, goat's cheese and some sharp yoghurt that he washed down with cool water. Then he set about getting out of the bed. He got to his feet, wobbly from having been in bed for so long. He had to reach out and steady himself at one point, but gradually his balance improved, and he stood upright.

He still wanted a bath very badly and wondered how to get one. He need not have worried; the slave woman who had brought him breakfast came with some towels and bade him to follow her. He padded along the corridors behind the wide swaying haunches of the woman. She was very dark, and had a tight mop of black curls on her head.

She led him to a darkened room that smelt of wood smoke and steam. She indicated that he should undress and get into the huge tub, filled with steaming hot water. This stood close to a large dark pool of water.

Sometime later Talon stepped out of the bath house, dressed in a clean soft cotton abaya, feeling enormously refreshed. He could not remember the last time he had felt so clean.

# Chapter 6

# The Fayoum

The second day Talon went directly to check on his horses. He found one of the syce watering Max's, while Rakhsh, his own, nickered at him in recognition from a stall. He smiled and went over to the horse and talked to him gently while stroking the fine skin on his neck. He was pleased to note that both Rakhsh and Max's mount had been well groomed.

He found great enjoyment in just being with these swift creatures. Yet he felt a twinge of conscience at having stolen them, and a faint anxiety grew at the thought of his hosts finding out. He need not have worried; as Malek came to join him at the stables, he said in a tone that was reassuring, "Your horses have been looked after by our syce, that boy over there; his name is Haytham." He indicated, pointing with his chin, a young lad who was attending to another horse.

"They are among the best I have seen for a long time..." said Malek, casually stroking Rakhsh's curious nose.

"If you mean they were expensive, you are right," Talon said with a smile. He wondered how much he really would have had to pay for one of these magnificent mounts.

But Malek did not seem in any hurry to interrogate him at this point, and instead proceeded to show him around the expansive grounds of the compound.

"This is an estate that goes back more than two hundred years in the Emir's family," he said proudly. "See those sycamores and palms? They have been here longer than any living man and probably were planted by my lord's great grandfather, who wanted an oasis of considerable size here, but he also wanted timber to sell to the Sultans for their ship building."

"Does he own other properties?" Talon asked casually. He watched children playing near to the servants' quarters. Life in the compound seemed a long way from all the conflicts he knew.

"Oh yes, he owns a salt flat here in the Fayoum, and another north of here which brings in good revenue. It is, near the sea. He has palaces, one in Alexandria and another in Al Qahirah. But they are places he visits only occasionally these days," Malek said.

"Why is that, Malek?'

"Because his first wife died in Alexandria while giving birth to his daughter Jasmine. She lived there with her grandmother and an army of servants for a long time. My lord Abbas was devastated and visited only occasionally, for the pain was great. Fortunately, with his new wife, my Lady Khalidah, he is beginning to take more interest in his daughter, who now lives here with us."

Malek continued, "His son Kazim is of prime importance, as he is the only male heir."

Talon was aware of the complex intermarriages among this society but did not probe further as they continued walking across the property. There was a virtual forest of trees around the walls outside the property, and within the walls themselves. There were many producing date palms, mulberries, lotus, and figs, and many different fruit trees growing in orchards, all well cared for. The sycamores, pines and cedars, Malek mentioned in passing, were used for buildings and ships.

To Talon's critical eye, that of a *Fidai*, the walls and defenses of the estate were poorly constructed and could do with a lot of improvements, but he assumed that the Lord was aware of this and it was not an issue. He felt uneasy that the family had been ambushed so near to home, however.

Later, Malek took him out into the countryside, after asking solicitously if he was up to it. Talon had nodded with a smile showing he was eager to. Now he was astride Rakhsh, comfortably seated and reveling in the feel of the strong, eager animal between his legs. They had ridden some miles west of the estate, looking over many fields of cotton and other crops of cereals and vegetables that belonged to the lord.

Malek explained that he was the steward of this land and that the good running of the estates was his responsibility. He asked if Talon was familiar with numbers, and when Talon had explained that he knew the elements of mathematics the man looked pleased.

"I have to count the crop listings and there are very few others who know how. Perhaps you could help me when the time comes?" he suggested, as though he thought Talon intended to stay a while. They rode even further west until they came to the shore of a huge lake that Malek called Birket Qarun. With a sweep of his arm that took in the whole area contained between the hills surrounding them, Malek exclaimed proudly, "This is a region known as the Fayoum, and most of it belongs to my master. The Nile has been draining into this lake since the beginning of time, during the wet season. But the river blocks that you may have already seen along the canal joining the Nile and the lake control the amount of water used for irrigation, and so we can use this fertile land to grow crops twice a year.

"The water level is low at this time, but in mid to late summer when the river rises, we work very hard to bring it into the channels and ditches."

The shoreline was wide and the water brackish and low. Obviously it was not time yet for the waters to flow. However, there were many birds wading along the shore or in deeper water, looking for fish. A few ducks swam in and out of reeds, while further out there was an assortment of birds either wading or floating on the calm waters. They walked their horses at a slow pace, contemplating the landscape and the placid waters of the lake.

They stopped on the shoreline and looked out over the immense, glimmering expanse of water. Talon could barely see the other side and the area seemed devoid of people, but when he looked a little closer, he could see ruins, blending with the red colored earth of the hills off to the north, a mile or so away. There was also a group of houses clustered together denoting a village.

He listened to the lapping of the waters on the sandy shore and the cries of the wading birds with real pleasure. He could hear the light breeze rustling the reeds along the shoreline. It was so quiet. There was something timeless and calming about the lake, as though the surrounding low hills protected it from the feverish activity of the outside world.

Malek, who had been sitting his horse quietly and enjoying the view as well, pointed out to the water, then waved his arm towards a plume of dust and said, "Over on the very west of this lake the water is not fit to drink, as it is heavy with salt. We now have a salt flat there. That one, plus the other one north by the sea, provide my Master with a good income. We send it to Al Qahirah and Al Iskandrîyah; I believe it is shipped as far away as Constantinople. But the export is not my concern; the infidels known as the Genoans take care of that." He continued, his hand outstretched towards the west.

"That is desert over those hills and it is blowing sand into the sky. See there, Suleiman?" he pointed, and Talon could just see a hazy brown column rising into the sky. "One day, unless we can prevent it, this area too will become unsuitable for cultivation. *Insha'Allah* it will not be for a very long time; and thanks be to Allah, we can still drink the water on this side of the lake."

"Why do you say this, Malek? I am no farmer, but the soil where you grow crops looks very rich. It is almost black! You yourself maintain the land as a good steward should, do you not?"

"Indeed, Suleiman, I try. It is not only my duty, but indeed it is my very life. But over the ages the water level of the lake has sunk deeper and the desert of the north and west has come closer. My Grandfather who grew up here told me it has lost much water in his lifetime. It is Allah's will. *Insha'Allah* he will arrest the desert before it kills this land." He finished on a fatalistic note.

A light wind came rippling across the waters of the lake and cooled Talon's brow. It also caused his robes to flutter. Lifting his head to sniff the air Talon murmured, "I find it very beautiful."

"You and I shall go hunting along this shore with falcons, and if you wish you can go fishing too, my friend," Malek said with a laugh. He lifted his face towards the horizon and continued with good humor, as if pleasant thoughts were on his mind.

"Over there, not so many miles at a small place called Ain al-Siliyin, the water comes out of the ground and is very hot. We sometimes bathe there. The local people say it is healing. When you and your companion have recovered sufficiently, we shall pay it a visit. They keep bees there and we harvest their hives, for the village belongs to the master. See those large jars over there? They are for our honey, which is much in demand in Al-Qahirah."

As they rode back to the buildings of the estate Malek talked a lot about the land and it became clear to Talon that he loved what he did and liked to share his love. Talon was content to listen and learn all he could about the man and the estates and the lord in question, Abbas. He wondered if he had not heard that name before, but frustratingly he could not recall it, so he dismissed the concern and turned his attention to Malek's tour and companionship.

"You should know that the attack on our party was no accident, Suleiman." Malek said in his gruff tone as they rode slowly along a track between cane stands.

"Allah alone knows what would have happened to our young Lord and our Mistresses had you not helped us. My lord will be very inclined to reward you for what you did that day. On the other hand, he might be inclined to cut my head off for allowing us to get into that mess."

"Who would want to attack your master's family, Malek?" Talon asked.

"My master is close to the Sultan, Salah Ed Din, may Allah protect him.. He holds the position of honorary Captain of the body guard. The courtiers at the palace are a venomous crowd, so there is a lot of jealousy He has one really bad enemy who is named Bahir and who is as mad as a hornet because my master took his wife from under Bahir's nose. They have been enemies since they were boys, but this made things worse, especially as Bahir's request to marry Khalidah was turned down not once, but twice. I suspect the attack is his work."

They arrived back just in time for evening prayers and Talon joined the row of murmuring men after completing his ablutions. He let his mind dwell upon the time honored obeisance to God.

After prayers, Malek, as though sensing that Talon was desperate to see his friend, beckoned to him and they walked towards a mud walled structure that ran alongside the main building. Entering the cool dark interior, Talon noted that the dirt floor was swept clean and the window shutters opened to let in the evening breeze. He saw Max lying on a pallet in one corner. Placed nearby on the floor was a jug of water and an earthenware bowl holding some bread and soup.

His eyes filling with tears of emotion, Talon forgot that Malek was present. He hurried to kneel at the bedside, to stare down at Max lying against a rolled cushion, asleep. Talon was shocked at the sight of his companion. Max, already thin from their previous hardships, had lost even more weight and looked pale and gaunt. There were bandages swathed around his chest and left shoulder. His light brown hair had been trimmed, however, and he looked clean. It was evident that he had been well cared for. He was only covered with a linen sheet up to his chest.

"Max," Talon whispered anxiously. He glanced behind him, feeling awkward at his display of emotions, but Malek had slipped away, leaving the two friends alone.

A full breath brought Max slowly out of a deep sleep and he peered blearily upwards and then focused on Talon, who was leaning over him. He gave a weak smile. "Ah Talon," he murmured. "God be praised. You live."

Talon glanced hurriedly behind him again, but there was no need to worry. Bending down so that he was close to Max's ear, Talon whispered, "I thought you were dead, my dear friend."

"And I you, Talon. I could not understand anything they said, so I assumed that you were either dead or taken prisoner and that I was alone." There were tears in Max's eyes as he looked up at Talon.

"Hush, my friend," murmured Talon, almost choking with emotion. "Now listen, and listen for our lives."

Max looked alarmed but he concentrated on what Talon said next.

"My name is Suleiman and I am a rich merchant's son from Anatolia. You are my bodyguard and a Christian. I shall pretend I am a Moslem. It will not be hard, as I was taught to be one. Do you hear me, Max?" He asked with some concern, for Max's eyes had closed briefly.

"Yes, Suleiman, I have heard. So... my name is Max?" His lips twitched in a tiny smile.

Talon grinned. "Yes, it is, unless you have a better one? But I do not want to lie more than I have to. They are treating us like heroes and with much kindness because we helped save them from disaster, but it is best that they do not know we are Franks heading for the Holy Land."

They could only talk a few more minutes, as it became clear that Max was growing very tired. Talon helped him drink some water from the jug nearby and offered him a spoonful of the lentil stew, but Max turned it away. Talon left him with the assurance that he would be back the next day and they would talk some more.

Leaving Max to rest, Talon walked slowly out into the evening light and saw Malek waiting for him with another man who had his right arm in a sling.

"Suleiman, this is Bilal, my brother," Malek said.

"I came to see you as I heard you were back on your feet. Allah be praised that both you and your companion are alive, and we can return your deeds by caring for you," Bilal said.

If anything he was stockier than Malek himself, and a little fleshier around his jowls, although it was clear he was a strong man. His hair was cut short and stuck out in a short bush around his head. His dark eyes regarded Talon with interest.

Bilal was unreserved with his praise. "You two came at just the right moment, like a pair of fiends. Thanks be to Allah for sending you."

"I thank you, *Oustez,* for your concern, but anyone would have done the same. We could not look on and do nothing," Talon replied.

"Ah, my friend, there are those who would have. Allah sent you," Bilal said with feeling.

Malek enjoined him to eat with them this early evening. They settled down near the stables on a patch of grass under a huge sycamore tree on cushions the servants had brought. The servants arrived with trays from the kitchen and put them down on a central rug. Malek offered him boiled cabbage and lotus seeds to start the meal.

They were joined by another man, much older than either of the brothers, who limped over leaning on a stick. He was helped to sit on a cushion by a solicitous Bilal, who obviously had great respect for the old man.

He was introduced as Khaldun ibn Mahmud Majd al Din, an old friend of the family and now retired, having been a close friend of Abbas's father when he had been alive. Malek and his brother called him Abu in an affectionate manner, which meant Father.

"I am asked to do little these days," Khaldun said, with a gap toothed smile. "Nor do I teach the young Kazim, because he is too energetic for me."

Malek chuckled at that and said, "The last person our Lady employed for the thankless task left a month ago. Only the Prophet knows, as I do not, where we are to find another around here to teach the young lord his numbers, reading and calligraphy...and his manners. He is falling behind in all four, not that he cares. Unfortunately, there are not that many scholars in these parts, nor do they want to move outside of Al Qahirah where most of them prefer to live."

"Ah! You are offering our new young friend the cabbage and lotus, brother," Bilal broke in. Turning to Talon he added, "This is a sign that he holds you in high regard, Suleiman. He will not even do that for me, his own brother." They laughed at this.

"We welcome a guest with our best food, Suleiman," Malek said, with a nod to Talon.

While they ate in comfortable silence, the servants brought spicy and scented foods that Talon had not tasted for a long time, and some never before.

Malek explained that the boiled cabbage was something Egyptians loved and they would always start a meal with it. This was wrapped around some paste that Talon savoured with pleasure. "That is the liver of one of those birds over there. Tastes good, does it not?" Bilal asked. He pointed at one of the large fat birds that waddled about near to the stables. We feed them much grain so they get fat and then...we eat them!" He laughed.

There was a plethora of other vegetables and fruits for Talon to choose from. He ate radishes, endives, and herb-encrusted morsels of pigeon meat that had been fried in expensive olive oil and heavily flavored with garlic, sesame seeds and onions.

There were several kinds of fish to choose from. Sun-dried and pungent, salted heavily, or even fresh, these fish were full of bones but very tasty. Malek kept urging him to eat, telling him, "These are fish from the lake and are good to eat. You look half starved, Suleiman, and must eat to regain your strength."

After the meal, Malek waved one of the hovering slaves over and ordered coffee. A brass coffee pot was brought. It had a long beak of a spout and the hot, black liquid was poured from a height to enhance its flavor. They drank it piping hot from tiny glazed earthenware cups.

Malek leaned back against one of the carpeted cushions and gave an appreciative belch of comfort before wiping his lips with a linen cloth. Then he looked over at Talon.

"I need to solve a small mystery, Suleiman. You must tell us how you and your companion came to be in the place where you were at that time. You say he is a Christian, but you are of the faith?"

Talon gave an inward sigh; it was time.

"I am a merchant, or rather the son of a merchant from Anatolia, who converted to Islam when the Turkish tribes came to the region now known as Rum. He has interests all over the Byzantium Empire and in Syria, including Al Iskandrîyah."

There were murmurs of interest as the others watched him and listened intently. He continued, "I had been visiting Iskandrîyah for the first time without my father when I was cheated out of my goods by some evil men on the outskirts of your fair city. My companion and I were chased for days because they thought we had a lot of money, which at one time I did have, but I lost most of that to them when we were attacked that day near the city. Despite our cries for help, no one came to our aid and they were too many, so we had to take flight. I was trying to reach a place where we could cross the great river but we were too far south of Al Qahirah. Now, I do not even know where I am."

"You are not so far south of Al Qahirah as you might think, my friend; this area called the Fayoum is south, only two days of hard riding from the city, if that was where you wanted to go," Khaldun said reflectively. "But tell me my young warrior... because that is what I think you are, how could you lose your own caravan and then be such lions when we were attacked?" His white-bearded face was thoughtful, his old faded eyes watchful.

"We were betrayed and surprised, *Oustez*. I lost more than one companion at that time and I mourn them deeply. I would not have thought that Egypt was so dangerous for a mere merchant hoping to sell goods," Talon said, looking him in the eye.

"What were you bringing to this country that we do not have already?" Bilal asked somewhat skeptically. "This is Egypt, after all," he added with a grin.

"We traded...nothing special, other than pelts and silver from the far north. I can buy those in Constantinople," Talon lied. He hoped that neither Malek nor his brother, nor Khaldun for that matter, had ever been there.

"Then there were carpets from eastern Anatolia, gems from Syria and filigree gold work from Damascus. The craftsmen there are without peer. I also trade in silk from... "

"Stop! I think I have understood what you were doing, Suleiman," Malek said with a laugh, "but where were you planning to go after you had been to Al Qahirah?"

"I was going to change some chits of paper for more gold with the bankers of the city. I have credit for more from the Jewish people in Constantinople and Damascus, but I will now have to find a way to prove that I am who I say I am when the time comes, as they don't give gold to just anyone who asks for it," Talon said with a rueful smile. "After that, I was going to take a ship back to Cyprus and do some more trading," he finished, hoping he had evaded the question sufficiently for the time being.

"You might find it very hard to find gold in that city anymore," Malek said skeptically.

"Why do you say this?" asked Talon, surprised.

Khaldun sucked on a date seed and chuckled. "Malek is right. Our Sultan, may Allah protect him always, is often at war. He needs money all the time to finance his battles and to pay off his Turkish mercenaries. Rumor has it he too is going to the Jews for gold. Not only that, Nur Ed Din, his distant uncle, wants to be paid back for the money *he* invested in the invasion of Egypt. It was a lot – around two hundred thousand dinars, if rumor is correct. Our Sultan spends money faster than anyone can provide it. But he will surely have the first pick through what is left in the souk of Al Qahirah."

Malek shifted the conversation back to Talon. "You seem to me to be an unlikely merchant, Suleiman, but if that is what you say you are – then I shall go along with it." He smiled and then enquired, "What about your companion? He does not speak our language like you do. In fact, we do not know what language he speaks; when he was in a fever he babbled in some strange tongues that none of us understood." He smiled drily at Talon, and so did Bilal. Khaldun smiled as well, but he looked thoughtful.

"My companion is from the Christian lands far to the west of here," Talon said, hurriedly. "He grew up in a high mountainous region, but came to Constantinople and met my father when young, and stayed with him. He acts as my bodyguard now. No, he does not speak the Arabic tongue and is slow to learn any of the other ones that we have encountered. I know the rudiments of his tongue and we communicate well enough. He is a brave and honest man who has saved my life on more than one occasion," Talon stated firmly.

"It is true enough; he was a terrifying sight when you charged in among our enemies," Bilal remarked.

"It seems that despite the continual fighting that goes on between the Christians and Moslem peoples that trade between us continues. For that I am glad," said Khaldun with a smile. Talon relaxed a little.

"We are in your debt and that is the truth. I hope you will stay a while and enjoy our hospitality. Our master is fighting in the south with his cavalry but will soon be home, *Insha' Allah,*" Malek summed up the sentiments of them all.

"Can you write and do calligraphy? Do you know the numbers, Suleiman? If you are truly a merchant's son you would know these things," Khaldun asked abruptly.

"I can write in the tongue we speak together – even though the dialect here is sometimes difficult to follow—Persian, some Latin, and Greek, *Oustez*. I was taught the numbers and know them well enough," Talon responded.

"Then, Malek, please bring some paper and a quill. I would see what our young guest is capable of," Khaldun said.

Talon realized that he was being tested, but had no qualms about the writing or the numbers; he felt he could acquit himself.

The thick paper was delivered, along with some ink and a large quill with a wide nib. He borrowed a knife from Bilal and trimmed it more carefully till he was satisfied that it was just so, then he eagerly began to use the lessons learnt in the past to demonstrate his knowledge in both the Arabic and the Christian languages. Khaldun looked on with growing approval and even complemented him on some of the more difficult calligraphy for the letters that he wrote down. Then he asked Talon to demonstrate his skill at numbers, which he was also able to do both orally and in writing.

At the end of the demonstration the old man nodded to himself, as though satisfied that he had learned what he needed to from the encounter, and said, "You had good teachers, Suleiman. Did you learn of the Astronomy and the medicine as well?"

"*Jo, Oustez*, I did learn of both but would not call myself a good student of either."

"That is a good answer, Suleiman. Humility in the study of sciences is to be respected more than showing off the ability," Khaldun said approvingly. "Now it is dusk and I must seek my bed, as my old eyes are tired."

He was helped to his feet by Malek, who then called over a boy from the stables to help the old man off to his quarters.

"Peace be with you, Abu," Malek said respectfully.

"Peace be with you all," the old man said as he hobbled off with the aid of the boy.

After he had gone, there was a high buzzing sound and something dark swooped low over their seating place. Talon started and Malek chuckled. "We have bats here that like fruit. That one was investigating our meal."

Talon looked around and noticed that indeed, there were several bats swooping and gliding in the darkening sky above them, further adding to the mystery of the evening quiet.

He went to bed that night trying to think of how he might be able to leave with Max, as soon as possible.

* * * * *

As days passed and Max continued to heal, Talon sought out the old man, who was gratified to have such an eager listener, for Talon made it clear he liked to spend time with him. Khaldun had travelled extensively, mostly down the Red sea and to the Jeddah, but also to Yemen and up the coast to Oman, and he had taken part in a Hajj. From the moment Khaldun revealed his pilgrimage to Mecca, Talon began to call him by the respectful title of *Hajji*. Khaldun appeared to enjoy the respect bestowed upon him and warmed towards Talon, sharing much information about the country he lived in and its history.

Talon took the opportunity to ask the burning question that had stayed with him since he had first seen the man-made mountains to the north.

Khaldun had laughed at that. "Indeed, you might well think of them as man-made mountains, Suleiman. They were constructed in the dim mists of long gone ages. It is thought they might be tombs of great kings; we Egyptians call our kings Pharaohs. You will see much of their history depicted on rocks and walls in this country, but especially the area of Giza."

"Hajji, there was also an enormous head sticking half out of the desert sand. It is hard to tell if it is a man or a mystical animal. What is that?"

"Long ago, before even the advent of Mahomet the prophet who brought us the true faith, our people worshiped many gods. Even now the ignorant are still superstitious and pay homage to their old gods, which they should not, but old habits die hard in a harsh world," the old man said.

"You mention Egyptians as though you are not of the Arab people, Hajji, but everywhere the language of the Arabs is spoken."

"True it is, Suleiman. Long, long ago we were many people clustered together along this river of life. There were many more *Dhimmi*, Christians and Jews, people of the book. My own ancestors were not Arabs from the desert, but times change, and so we have to change with them, and since the arrival of our Sultan we are now being told we should be good Sunni Moslems instead of Shia," he exclaimed with a shrug.

Talon did not miss the irony in Khaldun's voice and gathered from his comment that there had been some kind of upheaval recently. He asked many questions.

The old man was happy to answer them. Talon learned that he had been in Egypt before the invasion of the conquering army of Salah Ed Din's uncle. Hence he could also provide some answers to Talon's enquiries about the Ismaili who had been here before, and how the country had been ruled previously.

* * * * *

One day Talon decided to take a manuscript and read it in the garden, seated in the sun-dappled shade next to a pomegranate bush, which was overshadowed by huge sycamores. As he was engrossed in the text, he barely heard the light step of someone coming along the path towards him.

He went down on one knee when he realized just who it was.

"Salaam, my Lady. Peace be with you."

She inclined her head gracefully in acknowledgement and then said, "Peace be with you, Suleiman. Why have you chosen this place to read?"

"My Lady...a long time ago...or so it seems now, a friend once shared with me the shade of a pomegranate tree when in blossom. I find it is calming to read while sitting in the shade of trees. Moreover, over there is a fig tree which, according to legend, is also very soothing, so much so that should even a raging bull come near to the tree it too would be calmed."

She laughed with delight and waved an elegant hand at the pomegranate tree with its full red blossoms and exclaimed, "Indeed, Suleiman, I think you are right. It is both beautiful and calming to be near this tree! Who told you that? It sounds as though it might have come from a woman," she said archly.

Then without waiting for an answer she said more seriously, "I have heard from our wisest of men, the *Hajji*, that our warrior is also a man of letters. That is worthy of approval. Where did you learn to read?"

"My Lady, my first and best tutor was a Christian priest," Talon said truthfully, thinking of Jean de Loche, who had helped him through his first years in Persia, as he too had been kidnapped on the same raid.

"He taught me Latin, and then later I learned Farsi, and of course your tongue as well."

"So you are a warrior, a man of letters, and a merchant's son. You seem to be very young for all this," she said with a smile, taking a seat on a flat rock that ornamented the side of the path. The woman who had accompanied her moved so that she stood behind her mistress.

Talon could not help but to remark to himself that she was very beautiful indeed and her smile was captivating. He felt a pang of jealousy that the Emir Abbas should possess such a wonderful creature. But he suppressed it, not wanting to annoy or upset the mood of the conversation, which was light and pleasant.

"I was sent to a hard school when very young, my Lady," he remarked casually.

"My lord should be back before too long, and then he can reward you appropriately for your courage and for saving our lives," she said.

He opened his mouth to protest, but she lifted her hand and said, "Malek talked to me about how you and my son Kazim are becoming friends."

"He is a good boy," Talon said. His tone was neutral.

"But he does not spend enough time with someone who could teach him."

"I beg your pardon, my Lady?"

"I would ask you yet another favor, Suleiman."

"I shall do anything within my power to help you, my Lady, you have but to ask."

"Kazim is growing up and needs a little discipline, but also to be trained in languages and the ways of the world. Khaldun is very old and lacks the energy to teach one so young, and he told me that I should ask you if you would consider the post of Tutor.

"This would include some time spent with my daughter, because she too needs to be able to read well and to write and to use the numbers. I wish to have my daughter...Jasmine, educated well before she is married. She had some tuition while in Alexandria, but it pleased me very much that she herself has asked me for more. She will be the least of your problems... it is Kazim." She sighed and continued.

"I have brought old men in as tutors, but Kazim dislikes them because they want him to learn things that mean nothing to him at his age. You are young and I think wise beyond your years, Suleiman...could you help me with his teaching? At least until it is time for you to go," she added, a little vaguely. "I shall of course recompense you for your trouble."

He had been watching her while she sought the words to ask. He almost missed the last statement and had to ask again to be sure he had heard her correctly. She repeated.

"Will you teach him some of the things a young warrior should know, as well as other things about the world that you know?" she stated again patiently, and a little louder as the wind had picked up and was blowing noisily through the trees and making their loose clothing flutter. Once again he had the good fortune to see her face as her veil slipped, and once again he was struck by the perfection of her features. He just heard the last words she uttered.

"Or are you planning to leave us sooner, rather than later?"

He laughed but she misinterpreted it and gave a small frown. Seeing this he hastened to respond. "My lady, forgive me; I meant no offense. I am finding it astonishing that I should be asked to teach when it is I who should be taught. The *Hajji* is a far wiser man than I, and it is at his feet that I should sit rather than set myself up as a tutor."

She smiled then and he saw her beauty once more in her eyes as well as her form. "The *Hajji*, may Allah grant him many more years to his life, said that you were modest about your knowledge but that I should try to persuade you. How can I persuade you, Suleiman?"

He concentrated this time, and answered the request with a smile of his own.

"There is no need to persuade me, my Lady. You have given me back my life and that of my companion; I would repay you however I can. I would be honored to serve you. When do you wish me to start?"

* * * * *

One day news came that the war in the south was over. The army was on its way back to Al Qahirah to be honored by the Sultan, and this meant that the lord was coming home. The Sultan's fleet had even been seen sailing down the great river towards Al Qahirah the day before.

There was a palpable change in the atmosphere of the estate. Servants and men-at-arms were tense with excitement and anticipation, and so were Jasmine and Kazim. Malek, on the other hand, was not so happy, and his face was morose and worried.

"I do not know if I will have a head after he hears about the ambush," he confided in Talon dolefully one evening while they were eating in their favorite place under the sycamore near the stables.

"You should not worry so much," his brother said, punching him on the arm.

"Our lord is a just man and I am sure that her Ladyship will not allow it. She knows of your worth, brother."

"Malek, my good man, Allah is witness that you have proved your worth many times over to him. Do you not think he will take this into consideration when he comes to judge you ...if indeed he is inclined to?" Khaldun said as he munched some papyrus seeds, his white beard moving rhythmically up and down as he chewed carefully with the few teeth left in his mouth.

Talon threw an olive pit into the flower bed nearby and nodded.

"From all you have told me, and what I have heard from others, your lord is a good man who must appreciate how hard you work on this estate, Malek. It could not function without you and no mistake."

"I am glad that it is only the estate I have to worry about and not any of the master's other wives at the same time. That would be too much to deal with, for one man." There were chuckles at that.

"My lord Abbas only has one wife?" Talon asked incredulously.

"Yes, Suleiman, he has only one wife, but he has about five or six concubines here and there. Some are in Al Qahirah, and the others are in Al Iskandrîyah. However, I believe our master is deeply in love with our Lady, so his concubines are neglected." Bilal laughed and reached for another cabbage roll. He shifted and gave a small fart. Talon was appalled at his bad manners.

"Our Sultan, on the other hand, must have about eighty wives." Malek grinned at Talon's expression.

Talon pretended to be shocked. "Eighty is a lot for any man!" he said reverently with a grin in return.

"Well, he has his favorites of course, which means that the others die of boredom or use the eunuchs to satisfy them," Bilal stated knowledgeably.

"How do you know all this information?" Khaldun threw up his hands. "Whenever these two get together the subject always gets around to women," he said, pretending to be disgusted. "Suleiman, I expect better from you at least."

Talon looked solemn. "Indeed Hajji, I would not think of disappointing you."

Bilal grinned at the old man, and Malek winked at Talon.

# Chapter 7

# Abbas

With loud shouts and yells of excitement, the cavalry squadron swept down upon the small group of Nubian men who were running across the rocky plain. These Nubians were trying to keep up with their own retreating army much further ahead, which was partially hidden by the clouds of dust lifted by the fleeing army.

The stragglers, realizing that they were not going to catch up with the main body of their army, turned to face their aggressors and formed a tight group with their buffalo hide shields up and their spears pointing out, in a vain attempt to stop the charging cavalry. But their spears were not long lances, merely stabbing blades, and aside from the occasional breast plate of tough reeds, the tall Nubian men were almost devoid of armor and therefore an easy target for the long lances of the Egyptian cavalry.

The horsemen were able to smash into the group and easily break it up; the riders, using their mounts as battering rams, drove the terrified individuals to the ground, or made them turn and run, which was fatal. They hacked ferociously at the disorganized Nubians, beating with swords at the flimsy shields, and hacking down at exposed flesh. It was inevitable that the exhausted ranks of Nubians would disintegrate and flee in all directions. This was their undoing, as the Egyptian riders rode them down, stabbing at them, ignoring any pleas for mercy until none were left standing.

The dead littered the area along with the broken chariots, discarded military equipment, and booty that the raiding army had hoped to take home. The Nubian army was in full retreat with the hindermost being taken down by formations of cavalry such as this one. Abbas Abdul al Azim ibn Athir Faysal, Emir in his own right, reined in his excited horse, wiped his bloody scimitar with the end of his robe and sheathed it with a snap. He then turned his Arab war horse away from the receding dust cloud. He glanced back at his own men; like him, they were clad in flowing linen, or in some cases cotton robes, to ward off the sun and dust. Most of them wore a *kafeya*, a head wrap made of a wide linen or cotton strip, exposing only the eyes, eyebrows and foreheads, which were almost white with the accumulated dust. Their mounts were streaked with sweat and almost blown with the effort of the chase.

They rallied around him, shouting their victory songs and brandishing their bloody weapons, happy as a pack of hounds that had just made their kill. They had ridden hard to catch the Nubians and had succeeded in doing so just before they could escape over their own borders.

One of Abbas's men was brandishing a helmet taken off of a fallen Nubian. He waved it contemptuously in the air. "Look master, now they use crocodile skin for their helmets. These are no match for our steel. I had hoped for booty, but this is worthless."

He tossed the bloody and shredded helmet of hide into the dust.

The Sultan had forbidden his brother, General Turan-Shah, to follow the Nubians over the border, as he had other concerns, and one of them was not fruitless pursuit into the depths of the southern desert beyond the first cataract of the Nile. As a consequence, Abbas was honoring the command by not continuing the chase.

Allah be praised, he had lost very few men during the long day's running battle; the enemy did not fight back with any enthusiasm, being more interested in saving their skins so close to home than confronting the mounted devils that bore down upon them whenever they tarried.

Without speaking, Abbas raised his hand and turned his sweating, dust covered horse northward to lead his men back towards Aswan where the battle had commenced. Despite the chase, his mount was light on its feet and seemingly carried him without effort. Not for the first time he wondered at this breed that came from the deserts of the Arabs. He was followed closely by his Nubian warrior slave Panhsj, who also rode one of his master's fine animals. The man was so large that the horse seemed small under him, but he rode it well. As always, he stayed close, as his responsibility was his master's life. He, with Abbas's two hundred personal guards, arranged themselves behind their master in several loose rows as they began to ride northwards across the war strewn country.

Scattered all along the dry, dusty route among their unclaimed booty were the bodies of men who had been overtaken by the vengeful Egyptian cavalry during the last two days of fighting. Many corpses were already bloated and had attracted the inevitable flies and vultures, which landed their ungainly bodies clumsily. They waddled over to yet another body that was being steadily dismembered by others which were tearing at the flesh. Jackals lurked on the outskirts of the main feast, careful not to get in the way of one of these giant birds and risk being struck a fearsome blow by those sharp beaks. They would dart in when they saw an opportunity to seize a strand of flesh and run off to squabble with their own kind over the scraps.

Abbas allowed his men to take what they wanted from the dead as long as it did not inhibit the fast pace he was setting. By the time they were within sight of Aswan, his men did not so much resemble a company of disciplined warriors as a band of disreputable traders, clanking and jingling with all the metal, silver, gold and other goods they now carried. There had been more than one occasion when he had had Panhsj intervene and break up a knife fight over the booty the contenders had pilfered. By now their exhausted horses were in much need of a rest.

* * * * *

They arrived late in the afternoon two days later at Aswan to find the remainder of the Egyptian army already preparing to leave. Along the entire riverside was gathered a crowd of exhausted soldiers trying to obtain transport for themselves from the harassed quartermasters. Many were already embarking on boats and Abbas, who was in a hurry to get back to his estates, wanted to make sure there was a berth for himself and some of his higher up subordinates. The river bank was teeming with men, horses and camels, including a few elephants that had been discovered abandoned by their former masters. Many of the

Egyptian cavalry squadrons were squatting near their mounts in whatever shade they could find, resigned to the dust, the heat and flies, stoically waiting for the order to move off.

Leaving his horse with two of his men, Abbas walked down to the river's edge, accompanied by Panhsj. It took some tramping about in the mud and pushing aside people who got in the way before he was able to catch hold of one of the quartermasters who were responsible for feeding the army and transporting it up and down the Nile. He was a servant of Bark Abdul-Jalil, the newly elected Vizier to the Sultan, and knew Abbas well.

"I cannot take all your troops with me, honored Lord. Only you and a few retainers can board that boat over there if you want to go all the way down river to Cairo." He pointed to a large dhow that was loaded to the gunnels already with men and horses.

"Are you sure that boat can take us?" Abbas enquired skeptically.

"Oh yes, my lord, there is room for you, if you hurry and get on board within the hour."

Abbas thought about this for a moment. He was uncomfortable without his men, but he would take with him Panhsj and that should be enough as a body guard. He would place some of his cavalry on this boat but the rest he would send north under the command of Mustapha, who had proved to be trustworthy and would ensure they would arrive in Cairo in good order. He nodded briefly and gold exchanged hands.

"May Allah go with you, my lord. I pray he will grant you a safe and comfortable journey on the river."

"Allah protect you, Hassan, I thank you for your kindness," Abbas said absent-mindedly.

As he turned away from the boat to issue his orders to Panhsj, he saw General Turan Shah coming towards him, riding along the narrow sand strip that bordered the river before the steep banks rose sharply to the desert beyond. Fortunately, at this time of year, the river was sluggish and not in summer flood. The general was accompanied by a large party of brightly dressed retainers and soldiers.

Abbas's lip curled as he regarded the people who accompanied the general; he had a fighting man's contempt for all those who were not warriors but who paraded around as though they were. While he had no quarrel with the general, whom he believed to be brave and courageous, many of the others who accompanied him were targets of his dislike.

Most of them were Emirs and Chiefs who only came to the war because they had to. Not to have come would have been brought to the attention of the Sultan, Salah Ed Din, who would have punished them for cowardice. Abbas stiffened, as he could see that the general had noticed him, and was riding through the crowd towards him, looking purposeful.

Abbas waited with his men until the general was almost up to him before he placed his right hand on his heart and bowed low. Everyone else was already kneeling on the sandy shore with their foreheads touching the sand. As an Emir in his own right, Abbas did not need to be so servile to the general, even though he was the brother of the Sultan.

"Peace be with you. May Allah in his kindness protect Your Highness," Abbas said in a clear voice lifting his head to speak.

"Allah Protect you, Abbas, my good friend. You were successful in chasing the enemy forces back into their wilderness, I hear."

"My General, we chased them until our own horses were blown, but we took many lives from among their stragglers."

"Well...now that the enemy is safely out of the way, we can all go home. Would you care to sail with me, Abbas, or have you made some other arrangements?"

"If it pleases my lord I would be honored to sail to Cairo with you," Abbas said gratefully with another bow.

"Good, then have a word with Hassan. I saw him talking to you, and guessed that he would place you in some leaky old tub." The general grinned and gestured at the dhow in question. "You shall travel with me. I shall be sailing in that boat over there." He pointed towards a very large and well-outfitted galley that was anchored in the middle of the river a little further downstream. He smiled, and then turned his horse away; Abbas bowed and watched him and his entourage as they rode off. One among the group looked back at Abbas, and his stare was not friendly. He saw Abbas staring back at him; the man gave a short laugh and then turned away, spurring his fine animal to catch up with the General. Abbas watched him with slitted eyes.

The man's name was Bahir Ibn Hakeem, and although he was distantly related to Abbas there was no love lost between them. He noticed another looking at him, who lifted his fly whisk nonchalantly when their eyes met. It was Kemosiri ibn Jibade, a lean, handsome man with strong features under his short beard. He was a well-known officer in the Army with a very high pedigree and enviable record of warfare. It was known that he was a dangerous person to cross but a good ally to have. Abbas considered him an ally if not a friend; few got close to him.

Abbas decided that he wanted to travel with the General, as much to keep an eye on events as to ensure that Bahir did not stir up more trouble for him during the trip. There was always the risk that there might be trouble, but he was prepared to take that chance. He knew Panhsj would not sleep a wink for the entire three day voyage if he was asked to keep watch.

He became very busy making arrangements to ensure that some of the nearer retainers sailed while most of his men could travel with their booty and his own share overland. Satisfied with the arrangements, he joined his men while he waited for word to embark. He pondered the reason for Bahir's laughter, while half listening to his men murmuring quietly among themselves as they sat cross-legged in the shade of a clump of palms and ate their cold lunch of dried figs and dates washed down with water from the river.

The relationship between himself and Bahir had deteriorated while they were teenage boys. Abbas had come across Bahir bullying a young girl in the palace grounds. Bahir and another boy were teasing her brutally. She was crying and screaming at them to leave her alone, but they persisted with pinches and slaps to make her cry even more. Abbas, who was also in his early teens, did not greatly care for girls at that time, but was still disturbed to see the unpleasant behavior. He instinctively reacted angrily to bullying or abuse of the weak at any time. The girl's aged nurse was trying ineffectually to stop the boys, but was afraid of them, so all she could do was to flutter about like a plump goose squawking at the top of her voice and generally contributing to the noise, but little else.

Abbas strode up to the two boys and shouted at them to stop what they were doing. He was just a little younger than Bahir and the other boy, which gave him no authority at all. Bahir had pushed him roughly out of the way with the words, "Get out of here, Abbas, you runt, it's none of your business."

This had immediately incensed Abbas, who was even then not well known for controlling his temper. He smacked Bahir hard on the face with the flat of his hand. The loud slap stopped everyone in their tracks. Bahir had gasped and placed a hand over the rapidly reddening welt on his cheek. Then with a howl he had attacked Abbas, rushing at him with flailing fists and bared teeth.

The other boy, after a moment of hesitation, also rushed in to assist so that Abbas soon found himself on the defensive. However, he struck back as hard as he could, drawing blood from Bahir's nose, and a howl of pain from the other boy whom he poked in the eye. The two boys had run off whimpering and promising all sorts of dire consequences, but Abbas had not paid them any attention. He licked a swollen lip, but he was otherwise uninjured. The young girl, with huge eyes, had come up to him and stammered her thanks.

He looked at her and saw a skinny creature of about nine, with a tear stained face and dribbling nose and wondered why he had taken the trouble. Her nurse gathered the little girl up in her robes and dragged her away, still looking over her shoulder at him with huge gratitude in her eyes. She was calling upon Allah to protect him, as he would surely need it now.

"I am Khalidah, what is your name?" the little girl called over her shoulder.

"My name is Abbas," he had said abruptly, without interest.

"I shall remember you always. Allah protect you forever," she called, and then she was gone.

Abbas had made an implacable enemy out of Bahir from that day forth. They had fought again and again, with Abbas not always winning, as Bahir was sure to bring a henchman as backup. The hatred had endured, although they were separated upon reaching the age of fifteen, in order to go back to their respective families. The animosity had persisted during the turmoil of the new Sultan's arrival in Egypt, when most of the old families, once loyal to the former Fatimid rulers, were now jostling for positions within the new regime.

Abbas had been appointed to the position of Captain of the palace guard as a reward for soldiering well in one of the campaigns that the Sultan had waged across the North African regions. He had further earned his sultan's approval during the brief war with the Christians, when the sultan had called upon men from all over Egypt to come to the colors and defend the country. Many had not, because they considered him to be an upstart. They had stayed within the safety of the walls of Alexandria or Cairo, while the new sultan sallied forth with a small but determined army to arrest the progress of the invaders.

Abbas' first wife had died in childbirth after delivering a baby daughter. The grieving Abbas had spent his time away from his ancestral home, leaving his daughter to be raised by her grandmother on his wife's side, in Alexandria. The girl had been almost six years old by the time Abbas came back from the wars and his duties to the Sultan.

He had come across Khalidah again while visiting the huge estates of a longtime friend of his father. Abbas's father had died early in battle, making him the head of the family, so it was a duty for him to pay respects to the Emir, although he performed it tardily.

On one of these occasions, the Emir Al Hakim ibn Hudhafah Ghassan had invited him to come with him on a walk in the cool gardens of his small palace. They walked slowly in the shade of the tall pomegranate bushes and the palm trees. As they walked, the old man remained silent, allowing Abbas to become aware of the calm in the garden. He gazed up at the date palms and at the even taller sycamores; his eyes rested on the flowered gardens and the cool green bushes, newly wet by the busy gardeners. The perfume of the tiny white jasmine flowers and fruit tree blossoms wafted through the air around them as they walked almost shoulder to shoulder. It was a far cry from the harsh deserts Abbas was more familiar with these days.

Some way off, he could hear the sound of water from a fountain splashing into a pond and heard cicadas buzzing in the palm fronds. The whole atmosphere was one of peace and tranquility. It had been a very long time since he had known either. He sighed, soaking in the unaccustomed atmosphere with pleasure.

"How long is it, Abbas, my young friend, since you knew a woman?" the older man asked without looking at him.

Abbas had been taken aback by the directness of the old man. He took his time responding, as he was uncomfortable with the question.

"It has been a long time, my Father," he revealed reluctantly.

"I thought so. You have taken yourself away from your family and you have neglected your friends, going off to war as often as the Sultan permits you to."

"Father, forgive me if I have been negligent of my duties. Since the death of my wife, may Allah be kind to her soul, I have no desire left in me," Abbas muttered uncomfortably, wishing the conversation would go elsewhere.

The old man gave a skeptical chuckle. "Is it not Allah's will that we procreate and produce sons to fight our wars and protect our nation and daughters, who can in turn, give their husbands children?"

"It is written, Oh Father." Abbas agreed.

"Then you should marry again, and have a family with many children, my son," the old man suggested quietly with a smile, putting his age-spotted hand on Abbas's strong forearm.

Just at that moment they came round a corner and saw the fountain, and the sound of the splashing water came sharper to Abbas's ears. It was a very calm and lovely setting; the fountain was tucked in among flowering shrubs and pomegranate bushes with the palms behind lending a wide expanse of shade. It was also very private. But Abbas did not see the beauty of the fountain nor smell the scent of the fruit trees; instead he saw an apparition.

He saw a lovely young woman, who had unthinkingly dropped her veil. She was seated on the side of the pond, leaning out, with her hand in the water running it back and forth, teasing large carp that were moving languidly in the water. She was humming a tune, and seemed quite unaware of their intrusion.

Abbas stopped abruptly and stared. While he had known other women since his wife's death, he was awed by this beautiful creature. In one long glance, he saw her fine, light olive skin, her slim limbs and delicate wrists. He even glimpsed a finely turned ankle that was showing below the hem of an intricately patterned cotton dress. He sensed rather than saw she was a beautifully formed woman.

She noticed them just after they had stopped, and gave a small gasp. She hurriedly replaced her veil and stood up.

"Father, forgive me. I did not know you were coming with a guest!" she exclaimed.

"Do not be alarmed, my daughter," her father reassured her, and he turned to Abbas.

"Sir, please forgive my daughter's impropriety, she is young and rebellious and should be punished for her impropriety, but I love her dearly. She is the light of my life."

The old man had a twinkle in his eyes.

"This is Khalidah, my only daughter and my treasure. My daughter, this is Lord Abbas. Please be respectful to him," he said sternly. But the old man was smiling with pleasure at the sight of his daughter, who it was clear wanted to embrace him, but held back because of the stranger.

Abbas suddenly remembered. "Forgive my bad manners, my Lady, but have we ...are you the girl I met while in the garden of the palace of Prince Said?"

Khalidah laughed, and he felt his chest tighten. Her laugh tinkled and blended with the sound of the water from the fountain to make music in his ears.

"It is I, my lord. You saved me from a very unpleasant time; Bahir is such a bully, but... at much expense to yourself, I fear."

Abbas, who had already decided that he had paid no price at all, nodded, mesmerized by the young woman in front of him. He did not know what else to say.

"It appears that you two know each other," the old man said, but he seemed unsurprised.

Abbas nodded again and declared, "We met a long time ago, Sire. It was not the best of meetings."

"Well, my daughter does not seem to agree with you there, my son." The old man smiled and asked, "Khalidah, please would you see that the servants bring us refreshments, as we wish to sit here and talk together." He laid his hand alongside his daughter's cheek affectionately.

"I shall see to it myself, father," she responded.

She walked off gracefully, leaving some indefinable scent behind that teased Abbas's senses. His eyes never left the swaying form as it receded down the path.

The old man watched with a half-smile as the scene unfolded before him, then sat down heavily on the side of the fountain. He waved Abbas down beside him. He was pleased that he had contrived the meeting thus, and by the look of bewildered awe on the face of his young visitor, it had been a success so far.

He studied Abbas for a moment. He saw a determined visage, the lean body of a warrior well used to hardship, but the features were not coarse. The well-groomed beard and slightly hooked nose, the strong chin and deep set dark eyes commanded respect for one who was just thirty years old.

"Abbas, my young Prince. I have known you almost all your life and have heard good reports of you from all quarters, but it is time to discuss something that concerns me deeply."

Abbas made to speak, but the old man raised his hand for silence, and out of respect Abbas held his peace.

"There is something very important that I want to discuss with you, so please let me finish. In normal circumstances, your parents and I would talk about it and then decide and so on. But as your father is dead, I must talk to you directly, for time is of the essence."

"Allah protect you, Father, but if there is anything I can do to help then I am your servant," Abbas murmured, not at all sure where this was going.

"It is a delicate matter but it must be said. You need to marry again, my son. I have a beautiful daughter who is unmarried, and who is already somewhat older than she should be for marriage, but who is still young enough to bear children," the old man smiled with his eyes.

He left the rest of it in the air, waiting patiently for Abbas to collect his wits.

After looking all around the garden trying to regain his composure, he finally spoke.

"Father, you do me great honor. Your daughter has enchanted me and I would willingly marry her today but...would she want me?" He knew very well that it would not be up to Khalidah to choose, if her father decided to marry her off; nonetheless, he felt it should be asked.

The old man looked at him with approval.

"She has mentioned your name on several occasions, since another came to propose to me for her hand."

Abbas gave a start. "Who?" he blurted out, in spite of himself.

"Why, Emir Bahir of course, who else? He has known her since they were playmates at the palace of the Sultan many years ago."

"They were no playmates," Abbas burst out. "Oh, respected Father, as Allah is my witness he bullied her whenever he could."

"I was not unaware of this," said the old man calmly.

"You refused him?" Abbas regretted his abrupt tone immediately. "I...I am sorry. Forgive me, Father, I spoke rudely, but I do not like that man," he added impulsively.

"Indeed, nor do I! No, my son. There is nothing to forgive; but yes, I did refuse him the first and the second time, but...the third time might be hard to resist, as he has influence and could go to the Sultan and request the right to marry her. Besides," he added, "she would have turned him down in any case, as she has so many others. I was beginning to despair." He gave a dry chuckle. "I would not marry her off to anyone, Abbas. Her happiness is important to me."

"But if I propose and she...you accept, then he cannot affect this union, Father?" Abbas demanded, a little breathless now.

"Indeed, I believe that to be the case, my son."

Abbas stared at him. He hesitated and looked away, uncertain, but then made his decision.

"Then...then I wish to propose marriage to your daughter, Sire...if you will accept me as your son?" He said it in a rush, as he impulsively knelt in front of the old man and grasped his hand.

"She is beautiful indeed. So beautiful," Abbas said, as though to himself. He had barely seen her, but the vision of her leaning over the pond, the delicate limbs, the hint of full breasts, with an oval face and huge dark eyes, was still fixed in his mind.

As though by some invisible command, two servants appeared carrying large silver trays with sherbet and small honey cakes and *falafel*. Khalidah followed; she was now veiled as decorum dictated, and was wearing finely wrought slippers that slapped her heels at each light step.

Abbas stood up as she approached, as did her father, who spoke gently, but with much emotion in his voice.

"Come to me, my daughter, I have something important to tell you."

She glided over to stand in front of them, her head demurely down. He took her hands and held them while the servants departed, having made low tables of the large trays that had been laid on folding legs.

"My dear Khalidah, my lovely daughter. Prince Abbas has asked me for your hand in marriage! Though why he would want to marry a self-willed and stubborn girl like you, I cannot think," he was smiling and there were tears in his eyes.

She lifted her head then, and the veil dropped again, this time because she had rushed into her father's arms, all decorum forgotten, a huge smile lighting up her face.

"Oh, Father! Have you accepted?"

"My dear, please. Behave yourself. What will our guest think of you?" her father remonstrated, even as he embraced her tenderly.

Instantly contrite, Khalidah resumed her demure posture, and replaced her veil.

"Sir, please forgive me, I did not know what I was doing," she murmured with a glint in her eyes. She did not sound in the least repentant to Abbas, whose own happiness was growing in her presence, and he was having difficulty hiding his amusement at this display.

"My dear lady, please do not feel the need. It is clear that you are pleased that I have asked your father for your hand in marriage, which he has granted, and for that I, too, am very happy."

"My lord, Allah has been kind to me this day. I have waited so long for this moment," she exclaimed.

Decorum forbade him to kiss her, but the urge was hard to restrain, and he doubted that he could have controlled himself if her father had not been standing with them, beaming with his own happiness.

"Then, that is settled, children: although it is highly irregular to propose with my daughter standing nearby, I do give my blessings to you both, and we must ensure a wedding is arranged quickly."

Thus it was that Abbas married Khalidah, amid great rejoicing among both clans. A somewhat bemused Abbas found himself with a new wife, who was young but also very intelligent and had her own mind. Before long he grew to love her without reservation, and every moment was a torment while he was away. After spending some time in Alexandria at his palace, he took her to his estates down in the region of the Fayoum, not far from the west bank of the Nile, where his family had ruled for two hundred years.

Before they left, he heard that Bahir al Hakeem had thrown a massive tantrum at the news and had sworn to avenge himself upon them both. Abbas had smiled at the news.

He had told his new wife, before taking her to his palace, about his daughter and her lonely life in Alexandria. What he had not anticipated was the almost immediate closeness of the two when they did meet. He assumed it was some woman thing, but all the same, it was a great comfort to know that they liked each other so quickly. One night, after they had made love, he asked Khalidah how she had managed to win his daughter over so quickly, as only recently she had been a distant child with little to communicate to him on his infrequent visits.

Khalidah had turned in his arms and said, "You men. You think you know everything. Well...we women know exactly what we need to do and say with one another. Your daughter needs a friend who is a woman. I am going to be her friend and sister, not try to be the mother that she does not want."

He had smiled at that and kissed her lightly, then went to sleep holding her close, content that his wife was not only beautiful, but wise as well.

## Chapter 8

# Homecoming

Abbas took the same ship to Al Qahirah as General Turan Shah. Panhsj accompanied him, and Abbas told him to keep an eye open for trouble. His enemy Bahir was embarked on the same boat, with his own small retinue of men. Abbas knew that he was greatly outnumbered, but at the same time he was under the protection of the general, and he hoped there would not be any overt foul play. All the same, he stayed alert for danger, and he was comforted in the knowledge that Panhsj was doing the same.

During the northward journey the general kept them entertained with conversation and pleasantries. They discussed the battle and the deeds of warriors, and Abbas came up for mention several times, as his small but well-trained cavalry had acquitted themselves very well.

Abbas spent some time with Kemosiri, of a similar grade and position as himself, who seemed to be pleased to talk. They would lean over the side of the boat away from the other officers and men and discuss the recent battle and speculate on the chances of another war with the Frans, whom they believed to be the main threat to Egypt at this time. Somehow, however, despite their familiarity and seeming common agreement on much about the world they lived in, Abbas felt the man to be distant. Kemosiri was from one of the oldest Egyptian families in the country, claiming descent as far back as the Byzantium times. He lacked for nothing in terms of riches, palaces and ships, but no one seemed to be close to him.

As evening came, the winds died down to a light breeze, leaving the boat to be drawn down river by the current. The lamps were lit, food was laid out by servants, and the men feasted and indulged themselves with wine and women. Before too long every corner of the boat was occupied with the satisfied grunts of men taking the harlots who had accompanied the army southward before the battle.

Those who were disinclined to take a woman gambled with dice in a game known as al-zahr, meaning 'chance'. The air was filled with oaths, and the click of dice and the jingle of coins or other trinkets were to be heard falling on the mat for the betting, as the men played to applause followed by groans as they won or lost.

Abbas saw no reason to get involved with any of the women or the gambling, although some of the women were very pretty. His thoughts were focused on his wife Khalidah, and his longing to be with her only increased as the distance between them shortened. He spent long hours in the bow of the ship watching the distant western shoreline of the river.

The general liked to have beautiful things, especially women, around him; and while he observed the laws on drinking, he had few concerns about fornication or smoking hashish, which wafted over the boat from dawn to dusk.

It puzzled Abbas that Bahir acted with a smug attitude about something that he felt concerned him. His dislike and mistrust cautioned him to keep his distance and to watch his back. He caught Bahir watching him on occasion, with a satisfied smile on his face, but there was little he could do to find out why. The boat was not so large that it was easy to avoid Bahir, who was his declared enemy. Instead he took himself and Panhsj off to the front of the boat and wished they were already at his estates.

It was on one of these dark nights, with the boats slipping quietly downstream, the revelry done for the night, the general comfortably retired in his rear cabin, and most men asleep on the deck to take advantage of the cool breeze that came off the river, when trouble finally came. Abbas was fast asleep when he felt an urgent nudge in his ribs and awoke in the instant. His servant would never have done this unless it was of the utmost importance. Panhsj put his head very close to him and whispered.

"Awake, my lord, there are those who look as though they are seeking us; they come as shadows and possible killers." He turned his head away to stare down the length of the boat towards the rear.

Abbas drew his knife and rolled slowly over so that he could watch where Panhsj was indicating. His head was just level with his servant's chest so he could look over without showing too much of his face. They were under the curve of the side of the boat, so they were if anything in deeper shadow than many of the sleeping bodies lying around on the deck.

"We shall let them come very close, and then fight with knives," he whispered.

Then he saw them. There were two, and they were definitely looking for something, but it was also clear that they knew roughly where he was; because although they moved cautiously, they came inexorably towards him and his servant.

Abbas drew his feet under him and prepared to leap, and he felt Panhsj do the same, but they did it so unobtrusively that their attackers did not seem to notice. Apart from the slip of bare feet on the deck, the dark shadows crept up to them in silence, and when they were leaning over them one pointed down at the seemingly asleep Abbas. There was a slither of steel leaving a sheath, and then both men poised themselves to strike.

Abbas did not wait further. With a hiss he leapt to his feet and reached for the wrist of the man leaning directly over him, gripping it in a vice-like hold. The man grunted with surprise but then his other hand went for Abbas's throat. Alongside him Abbas could feel rather than hear the other struggle going on as Panhsj fought his opponent. The only sound in this dark corner was the slapping of feet on the wood deck and the rasp of heavy breathing.

Abbas could feel the grip of his opponent tightening on his throat and the consequent lack of breath, and he allowed the man to believe that he was succeeding in his attempt to strangle him. Then his knife came out and plunged deep into the man's exposed stomach. The dark form gave an audible gasp, but Abbas drove the blade deeper, released his opponent's wrist, slapped his hand over his adversary's open mouth, and drove the curved blade deeper still.

The man was about to scream, but Abbas gave a mighty heave and sent him overboard. There was a cracking sound and another splash as the second attacker followed his companion into the water, but he did not cry out either; his neck had been broken.

There was a shout from the rear of the boat as men woke up to the noise and shouted demands to know what was going on. Abbas quickly lay down with Panhsj, and they both pretended to also wake up from the disturbance.

"In Allah's name, who is making all this noise?" someone exclaimed irritably.

"Has anyone fallen overboard?" another enquired.

"I heard a splash but no cry, so maybe it was something someone threw overboard," someone else yawned.

Abbas placed his hand on Panhsj's thick muscular arm.

"Thank you, my friend. I shall not forget this," he whispered, and then they pretended to go back to sleep.

The boat continued on its course and the people who had been awakened went back to sleep, grumbling and muttering to themselves at being disturbed.

Abbas's mind was racing. He was sure he knew who had sent those killers, but he would not know without directly confronting Bahir. But what proof did he have? The attackers were now crocodile meat.

In the morning he received his answer when he saw Bahir's expression. At first there had been genuine surprise on the man's face, followed by the glitter of hatred in his enemy's eyes as he turned away.

It was clear to Abbas that his suspicions had been correct, and he resolved the day would come when he would make Bahir regret the previous night's attempt on his life. Now was not the time, however, to bring accusations, nor to allow the enmity to flare up in front of the general. Like his brother the Sultan Salah Ed Din, General Turan Shah disliked disunity among his senior commanders and often punished those who infringed the rule. Abbas decided that he would bide his time. Sooner or later Bahir would make a mistake, and he would capitalize on it.

As they sailed by the small river port of Beneade and the road which would have taken them to his home in the oasis Fayoum, he longed to jump off the ship and swim to shore and ride to the gates of his house. But as a commander he was expected to first appear before the sultan, make obeisance, and even join in the victory celebrations.

They arrived later that day at the citadel of Al Qahirah amid much rejoicing. The air was filled with the deep booming of kettle drums, accompanied by the ear-piercing shriek of reed horns. It seemed as though the entire population turned out to welcome and honor the victorious general. The sultan was there in all his finery, although Abbas knew that Salah Ed Din did not care very much for pomp and ceremony. This occasion demanded that he performed the honors and heap praise upon his brother and his army.

General Turan Shah gave a lengthy speech to the seated sultan. He stayed on one knee all the while in front of him, amid the silks and other booty that had been placed before his brother.He brought forward officers who had performed well on the battle field, and he was not short on praise for Abbas. After the welcoming ceremony was over, the sultan turned and beckoned Abbas over.

"I am told that you performed great deeds upon the battle field, my Prince. Allah be praised, we had a great victory," Salah Ed Din said by way of welcome, after Abbas had prostrated himself in front of him and then been permitted to stand.

"My lord, I only did my duty as a soldier. Allah was with the faithful," Abbas replied.

"Ah, thus speaks a modest soldier of mine, one of my most faithful of followers," the sultan remarked with a smile. "All the same, my brother said that you helped turn the tide of the battle and then chased the enemy back to their border. It shall be remembered, Abbas. What can I do for you this day as a reward?"

Abbas looked up at the face of the man he worshiped. The sharp dark eyes were kindly today, and regarded him with affection.

"My lord, I need no reward but to serve you. May Allah bless you with his kindness. But if I could take some time away to see my family that I have not seen for many months, I would be forever grateful."

"My lord Abbas! How can you abandon me in my hour of greatest need in this way?" the sultan exclaimed.

Abbas stepped back, aghast that he may have offended, but then he saw the sultan laugh. The general joined in the amusement, and Abbas knew he was allowed to leave his duties for a while. Salah Ed Din, who had almost no family life to speak of, never denied his officers time with their own families when war permitted.

"May God protect you at all times, my lord, as I shall when I return," Abbas said happily.

"May Allah speed you on your way, my loyal Prince, but remember to come back, as we have some unfinished business with the prison in Alexandria still to discuss."

Instantly cowed, Abbas put his hand over his heart and bowed in silence. Then he retreated backwards for a few paces before rejoining his men.

The words had stung, but he knew the sultan had let him off lightly. Another man might have lost his head over that debacle, he realized with chagrin. How could he ever live down the shame of that? He wondered in agony.

His reputation had been on the rise until that fateful night when the whole enclosure had gone up in smoke. He had received the messenger with the ill news even while on his way south to the war with the Nubians, and there had been very little he could do at that distance.

Even to this day, no one was entirely sure how it had happened. The messenger informed him that there had been some prisoners caught in their cells that had suffocated to death, while others had forced the doors and killed the guards, then gone on a rampage through the city. It had taken a large force of cavalry and footmen to round up most of them. Some had vanished, while others had been picked up nearby, too drunk to move or to know where they were by dawn.

Abbas retrieved his horse and those of his men who had disembarked from the other boats, then they set out from the city to the south and west where his lands lay. He took only the men who had come down river with him. The others would arrive in Al Qahirah a week hence and he did not want to wait for them.

They had a day and a half to ride to reach their destination. He rode with a light heart, knowing he would soon see his family after almost three months of absence.

* * * * *

They arrived late the next evening, finding the stronghold dark and quiet. As they approached the large wooden gates, he was pleased to note that the guards were alert and challenged them. Once the guards ascertained the identity of his party, the entire place became a noisy bustle. There was a distant return shout and then more excited calls from within the compound as the inhabitants woke up to receive their Lord and master. The gates creaked open and slammed back against the outer walls, followed by the jingle of harness and stamp of iron-shod feet as many horses entered the compound.

Within the house the awakened servants frantically made preparations to welcome the return of their Lord. Abbas walked his horse into the main compound and felt that he was at last home. The tall palms and even taller sycamore trees of great age that lined the road to the gate had initiated this feeling of homecoming, but now once within the gates the cool air of the night and the scent of flowers and watered earth gave him a sense of peace.

To complete the scene, he saw his wife descending the steps of the main building, her way lit by a torch held high by a male servant. His breath caught at the sight of her beauty, which was perhaps made all the more by the flickering flames of the surrounding torches.

He leapt off his horse and almost began to run to her, proper decorum forgotten, but then he remembered himself and walked with careful deliberation as she came to him. They met in the middle of the suddenly quiet maidan and he, in keeping with his position, tilted his head to acknowledge her presence.

His wife knelt at his feet, her head bowed and her face half hidden, her hand held up to him.

"Your beauty is twice what it was when I left, my princess. How is it so?" he whispered, as he took her proffered hand and lifted her to her feet to gaze down upon her features.

"You should not abandon me so often, my lord, nor for so long, for my beauty in your eyes would increase tenfold were you to remain with me," she whispered back, her eyes glowing with the pleasure of seeing him.

He chuckled with delight and then said, "Are you well, my wife? Has my son tested your patience since I left? Are you still friends with that daughter of mine?"

As he spoke, Malek arrived to greet Abbas and hastily prostrated himself in the dust in front of them both.

"Peace be with, you Lord," he said.

"Peace be with you. Rise up, my faithful Malek, and tell me how you are."

"We are well, my lord, and..." he cast a glance at Khalidah. "Allah be praised, we have been safe as well. Go you my lord with your wife, while I attend to your men and horses. Er...did you receive my letter, my lord?"

Abbas shook his head. "What letter? I have just come directly from the ship that landed in Al Qahirah two days ago. What do you mean safe? Are you not safe here always?"

"My lord," Khalidah said gently, "why don't you come into the house where we can wash away the dust of travel and war, and I shall tell you all."

Malek gave an almost audible sigh of relief and bowed deeply as his master walked towards the house with his wife on his arm.

They were accosted by a tousle-haired sleepy boy who rushed out of the house and threw himself at his father with a cry of delight.

"Father, you are back with us! We have so much to tell you! We were set upon..." He got no further, as his mother hushed him and put her finger to her lips, then turned to Abbas and spoke.

"We do have much to tell, my lord, but you should be allowed to clean off the dust of travel and eat before we speak of our adventure. Kazim, go back to bed, my sweet. We can meet again in the morning," she said firmly to the boy.

Abbas put Kazim down and ruffled his son's hair. "Obey your mother, my son, and get a good night's rest. Tomorrow you will come with me to inspect our land, with Malek."

The boy reluctantly went off with his maid servant and Abbas turned back to his wife.

"What did the boy mean?" he asked, looking puzzled.

"It was nothing, my lord, but I shall indeed tell you of it. Come, it is late enough and you must be very tired."

He smiled at her. "Not so tired that I cannot feel the desire of a man who is with a very beautiful woman, my princess."

She smiled and said, "I am at your command, my lord. I shall take it upon myself to see that you sleep well tonight."

One other person greeted them at the head of the stairs. Jasmine had stood waiting, but now she ran down the steps and into her father's arms.

"Father, I am so glad you are back at last," she said, her voice muffled in his shoulder. He stroked her long hair and murmured his pleasure at her greeting. She had mellowed and blossomed since Khalidah became her friend. Now his daughter was happy to see him.

"I am back, my child, and very pleased to be. I hope I find you well and keeping up with your studies?"

"I am well, Father, but Mother will tell you all. I shall bid you goodnight and let you go," she said in a very grown-up manner that made him look at her a bit closer.

He glanced at Khalidah. She noticed his look and nodded. His daughter was turning into a very beautiful woman.

Later, feeling refreshed, Abbas dined on the best food that could be prepared in the house.

The fare was infinitely better than the bare necessities he had had to live on for nearly three months hitherto. He munched on salted seeds that were sun dried, along with imported olives in oil. There were small cakes of pounded lotus, baked hard, which his wife knew he enjoyed, followed by dried salty fish morsels in a bed of celery and lettuce. The main meal consisted of stewed goat meat surrounded by rice, with plenty of onion and garlic and fragrant with spices.

Abbas set to with the hunger of a man who has been deprived of good food for too long.

His wife ate a morsel of food here and there to keep him company. When they were finished and the sweetmeats came, she called for coffee.

"My lord, it is time to tell you of events that came to pass," she said, her face pale.

She had the full attention of her husband; his lean dark face turned towards her without comment and watched her while she spoke.

"Remember that you sent me by boat to the junction of the two rivers, the one great Nile and the other our own, that flows not far from this very place?"

He nodded in reply.

"You did this for our safety, I know...but, my lord, we received word that robbers would be waiting for us in boats at the junction of the rivers near to Beneade. The information was reliable, but you must ask Malek how it came to him. In order to avoid the risk of attack, I ordered the servants to disembark a good three leagues beforehand. Malek told me he did not like the idea and wanted to go back to Al Qahirah, but I overruled him and we took the road instead, which I thought might bypass the danger. It was not so."

Abbas gave a start, and was about to ask a question when she put a light hand on his arm and said, "I beg of you, let me finish the story, my lord, and then you may ask the questions."

The coffee forgotten, he watched the emotions playing across her face.

"We...we were almost home when we came under attack by a large band of men who first killed our scouts. My lord, Malek and his brother are good men, and they took every precaution, but to no avail. The men came out of a large grove of trees and overwhelmed us.

"Malek and his men fought like lions, my lord, and those not killed were sorely wounded, but there were too many of them." She had tears running down her cheeks.

"The slaves dropped my palanquin and fled for their lives, and the robbers were about to kill me and your children, but for the intervention of Allah, may He be praised forever."

Abbas was pale. "What happened? How did you live?" he whispered through bloodless lips, his eyes on fire.

"I know not how it happened, other than what Malek and his brother told me later, but two men came down from the hills overlooking the road, riding like devils, and they began to attack and destroy the enemy right in front of us.

"The one, Suleiman, saved my life directly, and that of Kazim and Jasmine. The attackers were about to kill us when he came like an avenging angel and slew all about him. The other gave a good account of himself, but then he was badly wounded. It was

Allah's will, and he will recover, although for a time it was not at all sure that he would."

Abbas stared down at his wife who, having to relive the terrible events of the attack, was now shaking and weeping in his arms.

She huddled in the shelter of his arms while he tried to digest what had happened. Some things were beginning to fall into place and he did not like what he was seeing.

"I must talk to Malek at once," he said—all thought of sleep forgotten.

"You!" he called to one of the servants standing just outside the entrance to their room. "Bring Malek, and his brother, here at once." The servant scurried off.

Abbas turned back to his wife. Using a cotton cloth he wiped the tears away and said, "My lovely princess. Go to bed and I shall come to you when I have listened to Malek. I would know all there is to this treachery, for that is what it was, and I am sure I know who was responsible."

He leaned over and kissed her. "I thank almighty Allah that you are still alive, and praise him for his kindness in preserving you and my children," he whispered, as he lifted her up from the floor cushion and sent her on her way.

It was only a few minutes before Malek and his brother were prostrated in front of their lord and master, who stood above them with a face like thunder.

He kept them in that position for longer than usual, while he regained his composure, and then abruptly he bade them sit up.

"Now tell me in your own words what happened on the road recently," he said as calmly as he could.

"There is treachery somewhere in Al Qahirah, my lord..." Malek began fearfully.

*****

The dawn was beginning to glow in the east, throwing the palm trees into dark relief, and the cocks were beginning to crow in the gardens as Abbas came silently to his bed. He had not wanted to wake his wife, but as he settled down on the bedclothes with a barely audible sigh, she rolled over and placed her hand on his naked chest and began to caress him.

Despite his exhaustion, he smiled and took her into his arms.

Sometime later the two fell into a deep sleep that was undisturbed by the sounds coming from the courtyard. Everyone walked quietly, for the Lord had come home and was asleep.

# Chapter 9

# Arrest

Talon had heard the welcoming shouts and the noise of the gates opening. He wondered what the commotion was about and stepped out of his room to see what was going on. It was late, yet the servants were excited, and he guessed that it had to be the arrival of the Lord. He knew Malek would need to brief his master of the events of the last three months and give an account of the attack that had brought him and Max to this place. Thus he chose to remain out of the way for now, observing from the doorway.

He could not make out the features of the Lord Abbas in the flickering torchlight, yet there was something familiar about his demeanor. He wore a helmet with a nose guard that concealed his face, but even when the man took this off, Talon could not tell where he had seen him before.

Thoughtful, he went back to bed, as did most of the servants other than an unfortunate few who would have to stay up to serve as long as the Lord was awake. Calm settled over the house and compound as men and women returned to their unfinished night and tried to catch up on lost sleep.

Talon woke early with an uneasy feeling. He tried to put it aside and go about his normal morning tasks. After having paid Max a wakeup visit, he went to check that the horses were fed. Max was getting stronger and up to a little activity, so they spent time after a breakfast of dates and goats milk, cleaning their saddles and leather in preparation for another day out on the estate, perhaps with Malek or with Kazim, who had not yet appeared from the house at this early hour.

Having sweated over tack cleaning, Talon suggested they go to the bath house, which Max had learned to enjoy. It was a secluded place where they were able to talk in low tones about their plans for escape. Max felt well enough to ride, although his shoulder still gave him some pain. It remained a concern that if by any bad luck they were forced into a fight, it would still be difficult for him to assist Talon. "We will just have to disappear at night with our horses and put as much distance between us and the good people of this place as we can, Talon," Max said. "Do you think the master will try to stop us?"

"I don't know, Max, but I have an unsettling feeling about Lord Abbas. I could swear I have seen that man before, but I do not know where," Talon said in a frustrated whisper.

It was time for class and he was expected to join the children. He hurriedly dressed, leaving Max to go back to his room and rest. He made his way towards the spot in the garden where they held their class room. No one was waiting under the old fig tree. He changed direction and went to the stables instead.

Talon assumed the family was catching up with the news the Lord Abbas had brought with him from Cairo and the war, and thus the children would be late. He carried on with repairing the tack, chatting with the syce who was busy grooming the horses. Bilal dawdled over to exchange greetings for the day. He jerked his head at the house on the other side of the maidan as he said, "We will not see our Lord till late this morning, Suleiman. He kept us talking into the night, demanding a full explanation of what happened when we were ambushed, and then he finally went to bed. I am sure his wife was still awake waiting for him." Bilal winked and grinned. "But he will want to see you when he arises, so be available."

For some reason Talon did not want to hear the last part of Bilal's words; he shrugged it off as he watched Bilal amble away with a short wave as he went to collect his horse held by a syce. Bilal then joined a small group of men already mounted. They were going for a ride to inspect a far corner of the estate on the other side of the lake.

Talon stopped mending his tack and went to see the horses. As he approached the stables, he noticed a group of men lounging in the shade. There was a man who appeared to be from Nubia, for he was a deep ebony color and his head was covered with a tight frizz of black hair. Talon assumed he had arrived with the Lord. The large man was dressed as a warrior, in pants and boots rather than the loose abbaya that a servant normally wore. The men were talking and laughing and made no attempt to greet him as he passed, so he kept to himself.

Max had not shown up either, and Talon imagined he was still resting after his bath.

By mid morning Talon was just preparing to walk to the house and find out what was keeping the children when he saw Malek and another man come down the steps of the main house. Kazim was with them, and as soon as he saw Talon, he broke away and came running up to him.

"Suleiman, my father is here and he wants to see you," he squeaked, and he pulled on Talon's sleeve to get him to move faster in the direction of his father.

Talon came quickly, led by the excited boy, but as soon as he was near to the Lord Abbas he obeyed custom and went onto one knee, bowing his head to the man who stood in front of him.

"Rise, Suleiman, that I might see who it is who saved my family and my honor," said a voice that he recognized with horror. Slowly Talon lifted his head. Then he stood to face the Lord of the house. Recognition was instantaneous.

"You!" exclaimed the man. He actually took a step backwards, such was his surprise.

But he never let his eyes leave Talon, who was equally surprised. Talon looked around desperately, seeking some means of escape. He wanted to run and seize a horse and somehow flee the scene, but it was much too late for that, and besides he could not leave Max. These thoughts flashed through his mind as he stood rooted to the ground in front of Kazim's father.

"Seize this man!" roared the Emir Abbas to Malek, whose eyes were wide with surprise. "Seize him! Guards, to me now and seize this man!" he shouted again. His hand instinctively went to his sword and he half drew it.

Men came running, and within seconds Talon had his arms pinioned then forced behind him, while the Lord Abbas glared at him.

"There...there must be some mistake, my lord," Malek quavered. He was utterly shocked, but although he feared his lord and master had lost his mind, the sudden change in events forced him to say something on Talon's behalf, even if it meant danger for himself.

"My lord, this is the man who saved the lives of your wife and children! He is a good man!" Malek protested.

"He is a common criminal who escaped from my prison in Alexandria, and but for the Grace of Allah could have cut all your throats by now!" shouted Abbas. "I have been shamed by this...this prisoner."

He drew his sword and advanced upon Talon and his two guards. "Make him kneel! I would have his head. Now!"

The men forced Talon to his knees in front of Abbas, who was still trembling with rage and had his sword raised to strike. There was a deathly, shocked silence which extended to everyone who was witness to the scene taking place in the middle of the maidan. Talon's heart was beating furiously, but he was powerless in the grip of the two soldiers who had forced him down so that he could only see the dust in front of him.

A drop of sweat fell from his brow onto the dust. It seemed to fall in slow motion and he even saw the particles of dust rising as it landed. He knew he was to die but could think of nothing at all; his mind was blank. Then, just as Abbas raised his sword to strike, Kazim threw himself at his father and clutched him around his legs.

"No, Father! You must not do this! He is my friend and he did save our lives!"

"My lord, Allah be my witness. He saved your family from a dreadful fate. Would you reward him this way?" Malek begged. He was clearly frightened of his master's rage but determined to plead for Talon's life.

Abbas lowered his sword and stared around him as though dazed by his own anger. Then he said in a calmer tone.

"I have heard you, my son. I shall not execute him now." He pointed at Talon with the sword; it shook in his hand as he said in a cold voice, "Chain him and lock him up. If he tries to escape, kill him. I shall get to the bottom of this; in the name of the Prophet, I shall."

He stood aside while Talon was hustled off to have chains hammered onto his legs and wrists and then be tossed, none too gently, by the newly arrived soldiers into a feed room to await his fate.

"Don't even think of trying to get out! We will use you for spear practice," they told him as the door slammed shut. Just as a precaution, men stood guard outside the rough door. Talon fell against the sacks and drew in a huge gasp of air. He felt as though he had not taken a breath since he first saw Abbas.

Within minutes the door opened again and Max was thrust violently into the shed. He would have fallen had not Talon leapt to his feet and held him upright. Max was pale and in obvious pain from his wound. They had not been gentle with him. He groaned as Talon assisted him to sit on a sack of grain.

"What happened?" he asked, a bewildered look on his face. He held onto his shoulder, wincing in pain.

"It is as I feared Max, I did know the man. The Lord of this place is the very man who bound us in prison in Alexandria. He recognized me," Talon said. "He nearly executed me on the spot. But for Kazim and Malek, I would be dead now. As it is, I do not know for how long we are to live."

"Dear God." Max had paled even more. "Now we are in for it. We should have left days ago."

"In your condition, Max? I think not. You are barely recovered; any journey would have opened your wound, and then what?" Talon said in a resigned tone.

Talon sat on a sack of grain and rubbed his bruised arms. The chains clinked ominously on both of them, reminding them of their desperate plight, and he wondered why fate should have dealt him this blow. He thought of the opportunities he had had to leave, but had not. Max had not been fit to travel. Also he could not deny that he had been seduced by the comfort and calm of the place; he had been lulled into a false sense of security, and now they would either be executed here, or sent back to the prison to die.

They made the best of the sacks of grain and arranged them in comfortable enough nests, where they waited during the next two days and nights they were locked in the hut. They were given only a small amount of water and some flat bread for sustenance.

On the third day, Talon listened to the morning beginning in its usual rituals: the estate awaking at dawn, the cockerel calling, quickly countered by the call of the peacock from his stand on the tiled roof. From the distant mezzanine the call to prayers was floating on the still cool air, closely followed by the call to prayers by one of the older servants within the compound.

He heard the familiar sounds of the bustling household and the stables where the horses were stamping, impatient for their food. He listened with half an ear to the conversation of the guards and the occasional laugh, but other than having some food brought to them, he and Max remained under lock and key.

They were sweating in the heat of the storage room beneath the late morning sun, unsure what the day might bring, when they heard footsteps approaching the door. There were low voices and the latch was lifted. The Nubian bent his head into the entrance and beckoned Talon to come outside into the sunlight. When Max tried to follow, the man shook his head and motioned Talon impatiently to come with him.

"God save you, Talon," Max whispered. He crossed himself.

Talon did as he was told. He had to squint in the harsh sunlight. The Nubian took his arm and held him in an unbreakable grip while two men at arms accompanied them across the maidan.

They were followed by the curious looks of the servants around the compound.

"Do not try to escape, Kharagi, or I shall break your neck," muttered the Nubian as they reached the steps of the house.

Talon clinked his way up the steps, then Panhsj pushed Talon into a large room where the Lord Abbas was seated on cushions upon a raised platform, with his son Kazim on his right and his wife and daughter on his left. The women were veiled and seated almost behind Abbas. Talon noted with some surprise that Khaldun was also there seated to the right of Kazim. There were guards just inside the door, and more on either side of Abbas. Malek and his brother Bilal were off to the side by the windows, looking awkward and nervous. Everyone seemed either grim or very worried.

Talon was shoved roughly to his knees and held there in the silence that greeted their arrival.

"I recognize you very easily now... as this was the position you were in when I saw you last in Alexandria," Abbas grated.

"My lord…" Talon began.

"Silence! You have come into my house under false pretenses and it is lucky for everyone I arrived when I did, as Allah alone knows what mischief you would have accomplished if I had not," Abbas blared.

"You have caused me enormous trouble, shame, and even risk to my life; and yet I am told by my trusted servant Malek and his brother Bilal that you saved not only their lives, but those of my wife and children during a deadly attack a couple of months ago. If my wife had not confirmed their story in every detail, you would not be alive this minute. But you have lied to them all this time about who you are. You have deceived them. Now, what have you got to say to me?" He sat up and glared at Talon.

Talon, still kneeling, looked Abbas straight in the eye.

"My lord, you are right, I am the prisoner whom you arrested in Alexandria, and yes, I did lie to your honored wife and everyone here. But we were saving our lives from wrong done to us. I am the son of a merchant, and I was robbed. At the time of my arrest, I and my two companions were rightfully trying to defend what was ours. The men who deceived us have either died or have left the shores of Egypt with my money. In this doing, I have lost one good companion and friend, while my other companion was wounded grievously when we helped your men protect my Lady and the children. I have lost much and gained nothing in this land that is your home."

There was silence so he hurried on. "The story I told your family and servants was to protect myself and in no way meant to harm. My pleas for a hearing were not heard in Alexandria, so why should I think that I would be believed here? But ask yourself, my lord, why would I try to save your people when my companion and I could have left them to their fate and ignored their predicament? Having saved them, why would I then try to do ill to them? Especially after they helped me to get better from the swamp fever, looked after my companion, and I believe saved his life. Why would I want to harm people who have done this for us, my lord?"

"I suspect that you were responsible for the break out from the prison. I could have lost my head because of that," snapped Abbas, almost as though he had not heard a word Talon had said. But he did not sound so angry now.

Talon chose not to confirm or deny the suggestion. There was a long pause, finally broken by Abbas who continued, "You are a lucky man, Suleiman...if that is your real name. My wife, son and daughter and my venerated friend Khaldun here, even Malek and his brother, have begged for your worthless lives. Tell me, why should I not send you back to the prison again to die there?"

Talon again looked the man in the eye. He had nothing to lose now but his life, and it mattered little whether he did.

"Because I might escape again, my lord?" he ventured.

He heard a gasp of surprise from everyone in the room, but he had been watching Abbas carefully. His eyes gleamed with surprise and amusement. A smile twitched at his lips and he had to move his hand over his mouth to prevent it being seen.

He also noticed that Lady Khalidah had bent over and was struggling with her veil, as was Jasmine. Kazim was openly grinning. Khaldun began to cough into his beard, while Malek seemed to be having a heart attack off to the side as he leaned against his brother, whose face had swollen and gone dark as he too tried to control himself.

Abbas took a deep slow breath, composed himself, and then spoke, almost timing his words.

"When I saw you, two days ago, the first thing I wanted to do, before Allah, was to have you executed then and there. But you have ingratiated yourself with my family, and my servants speak very highly of you as a good warrior and indeed, a learned man of letters." He paused.

"While I shall ascertain for myself that this is all true, because I still suspect that you have bewitched them, I shall not send you back to prison, Suleiman, but I shall not let you go either. You are my prisoner and shall remain so at my pleasure.

"You will continue your duties of teacher with my son, who for his own peculiar reasons seems to think highly of you. My wife has told me that no one else has been able to teach him both to read *and* to ride a horse. That is something of an accomplishment...if it is true.

"Your companion will work for Malek on the estate, doing such duties as Malek deems fit.

"If either of you tries to escape, I shall catch you and turn you over to my trusted servant standing next to you, Panhsj, who will kill you, very slowly, while I watch. Do I make myself clear, Suleiman?" Abbas asked, silkily stroking his beard and watching Talon from hooded eyes.

Talon craned his neck to look up at the glowering Panhsj. Then he looked back at Abbas and said respectfully, "My lord, until the time comes when you give me my freedom and I can one day go home, then I am your servant. This I swear before Allah," he said sincerely.

Abbas nodded slowly then said, "Panhsj will take you to have the chains removed, and then you shall live in the servant's quarters. You will resume your duties tomorrow and I shall observe how well you perform them. Malek, see to it."

Talon managed to send a grateful look towards the veiled ladies and Kazim before he was hustled out of the room by a none too gentle Panhsj. He was marched back to the blacksmith, who struck the chains off. As Talon was rubbing his wrists and waiting for the leg chains to be removed, Panhsj growled, "My master is not to be taken lightly, Suleiman. I am not to be taken lightly, either. Slave I might be, as you are now, but I shall still do as he says if the time comes when you break your word."

Talon turned and looked up at the big man. It was the first time he had been able to observe up close the features of the black man who stood in front of him. He was a good two inches taller, and although his scowl distorted his strong, even features, Talon took note of the tattoos and other marks decorating the cheeks and forehead. There was no friendliness, either in the words delivered or the dark hostile eyes that stared back at him.

He said evenly, "I gave my word back there, Panhsj, and that is not something I do lightly either."

The last link had been struck and Talon turned and walked off without looking back. He might or might not have an enemy there, he decided, but at this moment he was grateful to have his life.

Max came to his cell later, and the two talked for a long time in low tones.

"It could have gone badly there, Talon. I heard, at least I think I heard, that you were insolent and the master decided not to kill us? How is this?"

"It is true, Max, I was insolent, but he saw the truth of what I said. I told him that if he took me back to the prison I would escape again. He found that amusing, I think. In any case, our situation is that neither of us can escape. If we should try, he will have that black slave, Panhsj, kill us very slowly. Besides, I gave my word, so we are in God's hands for now."

"I for one do not know where to go or how to escape from here, and I know that you would not abandon me to these heathens in any case. I suppose we must try to live with the hope that with God's help we can escape one day, young master," Max said in an effort to comfort both of them.

"Max, I will make you this promise. I shall come for you when it is time, and if we do indeed escape back to the kingdom of Jerusalem, I shall stand witness to the Knights for your induction. You, more than anyone I know, should be a Knight Templar."

Max looked at him in surprise. "Master Talon, I am deeply honored," he said with tears in his eyes. "But that can wait. We have to do some living here, in this place. It could be much worse... we could be in irons and in prison again, or dead. I think Lord Abbas has shown great mercy."

# Chapter 10

# Slaves

Life resumed its course, but there were differences. Malek and Bilal now avoided Talon, and he ate alone with Max. Each morning, once he had seen to the horses, he met Kazim and Jasmine in front of the house and they gathered in the garden, trailed by the nurses, where they would wrestle with the calligraphy and reading, or the numbers, as they sat on carpets and cushions that had been laid for them in the shade under the fig tree.

Initially, Kazim had been very curious about Talon's adventures while at the prison, but when Talon discouraged the questions he soon settled back into their earlier relationship and concentrated upon his lessons.

Jasmine behaved haughtily towards Talon for a while, but he chose to ignore her when she was behaving in this manner and she found that the lessons were not as much fun, so she soon dropped the attitude. Before long the three of them were comfortably back in their little world of calligraphy, numbers and discussions. He continued enthralling them with tales of faraway places, much to their delight.

On this day, Jasmine wanted to hear her favorite story. "Suleiman, tell us the story of Isolde again. It is so sad and romantic," she sighed, with teenage dreams drifting behind her dark, heavily lashed eyes.

Kazim snorted contemptuously and rolled his eyes; his sister glared back at him.

"If there is time, Annessa," Talon replied, using the polite form of Miss, which he always did with her. "I want to demonstrate to your father that you are both good students, so that he will continue to employ me as your teacher. Will you help me do that?"

"What do we have to do, Suleiman?" Jasmine asked. "I like to have you teach us, and you keep my brother from being a pest," she said with a sweet smile at Kazim.

Kazim glowered and responded, "Suleiman, I will be good, I promise, but you wait, my sister, ...till later," he said ominously. Then he implored Talon with a whine, "Please do not make the numbers too difficult today!"

Jasmine snorted contemptuously. "I don't care how difficult they are, I can do my numbers." This she said with much confidence. "You shall see."

"We shall do the calligraphy and perhaps some numbers," Talon responded, with a suppressed grin. "I will not make them too hard, Kazim."

They were thus engrossed when Lord Abbas walked along the pathway that led to the small, shaded alcove where they sat. They were using a smooth board of juniper wood to support the paper. Kazim was laboriously working his quill over some complicated calligraphy forms that he was beginning to master. His ink-stained fingers clutched the quill tightly and his tongue was out at a corner of his mouth, he was concentrating so hard. Talon had promised him a small bow that he could shoot from a horse as a reward if he could master these letters.

Upon Abbas' approach, Talon bowed very low. Kazim looked up and said, "Father, have you seen what I can do?" He badly wanted to show off his skill.

Abbas stopped and looked on for a moment and said, "I am delighted with your work, Kazim. You have made good progress, and I am pleased." He turned to Talon.

"It would seem that the greatest champions for your life, my wife and Khaldun, are right. You are a good teacher. My son is making progress. And Jasmine, my daughter, are you doing well?"

"Oh yes, Father, I enjoy the numbers, and the calligraphy, very much," his daughter said dutifully. She proudly showed her work to him, which he observed with surprised approval.

"I am pleased with you both."

Abbas then spoke to Talon. "You will continue to work with the children as their teacher. When you are finished today I want you to come to the stables, and we will see what else you can do."

He turned and strode off, after patting Kazim on the head and nodding with a smile at his daughter. Talon bowed low again to his departing back. At least one test had been passed, he thought to himself as he exhaled.

The lesson of the day finished, Talon walked to the stables, where he found Panhsj and some soldiers idling outside, leaning against the walls and doors. He looked about him, seeking Lord Abbas, but he wasn't there, so he squatted in the shade of a wide sycamore. It was a hot day, and he was uncertain as to what Abbas had in mind for him. He kept a wary eye on the soldiers who had come back with Abbas from the wars, and he realized that he was the subject of their discussion.

Panhsj was grinning and looking his way, but it was not a friendly look. He said something and two of the men got up and came towards Talon, hitching their sword belts up. They had not drawn their swords, but neither did they look as though they were coming towards him with any good intent.

Panhsj sauntered along with them, and the men stood looking at Talon from a distance of twenty feet. He had risen warily to his feet as they approached, wondering what was going on.

"I hear you are good with a sword and shield, Suleiman. Are you a real warrior, though?"

"Real enough when it matters," replied Talon, coolly.

"Why don't you show us how good you think you are?" Panhsj asked. He beckoned to the soldiers and told them to bring swords and shields.

When the arms came, he tossed a sword at Talon, who caught it by the hilt in midair and then snatched one of the small shields that they also tossed his way. Panhsj muttered something to the two men. They were already armed, and without any warning they ran at Talon, who had just the barest time to position the shield and back away from the attack.

He parried a heavy downward blow and took another on his shield with a loud clang that jarred his arm, and then he settled into a watchful crouch. His heart was beating fast, adrenalin surging through his veins. He breathed deeply to counter the effect and watched the two men warily. Panhsj was trying to hurt him, and he wondered why.

This didn't feel right. However, he had no time to ponder the situation. The two men, their turbaned heads tucked behind their shields and their swords raised, came at him from two different angles.

Talon decided that he had to disable one of them to be able to manage the other. They were experienced men of war who knew combat, but were they fast enough? He feinted at the one then rushed in, catching the man for an instant off guard, and slammed his shield against him, pushing him back a pace while dodging the wild swing of the sword. The man had not expected this and took another pace back. Spinning on one foot Talon was able to strike at an unexpected angle at the other man, whose side was exposed. Talon sliced his sword into the man's flesh, inflicting a nasty wound that, although long, was not deep. It hurt, nevertheless, and the man yelled and stumbled. Talon drove the hilt of his sword savagely into the man's exposed jaw and felled him.

The man lay still in the dust on his face. There was a shout of surprise from the onlookers as they saw one of their own humiliated so quickly. A crowd rapidly formed and there were shouts of encouragement, but not just for the other man. Talon had become liked during his stay, and much to the annoyance of the soldiers, many of the syce and other garden workers now cheered for him.

Whirling about on the ball of his foot again, Talon parried a blow aimed at his head. The blades rasped and sparks flew; then he danced out of the way of another vicious slash at his exposed shoulder. Had the blade connected it would have inflicted a very serious wound. Talon now knew the way things were going, so he decided that he was going to fight this man on his own terms.

Having seen his comrade go down so fast, the other man was now more wary of Talon and avoided rushing in. Instead he played his blade in all manner of angles, slashing and whipping the blade back and forth, giving Talon few openings.

Talon knew the man could hold him at bay for a long time, wear him down, and eventually take the offensive to him. He probably knew a thing or two about extended bouts, but Talon was not in the mood to wait it out. Then, to his surprise, the man took the offensive and managed to flick his blade just past the shield and cut Talon on the shoulder. He felt the sting and heard the cries of the watching crowd, but his own vicious return stopped the man from counting his victory too early.

Talon could now see respect on the face of his opponent. He also noticed that the man would advance with his left leg well forward and then use it to spring his weight forward, just before he struck. He parried several attacks to see how the man behaved and each time that leg came forward, exposing the knee for an instant before the rest of the body followed.

Keeping a wary eye open for an attack from some other quarter, Talon was ready for the next rush. He dropped to one knee, kept his shield high, then reached forward to cut into the side of the man's lower thigh as he came forward. The agony of the cut made the man stumble with a yell of pain right into Talon's shield that battered his own away, and then the haft of Talon's sword felled him too.

Thanking his dead uncle Phillip for teaching him the use of more than the blade of a sword, Talon placed his sword point on the neck of the prone man, ready to push it in.

He was interrupted by a commanding shout. It came from Abbas, who strode forward, pushing aside the onlookers, with an alarmed expression on his face.

"Stop! I order you, Suleiman, to stop, and you..." he pointed at the cluster of men standing watching, "get these sorry louts out of the way and make sure their wounds are dressed. It is clear they cannot look after themselves."

Men ran to pick up the two downed warriors from the dust. Both were dazed and bloody and had to be half carried.

Talon was still standing in the middle of the crowd of onlookers, his bloody sword in his hand, breathing deeply, when Panhsj walked up and carefully took it from him. Talon then dropped the shield on the ground with a low clang and waited. He was angry, but knew he could not do nor say anything at this moment, so he held his tongue. Abbas, in the meantime, was standing with his arms crossed, regarding him with narrowed eyes.

"Those are two of my very own bodyguards you have wounded, Suleiman. But it was a good fight and you did much better than I expected. Indeed, Panhsj, I think we have a warrior in our midst, do you not think so?"

"My lord, he did well," Panhsj said shortly, but his eyes gleamed and Talon saw how he was containing his rage.

Abbas nodded, then said, "There is nothing like the threat of real danger to find out what a man is made of, Suleiman. You have done well... now mount up, we are going riding. I want to look over my estates with you and Malek. Panhsj will be coming too."

* * * * *

Their mounts were made ready and they rode out into the country heading west towards the distant lake. Talon kept quiet, while Malek and Abbas looked over the cultivated fields and discussed the drainage and irrigation problems. He drew some comfort from the feel of his horse between his legs, and although his shoulder cut stung, he pushed the recent punishing fight into the back of his mind while he enjoyed seeing the open countryside. Panhsj rode nearby; he did not speak. Talon was left to his own thoughts.

He wondered at the implications of his enforced servitude. It could have been much worse—he was thankful that it wasn't—but his and Max's positions were now definitely that of slaves, not guests. The plan of getting to Palestine was now an indefinite thing until he could escape or was released, and Panhsj would not hesitate to kill him if he thought for a moment Talon was trying to escape. He decided that he had to make the best of it and leave the rest up to God.

Over the weeks, and then months, that went by with a slow rhythm, he accompanied Abbas often as he rode over the vast estates. His role was more as an armed escort, because he was allowed to bring his bow and sword with him. A small shield hung off the left side of the saddle, while the bow resided in a sheath he had had fashioned, under the flap of the left leg of the saddle. He found that he was being treated with respect by the other soldiers who had sseen how he dealt with the two of their number. These two did not seem to hold any resentment for their wounding and even joked with him on occasion while they were working the horses.

He decided to practice one thing, however, and that was to hone his skill at stealth. It was not long before the guards and others were finding him standing next to them, not having heard a sound. They began to talk about his way of moving about in the dark with nervous shrugs. He was very careful not to be seen nor heard when he did not want to be. To him it was a game with deadly intent, as one day he knew he would need it again.

But he had not reckoned with Panhsj, who, it seemed, still had reservations about him. One day when they were riding together some distance behind Abbas and Malek, who were discussing the crops, Panhsj edged his horse a little closer to Talons and spoke.

"My men, and even Malek and his brother, say that you talk softly, Suleiman, and walk even more softly. We have each seen that you can fight like a demon. There is more to you than meets the eye."

"I do not intend to harm anyone in the care of our master!" Talon retorted sharply, staring Panhsj in the eye.

"It might be, Kharagi. But there is more, and I wonder just who you might really be. Remember, I am watching," Panhsj warned as he pulled his horse away.

It had not taken very long for Talon to find that he was accepted again. Malek and his brother Bilal came and ate with him and Max. Khaldun would join them again, and they continued the long conversations Talon had so enjoyed at the beginning of their relationship.

A renewed friendship grew between Talon, Malek, and Bilal, and it included Max now, who was doing quite well with Arabic. Even Panhsj came and joined them on more than one occasion, and Talon was able to learn more about the taciturn black man from the south who grudgingly accepted him in their midst.

Malek told Talon that Panhsj had been captured during one of the periodic wars that sprang up between the Egyptians and Nubians while he was merely a youth. He had been wounded and near death when Abbas and his horsemen came upon him. He had tried to fight them nonetheless. Impressed by his courage, Abbas had held his men off killing him and granted Panhsj his life, but as his slave. It had been a good bargain for both of them, as there was now much mutual respect; Abbas knew that this man would give his life for him.

Malek and Bilal told Talon about a conversation the master had had with them, Panhsj, and the lady of the house.

"Our master is seething with anger and yearning for revenge for the attack, Suleiman," Bilal told him.

"But he is a wise man and will not rush in where fools will fall on their swords," Malek added, with a glance at his brother.

Talon shifted his position and prepared to listen. They were taking him into their confidence, and he appreciated the renewed trust.

"The master is very grateful to you for what you did, Suleiman, do not think otherwise," Bilal said, as he touched Talon on the arm.

"He does not stand in the sultan's favor for nothing, but he has to be very careful. He is trying to work out how best to plan a reprisal. But he is worried, I can tell. He told us that even here in the middle of his own lands he now cannot be sure that his family is safe, especially if he has to leave."

"Who is this enemy who wishes him such harm?" Talon enquired.

"His name is Bahir Ibn Hakeem; remember I spoke of him when we went riding out on the Fayoum that first day, you and I. He is a dangerous man who is as powerful in Cairo as our master, which is why our master chooses to move carefully," Malek informed him.

"That is also why you see more guards on the walls and gates, day and night," Bilal remarked with a belch. "Hmmm, that sweet cake is one of the best," he murmured to himself as he reached for another.

Talon nodded agreement. "I have noticed the guards, but I have to tell you, my friends, that the walls are as full of holes as a fisherman's net."

"How so?" Malek demanded, looking irritated.

Talon did not want to give away his ability to move stealthily but he said nonetheless, "I am not an expert in the art of defense, but you have to admit that it would not take much for a determined force to swarm over these walls, should they really wish to do us harm."

Both men and Khaldun stared at him in a long silence. Finally, Khaldun nodded his head so emphatically that his loose turban threatened to fall off.

"I think he is right. These walls are made of mud and are not high; they need repairs. Should our men be slow one night, and the enemy were to attack, we would be in trouble," he cackled knowingly. He peered at Talon through the wrinkles of his old eyes. "You see much, Suleiman," he stated enigmatically.

"We need to discuss this with our master," Bilal said with another glance at Talon.

The result of this discussion brought much activity around the walls; they were strengthened by workers brought in for that purpose.

Abbas, while he did not want to acknowledge openly from where or whom he had taken advice, still displayed a certain curiosity about Talon. One day he asked Talon to demonstrate his skills with the bow that Malek had purchased for him some months before. Talon explained that he had learned from the Seljuk Turks how to shoot arrows from horseback and asked for straw dummies to be set up at the end of the polo field.

He was confident that he could shoot a man-sized target from about sixty paces while cantering on horseback. Rakhsh was by now well used to the leg aids from Talon, so it was an easy matter to put four arrows into two widely spaced targets, and so quickly that there were murmurs of amazement from the watching syce and warriors.

His demonstration over, he rode towards Abbas. He could see the man was looking very thoughtful. Abbas called Panhsj over and the two spoke in low tones for a minute or two, often glancing Talon's way. Then Abbas signaled him to come over. Talon dismounted and went on one knee in front of the master, who gruffly told him to stand.

"I am very impressed with what you have done, Suleiman. You have shown me a new weapon for my cavalry. I want you to train some of my best riders to do as you have done."

Talon looked at Abbas and then at Panhsj, whose stern visage gave nothing away. Things were changing fast.

Talon was given a group of horsemen from Abbas's personal guards, and now he spent most of the afternoons working with them on the polo field. They were good horsemen and it did not take long before he had them maneuvering as a unit. Their bows were lighter than his, but they were highly competitive amongst themselves. They soon managed to gallop past a row of well-spaced straw figures and place an arrow in each from a distance of about forty paces, and this after only a couple of weeks of hard training. Abbas pronounced that he was pleased with the effort after watching a demonstration.

To rejoice in the bonding that the teamwork had brought upon them, that evening Abbas himself joined the polo game and evidently highly enjoyed it; he scored a couple of goals against Bilal's team, of which Talon was a member, and this put him in a good mood.

# Chapter 11

# Al Qahirah
## (Cairo)

The message arrived late one evening, almost three months after Abbas had returned to the Fayoum. He sent for Malek almost immediately. Malek walked into the main room of the house and bowed low, then he waited in respectful silence while Abbas continued to read the missive.

Finally Abbas looked up and said, "I am being recalled to Al Qahirah by the Sultan. You should know that the father of our Sultan, Najm Ad-Dīn Ayyūb, has died. He had a fall some months ago and never fully recovered." Abbas gave a wry smile and continued, "The Sultan also says that I have spent enough time with my family, that he needs me back with him, as there is the possibility of another campaign taking place soon.

"I will leave in the morning with half my men; but you, Malek, will stay and manage my lands. Your brother Bilal will bring my wife and children along with him within two days. I do not feel that I can leave them here while I am gone. It is too isolated, and the risk of my enemy striking at them again is too high. They shall come to Al Qahirah and live in my house there, until I know what is to happen. Make preparations for their departure as soon as possible."

Malek bowed low. "My lord, what of Suleiman and the *kharagi*, Max? Do they stay here, or go with you or the family?"

Abbas lifted his head. "Suleiman goes with Bilal. They will accompany my wife. He is to continue to instruct the children. The other man will stay here and work for you; be sure that he is put to good use."

"Yes, my lord. May Allah give you safe passage. Are you riding all the way there?"

"Yes. That is the best, as I would need too many boats for all my men. However, Bilal should take a boat. Make sure Bilal does not find himself in trouble again."

Malek kept his face wooden, but it was clear he was hurt. If Abbas noticed this, he gave no sign. Malek knew that the family was too important for him to be concerned about his own feelings on the subject.

But then Abbas seemed to relent. "I put my trust in Bilal, Malek, and don't forget that Suleiman seems to be a capable soldier too. Also my trust is in you to maintain and protect my property while we are gone."

Malek bowed deeply and said, "My lord, I shall be worthy of that trust, *Insha'Allah*."

Talon was informed along with the rest of the estate personnel by Malek, who took him aside afterwards and told him, "Suleiman, you and my brother are entrusted with the care of the master's family, and that is not a light thing he has done. Your companion, Max, is to stay here and work for me. Do not be concerned for him. Although he is an infidel, a *kharagi*, he will be safe here, and I will use him to help me run the estate.

"You will be taking a boat when you get to the great river, and it is at this point that I fear trouble might occur. Be alert for anything along the way."

Talon nodded. "It will be as you command, Malek. I shall watch Bilal's back for him, as well as the children and my Lady. Thank you for your words regarding my companion. I am grateful."

He hurried off to find Max and discuss the situation.

"So you must leave us?" Max asked him. They were in his bare little room and he was sitting on his pallet with his shirt off, rubbing his shoulder where there was still a livid scar. He turned his arm about as though easing the stiffness from the healing wound. Max did not sound at all happy at the prospect.

"Abbas is clever. He has separated us, knowing that I will not flee without you. He still does not trust me, despite me giving my word," Talon said. He was somewhat aggrieved.

"You cannot blame him, Talon. Would you not seek to escape if I were not here, despite your given word? He knows not whom to trust. He has many enemies and does not want his own people churning up the water as well," Max said.

"Perhaps you are right," Talon conceded reluctantly, and then he looked around at the room, avoiding Max's eyes. "Well, Max, my old friend, at least you will be safe here and have time to heal. Malek is a good man. He will give you work to do and perhaps you can become friends while helping him."

"I shall be glad of it, Talon. I too sense he is a good man. But when do you think you will be able to come back?" Max asked, concern in his voice. Talon looked frankly at his friend: Max's face had lost its former gauntness, his light hair and beard were now well trimmed, his ribs were no longer stark; he seemed to be putting on weight. Soon he would be fit to do heavier work and that would help time pass. Max, being unable to read, was bored.

"I cannot tell, Max. It could be a few months, it could be longer; God willing, not too long. What you must do is to get well and fit and stay on the good side of Malek until I can return. Do not get too fat lying about in this little corner of heaven." He joked to hide his sense of loss. "When I come back it will be to take you with me and to go to our original destination." He said this last very quietly as he did not know if they might be overheard, but they were talking French in any case. They continued to talk till it was late, neither happy at the prospect of being separated.

"You have grown in many ways since I first met you, Talon. You are as good a warrior as any I have seen, and as reliable a man as any I have met. The Templars could do with you when the time comes, so take good care of yourself. Protect the children and my Lady Khalidah as you intend, but come back for me before too long so that we can go on to Jerusalem. Go with God," Max said with feeling.

They embraced hard and Talon went off to his bed.

The preparations for departure went on late into the night as the warriors looked to their baggage, horses and arms, and the servants set about frantically packing for their lord. Finally it quieted, as people took to their beds to get what sleep was left before dawn.

Before he went to his own rest, Talon walked quietly onto the platform set into the wall over the gates and looked out of the compound. He nodded to the sentry nearby, who had barely heard him coming. Other than the usual greeting of *"Salaam Aliekom,"* they did not talk. Talon was too immersed in his own thoughts to want company, and the sentry, sensing this, gave him space.

It seemed quiet out there. He hoped that it would stay that way. Whoever wanted to strike at Abbas had an opportunity within the next few days to do so. He went to bed excited by the prospect of being on the move towards Al Qahirah, but at the same time depressed that he would be leaving Max for an unknown period of time. For the first time in weeks, his thoughts dared to move even further east than the Kingdom of Jerusalem.

For the thousandth time, he thought of Rav'an and Reza and wondered if they were still alive. He wished the emptiness that was ever with him would recede, but as long as he did not know their fates he could never know real peace. His cousin Aicelina, with a woman's intuition, had known so very well how Talon felt. He sent a small prayer across the sea separating them to his family and hoped that the Church had drawn in its teeth.

It was a short night.

The servants were up well before dawn and the compound was bustling with last minute preparations for the departure of the master and his troops. Talon was working with the horses when Panhsj walked up to him.

"I come to say safe journey, Suleiman, for when you depart in two days, but also to warn you against any attempt to escape. I shall find you should this happen," he said with quiet menace.

Talon turned from brushing the neck of his horse and looked Panhsj in the eye for a long moment, then said, "You seem to forget too easily, Panhsj. I gave my word, and I fully intend to keep it. Besides, the master's family is important to me and I shall protect them...with my life if need be. Now...do you not have to leave?" he asked pointedly.

Panhsj stood still, his dark eyes boring into Talon's. "I think I believe you. We shall meet again in Al Qahirah. Go with God." He turned abruptly and left.

Abbas and his men left before sun had risen above the eastern hills, leaving a void in the life of the compound. The greatly reduced household settled down to make preparations for the departure of their lord's family. Although they were taking a boat, the lesson learned from the last ambush was still fresh in Bilal's mind and he made a point to brief his men on how they would escort the family to the Nile. They listened attentively and then went off to get ready.

Bilal and Malek ate the evening meal with Talon and with Khaldun, along with Max, who had been invited to join them. This was a subdued meal, with little said. They all knew that it would be some time before they would meet again. The quiet, even contented routine of their days on the estate was at an end and another phase about to begin.

"I shall miss you, Suleiman," Khaldun said after a while, munching on some chick pea patties and green onions. His beard went up and down when he chewed, which seemed somewhat comical, but his deep-set faded eyes were sad when he looked at Talon.

"I do not know what fate has in store for you, my young warrior, but I hope that Allah is kind and keeps you safe."

"I shall miss you too, Hajji," Talon said with feeling. "I have learned much since I met you. May Allah protect you and give you many more years so that I might come and visit you from time to time. Please find some time to help Max with his Arabic, as he told me he wants to be useful to Malek while we are gone. Malek is getting old and needs support," he added, with a glint in his eyes.

This drew an indignant snort from Malek. He wagged his finger at Talon, who was grinning cheekily. Bilal clapped his brother on the shoulder and said laughing, "We will be back before long, my brother, to help you with the work load, never fear!"

"I am worried," Malek said, staring upwards thoughtfully. "I wonder if two novices like you two can really take care of the family of our master. Perhaps I should come with you to explain how it is done?"

"Please do not joke about that responsibility, brother. Suleiman and I will do the job well, *Insha' Allah*," Bilal said more soberly, although he was smiling at his brother's gentle jibe.

Malek put a hand on his brother's shoulder. "I am sure of it," he said, "but we will miss your jokes and your belches, but not...

your farts at our evening meals," he said, his eyes twinkling with amusement.

They all laughed; they were friends who were about to part and wanted to remember this moment with amusement.

"I would like you to come back, young Suleiman, and yes, I shall help Max with his learning," said the old man after he had stopped holding his sides and had regained his composure. He smiled his almost toothless smile at Max, who understood and smiled back.

Talon had a visitor that night. Malek walked in carrying a pair of saddle bags that looked heavy and dropped them on his pallet bed. They chinked as they fell.

"I do not know where you got this coin, Suleiman, but it is not mine and it came with you. It was on your horse and on your companion's. I have kept it safe because I think you should have it. So I give it back to you now."

Talon stared at him in astonishment. Malek could so easily have kept it for himself. Talon had just assumed that he had.

Then he recovered his surprise, and in one stride he walked forward and embraced Malek. "Any mortal man would have kept it and said nothing, Malek."

"Indeed, my young friend, but Bilal and I discussed this and decided that your need might be greater than ours. One day you will want to travel back to your homeland, whereas we are at home. I am content here on my beloved master's land, and Bilal my restless brother is equally content to serve our master wherever he goes. We have no need for it."

Talon did not believe him. "May Allah heap blessings upon you, Malek, for you are a very good and special man!" he said, almost overcome with emotion.

"I hope that Allah allows us to meet again, Suleiman," Malek said as he left. "Peace be with you."

Talon had one last visitor that night, but she did not stay long. Lamya, one of the women who waited upon Lady Khalidah, slipped into the room and kissed him without warning. She pulled back from him after the kiss, her huge black eyes smoldering.

"Will you see more of me in Al Qahirah, Suleiman?"

Talon grinned with surprise. She was a pretty young girl who clearly wanted to be with him, but they risked much should they get caught. "You must be very careful, Lamya. If they catch us together..."

"We will find a way. Will you see me?" she whispered fiercely.

He nodded, and she disappeared as quickly as she had come.

Talon sat down to ponder this new event. It did not make life any easier.

*****

The entire household was already up making the final preparations when the roosters crowed. The convoy left in the cool of the early morning just as the sun rose in all its reddened glory in the east. Once again the Lady Khalidah and Jasmine were to travel in a palanquin. Talon wished that they might have traveled in a wagon, but such things were not, it seemed, in great supply in this land of Egypt. So some of the burly eunuchs who were part of her retinue shouldered the palanquin and carried her. It was not long before these strong men were sweating in the morning sun.

The scouts ranged well ahead and behind, alert for any sign of trouble, while the main body stayed close to the palanquin as it moved slowly along the dusty road.

They arrived at the banks of the great river without incident and within three hours of leaving the Estate. Talon was relieved to see the large boat which was to be their transport to Al Qahirah moored alongside the solid wooden platform that jutted out into the waters of the river.

Talon was awed by the sheer size of the river and stared across its smoothly flowing waters with great interest. But his admiration of the mighty river was cut short; he had to help Bilal organize the loading of the horses and baggage aboard their ship.

The Lady Khalidah settled into the cushions arranged under the awning at the back of the boat where a little breeze from the river could be enjoyed. Her children stayed with her in the shade. Talon marveled at how cool she looked despite the blazing sun overhead. He was sweating in his undercoat and in the chain armor he now possessed; his helmet pressed into his forehead, threatening a headache.

The crew cast off and they set sail down river towards Al Qahirah. They passed slower, heavily laden dhows which glided downriver towards the same destination. The boats carried cargoes of palm fronds piled high, dates, flax bales, salt, and sometimes what seemed to be roughhewn marble blocks that weighed the hulls down to the point where their decks were almost level with the water. Others passed them going upriver, tacking in the wind and making much slower progress, fighting the current. The passengers and crews of these boats stared curiously at the rich trappings of the fast moving boat slipping past with its important looking passengers. Talon continued to watch carefully when these boats came too close, and Bilal would shout to them to stand clear.

"Tell me of this city we are going to, Bilal."

"It is a big city, Suleiman. There are some magnificent mosques, some have been there a long time; but our Sultan, Allah protect him, is building more...and palaces also ... and the great citadel is his too. The city was partially destroyed during the battle for control when the Sultan had to fight the Nubians, who were in rebellion."

"I thought the Nubians lived to the south of here, Bilal."

Bilal nodded and continued. "Their kingdom is there, but there are many Nubian slaves who live as soldiers — we call them Mamelukes — along with other races here. They were here in the Fatimid kingdom before the sultan's uncle won it. These men would not have wanted to go back home to the primitive conditions of their own land after tasting the power and riches of this country."

"So why did they rebel, why didn't they just become subjects to the sultan?"

"Because their former masters were in revolt; they liked it as it was before, corrupt and rotten to the core. You must remember that when Nur Ed Din, the Sultan of Syria, sent Salah Ed Din's uncle Asad al Din Shirkuh here, it was not in friendship, but to conquer and to change the people from being Shia heretics, and bring them back to the true faith, Sunni.

"Were you all then Shia once?" asked Talon, although he thought he knew.

"Many of us were, but for the most part it was the ruling families; the rest of us were Sunni or Christian or Jewish. Most have seen the light since; besides, it is better to be with the winning side in any case," Bilal said with a grin, his dark eyes flashing with amusement at Talon's surprised expression. "But there were many more Christians and Jewish people here before the Ayyubi family came and deposed the Fatimids."

He sobered. "But there is still some distrust of the 'Old' families, such as our master's, which his enemies try to exploit at his cost; but his loyalty is above reproach. He has proved his loyalty to the Sultan over and over again." He stared into the water of the Nile and continued.

"The men in power underestimated the young Sultan then, which led to a great battle in the streets of Al Qahirah that nearly destroyed a whole section of the city because the Nubians destroyed it with fire, to deny it to the Sultan's men. Even now that does not make any sense, but they did."

"Is he now completely accepted by all?" Talon asked.

"On the surface of it, Suleiman, he seemingly is, yes. But there are always elements who would like him to fail. The empire of the Fatima was here for almost three hundred years; many generations of the great families do not find it easy to just accept a man from elsewhere as their leader. They consider him an upstart. He might not be one of the hated Turks, but he is a Kurd; hence, not one of them. They had it much as they wanted before, because the previous sultans were weak and their viziers were corrupt. It is not easy to change everything within a short space of time. I think they underestimate him," Bilal said confidently.

The heat of the day made it difficult to see the detail of both banks, but Talon could make out the tall papyrus reeds lining the banks with the occasional mud beach where there lay some long dark shapes.

"Bilal, what are those things that lie on the sand over there?" he pointed.

"Those are known as crocodiles," Bilal told him. Talon had to have that explained to him, never having seen one before.

"They are the dragons of the water, Suleiman. They are fearsome creatures that can gobble up a child whole, but long ago my people worshipped them. We are still in awe and fear of them. It would not do to fall into the water anywhere near to them. They can swim very fast and they will seize an unwary camel, horse or man in their huge jaws, drag him into deeper water, and then roll until their victim is drowned and quite dead, then they eat him."

"Have you ever seen one do that?" Kazim piped. He had just joined them in the bows. He was obviously bored sitting with his mother and the ladies who waited upon her.

"Hello, young Lord," Bilal said with a mischievous grin. "Are you ready to be eaten by a crocodile?"

Kazim shuddered. "Bilal, I shall tell my mother. You are supposed to protect me!" he said uneasily.

"Fear not, noble lord. We are here to protect you and we will with the help of Allah," Bilal said soothingly.

He turned to Talon and said, "I once saw a foal being taken; it was drinking from the river. Its mother was grazing on the side of the bank and should have been watching for danger."

"I shall never forget the terror in the foal's eyes when it was seized. I was nearby, but could do nothing for the animal. We had not known a crocodile was so close. The poor foal squealed with terror and struggled desperately, but the monster pulled it in very fast and then there was a lot of spray and the animal disappeared for a while. Then I saw several of the monsters tearing it to pieces out in the deeper part of the river. The mother was running up and down the banks whinnying for her foal. It was very sad."

Talon felt a cold chill as he studied the long, rough shapes on the banks, while Kazim blanched and shuddered. "They look enormous," the boy said faintly, unaware that he had taken Talon's hand.

"Some of them are more than four paces long from snout to tail," Bilal said. "Is it small wonder that our ancestors used to pray to them?"

*****

They arrived within sight of the walls of Al Qahirah late that evening. The city appeared to be a dense mass of walls and buildings that extended up and down both flanks of the river, which, Bilal had explained to Talon, split up into many rivers that flowed through a wide fertile delta and eventually poured into the sea. Talon was surprised at the amount of traffic; the river was crowded with small boats. There were sails to be seen everywhere, boats going in all directions. Large war galleys were anchored well away from the banks, while smaller boats darted in and out of the clusters of shipping near the port.

The river trip had offered a respite from the heat, but now it returned, with the added unpleasant smells of a crowded city that were carried to them on the light breeze. Talon wrinkled his nose at the stench that wafted across the open water as they approached their destination.

"What are those round domes over there, with what looks like a cross on them, Bilal?" He asked and pointed to them.

"Those are the buildings of the Greek Christians. They are known as Copts; they are the Christians who have stayed in Egypt, Suleiman. They say that long ago many Egyptians were Christian. Our Prophet recognized the other faiths of the Book, so they still live here."

The ship was approaching a long wooden platform held up in the river by massive wooden piles. There was much bustle and noise on the bank, as gangs of slaves, bent beneath huge loads, carried cargo to and fro along the crowded quay. The skipper of their vessel skillfully placed the boat alongside the quay with only a gentle bump, and they tied up. Men shouted and whips cracked, as gangs of workers were directed towards their ship to help unload the horses and baggage.

An official looking man walked up to the boat, followed by a slave who was carrying a large book in his hands. This self-important man stood on the quayside and called over.

"Are you carrying any salt? Any flax loads, other cargo?"

"No cargo at all; only passengers for Emir Abbas Abdul Azim ibn Athir Faysal and their personal baggage," Bilal said as he walked down the gangway. He swaggered over to the man and a quiet exchange of words took place. Some coin exchanged hands before the man turned to his slave and said loudly, "No taxes from this ship!"

Bilal sauntered back and said sotto voice, "Puffed up bag of papyrus seeds."

Talon grinned. Bilal had done a good enough job of showing off his own importance.

It was unsettling to see slaves being driven with whips across the quay. They were prisoners from earlier battles or sieges who could not afford a ransom. He knew both sides did this, the

Muslims and the Christians. It was an easy resource to replace, because the wars never ceased and provided an endless supply of man labor. The prisoners rarely lasted more than six months, when they finally fell due to exhaustion or disease. The body would be dumped in a ditch to rot and be devoured by the ever present carrion birds, or, if they worked on the river, he imagined they became food for the crocodiles. He could not look at the men and neither did he want to catch their eyes, he felt so uncomfortable. But for the grace of God, he and Max could have been among these poor wretches.

The party finally proceeded slowly through the busy streets of the enormous, crowded city towards the house of Abbas, leaving on the quay a small mountain of bales and other goods to be carried to their destination by slaves.

Despite the combined efforts of Bilal and the other men on horses, it was a lot of work to persuade the surly citizens of Al Qahirah to move out of the way of their large party. Even if it was clear to everyone that someone of importance was trying to get through, people seemed to deem it their right to walk along the middle of the narrow streets and to give way to no one. Whips and the hafts of lances were used liberally upon those who were too slow and the way cleared eventually. The curtains of the palanquins were drawn close to keep out the choking dust and to ensure some privacy for its occupants.

The house that Emir Abbas owned in Al Qahirah was a small palace. Bilal informed Talon that Abbas's father, Emir Athir, had built it when Abbas had been a young boy. The house was now the home of his mother and the several concubines that his father had kept. His mother, Lady Emushire, had never left her home to travel to the other properties after his father died and now ruled the house with an iron hand, with the help of her chief eunuch, Chisisi.

The main building was constructed along elegant lines. The living quarters were spacious, well ventilated and multi-storied. The servants' quarters at the back of the house, although not as well appointed, were nonetheless very comfortable and also well ventilated, with wide verandahs to keep the sun off the walkways. Talon had been told by Bilal that the new house had been built upon the ruins of a Greek villa, hence the plentiful displays of intricate tiling. The baths had been kept almost as they were, for their plumbing was intact.

Talon liked the place immediately, from the cool of the high arched ceilings to the sound of water that could be heard splashing in the courtyard fountains and the inevitable chirp of the sparrows in the shaded trees dotting the gardens.

The front section of the palace area had three stories, two of which could look over the wall fronting the street, but their shutters were kept closed, keeping the heat outside. The balconies and shuttered windows were enclosed with an elegant carved wood latticework which allowed womenfolk from the inside to see out but not been seen. The whole palace with its stables and extensive gardens was contained within a tall mud brick wall that had wooden platforms along the inside where armed men could stand and watch the activity in the street outside or defend the walls from would-be attackers. Even the sounds from the busy street on the other side were muted.

The stables were situated along the back south wall of the palace, along with the accommodations for the syce and gardeners. Talon wandered down the line of horse boxes and stopped by his horse Rakhsh. While standing looking down the row of stalls he absently stroked the horse's soft nose. The horse nuzzled his midriff and half closed his eyes as Talon rubbed his ears and chin.

His mind was busy wondering how he could get away from this city and be on his way back to Max and then to escape altogether. It was now many months since they had staggered ashore half-drowned. Now Max was a virtual prisoner, while he was alone in Al Qahirah. It made him feel rudderless. He knew he could not complain as, although a slave, he could go anywhere he wanted to. In some ways that was worse than being imprisoned, but his word had been given and he would not break it.

The children had been whisked off into another part of the house by a gaggle of chattering women almost the moment they had appeared at the door along with their mother. He assumed the women to be either wives or concubines of the master, or perhaps servants. Talon had not even had time to say goodbye.

Later, Talon heard that there were other women here besides the concubines of Abbas. Abbas's father had had concubines in his old age; three of them lived in a relatively secluded manner on the second floor of the palace. There had to be at least fifty retainers of one kind or another, all of them subservient to the mother of Abbas, who used the eunuch Chisisi to keep order, which he did harshly.

Chisisi was a fat man with thick legs and huge chest and arms, topped by a smooth, shaved head which looked as though it was polished. His small black eyes were almost buried in the flesh of his face and his small pursed lips were disapproving. Bilal had mentioned to Talon that he was a bully who administered punishment directly with either his stick or a slap of his huge hand, hitting the offending servant's head, male or female.

Everyone feared him, for he had the ear of the mother and indirectly, her authority, which meant literally life or death for some of the lesser slaves.

The next day Bilal came to look for Talon.

"Suleiman, you are wanted at the house by Chisisi," he said, breathing hard. Bilal was becoming just a little portly.

"Do you know why, Bilal?" Talon asked.

"No, but you need to watch your back with that eunuch; he is no one's friend and makes a bad enemy."

Talon walked back towards the house deep in thought and found Chisisi standing in the main hallway shouting at a maid servant. The eunuch did not even look up when Talon came towards him. He continued to shout abuse in his high voice at the cringing maid and then dealt her a heavy slap on the back of the head which almost knocked her off her feet. She fled crying towards the kitchens. The huge man regarded Talon with suspicion; his small black eyes stared at him from his fleshy face.

"Ah, Suleiman, I have heard that you are a teacher, and the lady wants you to continue your work with the children."

"When does she want me to start?" Talon asked.

"Tomorrow. You are to report here in this hall in the morning and then go to the children. That room over there will be the class room."

Talon turned to go.

"You will wait here until I have finished with you!" Chisisi said loudly.

"Forgive me, I thought you had finished," Talon said.

"By Allah! When I have finished I shall let you know, and you will bow and then leave," Chisisi shouted for the benefit of passing servants.

Talon turned on the man, standing so close he could smell the onions he had eaten for his last meal and his other odors mixed with a stale perfume. Talon looked straight into Chisisi's eyes and spoke very quietly.

"I will tell you once only. You do not shout at me and you do not tell me what to do. I take my orders from my lord or from my lady, but not from you."

He saw what he wanted to see, hesitation and a flicker of uncertainty in the man's eyes. It was enough.

The household servants treated him with the respect due a learned person, but they kept their distance. He was neither one of them nor one of the family, so he was regarded with reserve.

The next morning after he had eaten, he reported for lessons with the children. They now looked forward to lessons as much as he did and accepted him as their tutor in all things. When he was not absorbed with them he felt isolated, other than the times he was able to spend with Bilal at the stables.

Despite the loud protestations of the eunuch, he managed to get them outside for most of their lessons, as he and they enjoyed the garden and its calm. The household was sadly a tense place, where the servants scuttled about in fear of retribution from Chisisi, who bullied them mercilessly. Chisisi had a couple of henchmen, Donkor and Jahi, who ran to do his bidding in all things, and more often than not joined in the bullying, punishing servants for the most trivial of offenses or for no reason at all. Talon took an instant dislike to them and decided that he would try to avoid all three at all times.

The one person he was careful not to offend in any way was the mother. Lady Emushire was not unkindly, but having had to run a house full of servants and bored, squabbling women for a long time, she had become hardened and rarely let her more kindly disposition show.

Talon noticed that Bilal stayed away from the house as much as possible, and he followed his friend's example. On the whole it was not so hard to do, as their quarters were nearer the stables, far to the rear of the house and its unhappy occupants.

*The city of beggars never sleeps*
*The noise goes on 24 hours a day*
*It is not safe to walk in the street of beggars*
*Because you can get robbed and killed*
*at any time of the night or day*
*The traffic is chaotic in the city of beggars*
*Thanks God there is no snow in the city of beggars*
*— Aldo Kraas*

# Chapter 12

# Beggars

Talon's duties were light, and by the time it was noon he was free to do much as he pleased. He took the opportunity to explore the streets of the huge city of Cairo. Noon was the time when the city virtually went to sleep. No one wanted to do anything for the two or three hours on the other side of noon. The oppressive heat placed a suffocating mantle over everything, which became even worse on days when there was a light layer of high clouds that resembled fish scales in the sky. On such days the city steamed. People with means retreated indoors and closed the shutters to the noises and stinks and either slept, or, as Bilal joked to Talon, enjoyed their wives, or concubines, or both. A heavy silence would settle over the normally noisy city.

"Night is for sleeping, but the afternoon is for making love," Bilal declared, and often as not, he too disappeared to follow up upon this philosophy with a servant girl to whom he had taken a liking.

Talon found it a good time to wander about the almost deserted streets and to explore the somnolent souk, where even the noisy hammers of the metal smiths were silenced. He would stride in his unobtrusive manner along the narrow streets and explore the dim arched passageways of the market place, observing the slow pace of life. Merchants might still be awake, drinking coffee or smoking hashish from a water pipe. They were mere shadows in the darkness at the back of their shop openings as they watched over their displays of goods with a stoic resignation, waiting for the cool of the evening to bring customers back.

Cairo was surrounded by high, well maintained walls which protected it from would-be besiegers, and that included the Crusaders. Bilal, who knew a little of its history, had told Talon that it was founded on very old ruins. The newer construction incorporated much of the older city walls and buildings that dated back to the time of Greece and even further back into the darkness of antiquity.

As evening came and the prayers were called from the many minarets in the city, Talon would join in to ensure that he did not stand out. When done with the prayers he would go and sit at a tea house, a chai khane, along Al Muizz Street among other chai khanes, where they not only served tea, lemon wine, or coffee, but where men told stories.

The men who told them were in some cases famous artists, because they could bring to life the characters of their tales. They would on occasion use a couple of musicians to back up their narrative, men who played a crude tambourine or a rababa, which squeaked and wailed to add emphasis to the story teller's tale. The tea houses would compete to have a particularly good story teller because he attracted more guests to drink tea or eat the spicy falafel and small, sweet wheat cakes with coatings of honey. The tea houses also served bitter, black coffee from tiny cups that were filled in a long stream from the elongatedF snouts of brass pots poured elegantly from the height of an arm length by harassed waiters. Students carrying books or rolled papers would pause to listen briefly or to talk loudly with one another about the latest depredations of the Turkish mercenaries, who were not liked in this city, or the Franks to the north. Older men came to smoke sweet herbal tobacco flavored with honey; others smoked hashish, sitting in the darker recesses, giggling to one another while telling crude jokes.

The crowd would hush these boisterous customers and any other noisy clients when a story teller arrived. He would climb onto a tall stool, which helped his voice to project and reach the people on the edges of the crowded floor. From this tall perch, he would mimic, intone, declaim, raise or lower his voice to emphasize, glorify or to generate tension or suspense, while at other times he would gesticulate vigorously in a comical manner as the tale unfolded with a faster momentum. A skilled narrator could keep the crowd silent in rapt attention and not infrequently bring the audience to its feet with tears and shaking fists as a hero was betrayed or when a heroine perished.

Talon began to look forward to spending time around these places. One in particular attracted him, for the artist was a Syrian and told enchanting stories from literature he was familiar with. This man knew tales from all the lands, including Persia. The favorite story of the crowd in this tea house was the story of the Congress of Birds by a famous poet named Farrid al Din Attar. This fable was long, with moral lessons, but also full of emotion and passion. Talon, often as not, took these tales back to his two young wards. It would be unthinkable for them to follow him into such a popular place, but he wanted very much to share the stories with them. The children were enthralled, and would mimic and participate in the story by acting between themselves. It made for lively and enjoyable lessons of poetry and folk lore.

Talon never revealed his explorations of the town to anyone, because even though he liked Bilal, he was not sure that he would approve of him wandering about the city in this manner. These places were for the lower classes and the merchants. Sometimes while in a tea house, Talon's thoughts would wing away to Hamadan or Isfahan, where he and his two companions Rav'an and Reza used to sit for long hours talking together, enjoying the atmosphere of the chai khane, as they were also called in Persia, and then his heart would grow heavy, as he did not know of their fate.

He sometimes walked along the river bank below the city walls to watch the boat builders and rope makers running the length of the beach with their rotating, twisting tools held high during the fabrication of a new rope. The smell of new cut wood and the activity drew him to watch the forming of an elegant prow and then the attachment of the formed strakes. He admired the symmetry of the bow and the curves that these craftsmen were able to create with very basic tools, seemingly without recourse to any plans.

Talon made two important discoveries during his explorations. The first one was that along the north wall of the city, on a hill, there was an impressive construction site in progress. Talon had asked Bilal about it.

"The sultan, may Allah be his guide, ordered the work of this 'Citadel' – which is to be called Qala'at Salāḥ ad-Dīn. It is being repaired, and on the highest point of the city. It will be made impregnable, especially from the depredations of the infidels. They have on several occasions tried to take Al Qahirah before, did you know?" Bilal glowered then he carried on. "The design is taken from that of the infidels who build huge castles in the area of Jerusalem, Allah curse them. But even if they are barbaric people they certainly know how to build castles," he had remarked dryly.

Talon noticed that every time someone in this country talked about the Christians he always seemed to add an expletive. He decided he might have to emulate Bilal someday to be like everyone else. "Why does the Sultan not take Alexandria as his capital city, Bilal? It is a very beautiful place with a huge sea port, and cleaner air than here," Talon ventured.

"I think it is because it is not at the center of things, Suleiman. Al-Qahirah is in the middle of the great river delta, so it controls the river; all the ships passing through have to pay a tithe, which means good revenue; and besides, the Sultan is ever looking east. Alexandria is too far to the west to be useful strategically, other than as a bulwark against the barbaric Berber tribes of the deserts, Allah's curse be upon them."

"Are they not Muslim too, Bilal?"

"They are, but they covet the riches of Egypt and would plunder our country, notwithstanding."

Talon thought he understood. Although he did not as yet have a good map of Egypt in his mind, it was formulating, and it did seem as though Cairo fulfilled several vital functions for the sultan. However, he didn't like the climate much: it was distinctly humid and oppressively hot here, whereas he remembered the cool dawns and evenings of Alexandria during his short stay, before he was tossed into jail. Not only was Cairo a steam bath, but with its seething mass of humanity it seemed about to burst out of its walls.

He agreed with Bilal about the Citadel; it was indeed a formidable construction, swarming with workers, masons and slaves, even during the hottest time of day. Talon did not doubt that many of the slaves were Christian prisoners. The walls of three sides were already built; their color was almost red, like most of the city buildings.

The shape of its towers and battlements did resemble the castles he was familiar with, as he remembered his former home in the kingdom of Jerusalem; but this castle was going to be far larger than anything he had ever seen before, including the castle of Carcassonne in Languedoc that he had come to know. The Citadel was already massive and dominated the entire city.

While ambling around the fortification, observing its strengths, his trained eye looking for weaknesses, Talon arrived at the main frontage and noticed that men were playing chogan at the bottom of the hill on a large flat field. He paused to watch. He remembered how much he had learned to love the game while in Isfahan, during the short respite while he and his friends Rav'an and Reza had been running for their lives. Although he had played at Al Fayou, he was not certain he would be able to play here in Al Qahirah. He was envious of the riders on this field.

The same field served as the place of execution for common criminals and traitors alike. The last one he had witnessed only a few days ago had been for a senior mason who had neglected to construct a portion of the citadel wall properly. The section had fallen away in a landslide of rubble the previous week and killed slaves and citizens on the path below. The embarrassing pile of rubble was still there being cleaned up by a gang of sweating slaves. Talon walked around the still bloody scaffolding that had been placed at the base of the steps leading up to the main entrance. He guessed that there would be another execution that day.

He did not stand out as a stranger in this city, for his mode of dress was just like that of any other male of moderate means on the street, a light shirt of much washed white linen, over which he sometimes wore an expensive cotton embroidered waist coat, pantaloons, and his calf length riding boots. His loose turban hid his lighter hair while his light beard and eyes, although not common, did not attract much attention in this city of so many differing peoples from many different countries. He was allowed, by virtue of his position of tutor and bodyguard, to wear a sword, and he carried a knife in his sash and another hidden in his boot.

Since the Sultan had decided that this was to be his capital, Cairo was undergoing a comprehensive renovation. As Talon walked the streets he noticed that there would often be a very old building alongside a relatively new one, both of similar style. The houses were for the most part constructed of mud brick walls on the ground floor, while the second floor was a wood frame.

He walked the tree lined areas that catered to the rich, and wandered across the several wide and spacious maidans that provided a setting for the very beautifully decorated mosques. He saw new ones being built in several locations around the city and imagined they were on the orders of the sultan. These open spaces, shaded by trees and with gardens, were ideal for family outings.

On occasion, when Abbas was not somewhere carrying out his duties for the sultan, he would take his family to the Al Azhar Mosque. Talon had seen that the children clearly enjoyed these occasions, as they were able to escape the confines of the palace and see more of the city. It was an adventure for Kazim and Jasmine. It was on these rare occasions that he could set eyes on Khalidah, although most of the time she was well hidden behind the curtains of the palanquin. Talon, Bilal, Panhsj and several soldiers would attend the family on those outings as bodyguards, clearing the way through the crowded streets for the entourage. The entire family would settle into an area in the spacious maidan of the huge mosque and enjoy the surroundings. Friends would come by and talk, always performing on arrival the elaborate greetings that Egyptians seemed to enjoy so much.

The various scholars who interpreted the Hadith and read from the Koran would be there surrounded by their faithful students. Abbas would sometimes go over and listen to this or that scholar whom he respected, even entering into discussions that would on occasion last a whole afternoon.

Talon noticed that there was another side to Cairo. Many of the streets were not in good repair. Most of them were unpaved tracks, dotted with pot holes and ruts from the last rains, so he was forced, as were other pedestrians, to pay attention to where he trod. Many were mere passage ways, filthy and crowded with beggars: crippled and maimed ex-soldiers and other ragged people of the poorer kind who were hurrying to and fro.

He encountered the usual heavily loaded donkeys trotting ahead of their drovers, and camels which refused to be hurried and ambled along at their own pace. The air was charged with the smell of cooking oil and food, spices and baking bread, which vied with the unpleasant stinks of the hot street. Rats were everywhere, and they were huge. They were quite unafraid of people and simply sat on their hind legs and stared balefully at passersby with their beady red eyes.

The heat was constant and suffocating within the confines of these narrow streets. The walker was constantly beset by flies that seemed to come from everywhere to attack the eyes and mouth. He deemed it prudent at these times to wear a covering over the nose and mouth, both to repel the flies and to filter the putrid stinks that emanated from the puddles of stagnant water that remained in the deeper pot holes. Talon longed for the desert and began to miss the Fayoum.

As the afternoon progressed and the sun lost some of its ferocity, the city would slowly wake up and more people and their animals showed up on the streets. The racket of many hammers tapping on metal started up again, construction work intensified and vendors shouted their wares to the growing crowds emerging onto the streets. The occasional camel train would saunter by, its owner tugging at the lead camel's chin rope, shouting for passage way. The huge loads on their backs almost filled the street from side to side and a person had to get into a doorway or take another street to get out of the way. The noise of people talking animatedly and the shouts of the drovers along with the screams and yells that came from inside the houses hurt his ears.

But his explorations always led him back towards the souk. This place was more of a caravanserai but much larger than anything he had seen in Persia. This was a warren of huge stone blocks and in some cases ancient looking pillars that denoted some extravagant building at one time, perhaps a temple, upon which masons had added mud brick to form arches and covered streets, some so narrow that only two people could negotiate the path at the same time, so that one had to move into the merchant's open shop space to give room when a loaded donkey came by.

His next discovery was the world of the beggars.

One day while he paused at the entrance to the souk to admire the stone archway that framed the entrance to the depths of that warren of covered streets and shops, he felt a tug on his leg. He instantly looked down and saw one of the numerous beggars sitting on the ground.

This one, however, was a boy, and it seemed he had lost a leg: there was just a stump below the knee. His crudely made crutch was laid alongside him, but he had managed to shuffle right into

Talon's path from his place off the nearby wall. The boy looked desperate, and his gaunt face had none of the cunning Talon had come to associate with most of the beggars he had run into so far.

"What is it?" Talon asked.

"In the good name of Allah, can you spare alms or food, *Oustez*?" The boy asked him in a rasping voice tinged with desperation. He looked sick.

"I can give you a dirham, but can you go and get the food with it?" Talon asked, looking hard at the boy. The creature wore a few filthy rags and his remaining foot was bare. His hair was matted and filthy. He tossed the small copper coin to the boy, who snatched it in midair and then hauled himself up pushing his back against the wall. Talon walked over to a street vendor who was selling chicken kebabs on thin reed sticks that were cooking on charcoal.

Buying one, Talon took it back to the boy, gave it to him, and admonished him to eat it slowly and go rest somewhere.

"May Allah be kind to you, Jo *Oustez*," the boy said, looking stunned, with tears in his eyes as he took the meat and began to devour it.

Talon continued his exploration of the souk without giving it another thought. But in subsequent days he noticed the boy at the same place every time he went near the place. He made a point of even walking across the busy street to give the boy a small coin or some food he had stolen from the palace, and before long the boy would smile at him and bob his head with thanks and then heap praise on him as he left.

One day, remembering his time in Isfahan, Talon decided to try something out. He was on his way as usual during the afternoon to walk the souk; the boy was at his usual place; it was quiet at this time of day with few people moving about, so he walked up and stood over him.

The boy was not paying much attention to what was going on around him, but he noticed the shadow and glanced up, squinting in the still bright sunlight. "Ah, it is you, *Oustez*. May Allah be kind to you in this life and the next." His thin features registered pleasure at seeing Talon.

Talon noticed that the boy did not look as unhealthy as he had been the first time, which was good. He asked the boy, "Are you always here in this place?"

"Yes, *Oustez*. This is my place."

"Can you not go somewhere else?"

"No, *Oustez*. The chief would not like it; he is my protector, and besides, this is a good place for me."

Talon had to agree. The boy must receive several coins on a good day when passersby were feeling generous or their faith prompted them to provide alms. Anyone who wanted to go in or out of the souk had to pass in front of him.

"I want to meet your protector, but I also want to pay you a little more to keep me informed about what is going on in the street when I need to know."

To reinforce his request Talon produced a slightly larger coin and placed it in the wooden bowl held in the boy's hand.

"What is your name?' he asked

"It is Kontar, *Oustez*."

"Then, Kontar, I want to meet your chief sometime in the near future. Can this be arranged?"

The boy looked at him, his deep-set eyes wary.

"Why do you want to meet him, *Oustez*?"

"Because I think we can help each other. There is coin to be had for him, and I will need information from time to time."

The boy nodded, but he did not seem very comfortable at hearing this.

"I shall talk to him, *Oustez*. Be back here tomorrow at the same time, and, if he wants to meet you, he will be here."

Talon nodded and moved off casually. He didn't want to be seen conversing with a beggar. The next day he arrived a little earlier than usual. Keeping out of sight of the main entrance, he checked to see if there were any suspicious people about who might be waiting for him. He noticed the boy propped up against the wall and observed that he appeared tense; his head was swiveling to and fro as though watching for someone.

Then he saw two other men hanging around close by and apparently idle, but their studied expressions gave them away. He decided that they must be the ones waiting for him. He searched the crowd hard for others but did not see anyone who looked as though they might be the chief. He decided that he had to take the chance that the chief, whoever he might be, was waiting for him elsewhere and he would be shown the way, somehow. He walked casually up to the boy and greeted him.

"I am here, Kontar, where is your chief?"

Just as he said that the boy's eyes flicked onto something behind him and he felt something sharp pressed into his back near his kidney.

"You will do as you are told. My knife likes to drink blood," someone hissed from behind him. Talon did not move or say anything.

"Move forward," the same voice instructed him.

Talon was pushed along the quiet street into the dim light of the long arched tunnel of the souk. Someone shoved him into deeper shadow off the main street. He glimpsed the frightened face of the boy as he left.

Two more men joined them, and these two checked his robes for any weapons. Talon had left his sword behind and only had the knife in his sash, which one of them removed, but they missed the one in his boot. There was a grunt and one said, "He is clean of weapons, let's keep moving."

A blindfold of some dirty cloth was bound over Talon's eyes, then he was pushed forward. They walked deep into the depths of the souk; this time he was held between two men and assisted over steps and down slopes. The air was stale and dusty to breathe.

They began to move downward and the air became cooler, with a light draft flowing up from underground. His heart was beating hard and he began to question the wisdom of his plan, but he was now committed, so he mentally shrugged and walked on with his escorts.

Talon felt as if they were moving along narrow tunnels and the familiar sounds of the souk began to recede; finally there was just their breathing and the tramp of footsteps followed by a dull echo. He could also hear the rustle and squeak of rats in the darkness. After what seemed to be many long minutes of walking, they finally came to a halt. The blindfold was removed and Talon blinked in the light of many small oil lamps.

He was at the entrance of a large underground space like a nave. It had many supporting pillars, which arched into the darkness of a roof above. The lamps were smoky and could not light up the entire area, which seemed extensive. The air was dense with the smell of people, cooking cabbage, and smoking oil lamps.

There was a smell of warm, sweet, nutty baking bread; his nostrils hung on to the memories of it. There were also acrid smells of smoked meat on open fires.

He was astonished. It was an underground village.

Lying on pallets in the back he could see the forms of sleeping people, while nearer at hand there were women preparing food over small fires, the smoke being drawn up through holes in the darkness above.

He heard the sound of running water somewhere in the darkness ahead of him, perhaps from an underground stream.

Talon tried to see to the end of the room but his captors pushed him roughly forward towards a low platform strewn with red and black colorful woven mats and carpets, where he could see several men seated among scuffed and patched cushions. Some were smoking water pipes; there was a strong smell of hashish in the air, while others were sipping tea. They all regarded him impassively as he was prodded one step at a time towards them.

His captors stopped at the edge of the platform, and one of the men lounging on the platform, leaning comfortably against some huge cushions, regarded him without enthusiasm. He was a very large bearded man with only one eye; his other was covered by a dark patch held in place with a leather thong. He said gruffly, "Who are you and what do you want with my boy?"

"I learned some time ago from a friend in Isfahan that a man who had the beggars as his friends knew all that was happening in a city," Talon replied.

There was a chuckle and the man's huge belly heaved.

"Your friend was right." There was silence after that and Talon sensed his captors behind him, waiting for the next sentence to decide his fate. He tensed, ready to react very quickly should his life become endangered.

Then the man said, "You are either a very brave man or very stupid to want to come here and talk about this. Why should I not just cut your throat and toss your body in the river for the crocodiles to eat? Why should I trust you, and what is in it for me?"

Talon shrugged. "I am a slave anyway and it makes little difference to me whether I am believed or not. I do know that on one occasion my lord's family was in grave danger and they did not know from where the danger came. I am trying to prevent that happening again, and in so doing I am protecting the family."

"Whose slave are you?"

"I am the tutor for my lord Abbas Abdul Azim. I am the teacher of his children and to some extent their guard."

"A tutor and a guard, that is unusual. I know of Lord Abbas. It is said he is a great warrior and that he is a fair man. I suppose that is as good as one can expect from his kind." The man motioned Talon to come forward.

The guards relaxed then, as did Talon; it was as though he had passed some kind of a test. He strode onto the carpeted platform and sat down cross-legged in front of the one-eyed man and his companions.

"Knowledge comes at a price...what is your name?"

"My name is Suleiman."

"Is that all?"

"It will do for the moment."

The one eyed man motioned to someone in the shadows and a very small cup of steaming coffee appeared on a tray in front of Talon. The aroma indicated that there was cardamom spice in it. He relaxed a little more. He knew that if he had not been offered anything he would have still been in danger. But these people were not of the Bedouin, so he really couldn't be sure.

He bowed from the waist to the man and sipped his coffee. The man gave a curt nod in acknowledgement. His many jowls rippling as he did so.

"You seem very young to be wandering about the city asking questions and talking to me about knowledge, Suleiman," the man remarked. His voice was throaty. He was well into middle age, about forty, comfortably dressed in good clothes. The people all around him treated him with respect.

"It was a hard but good lesson I learned at that time, as it saved not only my life but some of my companions as well," Talon replied. "I am not rich, *Oustez*. But I am prepared to pay what I can for information from time to time, and I wanted to meet with the leader, you, to make sure that it was something we could agree upon. *Insha'Allah*?"

"You have looked after my boy, and he told me about the food you gave him when he was sick," the man said reflectively.

"I am glad that Allah deemed fit to make him well again," said Talon. "To whom do I have the honor of talking, *Oustez*?"

"My name is Mukhwana, and that will have to do for the moment."

His good eye twinkled behind his beard. "I am the leader of a large group of the beggars in this area of the city. Perhaps I can help," he offered reflectively. "But I shall want payment in silver or gold. How can a mere slave do this?" he asked. His tone was skeptical.

"As it happens, Allah has provided for me and I can... within limits." Talon had already deposited his silver and gold with a Jewish banker in the souk some weeks before as a protection against theft. His chits were carefully hidden in the palace where he felt they would be safe until he needed them. He did not trust the eunuch or his companions.

"Do you have something you need to know at this time?" Mukhwana asked of him.

"Does the name Bahir Ibn Hakeem mean anything to you?' Talon asked.

He was not expecting the reaction he got. The old man sat up quickly and dropped his pipe.

"Yes, I know of him!" he snarled. "He is responsible for my lost eye. May Allah curse his aristocratic hide and send him to Jehannum when he dies."

"How can that be?" Talon asked politely, but with interest.

"Never you mind. What do you need to know about him?'

"I want to know where he lives."

"Is that all?"

"For the moment, *Oustez* Mukhwana, yes."

Talon smiled and Mukhwana laughed quietly.

# Chapter 13

# Chogan

Talon sat his restless horse Rakhsh alongside that of Abbas and of the other members of the team, listening to the excited chatter of the crowd that surrounded the large dirt maidan where the game was to be played. He patted Rakhsh's already sweating neck and murmured words to settle him. The horse flicked his ears back as though listening and calmed down somewhat, but then another horse behind them gave a nasal snarl of irritation and tried to bite its neighbor. There was a brief moment of pandemonium as shouting riders fought to bring their horses under control, glaring at one another as they spurred and whipped their mounts back into line. Talon held Rakhsh on a firm rein, sitting deep, and the horse listened to him, trembling but not moving from his place, even as he was jostled by other horses.

When the horses were finally quieted, Talon glanced up at the massive fortification that dominated the maidan where they were going to play. His eyes studied the high walls and he could see that it had been refurbished. Its two huge rounded gate towers flanking the front of the Citadel were, for this occasion, decorated with banners that fluttered in the light breeze, lending a festive atmosphere to the already palpable excitement in the air. Small figures stood on the battlements looking down on the crowd below. The breeze did little to alleviate the heat that blanketed the wide, flat field.

Thousands of people had come from the city, and every soldier who could escape from duty had arrived from the army barracks to watch the game, and to support Abbas, for he was a popular commander. Bets were being taken everywhere by the excited Egyptians, who loved to gamble. It was well known that this was not just an ordinary game of chogan, but a grudge-match between two well known noble houses, and the crowd was buzzing with anticipation.

The first ball would be thrown by the sultan himself, who now stood in front of them, looking down on the two teams of six men lined up in two jostling, irregular lines almost knee to knee, waiting for the ball to be thrown in to start the game.

Talon's mind flicked back to the evening three days ago when the challenge had been delivered to Abbas.

On the way home Abbas had been raging, "That jackal, Bahir arranged this," he growled to his men. "But I do not know *why*! It is as though he knows something I do not." He said this to no one in particular, but Panhsj and Talon had looked at one another as though they were expected to reply. Neither knew what to say, so they had remained silent while their master fumed.

Later, at his palace, Abbas had held a conference with Talon, Bilal, and Panhsj. "The family honor is at stake. We have only the rudiments of a polo team. You Suleiman, and you Bilal, and of course myself, but who will we use for the other three?"

Talon and Bilal had not been short of ideas in that regard.

Talon dragged his thoughts back to the present, his instincts telling him to pay attention. The sultan was saying something and he strained to hear.

"This is a game of great importance. The match is to be friendly, and is to finally settle disagreements that have arisen. I prefer to have my lords working for me, instead of against each other. Let this be the end of the grudge, my lords. Play well."

He then threw the fist-sized ball of willow wood on the ground so that it landed deep among the cluster of men and horses, whereupon the fighting began. Talon had been prepared for this, but even so, he noticed that the players on the other side were using their mallets as weapons, striking at man and horse in a manner that indicated that this was a grudge match indeed. Around him, men tried to get at the ball and clear it from the melee of pushing and shoving horsemen. They cursed and hacked at the ball, which bounced around between the horses' feet.

Abbas managed, with the help of Haytham, a syce only thirteen years old who was a fearless player, to tap the ball free of the struggling mass of riders. Then the game immediately opened up, as men began to chase Talon and Haytham at a stretched out gallop down the field towards the opposition's goal. Talon knew a feeling of exhilaration as Rakhsh pounded after Haytham, who was racing down field on his white mare, hitting the ball well. But Talon knew that with the uneven ground he would sooner or later lose control of the wildly bouncing object, and then the rider behind him would have to take it. Talon could barely hear the crowd screaming at them as they charged down the hard packed, dusty field.

He turned in the saddle to see who was following, and saw that Bahir was right on his tail. Rakhsh responded to the light touch on the bit from Talon and eased his pace just enough to keep in line. Haytham had lost the ball and was trying to stop his horse on its haunches as he crossed over the ball, taking a wild swipe with his mallet.

Talon concentrated on the bouncing object as he kneed Rakhsh closer to its line of flight. They came upon the ball at a fast gallop and Talon managed to tip the ball forward, but not enough to strike it the rest of the way between the two posts that represented the goal.

As he slowed to try again, Bahir rode right into Talon's left side. The force of the other horse drove him off the line of the ball. Talon turned and drove Rakhsh back into Bahir's horse and they swayed off in the opposite direction. This time, Talon stood on his right stirrup and leaned far out, managing to tap the ball once again, but it bounced out of reach. The dust was everywhere by now as the group of other players, with one of Bahir's team in the lead, raced down upon the now stilled ball.

Bahir and Talon were knee to knee until Talon broke free. To Talon's shock, Bahir suddenly lashed out at him, striking at his face with the haft of his stick. Talon managed to deflect the blow enough that the haft of the mallet struck the top of his forehead instead of his nose. The blow was absorbed by his turban, but nonetheless it knocked Talon back in his saddle and he pulled up Rakhsh, feeling dazed and groggy. He shook his head to regain his senses. Meanwhile, Bahir had ridden off to join the milling and shouting men who had regained the ball and were chasing it in the opposite direction.

Conscious of being left out of the game, Talon put Rakhsh into a gallop to catch up with the others, who had all but disappeared in a cloud of dust towards their own goal posts. He was too late to help his team. He heard a huge roar from the crowd and the game was stopped. A man between the goal posts was waving a flag to indicate a goal had been scored. Talon was riding towards the middle of the field, still trying to clear his head, when he was accosted by Abbas as he galloped back to the center of the field from the other direction.

"What happened to you, Suleiman? They have the first goal and we need all our players with us," Abbas said sharply. He was obviously put out by the speed that the first goal had been scored against him.

"I am sorry, my lord, but your enemy struck me in the face," Talon said, shaking his head one more time.

Abbas looked hard at him. "Yes, by the Prophet, he did. You have a large lump growing, and there is blood on your forehead, Suleiman. I might have known he would not play well. Will you be able to continue?"

"Yes, my lord...now that I know the rules," Talon said with a weak grin.

Abbas laughed grimly.

"Good." He turned to his team. "Men, look to yourselves. We have not a game but a war to win." There was a light of battle in his eyes as he went for the throw in with the others following him.

Bilal rode alongside Talon. "I fear that this is just the beginning, and now I worry that it might become much worse, Suleiman." He showed Talon a welt on his forearm.

"I too, Bilal. I shall be watching for our lord's safety, as I smell something bad here."

The fight for the ball went one way and the next for what felt like many minutes. The crowd, having heard about the enmity and witnessed the blows, appreciated that this was a serious grudge match and screamed their support for one side or the other.

Talon and Haytham became the men the other players would try to pass to, but often they themselves needed to extricate the ball and take it up field. There were times when Talon could almost feel the ground with his foot, Rakhsh was leaning so far over as they went into a turn. He or Haytham would be tapping the ball, leaning out at impossible angles, literally hanging on by their ankles hooked onto the saddle, their horses seeming to be there just when it could have meant a fall, and then they would rush off in another direction.

The second goal was scored by Haytham, with the help of a long pass by Talon, who lofted a long hit from under Rakhsh's neck that dropped the ball right in front of the boy. Haytham had placed himself near the opposition's goal on hearing the shouted instructions from Talon. Holding position, and quite unmarked, the boy just leaned down and almost stroked the ball through the posts from only thirty paces, then nimbly danced his horse out of the way of the charging steeds who swept past him, too late to stop the ball from going in. The crowd shrieked their approval of a very neat maneuver, and Talon grinned at Haytham, who laughed with excitement.

As they cantered their horses back to the center line, Abbas nodded to Talon and Haytham approvingly. "That was good team play, Suleiman. You are right about the boy." He smiled at Haytham as they rode. "Well done...now let's get some more."

The boy was flushed with pleasure at the compliment. The players were already covered with a fine coating of dust, and it was difficult to swallow. Talon wrapped his kafeya tighter around his face.

The game became harder, as the opposition team, instead of going after the ball, seemed to concentrate upon incapacitating Abbas's riders.

In spite of this, they managed to get another goal, and this time it was Abbas himself who scored with a long high shot that sent the ball about fifty feet into the air and down between the opposition goal posts. The crowd was ecstatic, and roared their approval. Money began to change hands again among the crowd.

The faces of Bahir and his team mates was all the reward Abbas and his team needed, but their looks were murderous. Bilal again rode alongside Talon and said, "It will not be long before they try something ugly, Suleiman. Be on your guard."

His face was sweating profusely, his back streaked with sweat; he mopped his neck with the tail of his turban. It was the end of a chucker and the players were given some time off to obtain fresh horses, and then it was back onto the field and the game continued.

"By Allah, I am too old for this game, I swear it," Bilal gasped at one point when they were changing horses for the second time.

Talon took back Rakhsh, as he felt he would need the responsive animal for this round.

He was right. The game became even more vicious, and the first casualty was Jawad, one of Talon's archers and a superb rider, even if an inexperienced player. Jawad was trying to tap the ball in a half circle to change direction, leaning far off his horse which itself was over at a sharp angle in a tight canter. One of the opposition rode straight into his horse, bringing it down in a tumbled heap with Jawad caught beneath the animal.

Jawad's scream of agony was muffled by the noise of the pounding hooves. Few saw the attack because of the thick dust. But when the game had stopped and the dust had settled, it was obvious to everyone that there had been a bad accident.

Talon was furious. He dismounted and ran to the prone man, whose frightened horse galloped back to horse lines. Jawad lay on the ground in a tight bundle, clutching at his arm which was twisted at an unnatural angle, and he was pale under his dark features. He rocked back and forth, crying with the pain. His turban had fallen off and Talon could see that his face was screwed up in agony and there was a rapidly growing welt on his cheek.

Talon was quickly joined by Abbas and the other team members.

"It was no accident, my lord. I saw it happen. I was behind that man when he rode straight into him and then struck him as he went down. It was like he wanted to kill him."

Abbas's face was dark with anger. He pivoted his horse in one swift move and rode hard into Bahir's horse, not even bothering to stop at any distance. Bahir exclaimed angrily as his mount staggered back, but then seeing the murderous expression on Abbas's face, he reined his horse away even further. Abbas followed, shouting and pointing back at his man, who was now being helped off the field.

"Your man tried to kill him. What are you trying to do?"

"It was an accident, and you know it," Bahir shouted back at Abbas. "If you put children on the field, you must expect them to get hurt by real men," he sneered. But he kept his distance. His men rode up to gather behind him, and the threatening group deterred Abbas from continuing.

"My man saw what he did and it was not an accident. By Allah, I shall defeat you anyway, you scum!" Abbas shouted. He turned and cantered back to his lines to arrange for a substitute.

They rode back onto the field in a somber mood. "Each of you must pay attention to their dirty tricks. Protect one another. Suleiman saw what they did, and it was malicious, so be careful. I want to win this game." Abbas said. His lips were set in a tight line under his beard, and his dark eyes flashed with rage.

The crowd murmured, but the Sultan did not interfere. The game of Polo was for men, not children, and while this one seemed inordinately rough, it was a good game and he wanted it to continue. In any case, the crowd would have rioted if he had decided it was enough at this point. They were wildly excited; betting was frenzied as the citizens of Cairo scented blood.

The trumpet blew to resume the game and the ball was thrown in from the center by a herald. Bahir was now a goal down, but for some reason Talon had the feeling that his team was not really concerned about the goal difference.

On more than one occasion, he noticed that two of the opposition players were homing in on him, but each time he managed to evade them by urging Rakhsh to outpace them. And once, with the help of Bilal, they managed to ride one of the opponents out of play. This enabled him to head for the goal by tapping the ball along as the others rode furiously after him. The ball rose into the air just in front of him and he tapped it again, moving it ten feet forward, and then tapped it one more time at a flat out gallop.

Then an opportunity presented itself that he could not resist. The man who had attacked Jawad earlier was galloping directly towards him, almost in line with him and the ball, which was bouncing lightly in front of the galloping Rakhsh. He took his time and made sure his mallet connected just as the ball rose a couple of inches in the air. He struck hard and the ball was hurled forward to drive itself into the shocked face of the man coming towards him.

Talon actually saw teeth flying as it struck the oncoming man right in the mouth. The shock was too much for the player. He toppled over the back of his horse to tumble to the ground in a heap.

Talon guided Rakhsh nimbly out of the way of the oncoming horse and galloped down field, hoping that someone would take advantage and hit the ball to him. Sure enough, Abbas drove the ball down the field to drop it a few dozen yards in front of the goal. Talon merely tapped it in to score. He slowed Rakhsh to a trot, and patted the still eager but blowing animal on his foam-flecked neck, talking to him gently. Rakhsh's ears flicked back and he tossed his head as though to say, "I am not done yet, let's get on with it." Talon laughed with delight.

As they rode back to center, a jubilant Bilal rode over and shouted. "You took all his teeth out, Suleiman. What a dreadful thing to do! Ha, ha!" He clapped Talon on the back, as did the other jubilant team members, including Abbas who was roaring with laughter as he said, "He got what he deserved there, Suleiman. Did you mean to do it? I wonder about you sometimes. Allah is sweet with his punishments. He is going to look like a dog with no teeth for the rest of his life."

They barely heard the delighted screams of the crowd who had seen the whole thing, despite the rising dust. The man was still stumbling off the field holding his bloody face when they arrived at the center to be met by a glowering Bahir and the remnants of his team.

"I saw that, Abbas. There will be a reckoning." He pointed with his mallet at Talon.

"It was you who told me that this was a game for men and not for boys, Bahir. Your 'boy' deserved all he got," Abbas responded.

Now Abbas was two goals up, and the game had only a few minutes to go. His ecstatic team members were yelling encouragement at one another through their dirt and sweat-caked faces when the ball was thrown in again, their confidence fully restored, ready to finish it. Everyone was panting from exertion, covered with dust and wound up tight with the tension of the game. It could go either way at this point, but Abbas and his men were determined not to lose the advantage.

Talon raced up field at the shouted command of Abbas, with Haytham close behind him in anticipation of a long pass, which soon came. The ball appeared out of the cloud of dust like a missile and flew past Talon's ear so close he felt the wind. With a whoop he gave chase, the boy yelling and screaming advice right behind him, their horses extended at a fierce gallop. The ball bounced once and then Talon connected with a lazy strike that lofted it high into the air. There it was, flying like a bird over the opposition goal posts in a sudden silence from the crowd. Then they roared. The supporters of Abbas went wild, screaming and waving and hugging each other, while those supporters of Bahir glowered and swore; money changed hands once more.

Haytham rode alongside Talon and embraced him with tears streaking down his sweaty, dust-caked face. Talon laughed, slapped the youngster on the back, and grinned at Abbas and the others as they gathered around to congratulate him.

"We have won the game my friends," Abbas said with satisfaction. "But they still have to blow the trumpets, so we must fight on till then."

Talon almost missed the moment when danger threatened. His glance backwards told him that something bad was about to take place from the intent faces of two of the better players on Bahir's team, who now ignored the ball altogether and rode very hard in intercepting lines towards Abbas, who had not noticed them.

Talon twitched his reins and sat deep. Rakhsh responded well. He promptly sat on his haunches and turned so fast Talon had to grip hard with his thighs to prevent himself being left behind. He never took his eyes off the two men, who were now riding on a collision course with Abbas, who in turn was getting ever closer to Talon. Abbas shouted something to Talon, but Talon just pointed with his stick at the men.

Realization dawned on Abbas's face, but it was too late. The men crashed into his horse, which staggered from the force. Talon had to haul Rakhsh out of the way as the three men careened past in a thunder of hooves. Rakhsh sat back on his heels, then jumped into a gallop to catch up, and Talon was able to race alongside the man on Abbas's right and engage him, but it was still too late to prevent what happened next. The men had planned it well. The riders were still close enough to the main party of polo players to be unnoticed by anyone watching from the sidelines. The two attackers took full advantage of this fact.

Inevitably, because one of the riders was riding across its path, Abbas's horse stumbled and began to go down. As he sensed his horse falling, Abbas made to get his feet out of the stirrups and prepared to dive and roll, his only defense in these circumstances. However, the men on his left and right both struck at his neck and head from either side. His horse somersaulted and Abbas was not able to get free in time. Talon watched in horror as time seemed to slow and Abbas was carried beneath the falling body of the horse. He did not scream. He could not. His body was crushed under the weight of the horse that lay there for seeming endless moments before finally it rolled clear and staggered to its feet to stand shaking, its reins trailing and its saddle askew, leaving Abbas lying in a huddle on the ground.

Both the men who had carried out the attack reined in fast and leapt off their horses to run back to the still prone body of Abbas. But Talon was faster; he jumped off Rakhsh at the gallop and landed at a run next to Abbas. He halted a couple paces in front of the prone body. He knew they were coming back to finish Abbas off and he needed those vital seconds it would take for Bilal to come to his assistance and stop them from completing their work. His heart pounding, and his breath rasping with the effort, he braced himself for the fight to come.

The men hesitated, but then with a muttered curse they came on. One drew a knife from his sash and held it low along his thigh as they moved towards him. Talon was aware of the eerie quiet that had befallen the crowd. People were aware that Abbas, the nobleman, had crashed and had seen, despite the dust, how the horse had carried him down. But the events happening on the ground were still obscured by the pall of dust hanging over the area.

Talon reached into his boot and pulled out a long thin knife which he held low in front of him. Silently he faced the men; then to his relief he heard hooves behind him, and Bilal called out, "Stay there, Suleiman, watch them. I will be with our Lord Abbas."

He heard Bilal's sharp intake of breath as he knelt by Abbas.

"Dear Allah, I beg your mercy for my master... please...!" he muttered.

The two men in front of Talon hesitated, as though trying to decide what to do, but it seemed to occur to them that to try anything now in front of the huge crowd and the sultan himself would be insane, so they shrugged, shook their heads and remounted their horses. They rode off towards Bahir, who had stopped his horse about forty yards away and was watching the situation through narrowed eyes. The men rode up to him and there was a muttered conference, then at a gesture from Bahir, the men rode off the field as though they did not want to be seen any more.

Talon watched the men leave through red-rimmed eyes, and he resolved to remember their faces. He turned back to Bilal. "Is he alive, Bilal? Have you checked to see if he is breathing? Do not move him. You must not move him...do you hear me?" he said urgently.

Bilal grunted acknowledgement, then he gasped and said, "I think he lives, Suleiman, but I fear the worst. Something is badly wrong."

Talon turned and knelt by Abbas. Bilal was right, something was dreadfully wrong with the way Abbas lay on the ground and Talon felt a cold sweat form on his brow. Abbas's body was twisted unnaturally, sprawled in such a way that Talon was sure his back was broken. The last time he had seen this kind of thing had been in Isfahan, a long time ago. In all probability it was a fatal injury. He remembered to check for a pulse, put his ear to Abbas's chest and listened with relief to the faint rasping of breath, but the man was still unconscious. There was blood trickling from his nose and that worried Talon. He knew it might mean a ruptured lung.

He was not aware that the sultan himself had run onto the field and was standing nearby, silently watching. Those gathered around were on their knees. Talon, still kneeling, spoke in a loud voice, "He lives, but we will kill him if he is not placed very carefully on a wood board the length of his body. Someone go, get one, we cannot move him before that."

He glanced up to see a figure leaning over him. As the sun was behind him, Talon could not tell who it was.

"You there, get me a plank, it is the only thing that will save my lord's life," he said.

The man nodded and said. "It will be as you command."

He began to issue orders to people all around. Too late Talon realized that he had been talking to the sultan. "My...My lord! I did not know it was you...the sun," he stammered.

Sal Ed Din placed his hand on his shoulder and said. "You are a loyal and it would seem a competent servant of your lord, who is very important to me. I shall ensure that your wishes are carried out. My very own physicians will take him into their care at once. *Insha'Allah* he will live?"

Talon nodded. "He might live, my lord, but I think his back is broken, and perhaps more than that. We have to have the best physicians, and much help from Allah."

The sultan gave a sharp intake of breath at the news, but then men came running with a large wide panel and laid it on the ground. Talon, hoping he was doing the right thing, directed them as to how they should lift Abbas and place him on the panel, and then he instructed them to tie him down, so that his body was immobilized. He then bowed very low to the sultan and followed the men off the maidan towards a palanquin that would carry Abbas to the palace of the sultan.

Talon did not hear the announcement that declared Abbas the victor, but the shouts of applause from the crowd told him this was so. He left the organization of the horses and the remainder of the team to Bilal. At his side now was Panhsj, who wore a ferocious scowl of worry and anxiety at what he had witnessed from the sidelines.

He held Talon's horse for him, and they mounted together to follow the palanquin. As they rode, Talon told him what he had seen, and what he thought of the situation.

"I am still unsure as to why they would try to kill him on the field, Panhsj. Why there, in public, when all they had to do was to kill him somewhere quiet with no one watching?"

"You did not know this, Suleiman, but Bahir and his dog-eating scum tried to kill our master and myself while we were on our way back from the southern campaign. They did not succeed, so I suppose they wanted to do it here and cover it as an accident."

"There are far easier ways to kill a man than on the Polo field, Panhsj," Talon said quietly, "and look, they might have crippled him, but he still lives."

There was something else that eluded him, but he was exhausted and just wanted to make sure that Abbas was safe with a physician who knew what he was about before he went back for a bath and rest.

"I shall stay with him when we get to the palace of the sultan." Panhsj leaned over and placed his dark hand on Talon's shoulder and gripped it. "I saw you hold those two men at bay after the accident, if that is what it was. I believe you saved his life by doing that." Panhsj was looking hard at Talon, his black eyes fierce, but for the first time with a warmth that had hitherto been missing.

"Perhaps, but if his back is broken, my lord Abbas might not live much longer in any case. It is in God's hands now," Talon said in a resigned tone.

"You could have let them kill him, Suleiman. You might have gained your freedom by letting him die, but you did not. I have been untrusting of you, because I think there is more to you than meets the eye. However, after what I have witnessed, I believe that you are an honorable man." He held out his hand to be clasped by a bemused Talon. They gripped hard and Talon smiled.

"I would prefer to have you as my friend, Panhsj. I am glad it is now so. It is my feeling that our master has more than one enemy and that the attack on him today was meant to be seen as an accident," he mused. "But Panhsj, I do not know for what reason. One thing is for sure, we must make sure that he is never left unattended, as they may try to come back and finish him off."

Panhsj nodded grimly. "I shall guard him day and night, you can be sure of that, Suleiman." His face was furrowed with worry.

"We will go and see that he is with the physicians, and then you can stay with him if you want to. I am sure the sultan will make sure he is well guarded. I shall have to tell our lady of the accident and try to reassure her as to his condition."

"That will not be easy," Panhsj commented. "Watch out for that pig, the eunuch. He will seize the opportunity to be even more of a bully once he hears."

Later, after they had seen Abbas into the care of two physicians, Talon rode Rakhsh slowly back to the palace where he discovered that news had preceded him and the whole place was in an uproar. He left Rakhsh at the stables to be looked after by a syce and the eager Haytham, who took him away to be fed and watered. Talon placed his hand on the boy's shoulder before he led the horse away.

"You played a good game, Haytham. You helped us to win."

The boy nodded in silence. He was devastated by the event, but proud also.

Talon stroked Rakhsh on the nose before parting and murmured praise. He had been impressed with the bravery of the horse. As though he understood, Rakhsh pushed at his chest with his nose.

After seeing to the other mounts, Bilal came over to clasp Talon on the shoulder.

"Thank you, Suleiman. How did you leave him?"

"In the sultan's palace along with the sultan's own physicians and a very dangerous looking Panhsj guarding him. It is in Allah's hands and those of the physicians, but if it is as I fear, I do not know what they can do for him." He looked up at Bilal from under his lowered brow.

"We were right; they were trying to harm, even to kill him, Bilal. I do not as yet know why, but I shall find out, *Insha'Allah*. When I do..." he left the rest unsaid.

"You should be the one to go and tell our lady, Suleiman. I do not know how to do this thing." Bilal had tears in his eyes. "Can you do this?"

Talon nodded reluctantly. "We have to tell her...yes, I shall tell her."

He made his way slowly towards the palace across the garden in the dusk, oblivious of the many crickets and the few cicadas in the trees overhead. He was exhausted, and his head ached from the blow he had received. He wiped at the line of dried blood he felt on his forehead with the tail of his turban. His mouth felt dry; he was not looking forward to this. He could hear the clamor of weeping and crying from within the building, even as he crossed the garden.

Inside the palace there was pandemonium. The servants were running about wringing their hands and wailing, while Chisisi was shouting and laying about him with his cane trying to restore some kind of order. His henchmen were following his example, but they merely added to the general chaos.

When Talon made his entrance, Chisisi rounded on him and, forgetting himself, shouted in his eagerness to hear some news.

"Suleiman, at last there you are! Where have you been? You must give me news of our master immediately, as I have to take it to my Lady upstairs."

"I am here to speak to my Lady, directly, upon the orders of my master," Talon lied.

"But I am to take the news to the ladies. You cannot possibly go near them. It would not be right!" the eunuch shouted. He glared pompously at Talon.

Talon noticed a movement above them on the mezzanine. It was Lady Khalidah, heavily veiled, who stood at the head of the stairs looking down. Behind her were at least a dozen other women crowding the rail, staring curiously down at him.

Accompanied by two female servants, Khalidah began to walk down the stairs, placing her hand on the wall for support as she did so. As she came closer, Talon noticed that she seemed weak and shaken. He made a move to come forward to support her, but the eunuch stepped in and barred his way. When she reached the bottom step, Khalidah stopped, and from a distance of four paces she whispered,

"Suleiman, you have come from my husband?"

"I have, my Lady, and ...he lives."

Khalidah swayed and would have fallen had not two female servants rushed to her assistance and led her to a carpeted area near the far wall where there were cushions. She settled down on one and motioned Talon to approach.

Chisisi made to protest, but a sharp gesture from Khalidah silenced him. The room was so quiet that Talon imagined a feather would have been heard falling.

She looked up at Talon.

"You say he is alive...we heard that he had died on the Polo field."

He looked at her with her two servants kneeling nearby, the rich hangings on the walls and the lights of the oil lamps illuminating her pale forehead. Over the veil he could see her eyes huge and dark in the lamplight.

He went forward and down on one knee before her. "My lady, I have seen him, and he is alive...but very badly wounded from the accident with his horse."

She gave a stifled sob and her shoulders slumped as though a great weight had fallen upon her. "Tell me what happened, and do not spare me the truth, Suleiman," she commanded. Her eyes stared straight into his.

# Chapter 14

# A Visit

Two days later, in Bahir's palace, the men who had plotted the downfall of Abbas met once again. It was late evening. The meeting was tense and not at all cordial.

Al Muntaqim was coldly furious, and broke all etiquette by ignoring the usual greetings and customary expressions of good will. He made sure Bahir knew it.

"Is it that you and your men are utterly incompetent? Or do you have a death wish of your own?" he snarled at Bahir, who was already unsettled. Now his face paled.

"I...I don't know what you mean. My men would have had him if that cursed bodyguard of his had not come in between...with his knife ready," he stammered and then, offended he said, "No one is allowed to bring weapons onto the field, and yet there he was with a long knife, threatening my men. They could not get near Abbas, and then his team was in the way, stopping my men from finishing him off." His confidence returned and he almost shouted.

"By the Prophet, I do not know what else we could have done, other than to cut him down in front of the sultan and the whole army combined, in plain sight. It was your stupid idea anyway. We should have sent an assassin after him while he was hunting, or some such thing."

Bahir stopped, fearing he might have gone too far. He glanced at the poet who was seated nearby and noticed that he had paled at his temerity. No one spoke to Al Muntaqim in that manner.

Trying to calm things the poet stuttered, addressing Bahir. "That man's name... the one who stopped your men. He only goes by Suleiman...this is on everyone's lips."

"Men have died playing chogan. It is not that unusual," Umarah bleated. "Why did Abbas have to survive?"

Al Muntaqim glared at them. "Neither of you seems to understand that to kill him in public, or even assassinate him some dark night, would set in motion an enquiry we might not survive!" he shouted, the veins on his neck standing out in rage.

"Calm yourself, my friend," Bahir said, raising both hands. "We have had a setback, that is all. However, we must finish the work soon or we might find it harder to complete, once Abbas regains his health. If he does."

Al Muntaqim thought for a few long moments, took a deep breath and visibly regained his composure. There was a long silence. Then he said, "You are right, Bahir. Besides, he did not really survive it. I have heard that his back is broken, and he will be a cripple for life. He may even die from that alone." He continued with low intensity in his voice. "But he must be finished off. Alive he can still command respect and obedience from his men, who are still here in Cairo; and very soon we will need the ones who do not go to Yemen subdued and under our control. Time is not on our side so we must find a way to ensure that he seems to die from his injuries. There is no time to waste; we have to set the events in motion very soon."

"I shall send someone to do it," Bahir stated, trying to regain some control of the discussion.

"No! By Allah you shall not," Al Muntaqim barked. "This time I shall take care of this. You have tried and failed to kill him twice. I shall deal with it in my way." He glared at Bahir, his former anger resurfacing.

Bahir sat back as though struck. His face reddened. He dared not contradict this dangerous man. He glanced at the poet for support, but that man studiously ignored him.

"We cannot get near to Abbas at present. He is well guarded in the sultan's palace and under constant watch. I tried to pay him a visit...to ascertain his state, you understand, but that Nubian of his stands there like a great black pillar of wrath," Umarah said plaintively. "He does not even move, but his expression and his eyes are terrible to see. As Allah is my witness, I could not move past him. His glare seems to penetrate a man's soul and I would not want to be in his hands should he decide I was trying to hurt his master." Umarah was actually wringing his hands.

Al Muntaqim shot him a disdainful look.

"Of course we will not do anything while he is with the sultan, but when he is moved back into his own palace...we will deal with him then. *I* will deal with him."

"After this, his palace will be like a fortress," Bahir said, deferentially this time. "We will never get anyone in there."

"There are many ways to enter a man's stronghold without beating down his doors, but I do not intend to send a stranger into the palace, not at first anyway. I intend to find someone within who can be motivated by gold. Everyone has their price.

"Does our Lord Abbas not have a very beautiful wife?" Al Muntaqim asked no one in particular.

"You could say that," Bahir agreed reluctantly. He did not want to look at Al Muntaqim.

"It is doubtful that our friend can perform his marital duties any more, wouldn't you say?" Al Muntaqim inquired softly. "Does not the thought of this beautiful woman going to waste upset you?"

Bahir stared at him. "By my ancestors," he breathed. "Do you mean...?" He left the rest of the sentence unsaid.

Al Muntaqim nodded. "The takings will be ours when the time comes. But first we must deal with Abbas. After that, you can send as many people into the house as you like, because the sultan will be away and unable to stop you." Then his lips parted in a lascivious leer and hissed, "It is that little boy of his who must not live to inherit...but first I want to stroke his smooth young body."

"I would prefer to have a handsome young man than a small boy," Umarah commented with a nervous laugh, raising his eyebrows at Bahir.

Neither of the other two thought it strange that Al Muntaqim wanted a boy. It was not uncommon for boys to be part of the amorous life of a nobleman, and Abbas's son would make fine sport until he was no longer wanted.

Bahir announced it was time for refreshments. He clapped his hands and the door opened. Servants brought in wine in silver cups and an array of food.

"I shall drink to your success, my friend," Bahir said, without sincerity.

* * * * *

Talon walked up to the beggar boy Kontar. After dropping a small coin in the boy's bowl as though he were just a passerby, he murmured, "I need to see Mukhwana, Kontar. There is a problem and I need help."

"Come back this evening, Suleiman. That was a fine game of chogan you played. I was betting on you," Kontar whispered with a grin, and then louder he called after Talon's retreating back, "May Allah bless you, my lord, for your generosity."

The boy pushed himself up the wall, and then with the aid of his crutch he began to hobble off into the gloom of the souk.

Talon was taken before Mukhwana that evening, and this time it was a very different meeting. The fat man with one eye greeted him as an old friend, and he was given polite greetings by the other men about the place. Talon could have sworn that not one of them had moved an inch from their positions since he was last there.

After he had been accorded and had given the lengthy courtesies that were part of the Egyptian custom, he was invited to be seated and again offered coffee, which he sipped politely. He liked the bitter taste of the strong black liquid.

"Well, my young teacher-warrior, your name is now on the lips of many in the streets of Cairo. Did you know?"

Talon looked at him in surprise.

"Oh yes, Suleiman. You see, the whole world knew of the grudge that existed between Bahir and your master. The chogan game has been talked about in fine detail since your master fell, and one thing has stood out. For those of the crowd who could see, it was clear that you saved what is left of his life. Apart from scoring some nice goals, that is." Mukhwana grinned. "I lost money on your game. We thought your master would lose, because it is well known that Bahir, God damn him, had the better team. But there you were, scoring all over the place. I should be asking you for my money back."

He shook with laughter, followed by his companions, who began to snicker.

Talon wondered if the large man meant it, but then Mukhwana wiped his one eye and said, "But you gave the whore's son a beating, and that was good enough for me."

"I am sorry you lost money, Mukhwana, perhaps I can get some back for you in time, *Insha'Allah,*" Talon said with an insincere grin. "But I am here to make a serious request of you, if you will hear me?"

"Speak, Suleiman...I think I shall call you the Hawk. They are dangerous and some even have green eyes."

"I need to know if I can come to you for help."

"You want help now?"

"No, but I might one day, as I fear for my lord and in particular for his lady and her children. I do not trust the eunuch who works there, or his men; and Abbas's mother does not know me and will not listen to a simple slave."

"What is worrying you, Suleiman? You do not look like someone who is afraid of anything."

"Treachery I fear, but I do not know from where it will come, from within or from without. I am sure of this: my master is in very real danger. They did try to kill him on the field. I ...I just sense that we, the whole family, are not out of danger, Mukhwana. I will pay for information from the street," Talon added.

"Yes, you will pay me something for my help, but I like you, Suleiman, and will try to help you. Kontar will be part of the messenger route, but there will be another beggar or two, near to your gates from hence forth. You must pay them a coin once in a while when you leave the palace and pass along anything you need me to hear. I shall use them to pass you information if I hear anything."

Talon thanked Mukhwana and left with his escort, who out of habit blindfolded him on the way out, as they had on the way in. Talon did not feel it necessary to tell them that he thought he knew the way by now.

* * * * *

That evening, he and Bilal talked about the situation as they sipped coffee and ate tiny sweet cakes brought by his woman.

"We have more than one enemy besides Bahir, Suleiman. Did you know that?"

"No, I did not know that, Bilal. Who are the others?" Talon responded.

"They are the people I talked about on the boat, my friend. They asked our master once to join them in an attempt to depose our sultan's uncle, and he refused. I do not know the details but they, whomsoever they are, have excluded him ever since from their company. Abbas only serves the sultan," Bilal said. He checked himself with emotion in his voice. "As only he could."

"Do you know any names?" Talon asked.

"No, I do not, but they exist, and may Allah curse them for what they have done," Bilal said.

"Have you sent a message to your brother, Malek?" Talon asked.

"Yes, and I have told him of what you did, Suleiman. I warned him to be on his guard, as we do not know where they will strike next."

It was late when they parted to go to their beds, but Talon did not go to his that night.

He slipped out of the servants' quarters, sped across the gardens and over the back wall into the darkness of the street. Having paused long enough to check that he was not being followed, he began to hurry along the dark, narrow, and now deserted streets of the city until he realized that he was hurrying and making noise. He slowed and continued in silence.

His intent was to find the house of Bahir and discover a way in. Mukhwana had given good instructions, but even so, it took an hour of walking and missing streets before he eventually arrived in view of the gates of that man's palace.

Mukhwana had described the palace accurately enough. From the outside it looked similar to most of the rich palaces in the same area, with high walls and a view of the top floor and its shuttered windows; only this one had a high arched gate that distinguished it from the other more modest palaces. Although the walls were high, Talon decided he could climb them using the trees that were growing along the street. Their foliage also provided good cover to allow him to slip past any guards who might be above the walls, looking down.

He moved along some narrow alleys towards the back of the palace to where he supposed the stables would be, along with the servants' quarters. Each step was now dangerous, because he did not know the layout and he could be discovered at any time. Rats scuttled out of the way as he slipped through the darkness.

The rear walls presented no real difficulty; the guards were conversing at another corner and inattentive. Soon he was in the shadows of the barn that housed the horses. The familiar smell of horses and the midden heap was strong in the still night air. He stared towards the main buildings across a wide space that looked like a neglected garden, where a thick profusion of stringy shrubs and small trees grew uncared for. Evidently Bahir was not enamored of the wonders of nature, he thought drily.

He listened to the horses as they munched their food or stamped about in their stalls. Some looked out across the wide path in front of their stables. Although he knew the horses were aware of him, as some turned their heads in his direction, none of them nickered or made any noise to indicate that they were disturbed by his presence.

Moving swiftly from shrub to tree, Talon traversed the wasted gardens and approached the buildings of the main house. His mind flickered to the last time he had done this kind of night raid with his brother Reza, long ago in Hamadan. It would be fatal to be caught; he could expect no mercy, rather a high profile execution and a very painful one at that. He concentrated.

He was dressed in dark clothing and had his face covered, only exposing his eyes; he wore no shoes and carried only his knife. He was invisible to the casual observer, and just as well, for he heard a sound ahead of him and promptly faded into a scrubby bush.

Two night guards passed so close he could have reached out and touched them, but the men were talking softly to one another and were not paying attention, and certainly had no idea there was an intruder so close by.

Talon moved on silently. He decided he must find a way to the second floor of the multi-storied building to the living apartments of Bahir, and the only way to do this was to climb a tree and get from there to the narrow balcony that ran the length of several windows, and then into the building. At least the windows over the gardens did not have the fretwork boxing that the ones over the street had.

Talon took great care not to rustle leaves as he climbed the tree and gained access to the balcony. He glanced back. From here he had a good view of the unkempt gardens and of the stables. He also noted how many sentries patrolled the area.

Near to him some shuttered windows had the glow of lamps from within. One attracted his attention as he heard the tinkle of feminine laughter and the sound of people talking loudly from inside.

On his stomach he moved along the wooden floor, keeping his head well out of sight of any casual observer from below, until he came to the shuttered window. He lay there listening for a while, trying to make out the words of the conversation. It was difficult as there were several voices speaking at the same time. Lifting his head he put his eye to a chink in the shutters. It was clear from that short review that Bahir was not among the people in the room. He slithered along the entire balcony on his belly, checking each of the lit windows, but none of these rooms held the man he sought. He lay back against the wall to think.

To gain access to the rest of the house was a simple matter. He eased the shutter of one of the dark windows open enough to slip into the room. Every muscle tense, he crouched below the window sill and listened once again.

He spent the next half hour exploring the house, moving like a wraith, noting the men who were guarding certain rooms and the pattern of activity in the kitchens, even at this late hour. His eye fell on two men standing outside a heavy wooden door, they were clearly on guard. They appeared to be very alert. Then they were joined by a huge, well-muscled man with a diminutive servant behind him holding a tray of food. They snapped to attention, spears at the ready.

The door was opened and the big man pushed the servant inside. Talon decided that this room had to be his objective and he cast about for another entrance. He slipped along a corridor that seemed to run parallel with the room itself and discovered a deep recess in the wall. It was well out of the way and if he had not been so eager to find places to hide, he might well have passed it by. It was more of an alcove with a door. He gingerly tried it, and it opened. The space beyond continued into a short arched anteroom with a heavy curtain about eight feet beyond.

Praying that he would not be discovered in this trap, Talon cautiously moved towards the curtain, and paused. He heard voices and listened. The curtain was not fully pulled against the wall, so without disturbing it he could peer through the gap. He saw three men in the room. The light was dim and there were only a few oil lamps. These were placed in front of the men who were seated comfortably on cushions only twenty feet from him.

He took note of their shadowy shapes and tried to study their features which the poor light of the lamps did not reveal clearly. It was not hard to recognize Bahir, but Talon had never seen the other two before. The man who had his back to Talon was lean and strong. His loose clothing did not hide his strong physique, thick neck and broad shoulders. On his head he wore the loose turban that soldiers wore when not on duty.

The other one was a plump looking fellow dressed in fine silks that glistened in the lamplight as he moved. He sported a straggly beard and wore a huge turban. At one time one of the others addressed him as 'Poet.' Talon resolved to remember the title and the face.

Bahir himself was dressed in rich, elegant robes and a large turban. The light flashed off the many rings on his fingers. Talon was disappointed. He had hoped to approach Bahir alone. But with the other two so near, and sentries outside, he knew he could not possibly kill Bahir and get away with it.

The men were eating with their fingers from a silver tray and drinking from silver goblets. He recognized the smell of baked chicken and boiled cabbage. He could also smell the distinct odor of palm wine. As the men were deep in conversation and oblivious of his presence, he took a good look around the room. Talon paid great attention to the furnishing of the room and its layout, while listening for any clues from what the men were saying. He heard the name of the sultan's brother mentioned. The speaker had a strong voice, enough that Talon caught bits. "Tariq is leaving within a week for Yemen; it will be time..."

The same man continued but lowered his voice, making it harder for Talon to distinguish the words. "The officers and men are ready for my command...Abbas...."

Talon was instantly alert, but although he strained his ears, he could not hear more. At this point the man with his back to Talon shifted around, and Talon caught his profile. He determined to remember the face, as this man seemed to be the leader.

He wished he could get closer because they talked in low tones, but it would have been fatal to try. There was one other snippet of the conversation which intrigued him. Bahir was talking this time, but once again he was speaking almost in whispers and Talon had to strain his ears to catch the words, "...you are a man of letters, so you would be able to get close to Bakir, Abdul-Jalil. He must be..."

The words seemed to be addressed to the richly dressed plump man seated next to Bahir. At least Talon could see him clearly. He spent a half hour watching and straining to hear their conversation. His instincts told him it was time to leave, but then Bahir clapped his hands and a servant appeared like a djinn from the entrance to the other doorway, bowing very low and asking in a soft voice what his master wished.

"Bring me the women, Ali; it is time to entertain my guests." Bahir had raised his voice to issue the command. The servant vanished and Talon was about to leave the way he had come in when he heard voices outside of his hiding place. He heaved himself up onto a narrow ledge as three women tripped into the darkened anteroom. The servant was herding them along with a scolding voice.

"Hurry, you stupid whores, the master is impatient and wants to show you off to his guests. Make sure that you dance well, or you shall be whipped. Stop giggling, and watch your step. Do not speak. They don't want to hear you. They only want to see you."

Talon felt movement of the air as the girls went past, now silent. He caught the scent of cheap musk and oil, followed by old onion on the breath of the servant. He could not see far from his hiding place, but as the curtain was drawn, he glimpsed the three half-naked women. They were young, with nubile bodies that had been oiled under the diaphanous veils they wore with little else for covering.

* * * * *

Much later, while it was still dark, he slipped over the peripheral wall into the area of the dung heap for the horses of Abbas's palace and went to his own room. He began to crawl into

196

bed just as the cock crowed, heralding the dawn, even though it was still dark.

His night, however, was not over, as he found someone in his bed. It was Lamya. She awoke and sleepily muttered something into his ear. His tiredness evaporated. He was seeking release from the tension of the day and welcomed the girl into his arms. She was eager for his love and responded to his caresses with tiny moans and sighs. Lamya had a firm young body that was very quick to awaken. It was not long before they took from one another what they needed that night. Exhausted and spent by the time dawn began to light the room, Lamya left him, disappearing silently back to the room she shared with the other maids.

# Chapter 15

# A Story in the Garden

Talon arrived at the entrance to the main building where he met his students every morning ready for the day's classes. He was very tired but determined not to show it.

Jasmine and Kazim had their maids in attendance, and together they walked off to the garden, to the place that Talon had chosen. It was a quiet location near a small fountain where water bubbled out of the ground into a low wide earthenware pot and then trickled over its edges into a wider but shallow pond. Water lilies spread on the surface and small clumps of young papyrus grew out of the water at the edge. A few golden carp drifted about the depths of the dark water, their red and metallic scales sometimes glittering as the sunlight reflected. Dragonflies swooped in and out of the reeds, just touching the surface of the water and then darting away again.

Occasionally, a slim black cat that Jasmine had named Sultan would keep them company. He would sit at the edge of the pond watching the fish, and once in a while would tentatively dip his paw into the surface of the water, as though to find out whether he could catch one.

The shade of the sycamore overhead softened the fierce sunlight and today they were blessed with a cool breeze that found its way, like caressing fingers, into the garden, rustling the dry leaves of the bushes and the palm fronds above.

It was hard for Talon to concentrate. He kept yawning, and the children, ever sensitive to the mood of their adults, reacted by quarreling.

At one point Jasmine turned to Suleiman and asked, "Suleiman, why cannot women sit at meals with their husband?"

"Because they are women and silly; and girls are especially," Kazim said contemptuously, smirking at his sister, who poked her tongue out at him.

With an effort of concentration, Talon thought about it. He could see that she was in earnest, and it demanded a serious answer.

It was clear that while he had not been paying attention, the two of them had been squabbling.

"Kazim, please mind your manners, a Lord must always be polite...especially to his family," Talon admonished him for the hundredth time.

He turned to Jasmine, who was glaring at her brother, her eyes narrowed with anger.

"Your father ate often with your mother while we were at Fayoum, and their conversations went on for many hours from what I can tell. This I know, because Malek talked about how much respect and love your father has for your mother."

Kazim replied with a dismissive wave of his hand. "I shall be a warrior and ride beautiful horses like Rakhsh into war. I shall have no time for women or for wives."

Jasmine glowered at him in silence, but then her gaze went down the pathway which led back to the house.

"Mamma!" She called and leapt to her feet to rush to embrace her stepmother. Talon jumped to his feet and bowed low to Khalidah who approached them, her hand touching the petal of a flower as she passed. She seemed to enjoy the scent of a rose as she bent to it. Tamir, the ancient, wizened chief gardener, was hovering nearby, his bald head bobbing on his skinny wrinkled neck as he nodded his agreement with her wishes. Khalidah was accompanied by a maid servant, also veiled, who kept a few paces behind.

Even under the veil that only covered the lower part of her face, he could see how tired she was. Her huge eyes had dark circles under them and there was a pinched look between her eyebrows that he had not seen before. She greeted each of the children with a gentle embrace before turning to Talon.

He received that direct gaze from Khalidah that, despite his self control, made his blood move faster in his veins.

"Master Suleiman, I greet you. How are the children doing with their lessons? I have not joined you for some time; forgive my negligence."

Talon smiled politely. "Salaam, my Lady, may Allah preserve your health. You have had much else on your mind of late, but your children are doing well. We were discussing manners and how we should behave towards our family."

"Ah, I see...Kazim, does that mean that you were being reprimanded?" she asked with a twitch of a smile in her eyes, pretending to sound stern.

Kazim had the grace to look embarrassed; he looked down and nodded reluctantly. Khalidah smiled.

"Your tutor Suleiman can teach you much, my son; listen to him carefully. One thing you should know is that the sign of a great warrior is not only his fierceness in battle, but his kindness towards his family and servants. Your father is one such person, and therefore he has the loyalty of his men, who would die for him."

Kazim looked up at his mother with adoring eyes. "I shall, Mother." He glanced at his sister and at Talon from under his dark brows to see what their reaction might be. Talon pretended to look stern but had difficulty hiding his grin and had to look away.

"Suleiman, I have come not just to see my children but also in the hope that you would distract us with a story...perhaps one of those fables you know from Persia?" Khalidah asked politely, but to his ears it sounded more like a plea.

He bowed again. "I shall be happy to, my Lady."

The mood changed immediately. Jasmine clapped her hands and Kazim laughed with delight. They were going to be excused the arithmetic because their mother in her infinite power had persuaded the stern Suleiman with but a word to tell a story. Despite their pleas in past times he had been adamant about their lessons, only telling stories when he felt they had deserved it. While waiting for Khalidah to settle on a cushion and the children to sit close to her in the shade, he thought about what story to tell.

"Today I shall tell you the story of King Solomon and the Queen of Yemen, whose name was Balkis."

He waited until the fidgeting stopped and his audience was listening with attention. Even Khalidah seemed for the moment to have put her cares on hold and waited with anticipation on her face.

"There was once a king called Solomon, who, as everyone knows, spoke the language of of all creatures, including birds.

"He traveled about his kingdom on a magic carpet, and one day he flew over an ants' nest and heard the ants complaining about the number of flying carpets and humans in the area and telling the other ants to get underground and out of the way. Solomon guided his carpet down in such a way as not to disturb the ants. He was hungry and thirsty and needed water. He always travelled with the king of the hoopoes, for he was very good at finding water."

"You always bring the hoopoes into the stories, Suleiman," protested Kazim, who preferred a story about battles.

"Kazim, do not interfere with the story teller while he is in the middle. Behave yourself or you can leave," Khalidah said sharply. Kazim subsided and Jasmine smirked at him, upon which he poked his tongue out at her.

After a brief pause Talon continued. "As I was about to say, the king of the hoopoes is there with King Solomon because he is very clever at finding water and cool places to rest.

"The king of the hoopoes set off in a hurry to look and see what he could do for Solomon, and in the process discovered some beautiful gardens. While investigating them he met up with another hoopoe, a female, who told him the gardens belonged to Queen Balkis of the country of Yemen, which, as you have probably surmised, was a very long way from the king's palace. This female hoopoe persuaded the visiting hoopoe to tarry, but while he was enjoying his time in the gardens, King Solomon was becoming impatient and tired of waiting. He asked his eagle to go and find the hoopoe and bring him back with water, as he was thirsty. He was becoming upset at being left in the desert along with a bunch of grumbling ants for company."

Talon waved his arm to the sky and continued.

"The eagle soared up into the sky and finally, after flying for a while, with his long sight he noticed far away the king of the hoopoes flying back. He tried to catch the bird in his talons but the clever bird evaded him and managed to land next to King Solomon, to whom he displayed great homage.

"This mollified the king somewhat, and he asked the hoopoe where he had been. The hoopoe told him about the beautiful gardens and the luxurious palace of the Queen. He also slyly told the king of her lovely bed of silver, the frame of which was encrusted with jewels and gold, and whispered that her people were unbelievers who worshipped the sun and the moon.

"The king's curiosity was piqued so he decided to send a letter to the Queen via the king of the hoopoes, who took it all the way back to Yemen, tightly held in its beak. This was done, and the resident lady hoopoe advised him that the best thing he could do to attract the Queen's attention was to deliver the letter to her bedroom window, and by the same token see for himself how beautiful she was.

"He did this and delivered King Solomon's letter. The Queen was curious about King Solomon, so she sent in return some curious gifts to test him. She sent the hoopoe to fly back with her message of good will and promises of gifts; those she dispatched by road.

"She promised to send some pierced and un-pierced precious stones in a casket and asked him to thread them all, without opening the boxes and without the aid of man or Djinn.

"She also decided to send four bricks of gold to show him how rich she was.

"Solomon received the messages of good will and the promises of gifts with interest, and then he issued orders.

"He told the Djinn to construct a long road of gold bricks all the way up to his palace, leaving space for only four bricks near his throne.

"The envoys from Queen Balkis of Yemen arrived and observed the road of gold with dismay and then fitted their four bricks into the space left for them."

"He must have been unbelievably rich!" exclaimed Kazim.

"It is my understanding that he was," Talon replied.

"Let him continue with the story," said Jasmine impatiently.

"Ah yes...well, the gifts were delivered to him. Solomon knew what was in the caskets, since he had been told to thread the jewels without the aid of man or Djinn, so he asked a worm to enter the caskets and bore holes through the remaining jewels, which it did. For its help, it was rewarded with the privilege of being forever able to live in trees, because the king gave him eternal rights to do so.

"Then the cunning king asked the humble maggot to go into the caskets and thread all the jewels, which it did; and upon being asked what it wanted for its reward, it said it wanted the right to live in fruit—which it has been doing ever since."

"Ugh!"

"Be quiet, my Kazim, I do not think Suleiman is finished yet," Khalidah gently admonished her son.

Talon had to suppress a grin.

"He ordered all the presents to be sent back to the Queen and told her to stop worshipping the moon and to convert her people, or he would slay them. However, when he arrived to enforce this ruling, he saw how beautiful she was, fell in love with her and married her, although he did insist upon the conversion of everyone in Yemen. She, clever woman that she was, managed to keep all the jewels and the gold. Peace be upon them."

Khalidah and Jasmine clapped happily, as did Kazim, but he was disappointed. "I was hoping there would be a battle or a hero, Suleiman," he said, pouting.

"Kazimi, my dearest," Khalidah said, "Suleiman was telling the story for the benefit of us all, and I thank you, Suleiman, for the telling of it." He had not seen her smile for a long time, but now she did, and some of her cares seemed to have left her brow—for the moment at least.

Talon bowed low as she rose and left with the children in tow.


Later that day, he practiced with his sword for over an hour till his arms ached and he was drenched in sweat. Bilal came by and challenged him playfully to sword practice and they sparred for another half hour, whereupon Bilal, who was himself now puffing and sweating, called a truce.

"I am still sore from the game, Suleiman. You do not seem to be sore at all," he complained with good humor.

"I am a little tired, Bilal, but I think I agree with you about our enemies. There are more people than Bahir who are involved. Do you know a man...?" he tried to describe the two men he had seen with Bahir without letting Bilal know where he had seen them. Bilal could not identify them.

Later that day a messenger arrived from the estate with a letter from Malek for Bilal and one for the lady Khalidah. After his failed attempt to deliver the letter directly to lady Khalidah that the eunuch intercepted, Bilal came back to Talon, shaking his head, and said, "I should have delivered the letter to my Lady, but I could not get past that scab and his cronies. They are becoming insufferable. One of these days...." He didn't finish the thought but his expression told Talon what he was thinking.

He opened the letter from Malek and read it to Talon.

"My brother sends his greetings and those of Khaldun and says that all is well at the Estate. Al Fayoum and the crops are doing well." He glanced up with a grin. "Max is improving well with his wound and is now able to practice swords with him and ride, although he still tires easily and must rest in the afternoons.

"I wonder if he has a servant girl to come and massage his aches," Bilal asked rhetorically with a wicked grin.

Talon let out his breath. Max was regaining his health; that was good news. He grinned back at Bilal. "And what if he is?"

Bilal snickered and continued in a more serious tone. "Malek also says that they have had no trouble from the quarter we mention, but there is great distress at what has happened. He wants to know if he should send more men."

"Do we not have half of Abbas's division here in Cairo with us now?" Talon asked.

"Indeed we do, Suleiman, and I am sure we could have more men if we should ask for them, but there is little enough room as it is, and they really belong to the sultan, may Allah preserve his soul, so we must be circumspect as to how many soldiers we ask for."

"Why do you say that, Bilal? Would the sultan, Allah protect him, not grant us enough to fill this compound should we need them? Is not Abbas one of his most favored officers...and especially now?"

Bilal looked up from the letter, his face serious. "I should think so, but have you not heard? The sultan intends to take an army and harass the Bedouin in the Negev because they are helping the

Frans against us, Allah damn them. His brother has taken a large part of the army south with him to Yemen, which leaves him dependent upon those who are left, and that includes the division that Abbas commands."

Talon was taken aback. Pieces of the puzzle were moving into place, but he could not quite fathom the pattern as yet.

"When does he intend to leave?" he asked.

"The officer who came to talk to me yesterday mentioned that the men were preparing for a move in less than two weeks," Bilal quickly replied.

"Then we have to have the master back here before then. Although I do not believe he is safe anywhere, it will be better here than in a deserted palace of the Sultan," Talon declared.

Bilal nodded. "We should visit the master soon, in any case. Perhaps we can also have audience with the sultan, and ask for Abbas's transfer."

They were interrupted by a servant, who announced to Bilal that they had a visitor. Lady Emushire requested his presence as an honorary guard while they entertained this male visitor.

Bilal glanced at Talon. "We have had a procession of visitors today; yet another one has come to commiserate with the lady of the house. I must hurry and look smart."

He hurried off, leaving Talon curious. He wandered towards the main building, making sure he did not run into Chisisi or his henchmen along the way. He was accosted by Lamya instead. She gave him a sultry look as she approached and kissed him in the cover of a pomegranate bush. He walked with her until she glimpsed Donkor, Chisisi's henchman, in the distance and made a face of disappointment.

"I must go. Suleiman, we must meet again...will you sit with me one evening and tell me the stories you tell the family?" she asked coyly before slipping off into the servants' quarters.

He grinned. "I will be happy to," he called after her.

He could see the visiting retinue as he came in sight of the gate. It was a strong guard of mounted men in rich livery of blue linen shirts, the sleeves edged with gold under their polished bronze plated jerkins. They now squatted in the shade of the walls while their good-looking horses were being watered by several of the syce.

"This must be an important visitor," he thought. But he did not see any other activity and did not want to incur the wrath, justified or otherwise, from the strident Chisisi, so he drifted off.

Later, when he and Bilal were alone again eating snacks and drinking tea, their duties for the day completed, they talked.

"Who was the grand visitor today?" Talon asked.

"A great nobleman of ancient family who came to pay his respects to our Lady Emushire and Lady Khalidah. He is famous for his fighting skills and is an important man in the army."

"But what is his name?" Talon persisted.

"I forgot to mention it... Kemosiri bin Jibade. He has been a friend of our master for years. They have fought in many of the same battles alongside the sultan. He actually wept in front of everyone assembled today. He offered to protect our lady from our master's many enemies until he is fully recovered. May Allah protect him and bless him for standing by our side in our hour of need," Bilal intoned with respect.

But then he switched stride and pointed at Talon, saying with a sly grin, "You know that Lamya likes you?"

Talon concentrated on his honey cake. "Bilal, I am a slave here, and it would be more than my life was worth to go after even another servant. That would really give Chisisi an excuse to punish me."

"Not in my eyes, you are not. I am sure that would not deter you if you were in earnest," Bilal remarked with a leer. "Do you not like her? Is she not very pretty?"

"She is very pretty, indeed," Talon agreed, rubbing his shoulder, "but is it not forbidden?"

"Only if you are caught, and I am on your side in any case. So even if they did catch you at it, with my intervention, should it be timely enough, they might only cut it off." Bilal roared with laughter at his own wit.

# Chapter 16

# Return

Two weeks later, Emir Abbas Abdul Azim Ibn Athir Faysal was brought back to his house. The palanquin that carried him was supported by four brawny Nubian slaves and was heavily protected by men of his own personal bodyguard. The sultan had granted permission for Bilal to have extra men, not only to guard Abbas on return, but also to remain on duty at his home.

"I think the sultan's preoccupation is now with the forthcoming expedition to the Negev and it seems to me that our master is no longer on the list of the sultan's priorities." Bilal grumbled to Talon as they made their way to the palace to accompany Abbas on his way back home.

Panhsj looked exhausted but pleased to see them. "He is awake, but you will not like what you see," he warned them.

Abbas was conscious and they found him lying flat and secured with fine padded cotton straps on the hard bed that was placed carefully on the palanquin. The physician Yazan Abdul-Hayy, a man well known for his skill in medicine, had argued against moving him at all. He fussed about in his silk robes, waving his slim, dark fingers in the air like some agitated praying mantis whenever he thought the servants carrying Abbas were being in the slightest bit clumsy. He berated them in his high-pitched voice, clearly frightened of increasing the damage to his patient as they jostled the injured man down the steps. He asked them to stop for a moment to give the patient a little respite.

Bilal approached Abbas and knelt in front of the platform. Abbas weakly held out his hand and whispered something to him that Talon did not catch. Talon realized that Abbas was paralyzed from the waist down and thus would never be able to move of his own accord again.

Bilal nodded, stood up and waved Talon over.

Abbas was gaunt, his eyes sunken in his dark features, but his will still burned in his eyes. He moved just a little and winced. Talon knelt in front of him and came closer to better hear his voice.

"Ah, there you are, Suleiman," Abbas whispered.

"My lord?"

"Panhsj told me that you saved my life," Abbas croaked.

"Allah was there to preserve your life, Master." He did not think he had done Abbas a favor, considering his condition, but he held his peace.

"You could have let them finish me. I shall not forget. Does my wife know?"

"Yes Lord, she knows. I could not lie to her."

Abbas sighed, and as though accepting the fact, he relaxed a little and closed his eyes. They lifted him in the palanquin and began the long slow journey to Abbas's home.

The entire household turned out to greet their master, and although the womenfolk, including Khalidah, were still out of sight, Talon was sure that they were watching from behind the intricate fretwork of the closed shutters known as *mashrabya* and saw everything that went on in the compound.

Chisisi and his henchmen were present to obsequiously bow, scrape and wail with feigned distress, while the palanquin was lowered down gently to the ground by the four slaves.

With great care, the slaves lifted the bed off the palanquin and carried the master into his house.

His eyes were shut as though sleeping, but Talon understood his pain and that it took Abbas all of his strength to endure being moved in this way. They brought him up the stairs onto the second floor, across the mezzanine, and finally to the large spacious bedroom he shared with his wife. There were whispers and even shocked comments on the number of men who now stood on that floor. These exclamations came from the assembled heavily veiled women, as they clustered in every corner of the wide space.

Khalidah ignored them and she in person met the procession at the head of the stairs. She gazed down on her husband with tears pouring down her cheeks, although she said nothing and simply laid a hand upon his shoulder. She nodded to the men to continue towards their bedroom.

There they laid the platform down before moving him onto a hard bed that had been especially constructed to prevent movement to his back but still allow him to rest. It was the best anyone could do, as there was no cure for his injury, other than perhaps time. Talon considered it a miracle that Abbas had survived even this long. He had been told by the palace physician that complications often followed a broken back, which appeared to be unrelated, and these were what killed the patient in the end.

Abbas groaned and opened his eyes wide with the pain of being jerked about. He caught sight of Khalidah leaning over him. He tried to raise his hand to her but was too weak.

She took his hand and kissed it and then kissed him on the forehead, unmindful of the watching crowd. The physician drove everyone out, leaving the two together for a moment, but he warned her not to tire Abbas. The last Talon saw of them that day was Khalidah crouched beside Abbas, talking to him and holding his hand cupped in hers.

It had been decided by his mother, Lady Emushire, that Abbas should be cared for in his own bedroom, accessible via the wide steps leading up from the ground floor to the mezzanine. This had created some difficulty at first with regard to men going into the private area of the household, but Khalidah had stepped in and insisted that a body guard and the three of Abbas's senior men would have access to the master while he was an invalid.

Her mother-in-law opened her mouth to protest, and indeed Chisisi said, "I think, my lady, you should reconsider. We never let the men into this area."

Khalidah rounded on him in cold fury, her eyes flashing. "If you ever contradict me again you can expect a whipping. Now get out of my sight!"

Both he and her mother-in-law had left in stunned silence.

Talon talked about it with Bilal later in the day, once the guards had been posted to Panhsj's satisfaction before he staggered off to bed for a long deserved rest.

"I am full of admiration for our mistress," Bilal said while they sipped tea in their favorite place by the stables in the shade of a fruit tree. "That Chisisi has been in charge here for so long, he thinks that he even can tell my Lady what to do."

"She has made an enemy of him, for sure," Talon said. "We have to watch him. If he harms her or the children…"

"Then he is a dead man!" Bilal said with finality. "I shall personally stab him to death with a blunt piece of wood."

"You will have to beat Panhsj and myself to the doing of it," Talon said with a grin.

He glanced over at Anyess swinging her hips as she walked away, having brought them some tea.

Bilal noticed the glance. "That one has taken a liking to you also, Suleiman. I think you should bed her and ease her itch, and perhaps your own…you have always been hard to read in that area, my young friend." He grinned at Talon's discomfort. "You do like women don't you?"

Talon went red. "Of course, Bilal, but, well, there hasn't been a lot of time for that recently, and we did talk about it before. First you tell me Lamya wants me, and now it is Anyess. Are you trying to get me in trouble?"

"Pshaw!" Bilal laughed. "Every one of the serving girls would hop into your bed at the snap of your fingers, Suleiman, even that fat old thing from down south, and I am sure that you know it. I, on the other hand, a decrepit old man, must beg favors from where and whom I can." He put on a plaintive voice.

Talon laughed outright at the lugubrious expression on Bilal's face and pointed his finger at him accusingly. "You? I have seen you fighting and playing chogan, so you are anything but decrepit, Bilal. I have no doubt that it is you who could have any one of them whenever you wanted, and probably do. What nonsense is this?"

Bilal leaned forward to pick up his tea cup, which looked small in his large fingers; he grinned over its edge as he took a sip. "Well…all right, but the one who did come to my bed asked me one evening if you preferred boys."

Talon had been sipping his tea but now he choked, and for several seconds he was coughing hard. Meanwhile, Bilal chuckled at his discomfiture and even offered to smack him on the back if he needed it. Talon glared at him.

"Well, it seems I have the answer...which one do you want me to send to you first?" Bilal said solicitously. He let out a huge fart with a relieved look on his face that turned into a beatific smile of satisfaction.

Talon was startled; it was so loud and sudden, his face registering his surprise.

"I felt I was pregnant, had to let it go," Bilal explained. "The food here is so strange; I miss the food at Fayoum. I don't trust the cook here. Allah be my witness, I think he is trying to poison us all."

Talon could not help it, he laughed. His affection for the big, bluff man, with his earthy sense of humor and appalling bad manners, continued to grow.

The conversation veered to how best to protect their master, from what Talon was not sure.

Bilal was uncertain too. "Suleiman, listen to me, he is a favorite of the sultan, who has given us men. Look around you at the number of them."

"There are ten more well-armed men loafing about the stables with the already sizeable group who came with us from the Fayoum."

Talon glanced over to where he had indicated with his thumb. The new men had settled down near the stables, making themselves as comfortable as possible for the duration of their stay. Cooking fires were lit and more food was being brought to them from the kitchens.

"They are even trampling some of the nearby gardens, which will annoy the old gardener Tamir no end when he sees the damage," Talon said, pointing this out to Bilal, who shrugged.

"Who would dare to attack us while we are under the protection of the sultan? At least while he is still here in residence, and with as many men as we have now?" Bilal continued.

"I know what you are saying, Bilal, but I am just not sure it is finished."

Bilal looked at him skeptically. "You might be right. We do not have much to go on, but I think he is safer here than in the Sultan's palace; especially as Salah Ed Din is leaving for the Negev next week, may Allah protect him as he battles those Frans, God damn them."

"Yes, God damn them." Talon smiled to himself, having fulfilled his self promise. "I agree with that, Bilal, and no, I do not have a good reason for worrying about it, other than that during the Polo game we both know they tried to kill him. Perhaps they have decided that he can do no harm to them now and will leave him be?"

Talon did not sound convincing to his own ears, but he could not tell Bilal what he had done several nights before. No one must know that he was a Fidai of the Assassins and that he could move like a shadow in other people's houses.

"In Allah's name, I hope so," Bilal said getting up. "I can see your young master heading this way, so I shall make my escape now." He grinned at Talon before he left.

"*My* young master?" Talon asked him.

Pretending not to see Kazim rushing down the path towards them, Bilal hurried back towards the stables, shouting orders and waving his arms at the troops, leaving Talon to get up and bow to Kazim, who arrived breathless, his face tear-streaked and desolate.

"Suleiman, I have seen father. It is terrible...! What are we going to do?" He choked, trying unsuccessfully to keep tears from flowing again.

Talon stood between the boy and the men who were beginning to stare curiously from the stable area. Some of them had never seen Kazim, but they knew of him. Talon said in a quiet but firm voice, "Kazim, hide your tears from the men. You are the young master while your father is ill. They must not see you cry." He tried not to sound too severe.

Kazim stared up at Talon with scared, wet eyes, but he listened. Wiping the tears away with his sleeve, he sniffed and straightened his shoulders.

"That is better. Now would you like to inspect your men?" Talon asked him.

Kazim stared at him in surprise but then gave a mute nod, and walked alongside Talon, who took him to the stables and introduced him to those men who were his father's, which gave Talon the opportunity to find out the names of the others who had arrived at the orders of the sultan. Bilal was forced to attend. He grimaced back at Talon, who winked. Bilal was not fooled; he understood.

Talon noticed that the men reacted well to seeing Kazim, who soon forgot his grief and began to enjoy the role as the young lord. The boy seemed to like meeting the men, who bowed elaborately to him as he was introduced and called praises down on the head of his father.

Later, while walking away, Kazim took Talon by the hand and looked up at him.

"Thank you, Suleiman. Allah protect you," he said. Releasing his hand, the boy ran the last few yards into the palace.

"Allah protect you too, young lord," Talon muttered, as he watched him go. He wondered how the mood was with Khalidah and Jasmine in that house of wailing women and shrieking eunuchs.

The sultan left that week, a little earlier than Bilal had anticipated, leaving a small garrison to man the Citadel and a few thousand regular soldiers behind. The city seemed quieter with the main body of the army now marching off to harass the southern reaches of the Kingdom of Jerusalem. Talon and Panhsj, who had by now recovered from his self-imposed lack of sleep while guarding his master, worried about the future.

"Did Bahir and his men go with the sultan?" they asked Bilal later. He did not have an answer. "Perhaps he did, but I have not heard," was all he said. Talon wanted to be sure.

* * * * *

Talon again got in touch with the boy Kontar, and soon he found himself back in the depths of the city, drinking coffee with Mukhwana.

"Allah protect you, Teacher. How have you been?" Mukhwana asked as he slurped his drink.

"May Allah protect your soul and heap blessings on your house," Talon answered. He sat comfortably opposite him and glanced around. It was strange, but nothing seemed ever to change in this underground cave. Everyone who had been there was always still there, even after several weeks of his absence. Perhaps they were all a dream, he wondered. The smoke from one of the pipes reminded him that there were dreams to be had from a pipe. However, Mukhwana was alert and keen to hear from Talon the condition of his master.

Talon told him freely, not forgetting to thank him for the unobtrusive escort that watched them into the palace some days ago. Mukhwana shrugged it off.

"You are here, I take it, to find out if my lord Abbas still has enemies in the city, or did they leave with the sultan?"

Not for the first time Talon wondered at the extent of the man's underground intelligence.

He nodded. "I still feel uncomfortable and uncertain about Bahir's intentions towards my master," he said.

"You have reason to. Did you er...ever visit his place?"

"I did."

Mukhwana looked hard at him with his one eye. "When did you go? And did you enter his palace?"

Talon told him, whereupon Mukhwana grunted with surprise. "My people watch Lord Abbas's place from all around and they did not report anything to me. You gained entry to Lord Bahir's palace?"

"I passed your men easily, they were asleep. It is hard work being a beggar, I suppose." He grinned disarmingly. "But I did not gain entry; I just wanted to know where it was for future reference," Talon lied.

"I shall send Kontar to meet with you if I can find out anything," Mukhwana said.

"I would like to know who the friends of Bahir are, who visit him late at night, if possible."

Mukhwana nodded. "We shall see what can be done, Heru." Talon looked at the man, who had given him this name. It meant falcon.

"May Allah protect you, my friend," Talon said, getting up and leaving a silver coin on the carpet next to his cup.

* * * * *

The fifth evening, as the sun was setting and while he was looking after *Rakhsh*, Talon noticed that street outside had become unusually quiet. Although the palace compound walls were thick, the noises of the city could still be heard: some hawker shouting his wares, or the sound of horses going by. This evening, however, all was still; it gave Talon a sense of unease.

He decided to see if Abbas was well guarded, although he knew that Panhsj would have taken care of that without his help. Perhaps it was because he wanted to talk to Panhsj that he went into the palace. He entered from the back maidan and then went along passages that would take him to the main hall and up the stairs. The servants had lit the wall sconces, and the dancing light cast strange shadows.

Then he saw the heavy form of Chisisi ahead of him in the dim glow. There was something furtive about the way the man moved, as though he didn't want to be noticed. This was unusual, because Chisisi normally swaggered about the palace. Now, however, he was slipping along, ahead of Talon, and was carrying a large round basket gingerly with both hands. Talon didn't remark the basket but he resolved to keep Chisisi in sight as he hurried into the main hall and then climbed the stairs obviously intent upon an errand. He still had not noticed Talon, who walked in silence behind him.

Chisisi was met half way up the stairs by Donkor, one of his henchmen, who nodded as he went past but said nothing. Chisisi seemed to take this for a signal because he grasped the basket tighter and hurried on. Donkor glided down the stairs without noticing Talon and stepped outside, and before the large doors closed behind him, Talon saw Donkor heading towards the main gate. Talon's interest was now thoroughly piqued. What was Chisisi doing? What intrigue were they up to? He hastened up the stairs, ignoring one of the startled women, who exclaimed indignantly as she drew her veil more closely.

At the top of the stairs there were passages leading off in several directions. Talon was sure that the eunuch had gone towards the master's bedroom, and he took the short corridor that led to the bedroom of Abbas and Khalidah.

The oil lamp by the door was burning palm oil that was smoking, and here there should have been a guard but there was no one, and Talon felt a chill creep down his neck. He drew his sword and rushed towards the door, which to his surprise opened and out stepped Chisisi. The man was perspiring, and jumped with fright when he saw Talon. His eyes were wide and there was clearly fear mingled with something else in his expression. Was it triumph?

Talon decided to take no chances. "Where are the guards and why are you here?" he demanded. "Guards!" he shouted. "Where is everyone?"

Chisisi seemed so overcome with fear now that his whole body trembled. It was clear he had not expected Talon, and this interfered with whatever he was up to. He opened his mouth to say something but nothing came out, and then he lurched to the left as though to escape. Talon's sword came up and the blade settled on Chisisi's neck; there was a tiny dribble of blood from the place where the razor sharp blade touched the skin.

"You cannot go in there. The ...the master is asleep, and cannot be disturbed," Chisisi said, his voice high with agitation.

Bilal appeared at the end of the corridor, having run up the stairs. He had heard the shout and came immediately. "What is it, Suleiman, and where are the guards?" he demanded.

Talon did not rest on ceremony. "Bilal, there is something going on. Watch Chisisi. Call for Panhsj. I do not know where the guards are either. I need to go in and see to the master."

He heard the slip of Bilal's sword coming out of the sheath. "Go, I will watch him."

Talon's eyes never left the face of the eunuch as he pushed the man out of the way and seized the door latch. He glanced at the bed, half expecting to find Khalidah in the room with Abbas and he was ready to go on his knees to ask forgiveness. But the room was empty, other than Abbas. Talon froze with horror.

Coiled on Abbas's chest was a large snake, its head raised to strike. Abbas was writhing, his face contorted in terrible agony. His color was gray and his eyes were starting from their sockets with horror. He was trying to get away from this nightmarish creature that hovered above him, about to sink its fangs into his face. Talon could now see that the snake had already struck. Abbas's arms jerked and his mouth moved but no words came.

Talon drove himself to move, but it took a huge effort. His own fear nearly paralyzed him. He was quite sure the creature was deadly, and that it had been placed there to kill Abbas.

In one swift sideways slash with his blade, he struck. The steel sliced the head of the snake even as it moved. The jaws were gaping wide and the fangs exposed as the head flew off the long scaled body and dropped onto the pillow near to its intended victim.

Talon stepped forward and, although he was terrified, he seized the tail of the now convulsing serpent and threw it as far away from the bed as he could. Its body still writhed, twisting as it contorted in the air, and sprayed a thin jet of blood as it went. It landed with a dull thump on the floor in a corner. He leaned over Abbas and jabbed his sword into the snake's head with its staring eyes and still snapping jaws, and lifted it up, placing it gingerly at the end of the bed.

At this moment, the door crashed open and Panhsj charged in with his sword held ready in front of him, intent upon killing anything that opposed him. His eyes took in the room and widened when he saw the form of the snake, still writhing in the corner.

"Suleiman, in Allah's name, what has happened? Why the blood, and why is your sword out? What are you doing?" He only saw Talon leaning over Abbas his sword dripping blood on the end of the bed.

"Thank God you are here, Panhsj, but it might be too late. Chisisi put a snake on our master. There!" He pointed to the head and then motioned at the now still shape in the corner.

Panhsj gasped, his black eyes fearful. "Did it have time to strike?" His voice quavered.

Talon leaned over Abbas, and held his trembling hand. He knew it was too late. Abbas stared up at him, his eyes pleading, but he was racked with agony and unable to talk. His mouth filled with foam and he gasped for air but his eyes remained on Talon's face for those dreadful few moments between lucidity and death. The room became still as Talon continued to hold Abbas's hand, but it was growing cool already. Panhsj fell to his knees with a great cry. This brought Bilal into the room and what he saw made him too fall on his knees.

"Who has done this terrible thing?" Bilal cried, dropping his sword and beating his chest, tears coursing down his cheeks, his grief overwhelming him.

Talon came to his senses then. "Cannot you guess, Bilal?" he said. His voice was like ice.

Bilal scrambled to his feet, his face suffused with rage. He snatched up his sword that lay on the carpet.

"I shall kill him. Bring him in here!" he shouted towards the door.

Two of the guards, who had encountered Chisisi running for his life, came through the door, their eyes wide with fear, knowing they themselves were dead men for having neglected their duty. They held tight to the arms of the wailing figure of Chisisi. The behemoth fell to his knees in front of Bilal, who had raised his sword to strike, quite forgetting that he was in his master's bed chamber.

"No Bilal! Do not kill him. We have to find out why he did this!" Talon shouted. "There is much we need to know before he is executed, he did not act alone in this treason. He was with Donkor a few minutes earlier."

Now Panhsj recovered enough to join Talon. His rage was terrible to see. His black tattooed features were distorted with grief and anger to the point where Chisisi fell forward in terror and started to drool, there was a patch of moisture on the front of his clothing where he had wet himself.

The noise had drawn others to the doorway, including Khalidah, who hurried in, not knowing the fate that had taken the life of her husband. She was shocked to see the men standing in her room with swords drawn and her eyes flew to Abbas lying on the bed. She saw immediately that he was dead, and her eyes took in the horror of the fangs and eyes of the gaping snake head at the end of his bed. With a wrenching cry, she threw herself on Abbas' body, her tears running freely onto his face as she clutched at him.

"What has happened? In Allah's name, what has happened?" she cried, her eyes roaming wildly over the stricken faces that surrounded her.

Bilal recovered his composure and nodded in agreement to Talon for what he had said regarding Chisisi. Then he went to Khalidah and touched her on her shoulder in an oddly familiar manner.

"My Lady," he said gently. She did not respond, and with an agonized look at the other two, he shook her with more force.

She turned and looked up at him, not comprehending. Her veil fell away, revealing swollen eyes and a face streaked with tears.

Bilal took a deep breath. "My Lady, Suleiman discovered the treachery, but he was too late to save our master. May Allah now cherish his soul, but we have to find out why and who ordered this foul deed. It must be done quickly, as we do not know how much time we have. We will leave you now to your grief."

Khalidah did not really comprehend, but she nodded and turned back to her husband's body, staring down at it and plucking distractedly at the material of the bed near his shoulder.

Bilal was visibly touched, but he pulled himself together and shouted, "You there, get out of the way, we are coming out with a prisoner. Guards!"

He then seized Chisisi by the neck and, despite the man's weight, almost lifted him up onto his feet with his left hand.

"Take him to the back of the gardens by the stables, we will find out everything we need to, then finish him."

Several more soldiers arrived and they unceremoniously shoved the wailing women servants and concubines out of the way. Talon was glad that neither the children nor Abbas's mother had arrived, although it was only a matter of time, as the noise was now considerable.

"Find the other two, Donkor and Jahi at once, and bring them to the stables. Tie them and do not on your lives let them escape!" Bilal roared.

Although he felt revolted by its menacing shape, Talon forced himself to pick up the head. He first found a strip of cloth to protect his fingers from poison before doing so. He held up the grisly object to observe it more closely and asked Panhsj. "What is this that could kill so quickly, Panhsj?"

"I do not know, Suleiman. I do not know its Arab name. Perhaps Bilal can tell us."

Talon held it for Bilal to see. He stared down at the head lying on the cloth as though he was seeing something grossly evil. The serpent was the color of dirty sand, with two seeming horns that sprouted just above and behind the glazed dead eyes. Its jaw was wide and its head formed like a scaly triangle with a blunt nose at the point.

"It is a horned viper, and deadly. Our master never had a chance. Only one strike was needed. Ah, God, in all your mercy, why?" Bilal groaned, his head flung back beseeching God for understanding.

Bilal saw to it that Abbas's eyes were shut, and his hands lay across his chest. Then he knelt before Khalidah. "Please accept my sorrow at the loss of our great Master, may Allah have mercy on him, and you, my Lady." He dashed tears from his own eyes as he spoke.

He stood to leave, followed by Talon and the others, when they heard a loud commotion from outside of the building. There were screams and yells mingled with the clash of steel, and the sound was drawing closer by the minute. Talon understood what had happened before his companions. "Donkor has let the enemy inside our compound; we are betrayed."

Panhsj and Bilal stared at him, uncomprehending.

"I saw Donkor leaving to go towards the gates, while I was following Chisisi to the Master's room, but I thought nothing of it at the time. He must have killed the gate guards and let the enemy inside."

"They are after our Lady, and the children. They know about the killing we have just seen," Bilal groaned in anguish.

*Endless steps are taken*
*The light seems unreachable*
*Hope has escaped*
*But faith remains unfailing*
*Together they defy the unknown*
*Trudging in darkness unafraid*
*— Lady Lyn Rosete*

# Chapter 17

# Tunnels

Bilal whirled around, his eyes darting to Panhsj, to Talon, to Chisisi. He was wild with rage and uncertainty as he tried to decipher the situation.

"Do not let him go!" He shouted, pointing at Chisisi. He rushed to the head of the stairs, Talon and Panhsj on his heels. They stood there a brief moment, their senses riveted by the yells and screams coming from the courtyard and the gardens. Bilal glanced about, taking note of the few men available at his command, and he realized that the rest of his contingency were leaderless and fighting for their lives outside in the gardens; and by the sounds he was hearing he feared the forces against them to be overwhelming.

"Who would do this?" he raged, but then he answered his own question. "Bahir and his scum, without doubt. May Allah curse them all for their treachery."

Furious, he swung around and glared down the stairs, anticipating an attack within the building; as he did, there was a crash and the door to the entrance sagged open. The fighting men boiled into the ground floor. The battle was now inside the house.

"Suleiman, Panhsj, find the children and take my Lady away from here," Bilal said in a tight, controlled tone. "You must escape. If they take the children, or my Lady, I do not wish to contemplate the consequences. Now go, and find a way out. I shall defend your backs from here."

"I shall stay with you!" Panhsj shouted. He had recovered his wits and in his anguish felt invincible and wanted to fight anything and anyone who came to him.

"No! You and Suleiman are their only hope. Go quickly. I should have listened to you, Suleiman. You were right; our enemies are here to destroy us. I will stay here and hold them off for as long as I can."

"Allah protect." Talon gripped Bilal's arm, knowing there was little chance he would ever see him alive again. He quickly turned to Panhsj. "There is a way down the back for the servants."

"Go safely, Suleiman. Leave Al-Qahirah. Take them back to Fayoum!" Bilal shouted with a fierce look that settled on Chisisi.

"One last thing to do," he grated.

Chisisi, who had perhaps begun to feel more hopeful for his life when the mob entered the building, suddenly realized that it was about to end. With a shriek, he struggled with his captors and was able to shake them off. He lumbered towards the stairs in a vain attempt to get away, but Talon tripped him so that he fell on hands and knees in front of Bilal, whose sword was already raised to strike. With a huge downward swing, he sliced down on Chisisi's exposed neck. The man's severed head jumped away from his body to bounce down the steps, where it landed at the feet of the first of the enemy about to climb the stairs. Chisisi's prostrate body twitched, much as the snake's had done, and spouted blood from the severed neck, which splashing down the stairs.

"This is what awaits you up here, you dog turds!" Bilal shouted, brandishing his bloody sword at the men now clustered below.

Talon wished he had his bow with him. He could have done great damage, but he had left it in his room and now there was no time.

"Allah protect you, Bilal!" Panhsj shouted as they ran with two guards to find the children and lady. They charged through a panic stricken cluster of women, their wails adding to the din of the battle below and to the war cries of Bilal and his men.

Talon and Panhsj found Kazim and Jasmine huddled with their mother at the entrance to the bedroom where the body of Abbas lay.

"My lady, you must come with us; we must leave immediately. I shall explain later, but you and the children are in great danger," Talon said in an urgent tone. "We must leave!"

Khalidah stared at him for a short moment; she was still numb from her husband's death, but then she heeded the urgency in his voice. She nodded, grasped Kazim by the hand and pushed Jasmine in front of her.

Ignoring the wails and shrieks of terror from the other women, they hurried down the corridor to the place where Talon knew there was a narrow stairway that led down to the kitchens. He had found it in his silent wandering of the house some time ago. He led the way down the dark stairwell with his sword held ahead of him. He prayed that they would not encounter the enemy waiting for them in the darkness at the bottom. Khalidah and the children followed close behind, Panhsj taking up the rear with Bilal's two men on his heels. He listened to the now distant clash of steel on steel and the shouts, as Bilal and his men fought for their lives and those of Abbas's family. He knew they had very little time left.

He reached the last step and strained his ears, but there were no sounds from the kitchen; he eased the heavy linen curtain aside and edged into the room. The cooks and other servants had all fled. He wondered briefly if Lamya had escaped with them. He hoped so.

The cooks had left in such a hurry that there was a pot of soup boiling over on the large cooking fire, the liquid hissing and sputtering in the flames. But Talon had no thought for the aroma of chicken stew. His focus was on the urgency of their escape. He led the way across the tiled floor past the ovens and cooking items, ducking under braids of onions and other dried plants and herbs. They headed towards the back of the kitchen where he knew of a corridor that led behind the servants' quarters. He hoped too that they could get over the peripheral wall; to linger in the compound would be fatal. But his hopes were almost dashed when he encountered Jahi, one of Chisisi's henchmen.

The man was facing the wall, adjusting his clothing in such a way that suggested he had been relieving himself, and he did not see Talon until it was too late. Talon snatched out his knife and hurled it at a distance of fifteen feet. The blade flipped once and buried itself in his throat. The man stiffened and clutched at his neck with both hands, his eyes wide with shock, and then he fell over backwards with a strangled gargle to crash onto the floor. His body convulsed once then became limp, and he died with his eyes wide open.

Talon strode over and removed his knife from the man's neck, wiping the blood on the robe of the corpse before putting it away. He took an oil lamp off a ledge and turned to encourage Khalidah and the children to keep going, barely noticing the shock on their faces. They were frozen with fear and Panhsj had to give Khalidah a gentle push. "He had no choice, my Lady," he said. "That man was a traitor to your husband. He deserved to die. Now we must follow Suleiman. Please, we must hurry."

The urgency in his voice brought them back to reality. They stepped over the corpse one by one, each trying not to look down at the body. Talon had to admire Khalidah's composure. Although she was pale and her eyes were wide with shock, it was clear to him that she understood that their lives depended upon fully cooperating; but Jasmine was mewling and trembling, while Kazim was as white as a ghost. They just did not comprehend what was happening around them.

Urged on by Panhsj, who chivvied them forward, they crept out of the building and into the darkness along the narrow pathway at the back of the kitchens and soon reached the outside wall, which they hugged for a short distance, until they came to a mound of debris and rubbish piled against the wall; its height here was only about nine feet.

Talon stopped. Even from this far away at the back of the gardens they could hear the shouting and screams with the faint clash of steel in the distance. Bahir and his men were still giving a good account of themselves, it seemed. Talon clambered onto the pile of rubbish, hoping it would hold, and motioned for Panhsj to come close. He cupped his hands in front of himself, having squared his weight, and Panhsj placed one foot in them and leaped up to scramble onto the top of the wall. The man's weight drove Talon almost down to his knees. No sooner there, Panhsj seated himself firmly and leaned down, holding out his hand.

Talon motioned to Khalidah to take Panhsj's hand while he offered to lift her up. Compared to Panhsj, she was as light as a feather. The children went next, then the guards. Talon scrambled up to join them. While they were on the wide top, Panhsj stared back towards the house. There was an ominous reddish glow coming from the building. Some of the light reflected off his ebony skin, so that even in the darkness, Talon could see his face set in grim lines.

It was an easy matter to lower everyone down the other side, and then Talon and Panhsj jumped as quietly as they could to land and roll, coming silently to their feet in the dusty street. Again they listened intently, but no sound came to warn them that they had been observed. Talon glanced at Khalidah and the children; Jasmine and Kazim were as quiet as mice. They were subdued, but seemed in control of themselves.

"I have friends who might be able to help us, but we must hurry and get away from here," he whispered to Khalidah and Panhsj. "It is about a mile. We cannot be discovered on the streets or they will hunt us down, so we must move quickly."

Khalidah nodded and grasped Kazim by the hand. Panhsj took up the rear, while the two men stayed close to Khalidah and to Jasmine, who appeared to be close to collapse. The group scurried from shadow to dark shadow, always keeping watch for pursuit.

Talon led the way at fast pace towards the souk. Even though he was alert for the slightest sign of danger, his mind was working furiously.

He was puzzled and angry, wondering why they had had no warning. Mukhwana had promised that he would at the very least warn him. Talon wondered what had happened to the boy Kantor. Could the enemy men have killed him as they came to the palace? By now he felt sure that Kantor would have tried if at all possible to warn him. All the same, he meant to demand an explanation. In the meantime, however, they needed to disappear, and Mukhwana was the only person in Cairo who could hide them and with whom he thought they might be reasonably safe. He prayed that he was not leading Khalidah into a trap.

The street they were hurrying along led to a larger intersection which was some distance from the main entrance of the palace. It was quiet at this hour, for which Talon was grateful. He did not want curious people to remember them passing this way. In Cairo there were always eyes somewhere watching.

Apart from the occasional muffled exclamation, as one or another of the party stumbled, they made little noise. Kazim sniffled and Jasmine tripped once, losing a sandal, but one of the guards retrieved it and they hurried on.

It seemed like an eternity before they came to the dark and imposing entrance of the souk. There were few people about, as most of the shops were now closed. A few remaining merchants who were on their way home and some late night revelers paid little attention to the small group walking at a quick pace towards the dark, poorly lit opening that led into the depths of the souk. In any case, one look at Panhsj and even a man well into his drink would sober up and hurry off in the other direction.

Talon tried to remember the way to the caverns buried deep inside the guts of the souk. He found what he was looking for quickly enough, and made the others wait while he set about stealing an oil lamp to light their way. There were oil lamps aplenty placed in niches along the walls of the main street, but most of them were burnt out and would not be replenished until the next day. He helped himself to a couple that appeared to be well filled with palm oil and returned to his party.

"Do not be afraid. We are going deep into the souk where I have friends," he whispered to them as he handed a lamp to Panhsj. He hoped that he was right.

Khalidah's look questioned how he had friends here, but he pretended not to notice. Panhsj's features registered deep puzzlement, but Talon gripped his arm and said, "Trust me, Panhsj. Here I we may be safe. Follow me carefully."

He led them stumbling along the dark narrow tunnels over debris from roof falls and across gurgling underground streams. They descended rapidly at one point to where the ceiling dripped water and the walls were wet. Their pathway became muddy and slippery. The children clutched at the proffered hands of the two escorts, while Khalidah took Talon's arm for support.

He felt pity for them. While the warriors were in riding boots, they wore only light house slippers which were quite useless on this mucky floor. The air was stuffy, musty and dense with the stink of rotting objects and filthy, stagnant water holes.

The squeaking of rats and low flying bats that flew close to their faces unnerved Jasmine and she let out a stifled moan, but Khalidah whispered a warning to her. At one time Khalidah gripped Talon's arm fiercely, almost like a spasm, and he guessed the same had happened to her; he was holding the oil lamp high and from the corner of his eye he saw a furry creature scuttle away into the darkness from under their feet. The eyes of the rats glowed red in the lamplight, increasing the sense of menace in this alien world they had entered. He was relieved that they did not encounter anyone coming or going at this time of night. It might not have gone well.

Finally, when he was beginning to think he might have taken a wrong turn, Talon sensed a light draft of air carrying the whiff of hashish. It told him that they were near their destination. He held the lamp over his head and motioned the party to stop, cautioning them not to make any noise and to remain still while he went forward to find out what awaited them.

He eased his way along the tunnel until he came to the familiar opening into the larger series of wider archways where Mukhwana held court. His eyes searched the poorly lit area for any sign of activity, but it seemed that despite the several oil lamps still burning, everyone had gone to bed.

He looked for guards, but he saw none. He guessed that the people had a sense of security here in their underground home. He eased out into the opening to go to where he usually sat with Mukhwana, when a small movement alerted him. Someone had entered the cavernous hall from another area. Talon drifted into deeper shadow. Then he recognized Kontar hobbling quickly across the uneven surface of the cavern floor.

"Mukhwana!" Kontar screamed as he hobbled as fast as his crutch would permit him towards the platform where Mukhwana usually seated himself.

"Mukhwana, they have attacked the house of Abbas," he sobbed. Then he tripped and sprawled on the floor. Talon moved quickly forward, lifted him to his feet, and retrieved his stick.

Kantor stared up at him, not understanding that it was Talon. Then he gaped in surprise, "Suleiman! Where...where did you come from?" Fear and uncertainty were written across his tear stained face. There was obvious distress, but there was no guilt.

"It is all right now, Kontar, we have escaped." Talon patted the terrified boy reassuringly on his shoulder.

Kantor's screams had brought others, and they were soon surrounded by bearded men, still half asleep, clutching an odd assortment of knives and old swords and spears, gathered into a hostile cluster around the two of them. A dozen voices demanded that Kantor tell them what had happened, and who was this person with him? Then a roar from nearby stopped everyone in mid-sentence.

"What in Allah's name is happening that you should disturb my sleep?" Mukhwana bellowed. A path immediately opened for him to advance towards Talon and Kontar.

Mukhwana lumbered towards them, disheveled and obviously in bad humor at the noise. His eyes rested on Kontar, who was still sobbing and shaking. Then he saw Talon and his one eye widened.

"How in the name of all the Djinn did you get here?" he demanded. "Who brought you?"

"I know the way, my friend, and Kontar is right, we were attacked and the house is overrun by the enemies of Abbas."

Mukhwana stared at him for a long hard moment and then looked back at Kantor. "What happened, boy, why did you not warn them? Those were your instructions." He demanded in a low voice filled with menace.

Kontar sniffled and wiped his nose with his filthy ragged sleeve. "It...it was late and we were together eating at a corner nearby when some men came towards us. They were very quiet and caught us by surprise. We were afraid because we quickly understood that they wanted to have some sport with us. I was pushed into a dark corner while the others ran off to distract them from me. But the men went after them, Salem and Hussein. They killed them right there, not far from me on the street." He sniffled again. Talon reassuringly tightened his arm over the shaking boy's thin frame.

"We were betrayed from within, Mukhwana," Talon said. "The eunuch and his cronies first murdered my master and then opened the gates to the marauders, I only just escaped." He did not mention the lady and the others, because he had yet to ascertain if he could trust Mukhwana. After this night, he was not sure whom to trust.

"Go and get fed and then rest," Mukhwana growled to the boy, and then he said, "Suleiman, you are deserving of the name Heru. I do not know how you found this place, but now that you are here, you are safe. Come, we will have tea and you shall tell me all."

The curious crowd was beginning to disperse now that the excitement had cooled.

Talon stepped close to the man and said in a very low voice. "I thank you, Mukhwana, from my heart. May Allah's blessings be with you always...but I have others with me. Can I trust you to provide them with your protection?"

Mukhwana glared at him with his one eye. "I am the law here and if I provide you with protection that goes for anyone who came with you, other than my sworn enemies."

Talon bowed low. "Forgive me, *Oustez*, but tonight has been one of treachery and murder. I have with me the wife and children of Abbas, and their surviving guards. I place us under your protection."

"Who did you say?" Mukhwana asked with a stunned look.

"My Lady Khalidah, with her children and her guards," Talon repeated.

Mukhwana recovered enough to say curtly, "Bring them to me." He lumbered off shouting to some women nearby, "Prepare food and tea, we have guests. Be quick about it!"

As Talon went to collect Khalidah and the children, the people nearby began to chatter again. This was indeed going to be an interesting night.

By the time Talon brought his party to the middle of the cavern, Mukhwana had seated himself on his makeshift throne and looked a lot less disheveled.

Talon led Khalidah towards him. She was pale and exhausted. Her clothing of expensive cotton cloth was rent and dirty, her face smudged, and her hair barely covered by her veil. Despite this, the crowds of beggars who had gathered nearby were clearly awed by her beauty and her dignity. Mukhwana himself was obviously very impressed.

"My Lady Khalidah, wife of Emir Abbas Abdul Azim ibn Athir Faysal, we are now under the protection of Mukhwana, Lord of the beggars of Cairo," Talon intoned by way of introduction.

She stared at him to see if he were joking, but in the lamplight his face was dead serious; so she took her cue from that.

"My lord Mukhwana," she said, "I am indebted to you for offering your protection. I regret that I and my children have had to come to you in this condition but we had no choice, and my servant...my children's tutor, Suleiman, told me that you were an honorable man."

Her voice was melodious and clear despite her fatigue, and it had the desired effect. The people were captivated. There were murmurs of sympathy from nearby women.

Talon glanced at Panhsj, who himself had caused much comment on his arrival because of his large and fearsome bearing. Panhsj nodded silently as though agreeing with Talon's questioning look. There was silence for a moment in the wide hall.

Mukhwana seemed to have been lost in admiring her beauty. Then he finally found his voice and cleared his throat.

"Ahem... my Lady. You are the wife of Emir Abbas, whom we all respected, and you are a friend of Suleiman. That is enough. You have my protection for as long as you stay here. We can protect you from all enemies, *Insha'Allah*."

Khalidah gave a small sigh and seemed to slump. Talon was instantly by her side, but she placed slim fingers on his arm and said quietly in return to Mukhwana, "I...I am grateful. I shall repay you in great measure for your kindness once we have taken back what is my husband's. I give thanks to Allah for his benefice and for bringing me into your care."

Mukhwana shifted uncomfortably. He was not used to being treated as an equal by persons of aristocracy, even if they had fallen upon terrible times like this beautiful woman standing before him.

"Allah in his infinite mercy and wisdom will see you through this terrible time, my Lady. You will take some refreshment as my guests before you retire? I shall have an area set aside for you while you remain here."

He beckoned to some women, who carried trays of hot tea and small bits of food. Where and how they had conjured it up in such a short space of time? Talon had no idea. The children were introduced to Mukhwana, who was beginning to enjoy his sudden stature, and he behaved kindly to them.

Jasmine was ready to collapse, but managed to sip some tea from a not so clean little cup, but she refused the food. Kazim was too dazed to do more than take a bite of the food, which he must have liked because he took a second bite.

Soon Khalidah and the children were led off by the same women who had brought the tea to a place of privacy somewhere in the deeper reaches of the cavern, while the men stayed behind and talked.

Before she left Khalidah whispered to Talon, "This is the second time you have saved our lives, Suleiman. I and my children are placed ever deeper in your debt." She turned to Panhsj. "Ah, Panhsj, you grieve too? My husband's faithful companion, I am in your debt as well. May Allah's blessings be upon you."

The two men bowed silently and would not look at one another as she left, because they were embarrassed by the tears in their eyes.

Talon and Panhsj, with the two guards, who were named Hanif and Aahmes, were enjoined to eat and to tell of the events that had taken place. They sat cross legged on the frayed carpet in the wavering light of the oil lamps and nibbled the small pastries and sipped the hot tea. Kantor now sat with them, although he looked shaken from his own experiences. Talon and Panhsj asked him to tell what he had seen before he had to flee.

"Did you see any of their faces?" Panhsj asked him, but Kontar was so scared of his fierce features, despite the unthreatening intent, that he shifted closer to Talon, who laughed and said, "Kantor, this is my friend Panhsj, who is a great warrior, none fiercer in battle but none kinder to his friends. You are safe with him. Tell us what you can."

"It was dark, Suleiman, but we could see enough to know that there were many of them, mostly on foot and carrying spears and bows. That is why we were surprised; if they had been on horses we would have heard them and had more warning. They were moving very quietly and only when it was too late for us did we know the peril."

"Did you see the faces of anyone you might know?" Panhsj asked, this time with a smile that he hoped would relax the boy. In fact, when Panhsj smiled it was perhaps even more intimidating. Kantor gave him another of his fearful looks.

"*Jo Oustez*, I did not," he said respectfully. "I only know that while I was in the dark hole, two men came by later; these men were on horses, and one looked like the man who you played chogan against, Suleiman."

Talon started. "Are you sure? Which one?" he demanded.

"The one who led the other team...I think."

Panhsj almost leapt to his feet in his agitation. Kantor flinched and said pitifully, "Suleiman, you know we would have warned you, and we were about to. As Allah is my witness, we would have…" his voice trailed off.

"You know what this means, Suleiman," Panhsj grated, ignoring the boy.

Talon nodded. "With the sultan gone, Bahir came to settle accounts. He is probably enjoying the spoils of that, even now as we speak."

Panhsj gave a low menacing growl. He understood what that meant only too well. "We should go back and kill him tonight before he can do more harm," he said through clenched teeth.

Talon touched Panhsj on the knee. "You forget, my friend, in your hurt and pain that we have another task, and that is to care for my Lady and her children. We will not do any good to her by rushing back and killing or being killed tonight."

"I am anguished at the loss of my lord," Panhsj almost shouted.

"I too, but we will deal with them in our own time. For now we have the protection of Mukhwana, and we should rest. Tomorrow we plan."

"I agree with Suleiman," Mukhwana said. "There is nothing you can do to bring your master back, and rushing out there to be killed will do no one any good." His voice was quiet, but there was a firmness to it that brooked no more outbursts from Panhsj, who hung his head as though defeated.

Talon reached over and placed his hand on Panhsj's slumped shoulders.

"Be sure of one thing, Panhsj. Abbas will be avenged, as God is my witness, but now we must rest."

# Chapter 18

# Deep Sanctuary

Talon awoke in the darkness of the alcove that he and Panhsj shared and immediately began to scratch his ribs. Once more he was in a place that was infested with fleas and other nameless parasites; it was unpleasant to have them for company again; the memory of the prison was vivid in his mind.

He wondered how Khalidah and the children were faring. This must be an unpleasant experience for them after the comfortable life they have lived hitherto, he thought.

He stretched, feeling as if he had rested well, and realized that he must have slept for six hours despite the events the night before, but he could not be sure. Nearby he heard a low snore and realized that Panhsj was still sleeping the deep sleep of the exhausted. Talon worried about his friend. He considered Panhsj a friend now. He would have to keep a check on Panhsj's hot temper during this difficult time; especially when they had to find a way out of Cairo and find their way to the estate. Talon wondered if unspoken guilt would weigh on Panhsj and cause him to do reckless things that would place them all in danger.

He got up and walked quietly away, leaving his friend to sleep. He found the communal hall under the wide crumbling arches of limestone almost empty of people. He supposed that the beggars— men, women, and children—would be out in the streets by now earning a few coppers. He saw a group of small children, ragged and dirty, playing contentedly around the few adults who were chatting amongst themselves, and he heard a baby crying somewhere in the gloom.

Somewhat to his surprise he found Khalidah seated on a cushion talking to Mukhwana, while nearby Jasmine and Kazim were in the company of Kantor. They were munching on food and there was steaming tea in a high brass pot, placed on a brass tray in front of Khalidah.

As he came up to them he bowed and said, "*Salaam Aliekom*, my Lady and my lord Mukhwana. I hope you have rested well."

"*Aliekom Salaam*, Suleiman. While you have been sleeping the day away we have been planning," Mukhwana said complacently. The men who normally sat around him were gone, and Talon supposed they had been sent to listen for information on the streets of the city. Mukhwana was evidently enjoying his new status and the company of such a distinguished woman who, despite her dirty clothes, bore herself with much dignity. Khalidah gave Talon a wan smile with her eyes.

"Good morning, Suleiman, I hope you slept well...enough," she said with just a tinge of irony. Talon was forced to look at the ground and control his smile. She clearly meant the accommodation. But when he looked up he could see that her eyes over the veil were hollow, tired, and somehow lost.

"Suleiman," Kazim said coming over to him, "when will we go home?" The boy had voiced what they were all wondering.

Jasmine smiled tentatively at him but said nothing. She still looked drawn, frightened, and exhausted.

"Soon, young master," Talon said, as he sat down beside Khalidah. This was not the place to dwell on ceremony. However he addressed Mukhwana politely.

"I apologize for our untimely arrival last night, but we could not linger out in the streets and wait for them to hunt us down."

"You are brave to have come here in the night. There are strange things in these tunnels, and Djinn stalk the night. Cairo has a city beneath the city and we live here with ghosts and other creatures that it is best not to encounter. We are safe in this place as long as we do not wander about alone; as it is then that the creatures come out of the walls and take unsuspecting people," Mukhwana stated, his one eye gleaming.

Kazim edged a little closer to Talon, and Jasmine looked even more frightened than before. Khalidah had tensed but otherwise showed a perfect aplomb.

"We have to leave Cairo as soon as we can, Mukhwana. I must take my Lady to her estates in the south," Talon said.

"You must wait, Suleiman. My spies are out across the town today. Will you have enough gold to pay me for the trouble I am going to on your behalf?" He laughed, and Talon smiled, but he knew that Mukhwana meant what he said and would need payment some time.

"Once I can get to the Jews in the bazaar I can pay you, my lord." He glanced at Khalidah, who was watching them. "What do your spies tell you at present?" he enquired.

Mukhwana's one eye swiveled to Khalidah. "My Lady, forgive me, I have not said anything up to this minute, but it has to be told. Although it is early yet, the ones who have come back tell me that the palace of your husband was sacked last night and all within either taken prisoner or killed. There was a fire too; no one can tell how bad it was, but you were very lucky to escape. Now the word on the street is that they, the soldiers, seek you everywhere."

Khalidah leaned forward over her knees and gave a small sob. "My servants and the other women? My mother-in-law?" she whispered.

Jasmine, who had been listening to their conversation, began to cry. The terrible events of the night before, and now the news of more deaths, and to learn that they were hunted, was too much for her. Surprisingly, she did not push Kantor away when he held his arm around her shoulders. "Is Grandmama dead?" she sobbed.

Kazim began to sniffle, but then he caught Talon's look; he brought himself under control. He lifted his head and said to his sister bravely, "Jasmine, if they have harmed Grandmama, I shall avenge her. I promise you."

Jasmine shuffled closer to him on her knees and hugged him, still crying, but Kazim held her hard and Talon for the first time realized that the boy really did love his sister.

"My Lady," Talon said in a low voice, "I share your desolation for the loss of the others, but if we had not left when Bilal told us to, you too would now be facing a terrible fate. As for the children..." his voice trailed.

She nodded and lifted her tear-streaked face to look at him. "There was no choice, Suleiman, and I understand, but Allah has punished our family in a terrible manner and I do not know who our friends are, other than those who are here." She glanced at Mukhwana.

"I thought of my husband's friend Kemosiri ibn Jibade, but I do not know how to reach him, if indeed he is even in the city now. He could be with the sultan."

Talon tried to smile at her. "We will find out in time, my Lady, but for now I think we are safe here. Try to rest, because our journey is not yet over."

He turned back to Mukhwana. "If you can find a ship to take us upstream, I can surely pay you for that."

Khalidah stared at him. "Where do you have the money, Suleiman?" she asked with surprise in her voice. There was no money to be had from the palace now, although her husband had plenty of cash in the estate, and of course with the bankers in Alexandria. However, that was useless to her unless she could get to it.

"You might not have known it, my Lady, but I am the son of a merchant and I carried coin."

He did not want this to sound like a rebuke. It had not been her fault he had been made a slave. "After your husband made me a ... servant it was taken off me; but Malek, may Allah bless him, made sure I brought it with me to Cairo. It is in the care of the Jews of the Bazaar."

Despite his careful tone, Khalidah bent her head, as though acknowledging the unjustness of his position, but said nothing.

Mukhwana laughed and pointed. "I tell you he is a cunning man, this Suleiman of yours; he only ever tells anyone just what he wants them to know. Perhaps I can find a boat for you. A swift one is what you need to get you out of the city and well on your way to wherever it is you have to go for safety. I have friends in the harbor who owe me favors. It might take a few days, but I should be able to do something...but it will take gold..." he said thoughtfully.

"Do you think we have a few days?" Panhsj had come up quietly and now spoke.

He bowed low to Khalidah and then to Mukhwana, who greeted him with a smile and a wave of a pudgy hand.

"You have no choice but to stay here, where you are safe, while the hunt moves away. It will give us time get to a boat. Allah willing, it will be soon. But I too have to be careful. If the authorities ever discover this sanctuary, my people will be scattered and lost. There is more going on in Cairo than just the attack on your home, my Lady," Mukhwana said.

Talon nodded agreement. "There is, but I do not quite know what. It has a lot to do with the absence of the sultan, of that I am sure, but beyond that I do not really know. In any case, we are powerless to make much difference and we need to look to our own safety first."

Panhsj seated himself, at a motion from Khalidah.

"Suleiman, we must go back and find out what has happened. I shall not rest until I have seen with my own eyes what they have done, and perhaps, Allah willing, I can recover the body of my master," he said in a low tone.

Mukhwana glared at him with his one eye. "You will be recognized immediately, and that will compromise the rest of them, including my people," he said. "You should not go out of here. Suleiman can go because he is as cunning as a jackal, and will be able to disappear easily in a crowd; despite that he looks like a green-eyed Frank. But I expect you back, Suleiman."

"I am coming back, my friend. As you have given us your protection, so I shall honor it and come back." Talon pretended to look hurt. Mukhwana laughed; he knew that Talon was acting.

"You will have protection on the way to the Jewish shop that you told me about, and on the way back." Mukhwana grinned at Talon through his badly groomed beard. He shifted his weight on his huge cushion so that he could see Khalidah more easily.

Talon agreed. "Panhsj, I can go because I will not be noticed. I can go as a beggar with some of the other people and be well hidden, but Mukhwana is right, you will be recognized immediately. It is too dangerous."

Even Khalidah weighed in on the side of the other two. "Panhsj, would you desert me and my children to rush off on some wild adventure when we need you nearby for our protection?"

After that Panhsj could not say anything more. He took Talon aside later and asked him what he was planning to do.

"Mukhwana will send a couple of men with me to the Jewish quarter to obtain gold, because, as he said himself, it will take more than good will for him to persuade a ship's master to take us anywhere. Then tonight you and I will go back to the palace and see for ourselves what has happened," Talon told him. "Have no fear; we shall bring back our master's remains, if it is at all possible. In the meantime please defend our Lady with your life. Oh, and don't forget the children. Defend them with your second life."

He danced out of the way of the huge hand that swung round to cuff him.

"Do not get caught, my young friend. I am beginning to like you," Panhsj growled.

"I do not intend to. And Panhsj, we will avenge our master, Allah willing."

He left the gloomy cavernous tunnels in the company of two men whom Mukhwana had ordered to go with him. Their instructions were to ensure he came back, and Talon did not doubt that Mukhwana meant if without him, at least with the gold. Talon had few illusions as to how far the protection of Abbas's family would go if there was no gold to lubricate the deal.

They went by another route that brought them out at the back of a flax merchant's shop. The huge bales of raw flax, which were for display only, concealed the passageway. Being near the docks, the warehouse made a perfect place to enter the souk proper.

There was no one at the back of the shop when they emerged. They did not pause but hurried out onto the street via a side entrance and disappeared into the crowd. With a little help from his escort, Talon rediscovered the way to the Jewish quarter. While the two men sat on the ground, begging and waving their wooden bowls, Talon stayed near a wall and pretended to look at wares. He glanced around the street and began to take note of the people. There was a familiar looking woman begging on the corner opposite, and another man, bulky despite his rags, leaning against a mud brick archway. Talon knew he had both legs, but somehow he seemed to have lost one during the night. There was a hefty looking crutch leaning against the wall nearby.

He was thankful that Mukhwana was taking no chances with his safety, or was it the gold? He knew he could trust the lord of the beggars; at the same time he understood that the gold would make a big difference in stature for the man. He hoped that the ship would materialize and that they could leave without difficulty. If not, Mukhwana would not enjoy the gold for very long.

He cautiously made contact with the Jew by sidling up and showing his face. He had discovered that these people, who themselves had been persecuted from time to time by the fickle Fatimid rulers, as had the Christian Copts, were good at remembering faces. So despite his change in garb, the man recognized him.

"God's blessing upon you, *Oustez* Suleiman," the older man said softly. He was slim and well dressed, although not ostentatiously, and in the local style, but there was a kippah on his head of black curls which indicated his faith. There were flecks of gray in his well trimmed beard and on his temples. The few lines at the corner of his eyes crinkled as he smiled a welcome and offered Talon tea.

Talon accepted the offer and went into the carpeted den, where he sat on cushions and tea was poured by a burly servant who, Talon guessed, served to protect as well as to serve tea. The room was filled with carpets and bales of silk which gave off a pleasant smell of dense fabric, mingled with the very light scent of some herbal incense that Levi the Jew appeared to like.

He and Talon spent at least five minutes in quiet greetings and observation of good manners, which Talon had come to expect and even to enjoy; it was only after the second cup that they came to the point.

"What can I do for you today, *Oustez* Suleiman?" Levi asked Talon. His eyes had not missed the dirty clothes, the rents in the cloth, the mud on Talon's boots, which he had taken off and left at the edge of the carpet, or the tired face of his guest. But he also saw the clean sword and the hard look: so politely he did not allude to Talon's condition. His servant hovered unobtrusively in the background, his eyes watchful.

Talon spread his hands and smiled disarmingly. "Levi, I am about to leave this beautiful city of Al-Qahirah and I will need cash."

"How much do you wish to take away with you, *Oustez*?" Levi asked politely.

"I shall need about one half of what I gave you, and chits to carry with me that I can use in other cities, perhaps in another country, maybe Jerusalem?"

Levi looked at him for a long moment then he nodded. "I see... Suleiman. *Oustez*, if I might be permitted to ask, is this anything to do with the death of Emir Abbas? We are hearing terrible rumors about this."

"How did you know I worked for him?" Talon asked sharply.

"How could I not? Your name was on everyone's lips after the game of chogan a few weeks ago. Even my people were there, and they recognized you and watched you play. Some even bet upon the game, just like the Egyptians." He looked disapproving at that but then gave a disarming grin. "Some of us bet on your team, and others did not. Their loss. I heard it was a good game to watch."

He paused. "Do not fear, Suleiman, I shall get your coin, but you must give me a day, because, of course, I do not keep it all here. I can give you some, but the rest will be available by tomorrow, God willing."

"What is the rumor on the street, Levi?" Talon decided to ask.

"That there was fighting at the palace of my lord Abbas. It is well known that he was a favorite of the sultan, who is away with his army, so it is thought that someone took advantage of that to settle a score. Everyone is wondering where the family of Abbas has disappeared to and who is creating the unrest in the garrison with the soldiers that were left behind. It is not good for business you understand...this uncertainty. It could be bad for us Jews."

Talon looked closely at Levi, wondering if he could trust the man, who seemed to have a very good idea what was going on.

Levi gazed back into Talon's eyes calmly, and said very quietly. "We Jews know how to keep secrets, our own and those of others; it is our stock in trade. How could we do business otherwise?" He smiled drily. "*Oustez* Suleiman, you have nothing to fear. Come back tomorrow and your cash will be here."

Talon let out a silent breath. He stood up and Levi escorted him to the far rear of the shop, where he offered to give Talon the money in dinars. Talon knew the dinar was still one of the most trusted of coins, better than the bezat minted in Constantinople, because it was almost pure gold. So he nodded, and Levi counted out five dinars in gold coin. As half a dinar could buy a ton of bread, Talon estimated that this would help Mukhwana to buy a ship's captain in a down payment and leave him some profit. Talon signed a chit, then bowed to Levi, and they parted with mutual expressions of good will.

Talon picked up his escort, who abandoned their positions along the crowded street, and while the two who had come with him shuffled along, others shadowed them to make sure there were not lurking enemies who might try to waylay him. He smiled to himself at the thought, but was grateful for the company—the more so as he would have had a hard time finding his way back along the route they had taken this time.

On their return to the hall, he found that Khalidah had gone back to her place with the women to rest, pleading exhaustion. He smiled to find Kazim holding court with several boys of about his own age. Apparently he had overcome his initial shyness and now was deep into an animated conversation with them. The boys were ragged and dirty, but they were for the most part healthy enough, so that, unlike his sister, Kazim did not feel bothered by their unclean condition. They asked many questions of him, and once he understood these were not threatening, he began to answer.

The ever-watchful Panhsj was seated nearby and had relaxed enough so that the boys included him in their excited chatter, his deep voice booming when he responded or even laughed occasionally. Talon watched from the shadows some distance away, both amused and surprised at how resilient Kazim showed himself to be. Far from being the arrogant, spoiled little brat he had first known, Kazim seemed to be taking the situation in his stride, the ordeal of the last night already a distant memory.

Such was not the case with Jasmine, although she seemed calmer today and less agitated. She was subdued. She was seated a short distance away, listening to Kantor, who sat facing her with some other older boys and girls, and Talon guessed she was glad of their company.

He made his entrance known by walking across the dirt floor and halting behind Kazim. Panhsj grinned and lifted a hand in greeting. Kazim glanced behind him and noticed Talon standing and smiling down at him. "You are back," he said, and excitedly scrambled to his feet. He seemed ready to rush into Talon's arms, but checked himself; his dignity was important just now, so he stopped and asked in a grown up manner, "Where did you go, Suleiman?"

He was interrupted by Jasmine, who had no such inhibitions, and ran into Talon's arms and buried her head in his shoulder. Talon was too surprised to say anything, so he patted her gently on the back. "I was so worried about you, Suleiman. Where have you been?" Her voice was muffled in his shoulder.

"I went up to the Bazaar, Jasmine. There is nothing to worry about. Are you all right?"

"I am frightened," she whispered. "Please take us away from this place...soon. Also, there are things in the beds that bite."

Talon chuckled and released her. She looked ready to cry, but he held her arms gently and said. "Come, Jasmine, you are older than your brother and he is being very brave. You are your father's daughter so I know you are brave too. As for the bugs, that will be over before long and we will be on our way soon to your home in Fayoum, *Insha'Allah*. Then this will be a distant memory. Be patient, my Jasmine, your mother needs you to be strong. Panhsj and I are here to protect you."

She sniffed and wiped her tears, but stayed with him and Panhsj while they talked quietly together. Talon noticed with some wry amusement that Kantor threw longing puppy looks at Jasmine while she sat with them, but she was too preoccupied to notice.

That evening when they had all eaten, surrounded on all sides by the army of beggars, men, women, and children, Mukhwana held court. Talon had delivered the gold to him and received his thanks. Talon got the feeling that Mukhwana had not really expected him to come up with gold in payment, but now that he had, the man was overtly more attentive to them as guests and plied them with food, which while plain, was well prepared for all that. He shared with them what his people had heard on the streets. He looked sympathetically at Khalidah as he began.

"The palace of Lord Abbas has been ransacked and plundered by people who belong to Lord Bahir Ibn Hakeem. There was a fire in the main house, but the stables and out buildings are undamaged. There is another man, who is called Al Muntaqim, whom we have heard about. Yes, he is called 'The Destroyer' by his enemies and friends alike. I know little of him, but my sources tell me that he is a senior commander for the sultan and oversees the troops left behind while the sultan is off fighting one of his wars with the Frans, God damn them.

"There are men from the army throughout the city who are looking for you and your children, my Lady," he said, glancing to her and bowing his head in commiseration. "There is also a rumor that the garrison is talking of rebellion."

There were audible gasps from Khalidah, Panhsj, and the two bodyguards, Hanif and Aahmes. "By our Lord Allah! How could that be?" Hanif burst out. "Our men are loyal to the sultan and would never think of rebellion. We belong to Emir Abbas!" He choked and all but broke down as he recalled that his master was no more, and that his own world was very uncertain now.

Talon was the least surprised of all. Now the pieces of the puzzle were beginning to fall into place. As long as Abbas was alive, even if he was unable to command his men, those left behind would have refused to be a part of any insurrection. Now, however, without a leader they would probably do as they were told, and support this unknown commander in a rebellion, if indeed that was happening. He wondered if the Sultan had made a serious mistake in leaving all of Cairo in the command of this man. Then why and how was Bahir left behind, when he should have been with the Sultan? Perhaps he was the commander? Talon thought about this as he listened.

There was gloom as they each digested this information. They were trapped, it would seem, in this maze of tunnels, unable to escape the city unless Mukhwana by some miracle managed to arrange a boat for them. It would be unthinkable to try the road, as it was likely that Bahir would be watching the roads south. He would expect them to return to their country estate, if they could.

# Chapter 19

# Ruin

Talon and Panhsj enlisted Kantor's help to find the shortest way to Abbas's palace. Their intent was to find Abbas's body and that of Bilal, if they were still there, and bury them as soon as possible according to the laws of Islam, for the benefit of their souls. Prayers needed to be said over the body in order for the soul to begin its journey.

Kantor, who knew the tunnels very well, took them to a street near to the palace. Leaving him at the tunnel entrance, they set out for the palace using every bit of darkness for cover. As they moved along the street, there was a distant rumble of thunder and sharp gusts of wind whirled down in between the houses, tossing rags and other debris into the air before dying out.

Soon they stood in the shadows of a side street close to the palace wall. Here they waited and watched to see if there were any signs of activity. All was silent, although there was a pungent smell of burnt wood and other materials in the air which confirmed the fire Mukhwana had talked about.

"It seems deserted," Talon remarked in a whisper. He was puzzled at the outline of the palace. There was something wrong with what he was seeing. The top stories of the palace could normally be seen from the street, but they were gone; he thought of the fire. He looked up. He sensed the night sky thick with clouds and wondered if it was going to rain.

"We must get in there quickly, before anyone comes back," Panhsj whispered to Talon.

"Then we go over the wall, and not through the gate."

Panhsj grunted acknowledgement, and they made their cautious way back to the wall they had formerly clambered over.

Getting back over the wall was more of a scramble as there was no pile of stones to take advantage of on the outside, but they did it silently nonetheless. They lay on the top listening for any noises that might betray another human within the compound. There was a faint sound from the servant's quarters which both men heard. They slipped down the inside wall and made their way back along the same narrow pathway they had escaped along to the entrance of the kitchens. Cautiously Talon and Panhsj moved into the darkness of the kitchen and listened.

The sound was there again. It was like a moan and then some thumping, followed by silence, then the sound of a struggle and a muffled cry. They looked at one another in the gloom, then as silent as ghosts they both moved towards the sound emanating from the servants' quarter beyond the kitchen.

As they crept along they heard the sound again and realized what it was. A commotion came from the open doorway of one of the alcoves the servants used for bedrooms. The one oil lamp placed on a ledge illuminated what they had expected. A woman, her clothes half torn off, was lying on a bed mat struggling with a man who himself lacked any clothes below his waist. He was attempting to rape her.

She was gagged, but her struggles were beginning to frustrate the man who, with an angry grunt, sat up and raised his hand to strike her. At that moment she saw Talon and Panhsj and her eyes went wide with surprise as she recognized them.

The man's hand never made its decent. There was a low "whop" followed by a snick, as Panhsj's sword swept through the air and sliced it off. The hand jumped off the arm and a small jet of blood followed. Before the shocked man could turn, Panhsj had driven his blade through his heart. Talon leapt forward to haul the man's body off the woman. It was Anyess.

He ripped off her gag while Panhsj dragged the body away into a corner and grabbed some clothes which he pushed at her to cover her nakedness.

"Don't make a sound," Talon whispered urgently to the terrified woman who now looked ready to faint. He turned his back to give her some privacy and to look at the body. It was the second of Chisisi's henchmen, Donkor. He looked at Panhsj and nodded his approval. Panhsj nodded with satisfaction and wiped his blade on the dead man's shirt and then went to the door to see if there was anyone else about. The room was lit by a flash of lightning that made Anyess flinch; it was followed by an ominous rumble of thunder overhead.

Turning back to Anyess, Talon whispered, "What happened? Why did you not escape with the others?"

But she was crouching on the mat shaking with silent sobs and he could not make her understand for a couple of moments. She composed herself and looked up at him with tears streaming down her face.

"They murdered the men back here and only a couple of the women escaped. I think they did, but I am not sure. There was so much screaming. I...I was terrified so I hid in the store room, but they came and found me. I have been tied up here since yesterday."

"Is there anyone else here in this compound?" Talon asked, wondering what might have happened to Lamya.

She nodded. "I am sure of it. They will be by the stables, I think. Donkor was not alone."

"Do you know what happened to Bilal?" Talon asked hopefully. She shook her head.

Panhsj eased back into the room. "We must leave her and find Abbas," he whispered.

Anyess looked terrified again. She gave a low wail, placing her hand across her mouth as she did so.

"We cannot leave her here, Panhsj. We can take her to the wall and get her on the top then attend to our business."

"Then help me hide this piece of dog shit in case others come to have some fun," Panhsj said, moving towards the corpse.

They took Anyess with them, back through the kitchens, and helped her onto the top of the wall, then left her there lying flat with instructions not to move until they came back for her.

This time they went the other way through the kitchens, but when they came to the stairwell that they had formerly escaped down, they found it blocked with debris and fallen beams. Peering up the well, Talon saw the darkening sky instead of the roof. A drop of rain fell on his upturned face.

They looked for another way to get upstairs. Their new route took them along the passages that lead to the great entrance hall. When they emerged, it was to see a ruin of what had once been two more stories to the palace. Their eyes were now well used to the darkness and they could see enough with the dim light that came down through the large opening where the roof and walls had once been.

The stairs had collapsed into a pile of rubble and they could see that the entire top floor had collapsed onto the other, obliterating any sign of Abbas and, for that matter, Bilal and his men where they were last seen. The stench of burnt flesh hung heavily in the stormy air. There were some charred body remains lying in the darkness but there was no way they could be identified. The stink of charred and rotting flesh was nauseating; death was everywhere, which truth was borne out by the black shapes lying about. The enemy had not even accorded their victims the respect due to the dead. Talon hoped that Bilal had died before being consumed in the flames. Panhsj was trembling with rage at what he was witnessing.

Talon was appalled at the destruction. He heard Panhsj's sharp intake of breath and knew he too was shocked. Just then Talon felt a drop of rain on his shoulder. It was quickly followed by a bright flash of lightning, then a massive crack of thunder and more hard drops; within a few seconds they were standing in a downpour. The rain made the charred building smell even more cloying. It was time to leave; they could do nothing further this night. Another flash of lightning briefly illuminated the ghostly devastation all around them. They both shrank back as they witnessed the gaping flesh-stripped skulls of their former comrades and other occupants of the house. The corpses were charred beyond recognition, their teeth bared, their eye sockets burnt into deep holes, and bones gleamed through the burned clothing. Talon shivered.

They needed no encouragement to hurry back to the passage leading to the kitchens. There was nothing they could do for the dead at this time. As they were moving through the kitchens, Talon remembered.

"My Lady wants clothes, and I also want to get my bow," he whispered.

Panhsj nodded and said, "Get me something to wear too, but be quick. I shall go and see if the woman is still where we told her to wait."

Talon ran noiselessly down the short corridor to his room, hoping that it had not been ransacked. It was in disarray, but who ever had rummaged through did not take many things. He hastily collected his bow and quiver that were fortunately still tucked away under his pallet. He hurriedly looked around for shawls and other clothes in an alcove nearby. He gathered up what he found, thinking that would have to do for Khalidah and Jasmine. He had tied a large bundle together when he heard a distant shout. At first he thought Panhsj had been discovered, but then realized that it came from outside near the stables. Panhsj had gone in the opposite direction.

He froze, wondering if he might have been mistaken, but the faint shouting continued. There were at least two men and they were yelling at someone else. Leaving his bundle behind but taking his bow and quiver, he eased himself out of the low building and out across the muddy path, to slip under a dense shrub. From here, despite the rain, he had a good view of the stables.

Parting the dripping wet branches he peered into the darkness to try and see what the men had been shouting about. Lightning flashed again and he could just make out a small group of struggling bodies near the horses, which to his surprise were still in their stalls. Perhaps they had been left on the orders of Bahir and his men to be collected at a later day. They had to be looked after; the horses could not be taken away without a couple of guards noticing and this seemed to be the case here.

There was a scream and Talon suddenly recognized the agonized voice of Haytham begging to be spared.

Not waiting any longer Talon sprung up, leaving his bow and charged through the bushes, running as fast as he could towards the men who now had Haytham on the ground and were about to stab him to death. His hands were across his chest for protection with his feet kicking high in the air in a desperate attempt to ward off the inevitable.

Talon ran straight into the first man with the blade of his knife roughly level with the man's heart. He drove it with a thump into the back of the man as he bent over the screaming boy. The other barely had time to see the menacing shape in front of him and to shout with surprise before Talon's sword blade had ripped through his neck. His half decapitated head fell over to the side. The corpses both fell away to splash in the mud, leaving Haytham flopping about, still wailing with terror.

Talon cuffed him gently and called over the noise of the pounding rain. "Stop yelling, it's me, Suleiman. Are there any others about?"

Haytham rolled onto his hands and knees and gaped up at Talon. Then he grabbed him around the legs bleating, "Suleiman, Allah be praised. It is really you? What has happened? Where... where are my Lady and my lord Kazim? Where is everybody?"

Talon extricated himself and hauled the boy to his feet. He calmed down enough to lean, weak and shaken, against the rough wall of the stables. His clothes were soaked and covered with mud, as were those of Talon by now, but Talon could make out no sign of injury.

"Are you hurt?"

The boy shook his head.

The horses nearby were reacting to the smell of blood by dancing restlessly around their stalls, but one nickered at the two men and pawed its stall door with a thump.

Talon glanced over and saw Rakhsh staring out at him. He grasped Haytham by the shoulder and dragged him closer to the stable wall where they had a little shelter from the downpour and where he could reach Rakhsh. There was another flash of lightning and the horse flinched, but Talon rubbed Rakhsh on the neck to reassure him and thought for a moment: perhaps Haytham on Rakhsh might get out of the city undetected whereas the Lady Khalidah would stand no chance.

Turning to Haytham he said urgently, "Haytham, listen. Listen to me. Why did you come back?"

"I came for a horse, Suleiman. I wanted to go south to *Oustez* Malek. I thought you were all dead," the boy gasped, wiping his eyes.

"Good boy," Talon said with some surprise. His estimation of the Haytham's courage went up another notch. "But are you not injured?"

"I can still ride, *Oustez*."

"Take Rakhsh, he knows you, and ride, ride for your life, but not south to Malek. You must go east and find the sultan. Keep going to the east, and ask people to tell you where he is. Tell him," he paused, "tell him Emir Abbas is dead—murdered by Bahir, but Lady Khalidah and the children are in hiding. Tell him that there is a plot of some kind here in Cairo. I do not know who else is part of it is, but a man called Umarah, I think they call him the Poet, is one of them, the other is Bahir. There is another, who I think is named Al Muntaqim, but tell the sultan he must come back at once. There is danger for him if he delays. He should be prepared for treachery. Do you understand what I have said?" Talon demanded.

Haytham nodded vigorously and rushed to do as he was bid. Talon collected his bow from the bush, and on his return took one of the swords from the dead men, then rifled their pockets and clothing for coin, retrieving a few coppers. Then he gave a hand to Haytham to saddle Rakhsh. The horse was not very pleased to be dragged out into the rain. He did what he was asked of, although he pranced a little and snorted his disquiet. Talon assisted Haytham onto Rakhsh's back, then he thrust a handful of coins up at him.

"Bribe the guards with this coin to get you out, and when you have found the sultan, which God willing you will, give him the message; after that you must ride for Fayoum. We will be going there soon. Trust no one." He handed up the money.

Haytham pocketing the coin and a gold dinar that Talon handed to him. Then Talon ran towards the back gate to check whether there was a guard there. Rakhsh and Haytham followed just behind him splashing through the puddles.

There was a guard, but Talon had strung his bow by now; and as the running, shouting man raced towards them with his spear at the ready, Talon loosed an arrow that sped the short distance to strike the man directly in the chest. The rain drowned out the sound of the strike and the man stumbled a few steps and fell forward to die face down without a sound.

Slapping Rakhsh on the rump, Talon urged the boy on. Haytham's words were lost in the pouring rain but Talon heard the last, "...protect you!"

Boy and horse galloped off down the muddy street and disappeared into the darkness.

Talon stared after the boy for some moments, oblivious of the rain, wondering if he would be able to make the hard ride to find the sultan. He realized he had sent the boy on a dangerous quest that he might not survive. Then he turned and ran back past the dead men to the servants' quarters, collected the sizeable bundle of clothes he had dropped, and hurried to where he found a very agitated Panhsj waiting for him in the dark.

"What took you so long, Suleiman?" He growled with concern in his tone.

"I ran into Haytham being attacked by the last two men who were guarding the horses. I sent him off to find the sultan on Rakhsh." He left out the details, but Panhsj understood.

"We should leave. That woman will die of cold if we do not get her back to safety; she has been laying up there for a long time now."

They finally made it back to the catacombs with a still terrified Anyess. She, shaking with cold and fright, was handed over to the women, who were once again woken up in the dead of night to deal with this new arrival.

The rain had created small rivers out of the underground streams, making their crossing difficult. Even the tunnels deep underground were not spared the effects of the storm, as water had seeped through the limestone walls and accumulated in dark, muddy puddles.

Khalidah awoke and came into the hall to hear the news; the children slept on despite the disturbance in the main hall. Mukhwana and the two guards came to hear what the returning men had to tell them. It was bleak news for them all, even with the small satisfaction of having killed the last of the traitors. To hear that Haytham was trying to get out of the city and east to find the sultan helped raise their spirits, and Talon was glad to see Khalidah's shoulders lift and brace courageously as she digested this news. She thanked Talon for the bundle of clothes, as it had become decidedly cooler with the damp in this underground hiding place.

Panhsj and Talon watched with concern as she walked slowly back towards her bed area. Her shoulders were bowed and her head was down; it was clear that she was weeping. They looked at one another helplessly; there was nothing they could do to ease the grief that tore at her.

# Chapter 20

# A Promise Kept

Talon knew he had one more task to perform while they waited for Mukhwana to find a boat for their escape. He decided not to ask Panhsj to come with him; although he trusted his new found friend to fight his way out of any trouble, he wanted to do this alone. Talon intended to go to Bahir's palace and leave a message for the enemy that would be unmistakable; but it had to be done without anyone else knowing its origin.

While everyone was occupied during the second evening, huddled over their food in the faint smoky light of the oil lamps and wishing that the dank and wet tunnels were less cold, he slipped away unseen. He deliberately left his own sword behind to throw people off the scent, and then simply vanished from sight. No one remarked his absence until he had been gone for at least an hour and then nobody thought he would have left the safety of the tunnels, for his sword was still by his sleeping blanket.

It was a long way to go from the sanctuary to the palace of Bahir. The air was cool after the storm of the previous evening. The usual filthy puddles had been refreshed with rain water and the recessed places, in the corners between walls and at the base of stone steps, were strewn with trapped debris carried there by the rushing waters from the storm.

He noticed that there were few people about, which was unusual, as the Cairo citizen liked to stay up late. Talon reasoned that it had to be due to the current uncertainty and fear that kept the merchants in their own homes and the revelers off the streets. He noticed groups of armed men at some street intersections and gave them a wide berth. It was easy enough to move by unnoticed, as they were often enjoying noisy games of dice and bones around a fire that warmed them against the evening chill. It became obvious as he made his way along the gloomy streets that the city was under some kind of armed watch and he felt that his suspicions about the political climate were confirmed.

Using all his skill, he kept out of sight, for he did not want to be intercepted either coming or going. Often as not, it was unavoidable that he should come very close to people, but no one noticed the inconspicuous shadow slipping by. Once again he was able to put his training in the school of the Assassins to good use.

He reached the tall walls of Bahir's palace and studied its fascia for a place to clamber over. It did not take him long to scale the outer wall unnoticed by the sentries who were on patrol on the top of the wall. They failed to notice the shadow that eased over the edge and slithered down the inner wall to disappear into the darkness of the bushes. He planned to gain entry into Bahir's chamber through a main door he had noticed while on his last visit, but he ran into an unexpected problem; it was now guarded by a large man, and unfortunately he appeared to be wide awake.

Talon wondered why there were guards everywhere, but then he supposed Bahir was probably concerned for his own safety after sacking Abbas's palace, and he was therefore taking no chances. Talon paused in the darkness offered by the heavy folds of some wall curtains to think how it was to be done and decided that he would investigate the servants first and see what they were doing that might offer an opportunity.

From what he had seen the last time, he doubted that many of them were asleep. He suspected that Bahir kept his staff running about on his behalf until late. He was right. There were still many of them awake. He avoided being discovered by moving quickly out of the way or walking past someone with his head down, as though on an errand himself. He knew this would not work for very long as sooner or later one of them would challenge him. In fact one did, but fortunately for Talon there was a large chest nearby and the inquisitive servant, now very dead, was swiftly dumped inside it and the lid eased quietly down upon the body.

Talon borrowed the man's linen overshirt and made his way to the kitchens to see what he could carry. It seemed to him that no one challenged anyone who was carrying around a tray of food or drink and moving purposefully in one direction. He was lucky, the sleepy cooks and a couple of other servants were huddled together at the entrance to the large cooking area getting some fresh air.

He noted a brass tray with cups and a brass pot that steamed, giving off the smell of fresh coffee, which had been placed on a stone shelf nearby. He quietly lifted the tray and moved back into the corridor he had just left. He slipped along the now familiar route to the main entrance of the room where the sentry was standing guard at the door of the same room he had entered the last time he had visited. He had assumed there was only one destination for the coffee. His face half in shadow from the turban loosely wrapped and now well over his brows, Talon indicated that he wanted entry.

The guard looked him over casually, his attention held by the tray and the aroma of coffee that accompanied him. Talon waited patiently for him to open the door and let him through; he felt his heart pounding.

The guard even leaned over and sniffed the coffee, clearly wishing he could have some, and leered, "By God, I wish it was me going in there...those two nymphs are from heaven, I swear."

Talon found the wits to give him a tight grin and sidled past gingerly, balancing the tray. He wondered if Bahir would recognize him from the game of chogan, where indeed they had come very close. At the far end of the room Talon could see a pool of amber light cast by two oil lamps. Bahir was reclining on the sleeping platform among the cushions and the rumpled silk bed clothes. He was partially undressed and had company.

Leaning over him and snuggling up to him were two very pretty girls. They were quite naked, the glow of the flame casting soft shadows on their limbs. They were giggling and moving their hands over Bahir's chest, whispering seductively to him. Keeping his eyes down Talon approached the bed and stood waiting.

Bahir noticed the presence of the servant as his nostrils caught the coffee aroma wafting across the room. He waved his hand for Talon to place it on a low table alongside the bed.

Talon did as he was told and poured a small cup of the black cardamom flavored coffee, which he offered to Bahir with a deep bow, keeping his head and his eyes down. Bahir, however, had eyes only for the two naked girls. His one hand was stroking the smooth inner thigh of one girl sliding slowly up to her hairless sex, while he enjoyed what the other was doing to him. She had him thoroughly aroused. Bahir glanced up and took the cup without a word, drained it, handed it back, and waved Talon off without even looking up.

Talon glanced around the room as he placed the cup back on the tray and withdrew backward, his head down. He had no intention of leaving, however. He could have stabbed Bahir then and there, but he knew he would have to kill the girls too, and he might not be able to prevent a scream from one of them.

There was a curtained archway that led to an open window perhaps twenty feet from the bed. He faded into this darker shadow, watching Bahir all the time, and then found himself with plenty of room on a balcony that looked out over a small courtyard where bushes and small palms grew. He assessed the options of escape. If he could get down the twenty feet to the courtyard he could easily get amongst the bushes and then over the main wall to the street. The curtains would provide him with a rope.

He made his plans for departure while listening to the increasing activity on the bedroom side of the curtain. The one thing he did not want was for Bahir to get off the bed and walk to the window. He settled down to wait and tried to shut out the moans of ecstasy, real or performed, that came from the bed. Bahir was a strong man and quite determined to wear both girls out. Their enthusiasm waned, for he was a brutal lover, leaving one semi-conscious. The other one shrank into a corner of the bed whimpering.

Talon's ears registered a shuffling outside the main door; he shrank back into the deeper shadows. A man came in and bowed very low some ten feet from the bed where Bahir was sitting up. The girls, probably relieved to have a break, were peering fearfully out from under the rumpled bedclothes.

"What is it, Akhom?" Bahir asked querulously, clearly put out by this interruption.

"Will there be anything else that you require this evening, my lord?" It was the huge servant and body guard whom Talon had seen on his former visit. "No. Go away and do not come for me until I call in the morning. Make sure the guards are silent outside the door," Bahir grunted.

The servant bowed again. "May Allah pour his blessings upon you this night, My lord, and give you great strength," he said unctuously, and backed out of the room.

The door closed quietly and Talon sensed that the rest of the house was going to sleep. Bahir chuckled and was quickly restored to full arousal and the passion on the bed became heated, but this time there was much slapping and even some crying from the girls as Bahir got into his stride. Talon yawned.

Later when the crescent moon was half way down on the western sky, Bahir got out of bed and went over to a large pot in the corner of the room, relieving himself noisily. He climbed back into bed and soon went to sleep, ignoring the girls. After a whispered conference they followed suit, but they huddled together on the left side of the bed as far away as possible from Bahir. Soon snores told Talon that Bahir had fallen into a deep sleep. He watched the girls for a few long moments to ensure that they too were asleep.

Moving out of his cover, Talon crept over to the bed, all the time intently watching the sleeping figures. His blade in hand, he was prepared for any one of them who might sense him and wake up suddenly; they would just as quickly die.

He was glad that Bahir was on the right hand side of the bed and that he was also lying on his right side. It was an easy matter to open the vein that pulsed on the sleeping man's thick neck. The convulsions were mild, as much blood had flowed before the victim awoke groggily to realize his terrible predicament. Neither of the girls awoke during the brief time Talon knelt on his chest and held a hand over the man's mouth. He stared down into the stricken eyes of Bahir which slowly glazed over as he died. Bahir's last image in life was to see Talon's dark figure leaning over him.

* * * * *

Talon arrived back in the tunnels and slipped by the two sentries that Mukhwana had posted on the advice of Panhsj; neither noticed him. He went to bed near the sleeping Panhsj and shut his eyes.

259

The next morning was much like any other in the caverns. They ate a plain breakfast of cabbage and lentil soup accompanied by large, wide disks of dried bread. Mukhwana had thoughtfully provided some fruit, stolen no doubt, but welcome.

Talon woke later than the others and joined them towards the end of the meal. There were questioning looks from Khalidah after the normal greetings, but she did not ask any questions. The children had not noticed enough to ask questions either. There was a resigned look about them, however; there was nothing to be done at this point but wait for Mukhwana to find a boat. Panhsj took Talon aside later and demanded to know where he had been.

"No one really noticed, not even that Lord of the Beggars, as you call him, Suleiman. But I know you went somewhere. Was it back to the palace? What did you do all night?"

"I wandered the streets thinking and watching; there are soldiers all over the place. It would be very dangerous for us to leave these tunnels except at night, and even then it has to be by way of the river. Allah knows what else our enemies are doing and planning."

Panhsj nodded agreement, but there was a bewildered scowl on his face. "I trust you now, Suleiman, although I was right, you are not what you seem." He paused and added in a conspiratorial tone. "I shall not say anything."

It was not long into the morning when a couple of beggars came rushing into the tunnel area shouting with excitement.

Mukhwana was holding court, as usual, with his old cronies reestablished in their respective places, lounging in front of him, smoking and drinking tea. It was almost as though they had never moved, Talon thought, as he contemplated them. He looked up, along with everyone else at the arrival of the newcomers. Nerves were on edge and this could portend an attack.

Men scrambled for weapons, as did Panhsj and Talon, although he was sure he knew the reason for the excitement. The two beggars ran up to the platform where Mukhwana was seated and without any preamble babbled out their news in loud voices. They were so excited that he had to stop them and make them tell it again.

"What in the name of Allah are you two idiots trying to say?" he roared.

"The Lord Bahir is dead! He was murdered! His head was found on the window ledge of his bedroom," they shouted back in unison. "The news is all over the city. They think it was the Hashishini. No one else could have done such a thing in this manner."

Mukhwana dropped the mouthpiece of the water pipe he had been drawing on and sat back gaping at them.

Panhsj turned slowly towards Talon, his eyes wide with shock. "You?" he exclaimed in a whisper that no one else could hear.

Talon put a finger to his lips and drew Panhsj away. "Yes, I killed him, and you must not tell anyone about it, Panhsj; fear would put people against us and even against my Lady. The man deserved to die, and I wanted to leave a message for the others involved in this that they could expect no place to be safe."

Panhsj said very quietly, "By God but you are a dangerous man, Suleiman—if that is your real name. I will support you because what you did is for my young lord's protection, but I think I too fear you. What should we do now?"

"I for one need an escort to go and get the rest of the gold, and then we will have to see what happens."

He gained permission to go see the Jewish banker Levi without problem, and a while later found himself facing the man over the inevitable cups of tea.

Levi again noted the dirt on his customer and the unkempt and even unwashed state, but refrained from comment. However, while they were sipping tea, seated on silk cushions placed on the colorful carpets, he could not resist mentioning the latest news.

"Suleiman, you must have heard? The street is abuzz with gossip, and it is all about the death of Lord Bahir. He was murdered in his bed but his head was put on display! You might remember you played chogan with him. Now both he and Lord Abbas are dead. Is that some kind of coincidence perhaps?"

"I am sure there is an explanation for it. I do not think the deaths are connected, though. I suspect as everyone else does, that Bahir offended the Hashashini. May God be kind to his soul," Talon said in a casual manner.

"You cannot believe how much the people on the street love this kind of thing, although nothing quite like this has happened before. The stories get more lurid by the hour. My servant tells me that they are talking about nothing else in all the tea houses. It has provided Cairo with a new crop of vulgar jokes. They find this horrifying, but funny, too." He could not hold back a small grin as he said, "Losing his head over a couple of girls. The people of Cairo have not had so much entertainment for a long time."

Indeed, it seemed that this latest event almost eclipsed the tragedy of Abbas in people's minds. Few, if any, made any connection. Levi, who obviously had his ear to the ground, and whose very existence depended upon being ahead of events, did not make any certain connection between the two deaths. He discussed the incident with Talon as though it was merely a coincidence.

Talon was listening carefully and looked interested, but none of what was being said all round him was of any real importance. He made his way back to the tunnels and handed the remainder of the gold dinars over to Mukhwana.

Later that evening, after the excited chatter over dinner had died down and Mukhwana had collected all the available facts of the matter, he held a conference.

Khalidah and the children were given the place of honor near him on the threadbare cushions, with tea to hand. To Talon, she looked pale and wan. The events and their predicament, combined with the filthy conditions they endured, were taking their toll.

Talon, Panhsj, and the two guards Hanif and Aahmes were standing nearby.

"It would seem that Allah in his infinite wisdom has seen fit to rid the world of a very bad man. May He not have mercy on his soul," Mukhwana intoned, his one eye resting on Talon for a long moment. "However, the danger to you, my Lady, is not lessened, as Al Muntaqim is a vengeful man, and if he even suspects that you had a hand in this, he will move heaven and earth to find you."

Khalidah spoke for the first time in some while.

"I do not understand how it could be possible for me to have had a hand in Emir Bahir's death, but as you say, Lord of the Beggars; Allah's will has been done and I am rid of the man who murdered my husband, or at least one of them, and for that I give thanks to Allah."

Her clear voice reached the people at the edge of the crowded cavern. Many muttered their agreement; there was much sympathy for her here. In the short while they had spent in this underground place she had behaved with dignity and kindness to all.

"Go about your business, all of you. I want to talk to these people in private!" Mukhwana bellowed. The crowd dispersed slowly to their respective caves while the group near to him settled in to listen.

"All the same, it is important to get you out of the city, my Lady, and in that regard I have not been tardy," Mukhwana said in a low voice.

"There is now a boat, but we still have to find a way to get you onto it. Once aboard, you will be safe, as it is a very fine falukah and can take you up stream faster than most boats. The trouble is that if you go to the docks, everyone will know that it is you, my Lady, and for sure recognize the boy here," he pointed at Kazim.

"Can we not go there via the tunnels and drains that reach across the city?" Talon asked.

The discussion went back and forth for some time in low voices, as they explored their limited options. They went to bed still wondering when they would be able to leave safely.

* * * * *

In another large house far removed from the tunnels, two men were having tea. The poet Umarah ibn Ali al-Hakami was pale with worry, and so agitated that he could barely hold the small and elegant ceramic cup of tea in his shaking hands. Opposite him sat Al Muntaqim, who glared at him as though daring him to whine. Between them was a low table with food on it, but neither had any appetite.

The poet had to voice his fear to someone, but the only person who could be included in his confidence sat opposite him and was not responsive to his feelings.

"Who could have done this dreadful thing? By God, I cannot think of such a horrible death for anyone. I pray Allah will be kind to his soul." His voice was faint.

"It is highly doubtful that Allah will be kind to his soul, poet, but I am just now more concerned for my own life, as you should be for yours." Al Muntaqim spoke drily, and carried on with disdain.

"As usual, Bahir bungled the attack on Abbas—although in the end it worked, as the whole place nearly burned to the ground. There is no sign of the eunuch I paid to do the killing, so I hope that he died in the flames. It must have been a lamp or something that fell over."

"How can you be so flippant about this ghastly thing?" Umarah said plaintively.

"I find it just as frightening as you do. I heard there were two girls in the bed with him and the assassin left his headless body on the bed; imagine waking up to that. Not many men loses their head quite so literally over a woman." Al Muntaqim grinned wolfishly at the agitated poet. That was too much for Umarah.

"I am leaving the city for my estates tomorrow. Perhaps I shall go abroad!" he wailed. "I am not a warrior and this is more than I can take. Will one of us be next?"

"You will stay in the city, and only go when I give you leave to do so, poet." Al Muntaqim said icily. "I will have the brigade from Alexandria here in three days and then the city is truly mine. Think of the irony. The sultan has built the citadel to prevent the Franks from retaking the city, but I shall be there instead. On the inside." He chuckled.

"The sultan does not have the army to take it off me when he comes back. He will find the men from Alexandria already in here. There is also a large contingent of Nubians, and you know how they feel about him."

"What if he hears of Bahir and decides to come back before then?" Umarah was in need of comfort food and began nibbling a sweet honey-coated cake.

"He will not come back because I have sent messengers to tell him that the Hashishini struck Bahir down for some quarrel he had with them. You know what they are like. If they decide to demand money after you owe them a favor and you do not pay in time? Your life is forfeit.

"I have also made sure that no more pigeons fly in that direction to warn him of the events here in Cairo."

The poet gulped. "That Sinan of the Mountains is a terrifying man. He was, or is still, a teacher, but they say he can do all manner of magical things, and I know he holds a deep hatred for the sultan. Perhaps we should ask him to take care of Salah Ed Din?" The poet shuddered elaborately.

Al Muntaqim smiled coldly. "I have anticipated you."

Umarah stared at him, his mouth dropping open, and some saliva began to dribble down his chin. He closed his mouth just in time and wiped his plump lips on a fine linen cloth.

"You have hired Rashid Ed Din's assassins?" His voice was incredulous.

"Remember those Ismaili hate Salah Ed Din because he and his uncle conquered this country and made it all Sunni under the caliphate of Baghdad. We are all in accord; you and I, and many like us detest the Ayyubi for having invaded this country and dispossessing many of the royal families. In effect, we are allies. Don't you see?" He raised both eyebrows and continued.

"I sent a messenger asking if he would send some of his men to kill the sultan using their skill and stealth, but as yet I do not know if Sinan Rashid has done anything. It is a long journey from the Jabal Bahra Mountains, well north of the Kingdom of Jerusalem. He has not sent a reply and I do not even know what he will want in payment, if he accepts the offer."

"I think you are playing a very dangerous game, Al Muntaqim. Sinan is more deadly than a cobra. If he agrees, then he will want a lot of gold for it," the poet said, regaining some confidence. "Do you know that the Frankish Templars, God damn them, extract a tithe from him every year? Oh yes. He will want a lot of gold."

"Impossible." Al Muntaqim was less cocky now.

"No, possible. Somehow those dreadful warriors have him within their sway, but I would not want to bring it up in any conversation."

"No indeed."

"You don't think, Oh Allah protect us, but do you think this was a warning not to cross him—in case we change our minds, for instance?" The poet reached for another sweet cake, he was so nervous.

Al Muntaqim was thoughtful.

"It is entirely possible that Bahir crossed someone and they dealt with him this way. But it comes so closely upon the destruction of Abbas and his home that I am puzzled."

In fact, despite his casual attitude, Al Muntaqim was deeply concerned. Something did not quite fit and his mind was worrying at the issue even as he put on a confident face before the poet.

"In any case, the woman Khalidah and the boy Kazim, his only heir, still live. I want those estates for myself and now that Bahir is out of the way, I will have them. I am sure the family has not escaped as yet, as none of my men who are watching the estate has sent any messages to tell me they have made their way back. I would know if they were on the road for sure, and the harbor is watched night and day. It's just a matter of time."

"You are without feeling, Al Muntaqim. Bahir's body is barely cold and you are taking the spoils."

Al Muntaqim smiled. "You could say that," he chuckled. "He tried to be in two places at once, and look where that got him... his head here and his body there?" He laughed.

Umarah looked as though he were going to be sick.

* * * * *

Deep in the poorer section of the city, but still quite close to the grand mosque of Al-Azhar, two men sat drinking tea.

They were slim, youthful men, but to the keen observer they were wiry and honed—every move or gesture denoted feline strength. They were relaxed at this time, their weapons placed still close to hand, and the dark clothes they wore loose and comfortable. They were waiting for another to join them.

It was not long before they heard the light tap on the door, but cautious men that they were, one glided towards the door to wait next to the wall near the door opening with his sword held high, while the other spoke in a whisper through the dried up wood. It was a code, and hearing the correct answer, he glanced at the other, then he opened the door to admit another man similar to both in dress and physique.

Their leader spoke in low tones. "What is going on in the street? We have heard chatter outside, but cannot get the gist of it."

"There is word about that our people killed a man called Lord Bahir. They say that his head was cut off and placed on the ledge of a window looking out over his gardens. I listened to people in the bazaar and they are sure that it is an assassination by our people."

"Our people? Has Sinan sent others to do some work we know nothing about?" queried the leader.

"If not our people, who could have done this?" The third man shrugged.

"Allah alone knows. They are joking that two women were in the bed with him when he was killed and neither was touched; they woke up to find him dead in the bed with them but without his head. The Egyptians seem to find that very funny; they are joking about it everywhere. They are strange people."

"What should we do? Is not our mission still to kill the sultan?"

"Yes. Those are our orders, but we would surely know if any of our brethren were here in Cairo doing something else. Would we not? Should we send a message to Sinan? Could it perhaps be our Persian cousins who did this?"

The leader nodded reflectively. "They would never tell Sinan if they were involved in something here in Egypt, despite our relationship. The Agha Khan is answerable to no one. We should be very careful. If they are here they might not want us around, and you know what that means. But one way or the other, we must find out who did this. Sinan will want to know."

* * * * *

Late that night Mukhwana summoned Talon. When he came up and joined the beggar leader, Mukhwana was looking tense. "You have your boat, Suleiman, but you must leave at once."

They woke the women and Kazim, who whined about being woken in the dead of night, but when told to stop grumbling and to get ready to leave he became quiet and attentive to his mother. She pulled the two nervous children to her and whispered, "Have courage now. Suleiman and Panhsj will protect us, we are going home; *Insha'Allah* we will be there by tomorrow."

Mukhwana lumbered up to them as they were about to leave the cavern. There was a lamp nearby so Talon could see his features, and his one eye gleamed.

"You have delivered me gold and I have kept my side of the bargain. We are even in God's eyes, Suleiman. Go with God and go in peace. I think my Lady and her children are in good hands and her enemies have much to fear."

Talon looked sharply at the big man, but just nodded and said, "May Allah protect you, my friend. You have risked much on our behalf, and I shall not forget it."

Khalidah placed a hand on Mukhwana's thick arm. "You have provided me and my family with shelter and refuge when you could have done otherwise, Lord of the Beggars. May Allah's blessings always be upon you. I shall find a way to repay you one day."

The man was very touched, it was clear; but he said, a little more gruffly than usual to conceal his emotion, "Go in peace, my Lady, and may your journey be swift and safe. Follow my guides and make no noise; there is still much danger in this city for you."

The guides took them by a different route. The system of tunnels often petered out and they would find themselves climbing out into a deserted ruin of a building or having to move swiftly but silently across open ground to follow a narrow street before being led through a dark passage and then back down into the entrails of the sleeping city.

Talon had been concerned about Khalidah and the children having to negotiate the rat infested passages, but they seemed to have adjusted to the extraordinary circumstances and it was Anyess who shrank at the squeaking creatures that ran across her feet as she stifled her instinctive cries.

After almost half an hour of slow-but-sure-progress, the guides held up their hands to stop and blew out their clay oil lamps, plunging them into pitch darkness.

They waited for long moments, standing ankle deep in some trickling water that stank, before one of them stepped out through a small opening and disappeared. The other whispered that they were near the docks and must make no sound. After a while there was a faint shuffling sound and the other man returned.

He leaned towards where Talon was standing and whispered in his ear.

"The boat is ready but not at the wharf. It is near to the canal which is a hundred paces away to the left of here. The boat captain is pretending that he has a problem with his hull and has had it pulled up some way onto the bank. You can trust him, he is a relative of our leader, but it would be good to pay him a little more when you get to your destination. We will have to push you off once you are on the boat."

Talon did not pass along the message but it was clear that they were to follow the two men very cautiously. Talon looked off to the right to where the main docks were located. They were exiting from a tunnel, more of a drain that emptied out into the river. It was situated at the extreme end of the busy wharf, which was dark and deserted at this time of night, but he did notice armed men at the far end clustered around a fire. Talon had no doubt that if they made much noise they would attract some unwelcome attention from those men.

They waded through some stinking mud and sludge that forced them to hold their breath, and there in the dim light silhouetted against the expanse of water they saw the dark hull of a boat pulled half way out of the river. The children were carried by the two body guards while Khalidah was assisted by Panhsj.

At the looming hull of the boat they were challenged quietly, and the guides responded. Then it was time to help Khalidah and the children up and over the side of the boat. Anyess followed, and the crew on board helped them down into the waist of the boat in silence. The men stayed on the ground and Talon gave some coins to the two guides, who were surprised and grateful.

"I shall pray to Allah to protect you, *Oustez*, and the great Lady."

"Allah protect you. Go in peace."

It was time to push the boat back into the water. The four of them heaved hard, but for a frightening moment it did not move. It seemed as though it was stuck in the glue-like mud, but then, as they applied all their strength, it began to move very slowly. The vessel slid deeper into the open water until it was finally floating free. Talon and Panhsj scrambled over the side, wet and filthy, and then assisted the crew of three men to quickly unfurl the sail, which flapped noisily but suddenly bellied as it caught the light wind coming off the warm shore, and the boat surged forward. The crew moved about their tasks with swift efficiency, silently ensuring that the sail took full advantage of the wind. Mukhwana's guides had vanished into the darkness of the shoreline without a word.

Talon realized that he had been holding his breath waiting for an alarm of some kind, but the shore was silent and the wharfs, now several hundred paces away, seemed to be asleep.

The crew hauled the sail tighter and the boat gained speed rapidly. The helmsman was watching the river intently as though remembering the channels. Before very long they were well out in the middle of the huge river of the Nile, and Talon began to relax. There was a sigh from Panhsj nearby as he too relaxed for the first time since they had embarked upon their escape.

"*Insha'Allah* we are now finally on our way home," he whispered.

"May He protect us as we sail," Talon responded.

# Chapter 21

# A Sultan's Army

Far to the east of Al Qahirah but only a few miles from the fortified Christian town of Gaza an army was camped. This was an army that was for the most part of Turkish and Kurdish cavalry; although a sizeable number were also Arabs. There were no tents other than that of the general in command, and that was placed in the middle of the encampment, protected on all sides by men loyal to the Sultan Salah Ed Din. With first light the messenger pigeons were awake and cooing for their handlers to feed them. These much prized birds were the communications link with Al Qahirah and other cities upon which Salah Ed Din relied for messages and intelligence, but no new pigeons had arrived for a full day from Al Qahirah, which was unusual.

As dawn broke and streaks of light illuminated the eastern sky the army stirred, and in this desolate place of stone and sand someone began to call the soldiers to prayers. As the camp awoke and men knelt facing the southeast murmuring their prayers, the sun peeped over the horizon about to begin its long journey across the sky.

With the arrival of the dawn a sentry on the southern perimeter of the waking army peered out at the dark western desert and wondered if he had heard a sound. Although most noises were drowned out by the voices of thousands of men murmuring their prayers he was very alert, as they were close to the fortress of Gaza. No one wanted to be caught unprepared by one of those fanatical attacks by the mad Franks who lived inside. He heard the sound again, and this time the unmistakable 'click' of a horse's hoof striking a stone.

"Who goes there?" he shouted loudly, knowing that others would hear him and come to his aid if there was trouble.

There was a hoarse cough as though someone had tried to speak and failed. Men who had finished their devotions joined the sentry, armed and ready for anything. The alarm was being sounded and the army began to hurriedly prepare for the possibility of an attack.

Then, to the surprise of the soldiers peering out into the darkness, a single figure on a horse came slowly towards them. The eastern sky was now well lit and the men could see that the figure on the horse was slumped over its neck and the horse itself, streaked with dried sweat and its head low, was moving very slowly, as though it too was near the end of its strength.

The group of soldiers chattered to one another, wondering if this was a trap, but as the horse continued to walk slowly towards them the details became clearer. They realized that the rider was truly alone and that no madmen were about to charge out of the west from behind him; however, there was something wrong, for he swayed in the saddle and was clearly exhausted, to the point where he was about to fall to the ground.

The sultan was alerted by one of his aides, who told him that a boy tied to a horse had arrived and asked to see the sultan, but the boy was almost dead from thirst and exhaustion. The sultan had only just finished his prayers and was being assisted into his chain mail by two servants. He paused and then commanded that they should bring the boy to him at once.

His eyes widened with surprise when he saw the ragged, inert form carried into the tent. It was indeed just a boy and he looked as though he might even then be dead.

"Fetch Jacob immediately," the alarmed sultan commanded and pointed to where they should place the boy. He stepped closer to the boy, who was now placed on the carpet among the cushions where the sultan normally held his council. Exhaustion was etched into the young lad's features, and although someone had given him water it seemed he might be near death.

"My lord, he rode in this dawn on an exhausted but a beautiful horse, while he himself looks like just a syce," they told him.

Jacob, the physician, arrived and immediately exclaimed at the boy's condition and asked for wet cloths to be placed on his forehead. He was burning up. The sultan stood over them.

"Who is he? Where did he come from and what is he doing here?" he asked no one in particular.

The boy stirred and opened his eyes, but they could not seem to focus.

"I must see the sultan; it is a matter of life or death," he whispered through split and bleeding lips. Salah Ed Din started with surprise and exchanged looks with Jacob.

"Who are you, and who send you?" the sultan asked.

"I am Haytham, syce of my lord Abbas, my lord. You must come back to Al Qahirah...there...there is danger," he whispered.

The sultan stared down at the boy whose head was now swathed in wet linen bandages and to whom the physician was administering a few drops of water at a time, although he seemed to have trouble swallowing.

"I have heard about the death of Lord Abbas and Lord Bahir... but what brings you here?" Salah Ed Din demanded; too late, the boy had fainted.

"See if you can save him, Jacob. It looks bad, but I must know what he is talking about. I shall be back in a short while; it is time for me to talk to my commanders," the sultan said as he strode out of the tent.

As soon as he finished his conference, the sultan returned with a few of his senior commanders and they sat facing the carpet where the boy lay. Jacob looked up. "God is keeping him with us, my lord, and he has said one thing."

"What was that?" the sultan enquired.

"He said that a man called Suleiman told him to warn you about a poet named Umarah, and Lord Bahir, and some other name. He said that these men are plotting against you, but he never finished. He cried that Suleiman had saved Abbas's wife and something about a fire. Suleiman told him to find you and to warn you that there is danger in the city of Al Qahirah. He did not know exactly what, but he is sure it is against you."

There was consternation among the commanders. They all stared at the ragged form on the bed, now gasping for breath.

"Who is this Suleiman he talks of? Should I know him?"

"Perhaps yes, my lord, he was one of the players on Abbas's side during the game of chogan," one of the sultan's officers said diffidently. "He made sure my lord Abbas was protected when he had the accident."

The Sultan smiled and said, "Yes I remember now, the one who looks somewhat like a Frank?"

"Yes my lord, but he is a loyal servant of my lord Abbas...I mean he was."

"But I have had messenger pigeons, admittedly two days ago, which told me about the death of Abbas. They said it was a murder by the Hashashini, Allah curse them. Although why the Hashashini would want to kill Abbas, only God knows."

"We also had a messenger sent here by Lord Kemosiri, your honor, who said the same thing about the murder of Bahir," another commander stated.

The boy tried to sit up, his eyes swiveling wildly as though he had heard the conversation. Jacob tried to restrain him but it was as though he was driven.

"Suleiman is hiding my Lady from them."

"Who are they hiding from?" This question came from one of the commanders.

Gasping for air, Haytham said, "One of the men ...was Lord Bahir, and another was called Umarah, but there is another. I...I cannot remember his name." Two small tears fell from his closed eyes in frustration.

"But the sultan must be prepared for danger when he comes back," the boy finished in a short breath and then lay back in the cradle of the physician's arms.

The sultan leaned forward, wondering if the effort might have cost the boy what remained of his life.

"My lord, I must ask respectfully that we cease asking questions for now and wait until I have helped him recover, or he will die. As it is, he is on the edge of leaving us," Jacob said to the sultan, who nodded in reluctant agreement.

"Bring me that messenger who was here," Salah Ed Din said abruptly; his face was grim.

Men ran to do his bidding. Meanwhile the sultan's lean face was thoughtful.

"Are we talking about the poet Umarah? And what has Bahir got to do with any of this?" he mused.

Men nodded uncomfortably. They were stunned by the news, but the manner of its delivery could not be more convincing.

A man rushed up to the entrance of the tent and was admitted at once. He fell to his knees as he came before the seated sultan.

"My lord. The messenger you asked about is gone. They say he left this morning."

"Catch him! Send men after him at once! I want to know more about this messenger."

Two of his officers and the soldier got to their feet and rushed out of the tent.

The sultan turned to look down at Haytham. "It would appear that he might have done me a great service. Allah in his kindness let him find me and deliver vital news. For this he will be well rewarded. Assuming he lives, *Insha'Allah.*"

He turned to his commanders and said. "Break camp. We are marching back to Al Qahirah at once."

* * * * *

That same dawn broke over the wide expanse of the river Nile. It was almost midsummer now and the heat was already beginning to be felt even on this vast water. The floods were about to commence, which would bring new hazards to the river traffic.

Talon and Panhsj leaned on the wooden side of the falukah watching the distant river bank. They were concerned that they might have been noticed and that even now the enemy could be riding along the main road that ran almost alongside the river to try to intercept them.

"The river will soon be overflowing its banks, but not yet, so horsemen can still ride along that road if they have a mind to," Panhsj remarked, pointing with his chin towards the embankments.

It had been a long, sleepless night for both of them. The family had found what comfort they could in among the bales of flax and cordage and slept restlessly, but the two men stayed awake searching the waters behind them for any sign of pursuit. Talon's eyes were gritty with lack of sleep and those of Panhsj were red from the same.

It would be a few hours before they docked at the fort of Beneade, and that would be the most vulnerable time. Talon's bow was strung and his arrows near to hand.

He was surprised to see Khalidah walking towards him along the side deck of the boat. Panhsj seemed to sense that she wanted to talk to Talon, so he bowed and walked back towards the helmsman.

Talon bowed to the veiled woman in front of him and could not help but admire her composure. There were not many women, he reflected, who could endure the privations of the tunnels, suffer a night in a cargo boat, and remain seemingly calm and in control.

"My Lady?" he murmured.

"Do you think it will end now, Suleiman? Will my son be safe from harm once we are at my husband's estates?"

"Much depends upon whether the sultan comes back to Al Qahirah and how swiftly he unravels the plot against him, if there is one, my Lady," Talon said cautiously.

"You sent Haytham the syce boy to the sultan, did you not?"

"Yes, but much can happen on such a journey...I have no idea if he was successful; that is in Allah's hands."

"So we could be going into a trap?"

"It is possible, my Lady. I do not know if Malek has heard about the death of my lord."

"Suleiman..." She stopped and looked directly at him. "Did you kill Bahir?"

Talon looked back at her. He frowned. "Why do you think I did, my Lady?"

"Because of what Panhsj does *not* say. He has changed so much towards you, and he was very quiet when the news arrived about it the other night. He did not leave that night; however, I wonder if perhaps you did."

Talon shrugged. "Bahir is dead, my Lady, and deserved to die; what does it matter who did it?"

"It matters to me, Suleiman. You promised me revenge. I think, no, I am sure I now have that, so your obligations to my husband are paid."

She held his eyes. Then in a low voice, "Do you not hate, Suleiman?" she asked.

"Whom should I hate, my Lady?" Talon asked in a quiet voice.

"I hate them, whomsoever have done this to my husband and my family. Yes, I do hate them!" she responded fiercely. "But, you do not seem to; if you do, you hide it well. How then do you kill so easily?"

"I am a slave, my Lady. It is my duty to protect you," Talon answered in a wooden tone.

She stared at him for a moment longer, then she sighed as though accepting that she could not penetrate his reserve.

"I would give you back the freedom that was taken from you. I do so now, but I also beg you to stay with me until my son is safe and can inherit, without fear of being murdered. Will you do this one last thing for me, Suleiman?"

Her veil had slipped a little, exposing more than just her eyes, and he could see her perfect features clearly in the light of the dawn. Her eyes pleaded with him.

He smiled grimly. "I cannot refuse you, my Lady...I could never do that. Yes, I shall stay by you. I ask only that one day you allow me and my companion Max to leave."

Her eyes were solemn. "You have my word on it. May Allah bless you, Suleiman, for you are a good friend."

She turned and pointed. "Look, there is a blue heron! Jasmine," she called. "There is the heron. I am sure it is one of those that live not far from Beneade." Then she smiled at Talon, and he realized that he was no longer a slave.

The ragged and filthy children came at her call and stood with them at the bows of the falukah watching the life along the river as they sped south. They were unrecognizable from their former clean and well dressed condition, but there was a lighter mood in the air as they contemplated the hoped-for safety of the estate at the Fayoum.

Talon left them to join Panhsj, leaning against the side and watching the shore line intently. "We are not far from Beneade," he remarked.

"We should keep my Lady and the children out of sight, for when we come in closer to shore a sharp eye would see us from some way off, I fear," Talon answered as he rested against the handrail.

"What did my Lady need of you?" Panhsj asked him, his eyes watching the river bank.

"She gave me my freedom, but asked me to stay," Talon told him.

Panhsj's face was inscrutable. "I know this much about you now, Suleiman. You might have agreed to stay. But it is only for a while, and then you will leave..."

"Yes, my friend, but not until we are both sure that she and her children are safe."

Panhsj gripped his hand. "Allah be praised! Then I will not feel so alone," he said with a grin. "Go and ask her to endure one more discomfort and we shall ensure that they get to the estate safely."

Talon walked slowly back to where Khalidah and the two children stood; they too were leaning over the side watching the shoreline. Kazim was pointing at the east side at some long black objects lying on the muddy beach.

"Bahir told us about those creatures, Mamma. They can eat a horse whole!"

Talon smiled; at least their minds were off their perilous situation for a few minutes.

Jasmine gave a theatrical shudder. "They look like monsters. I hope we never see them doing that to an animal," she said.

Khalidah patted her on the shoulder. "We will keep away from the shore and only take a boat. Then *Insha'Allah* we will be safe," she told Jasmine with a smile.

Talon bowed to Khalidah. "My Lady, I have to ask one more thing from you before we land. Please go the center of the boat and hide there until we are sure we do not have an unpleasant welcome at Beneade."

Before long the small fort and cluster of houses that made up the village of Beneade came into sight. The men on the boat redoubled their intense scrutiny of the boats nearby, the banks of the river and even the fort itself. The mud walls of the fort gave little away. There was the usual bustle going on around it of a small but busy trading corner. The river that ran from Fayoum began here; hence there were many fishing boats and small cargo falukahs plying back and forth.

Talon could see bales of flax lying on the wooden jetty. There were salt ingots stacked high on the bank nearby. Some of the flax bales were being manhandled down into a boat that would carry them north for conversion to the linen cloth much needed in the city of Cairo. Another boat was loading salted fish and grain. Talon did not see anyone staring at them suspiciously, but that did not mean there wasn't anyone interested in their boat.

The boatmen skillfully brought their falukah alongside one of the more deserted areas of the quay and tied up. Jumping ashore and watching the busy quay with narrowed eyes, Panhsj kept his hand on his sword and told the two men with him, Hanif and Aahmes, to move along the quay to ensure that there was no one waiting for them on the river bank. After a tense few minutes, Hanif came back and waved, indicating that the way was clear.

Talon immediately assisted Khalidah and the children onto the quayside and they hurried along the boards, passing curious laborers and boatmen who must have wondered about these ragged people who were disembarking in such a furtive manner. However, no one wanted to ask the huge menacing Nubian any questions.

As they were clear of the small crowd, Panhsj ran ahead of them to the open gateway of the fort. There he used the authority of his deceased master to procure horses for them.

They waited in a group near the main gate for the horses to be prepared, the men standing in a protective circle around the family. Talon had been watching the docks, searching for any clues as to the presence of a spy, when he saw something that bothered him.

Two men were pushing off in a small boat. Nothing unusual in that, but his suspicions were aroused because of the intent way one of them was watching the group by the gate. He showed far too much interest in them for Talon's liking.

He decided to be sure. "Stay here!" he called out to Panhsj and ran towards the two men who, having seen him coming at them, scrambled hurriedly about their boat and pushed off hastily into the water. One of them was already on board and fumbled frantically to release the bindings for the sail which now dropped, and the small light boat surged forward out onto the river as the wind caught it. The second man, after pushing the boat out, fell into it and joined the other man hauling on the sail. They looked fearfully over their shoulders at Talon, who was by now on the beach.

Talon hesitated for a moment, but then notched an arrow and, taking quick aim, sent it speeding on its way. However the men were by now too far out, and apart from a distant shout of alarm from one of them as they realized what he had done, they were safe. The arrow dropped into the water a few paces behind them. They shook their fists at Talon, although they were careful not to stand up and present him with a better target.

Talon saw no reason to send another arrow after the first but he was sure that these men were heading back to whomsoever had sent them, with the news that the family of Abbas had come home. He watched them for a few moments more as their boat joined the other water traffic on the river and was soon out of sight. Finally he turned and hurried back to the fort to be met by a concerned Panhsj, who asked what had happened.

"I think they were spies who will sail back to the city and report that we have escaped and that my Lady is now here," Talon said angrily.

Panhsj sighed, "I had hoped for more time before this happened."

"I too. Allah's will, but we needed some time for the family to get over their ordeal. Now we have to think of a way to either defend the estate or go somewhere else."

"The first thing we need to do is to get them home," Panhsj said.

They sent Aahmes off at a gallop to alert Malek of their arrival, and to ask him to come and meet them with an escort. Then the group set off at a fast pace to get as much distance as possible between them and the great river.

It was but a half hour later that they saw dust ahead of them and stopped warily to see who it might be. They need not have worried; it was Malek in full battle regalia accompanied by a contingent of mounted men carrying lances, and they were galloping hard towards them.

Talon noticed someone else with Malek. It was Max, looking more like an Egyptian with his loose turban and clothes, but there was no mistake, it was Max. His heart leapt; his friend looked fit and well. Malek reined up, looking grim, and bowed from the saddle to Khalidah, his keen glance taking in their filthy and disheveled condition.

"Allah be praised that you are safe, my ladies, and you, my lord. We have not known anything for days and I feared the worst."

"We would not have even lived had it not been for Suleiman and Panhsj here, Malek. God be praised that we are home, although my husband has perished along with many others...at the hands of murderers," Khalidah told him, but her voice was steady.

Malek looked his shock. "We had heard that there had been an accident, my Lady, but not that my lord had been murdered!"

"They broke his back in the game, and then he was murdered in our own house," Khalidah stated shortly.

"May Allah in all his mercy speed his soul to paradise, my Lady. Our loss is beyond mere words and our tears shall flow like a river," Malek intoned, clearly horrified. He dashed some tears from his eyes and became focused.

"My Lady, I am sorely unhappy to find you in this condition, but how this came to be will have to wait until we have you safe in the walls of the estate. We are deeply honored to welcome you home."

With a tight smile to Talon and Panhsj he escorted them to waiting horses. Surrounded by the guards, they quickly covered the remaining miles to the estate, where they were greeted by the entire population, who clapped and ululated and called to the weary travelers as they dismounted. During the short ride back Talon and Max did not have the chance to talk, but rode alongside until they too dismounted.

Khalidah and the children were whisked away by her wailing womenfolk, who were horrified at their condition. They disappeared into the house where the cries and wails finally became muted by its thick walls. Max and Talon embraced hard.

"Ah, but it is good to see you, my young friend," Max said quietly, but his smile was huge.

"I have missed you sorely, my brother," Talon greeted him.

Then they turned and faced Malek, who embraced Panhsj. Malek had tears in his eyes when he opened his arms for Talon and his embrace was hard. He banged Talon on the back just like his brother used to do.

"There is much to tell, Malek, and little of it good," Talon told him.

"And there is still danger which you need to understand," Panhsj growled, after he had gripped hands with Max.

"My Lady will be well looked after, as will the children. I do not think she will want to talk until later in the day, so we can eat and talk about this, including...including my brother," Malek added, his face tight. He was stricken. Panhsj had told him of Bilal's fate as they rode. Nonetheless he clapped his hands for a boy to come running. The syce had taken the horses and they were walking towards the time honored place where they had always eaten in the past.

"Bring food for us, much of it, and be quick," Malek commanded. "Stop sweeping about, you are raising enough dust to choke us all!" he bellowed at a young boy who was whisking the hard packed ground near where they were going to sit with a tight bundle of twigs. The boy scampered off, his bare feet pattering. Malek, acting as the host, bade them be seated; his gesture included Max, who smiled at Talon and seated himself cross legged on a cushion alongside him.

They were drinking mint flavored lemonade while waiting for the food, all talking at once, when they heard a call. Talon jumped to his feet. Coming towards them was Khaldun. He seemed to have aged since they had been away, even though it had only been a few months. His thin white hair was falling out of his loose turban in strands. He leaned on the shoulder of a small Nubian boy who supported him with care as he hobbled towards them; his rheumatisms seemed to be getting worse.

"God be praised that my eyes see you! For shame, Malek, why did you not call me the moment they arrived?"

"Aba, forgive me," Malek was contrite. "We had to leave so quickly, and this is the time you like to sleep so I could not in all conscience wake you for the mere arrival of our friends," he said with an attempt at humor.

Khaldun wagged a finger at him and turned to Talon and Panhsj with a grin full of pleasure. "I am glad that we are together again! Allah be praised you are well, my friends. I welcome you home, even if that Malek has no use for me...an old man of no worth," he said, inclining his head towards Malek and with a mischievous look.

"Aba, how can you say that?" Malek held his open hands out and protested with a smile of affection for Khaldun.

He helped Khaldun to be seated and fussed over him to make up for his neglect, and then it was time to hear of their adventures.

Panhsj did most of the talking, Talon being content to let him, helping out here and there with the details. Panhsj told it well and at times emotionally so that there were many tears shed for the murder of their lord and Bilal's last heroic stand. Malek was devastated at the loss of his brother but intensely proud of his sacrifice. There was fury at the unknown people who had perpetrated the outrages against Abbas. Panhsj told of the attempt upon Abbas's life on the boat where it all seemed to have started. He did not fail to heap praise on Talon as the story unfolded.

The baskets of nuts and fruit and fresh herbs arrived from the kitchens and Talon enjoyed again the simple but excellent fare of the estate. Within minutes pistachio shells and other nutshells were strewn across the linen sheet that passed for a table cloth as they cracked them open and waited for the main meal to arrive. When it did, Talon's mouth watered at the smell of the stuffed pastries full of chicken and cabbage, the roasted quail and pigeon and a crispy, fatty, force-fed goose. The aroma teased Talon so that he salivated. He sniffed at the small salted and pungent fish and other delicious morsels of food with pleasure. Someone had killed a lamb in their honor, and they ate roasted kid meat with bread and vegetables growing this season. It was followed, hours later, by sweetmeats of many flavors, rose essence and citrus blossom essences, and sticky with honey. Meanwhile, Panhsj and Talon, in between mouthfuls, told the story of their escape and eventual trip back up the river. Piping hot coffee was brought as the men continued to share their experiences. Panhsj was very vague about how Lord Bahir had died and Talon cast him a thankful look. He had no doubt that Panhsj would tell Malek one day exactly what he knew, but not today. It was late in the afternoon when the sun had lost much of its heat that they began to close in on their present situation.

At one point Malek got up and disappeared to see if Khalidah needed him, as she was now the head of the household and he was very conscious of his responsibilities. He was gone for about half an hour, during which time Khaldun brought them up to date on the condition of the estate.

He nodded approvingly at Max and said, "Your companion is doing well with his language and understands most of what is said, although he will never be as good as you, Suleiman." He smiled at Max to take the sting out of his words. "He has proved his worth here and helped Malek a great deal."

Max glanced at Talon, flushing with embarrassment, but he was pleased with the praise. Talon punched his companion lightly on the arm. "We shall make time to talk together. How is the wound?" he asked.

"It still gives me twinges from time to time, Ta...Suleiman, but for the most part it is well healed," Max said with a smile, covering for his near mistake in using his real name.

"Suleiman has been given his freedom, Aba," Panhsj said casually.

Khaldun looked at Talon shrewdly, the wrinkles more pronounced than ever around his eyes. "I am pleased for you, Suleiman; it must have been for a great service. I am intrigued to hear about your relationship with the King of the Beggars. Indeed, it is amazing how little we understand that which goes on under our very feet. That is an unusual story; you must tell me more about that some time. Allah be praised that he led you to these people."

Malek rejoined them. "My Lady is fatigued and needs to rest, but in the morning she has commanded that everyone attend her to discuss the future."

The men nodded their agreement. It was time to find the baths and get cleaned up. Talon was desperate for a bath.

Later, feeling refreshed and clean for the first time in what seemed like weeks, although their ordeal had only been for a few days, he joined Max on the wall at one of the corners of the estate. The bats were already out hunting, high in the clear air, darting here and there, flying low over their heads. It was quiet, and the two men could lean on the crude mud wall battlements and converse without being disturbed while enjoying the cool breeze that now came in from the lake to the west of them. The light had become soft and the shadows were subdued.

"Max, you look so different from that last time I saw you! I went away concerned about you, but now look at you! You look fit and well, God be praised." Talon threw an arm over his friend's shoulders.

Max nodded and said, "There were some moments when it was very much in the hands of God, Suleiman." He used the name as though to keep his mind on it while they were in their current situation.

"Malek and the physician still had concerns for me, but as you can see I am well recovered. Malek has insisted that I practice with him at the sword and shield, you remember that kind of dance? Then we ride out every day to the estate, sometimes twenty or more miles. I must take you to the hot springs where we go sometimes to bathe. It is a wonderful medicine for my wound."

"What? You take baths regularly?" Talon pretended to look shocked. "Don't you know it is bad for your health?"

Max laughed and said, "I now understand what all that fuss was about that you made when we were in France. It is a good feeling...no?"

"I imagine that my Lady and her children would agree with you there, as I do Max; I do not have to favor the upwind of you anymore," Talon said drily with a grin on his face.

They talked long into the evening and then, because Max still needed his rest and Talon was weary to the bone, they walked back to their quarters through the garden shrubs, upsetting a cat about to pounce on a rodent.

Sleep was not to be just yet for Talon. He ran into Khaldun, who was seated on a large stone near the stables and called to him in the gloom. Talon felt he had been waiting for him.

"Suleiman, come and pass a few minutes with an old man who cannot sleep. I would hear from you what happened."

Talon could not refuse. "How is it that you are not abed, Aba? It is late. I am glad we have come back; I have missed the peaceful atmosphere of the Fayoum, so different from Al-Qahirah. And I rejoice to find you in good health."

"I, too, am glad to see you well, although you look thinner. From what Panhsj has told me you are now a free man, and that you earned it." He paused, staring at Talon with a face unreadable in the gloom, framed by his white beard and the loose linen turban.

"Tell me, Suleiman, tutor of my Lady's children, how is it that you seem to have known the beggars so well, and that my lord's enemies seem to die so mysteriously soon after you have disappeared on an errand, and that you play such good chogan?"

"I thought we talked about my years in Anatolia, Aba. That should be explanation enough as to my education; and for the rest, I learned to play chogan in Isfahan."

Khaldun raised his hand. "My boy, I do not seek to find fault, or to condemn you in Allah's eyes. You have been an avenging angel for the family of Abbas, and for that may God praise and protect you."

Talon said nothing.

"No...it is just that I sense there are two of you."

Talon tensed.

"There is the one who we know and have come to trust, respect, and perhaps even to love," the old man continued. "But there is someone else within you that we will never know, and that person is known only to Allah. He is the one whose soul I am afraid for, and that one is, perhaps, the real you, Suleiman? Are you someone we should fear?"

Talon sat in silence for a long moment in the darkness, and then he leaned forward and took Khaldun's thin and gnarled hand in his. Lifting it to his lips, he kissed it.

Khaldun made to pull his hand away but Talon held on to it with firm fingers.

"I have missed your wisdom and perception, Aba. But know this before Allah, I swear, may my life be forfeit, that neither you nor anyone in this place will ever have cause to fear me. However, that is not true for our enemies. May Allah's blessings and peace be with you. Good night, Hajji."

"I pray that Allah be kind to you, my young friend. Good night," the old man whispered as he placed his hand back on his lap and watched Talon leave.

# Chapter 22

# Assassins

Talon awoke to the call of the peacock. He could imagine it opening its huge tail majestically as it strutted across the rough roof tiles of the servants' quarters. Its call was answered by another in the gardens. Talon rolled over and lay quietly, listening to the sounds coming from the maidan: the horses stamping and snorting into their food, the clip clop of hooves on the hard packed ground as some were taken out to the polo field to graze under the sharp eyes of the syce. He heard the bark of a dog, and a yell, and then a sharp yelp as someone threw a stone that struck its target. He wondered at that. Dogs were tolerated but not treated well here, he had noticed. The syce chattered to one another and to the soldiers who were awake as they went about their tasks. He enjoyed the clarity of the sounds coming to him on the cool morning air.

Breakfast was a quiet affair. Malek, although pleased to see them, was deeply saddened by the death of his brother, and the rest of them respected his grief. Bilal had always been a cheerful presence at mealtimes. After the basic fare that they had had to eat with the beggars, the food they ate this morning tasted wonderful to Talon. Panhsj obviously agreed with that sentiment, as he ate a huge quantity of food in silence.

An hour later, Talon, Khaldun, Malek and Panhsj were seated on the carpet in the entrance room of the main house. Max had not been invited, as he was not yet part of the inner circle. They lowered themselves on floor cushions in front of Khalidah, who was seated on the raised dais formerly occupied by her husband. She was carefully veiled but seemed clear of eye and well rested.

Khalidah spoke. "By the grace of Allah we have survived and are home. I and my family mourn my husband and will always, but I and my children have much cause to be grateful to Suleiman, Panhsj, and in particular your brother, Bilal, who saved us from a fate worse than death with his sacrifice. It will not be forgotten." Malek bowed his head in acknowledgement of the words.

"All our tears flow for your loss, my Lady. I shall pray for their souls. May Allah be kind to them upon their arrival for judgment."

Khalidah nodded and then continued. "However, I am informed that we were seen when we arrived at Beneade by possible spies, and I am curious as to how you think we should react to this news. What say you, Suleiman, what does it mean for our safety here in Fayoum?"

Talon sat up straight, looked around at the men with him and then directly at Khalidah and the children. Everyone was looking at him.

"My Lady, if they truly were spies then I do not think we have much time. I would say perhaps a couple of days, but no more."

Kazim and Jasmine gasped with surprise. They had been confident that they were now safe. Khalidah gave a sigh of resignation, as though she had suspected as much.

"What do you advise?" she asked.

"I do not think we can defend this place against a well-coordinated attack, my Lady."

The argument began, as Malek and Panhsj were adamantly opposed to leaving the one place where they felt safe.

"We have food and defenses, Suleiman. Why do you say that we cannot defend ourselves?" Malek exclaimed.

"Our walls are thick mud and brick. We could withstand a siege, at least until help came from Cairo," Panhsj said.

"What help?" Khaldun interjected, his tone skeptical. "You have just come from there and the only help you had was from the beggars," he added, his head nodding to emphasize his point.

"Not only that, but we do not know if Haytham managed to get to the sultan, nor indeed whether the sultan believed him," Talon said. "Apart from Bahir, we don't even know who our enemies are.

One is gone, but we know there are others. There certainly is one very powerful man among them, and there might be more."

"What you are saying is that we cannot go back to Al-Qahirah even if the sultan has returned because we do not know who our enemies really are?" Malek exclaimed. He sounded incredulous.

"What if I were to throw myself upon the sultan's mercy and ask for his protection?" Khalidah asked.

"You could do this, my Lady. However we do not know if he has returned to the city, and we can't anticipate when another attempt might be made upon your son. I am sorry to be so blunt, but we need to be clear about our situation."

"My father lives in Alexandria. Why could I not go there?"

Malek seemed to like this idea. "I agree with you, my Lady. There you would be under the protection of your father, a powerful man who has much influence in the city. The children would be safer there and a message could be sent to the sultan explaining the situation and asking for his protection."

Panhsj, who had said very little up to this time, agreed with Malek. "My Lady's father lives in a small palace that could easily be defended with our men and his, Suleiman. It is better built than this estate for defense. Why should we not do this?"

Talon did not feel comfortable disagreeing with the rest of them. "I cannot argue against this idea, my Lady, although I do not feel good about it. However, I do not have an alternative to offer. If this is the decision we agree upon, then we should prepare to leave soon. Malek, you cannot stay either, as to do so might place you in grave danger."

"Which way would we go? Down the river by boat would be the quickest way, but it is perhaps also the most dangerous," Malek said.

"To stay here is to be trapped between the desert to the West and the river to the East. Anyone with horses could catch us with our backs to the lake and then we are finished," Panhsj said gloomily.

"Do we not own ships of your husband's anywhere?" Talon asked Khalidah.

"I cannot say. Perhaps, but as you saw we have none at present," she responded, looking embarrassed at not having the information at her fingertips.

"My Lady, we have only the feluccas, and they are small. We always relied upon the large cargo ships to take our crops and our salt to Cairo before," Malek explained.

"It is not for only your lives I fear," Talon said reluctantly. "This estate may be vulnerable."

"They are trying to hurt the young master, Suleiman. Once they discover he is gone from here, why would they try to destroy this place?" Malek asked.

Talon said nothing. The kind of enemy they were up against would have few scruples about burning the place to the ground and everyone within if they thought it would hurt the family. The property could be rebuilt later, but lives could not. He had quickly learned that the Fayoum was a green pearl in the economy of the entire country. The revenues from the farmlands encompassed by the property were enormous by any standards in Egypt and were a ripe fruit for the picking now that Abbas was gone.

The discussion went back and forth. However, it was clear that a decision had been made, and they knew that they needed to prepare to leave as soon as possible. They agreed not to take the river as there were no boats available for the entourage that would have to accompany a complete movement of household. Camels would need to be obtained, and then they would go overland to Alexandria. Eventually, when other options seemed exhausted, the men were given leave to depart. Khalidah asked Talon to remain for a minute.

She looked up at him. "Tell me, Suleiman, you who seem wise beyond your years. How long does grief last, and why is there so much pain?"

Talon was taken aback. He was not used to being a source of wisdom to people, and twice now he had been called upon to provide comfort.

"Perhaps you should ask Khaldun, my Lady. His life has been full and I am sure he has known both pain and grief of the kind that you are talking about."

She gave an impatient flick of her hand. "He is a dear and valued friend who is very wise, but his memories are dimmed by age. You, I think, know of these things and have felt them not so long ago."

"Indeed, my Lady, but a man like Khaldun would tell you that only time and Allah in his infinite kindness can heal the wounds of loss great as yours, so he is still the wiser man."

"How will the danger come?" she asked, quietly changing the subject.

"I do not know, but it might come as soon as tomorrow night, by which time we should be gone. I think it will be at night, when they hope our guard is down. In any case, you must not let the children sleep alone and you must have a guard at your door, all your doors. I shall talk to Malek and Panhsj about that and we will man the walls starting today."

"I will alert the servants for the need to be on guard," she said, rising. Talon stood too.

"Suleiman."

"Yes, my Lady?"

"My grief is for the life that we once led and for the loss of innocence of my children. It is shattered like a broken pot and can never be repaired. Allah has been cruel to us despite what Khaldun might say to the contrary."

Talon could think of nothing to say.

Silently and slowly, her head bowed, Khalidah withdrew to her chambers.

* * * * *

That evening Talon, Malek and Max were seated drinking scalding hot tea and having a serious discussion about how they needed to defend the buildings in the event of an attack. Talon was reminded of another time and place where the defense of a building had been crucial to their survival. One glance at Max told him that he was thinking the same thing. Khaldun and Panhsj joined them and a new council of war was held.

"We should make every attempt to leave by tomorrow, but we must also take precautions for tonight," Talon told Malek. "I think that our enemies will come by ship."

Malek agreed and immediately sent orders off for extra guards to man both the house and walls at once.

"My duty is to the young master, so I shall also be here at the house," Panhsj announced firmly.

Malek and Talon liked this arrangement; then they discussed how best to protect the property at night and keep an eye on the road where the attack would most probably come from.

Max had an idea. "Why do we not place watchers along the road and even in Beneade? We need as much warning as we can get," he suggested.

The rest of them looked at him in surprise.

"That is a very good idea," Malek said, and gave a wry smile. "It seems that both of you are thinking like soldiers, Suleiman." The others nodded vigorous agreement.

"We should post a horseman by the fort at Beneade who can ride back to the Fayoum and give us warning if anything suspicious happens there during the night."

He called over one of the syce and gave orders for two boys to take horses and ride fast to the village, where they were to remain unobserved, staying as close as possible to the fort while looking for any unusual activity.

"Suleiman, you seem very sure there is a real threat," Khaldun said to him once during the debate.

"Hajji, I cannot be sure, but Panhsj and I do know that there is a threat that continues after Bahir. From where and from whom, we cannot tell, but it would be foolish to ignore it as we prepare to leave. A few sleepless nights for some of us would not do any harm and might be to our benefit."

Panhsj nodded his agreement. "Indeed, Aba, we were caught off guard once, and your brother paid for it with his life, Malek. I for one would prefer to have a sleepless night than to wake up with my throat cut."

They smiled as his ludicrous answer.


Their spirits were dampened by the knowledge that danger threatened and that they must be prepared to face it. Meanwhile frantic preparations for flight continued. The maidan was now littered with huge bundles of household possessions and people's personal baggage. The camels would be arriving the next day from the town near the lake.

The soldiers of El Fayoum polished their spears and ran stones along the blades of their swords, waiting with tense anticipation for the night.

Talon changed into pants and boots, with a loose shirt held at the waist with a wide linen band into which he could slip his knife and sword. He wore, as did Max, a tight fitting helmet over which his turban was tightly wound. They each wore a light jerkin, in chain.

With Max he went to reconnoiter the thick walls of the estate to decide where they were most vulnerable. The outer sides were plastered with mud and very slightly slanted from the ground to a height of about fourteen feet, which to Talon was an invitation, but he didn't think the enemy horsemen would be inclined to dismount and climb it. He thought they might instead throw blazing torches over the walls, in the hope they could burn the roofs and smoke the inhabitants out.

Eventually people went to bed and the compound quieted. Panhsj had left for his duties at the main house while Talon and Max decided to stay on guard and let Malek get some sleep. Talon was unsure of how he felt about the threat they were possibly facing, and it worried him.

Life had become very uncertain again and he could not see into the future with any clarity. He looked up at the stars and wondered if his two friends might still be alive and sharing the same view in faraway Persia. That is, if they were there at all. He sent a prayer out for their safety and that of the child he would never see.

For Talon the night passed slowly, the waiting to be endured. Then around midnight the sentries at the gates sent an urgent message to Talon, who had been standing near the stables, that they could hear a horse in the distance.

He rushed to the walls and was joined almost immediately by Max. "Listen," the guard whispered.

Sure enough, coming towards the estate was the sound of a horse being ridden hard. Soon they could make out the shape of one of the riders who had been sent out earlier. He rode up to the still closed gates and shouted, "A galley has arrived at Beneade!"

Men rushed to open the gates and he trotted the sweating animal into the maidan, where he dismounted and was surrounded by men with flaming torches. Malek arrived looking disheveled from sleep and demanded silence. Then he asked the boy what he had seen.

"It was a large galley, Jo *Oustez*! Like...like one of those big war galleys we see going up and down the great river sometimes," the boy said in a high-pitched voice.

"Did you see men get off the boat?" Talon demanded.

"No, *Oustez*. We decided that I should come back immediately and Shebli would follow once he had counted the enemy."

Malek was silent while he thought about this, then he said, "For a galley to arrive at this hour is very suspicious. We should make ready for an attack. Man the walls and make sure that men are posted around the house," he ordered. "Put out all the torches and pretend that we are not awake. Perhaps we can surprise the enemy...if they come. Put archers on the walls with the sentries."

Talon asked the boy, "You said that he would follow you as soon as he knew the approximate numbers of the enemy?"

"Yes, *Oustez*. He should be here very soon. *Insha'Allah*."

"I shall report this to my Lady," Malek said and headed for the house.

Gradually the commotion in the enclosure died down, but now the inhabitants were wide awake. They waited for the second horseman to come, but when he failed to arrive after over an hour, Talon began to worry. He prowled around the maidan trying to think what might have happened. The one seductive possibility was that there had been no troops on the ship and it had been a false alarm. In which case, they could all go back to sleep.

But he had a hunch. He sensed there was something not quite right, but he could not put his finger on anything. Malek came up to him in the darkness with a puzzled grunt, as he too had expected the other boy to arrive. They looked towards the black shape of the gate as though it could provide answers. The men crouching along the battlements near the entrance were wide awake and tense. It had now been a good two hours since the arrival of the first boy. Time enough for the other messenger to arrive, and/or the enemy.

Talon heard a faint rattle of something on the walls at the other side of the estate, but there was no alarm called, so he relaxed when he heard nothing further. His eyesight in the night was enhanced by the blaze of stars overhead and the compound was not pitch dark. There were deep black shadows in some corners, and many dark places that were indistinct in the night, particularly near the buildings. He thought he saw movement in the area of the bath house which was situated between the servants' quarters and the main house. It was as though a shadow had moved. He stared hard at the same place and then he saw a furtive movement.

A shadow detached itself from the deeper darkness of the building and moved very slowly in a crouch towards the main house. Almost as though it was a trick of his eyes, the shadow disappeared from view. Talon gripped Malek's arm hard.

"They have arrived," he whispered.

"Who have arrived?" Malek asked, puzzled.

"Hashishini."

Malek tensed. "Where? In Allah's name, where?" he demanded in a fearful whisper.

"Raise the alarm, Malek. Raise the alarm, they are here," Talon muttered, and then he ran silently towards the place where he had last seen the shadow.

Malek yelled at the top of his voice. "To your posts, bring lights quickly, they are inside the Maidan!"

In the ensuing eruption of noise Talon arrived at the spot where he knew at least one assassin was lurking, or had been. But there was nothing. Every nerve taut, his sword held forward on guard, he swiveled his head rapidly from side to side. Could he have been mistaken? He didn't believe he was, but there was no one nearby. The house was waking up from the noise outside.

Then a door forty feet away from where he stood opened and light fell on the ground outside, as someone with an oil lamp came to investigate. Talon saw a shadow detach itself from the darkness of the wall nearby and the person at the door went down with a choking sound. He saw a dark shape swiftly slip past the body. The clay lamp that the victim had held fell to the floor and shattered. The oil spilled and caught fire, spreading up the length of the curtain at the entrance to the door with a speed that astonished Talon, who now ran as fast as he could towards the flames, his sword forward and a dagger in his other hand. Another shadow ran after the first, jumping over the flames and the dead servant. They disappeared into the darkness of the house behind the blazing doorway.

Talon had almost reached the door when a man in dark clothes leapt out to intercept him, a sword held high. Talon spun on his toes and slashed hard at the man, who spun out of the way of the blade and delivered his own downward blow to Talon's head. Talon blocked the blow with his sword and knife crossed over his head and then disengaged very fast; his blade flickered and the man fell back with a cry, his hand going to a deep cut to his neck, the main artery severed. Talon did not wait, but bounded into the flaming doorway, shouting a warning to Panhsj as he did so.

He leapt over the body of a fallen servant and ran down the corridor shouting as he went. He had a vague idea as to where the women's quarters were, but his ears picked up the sound of steel on steel and a cry of pain. He changed direction rapidly and headed along another corridor and saw bodies on the floor.

He mentally gasped at the sight of three servants lying in an untidy heap at the entrance of a room. He heard a cry of alarm and pain. Even as he raced towards the dead men, he marveled at how quickly they had been dispatched.

Blood was everywhere on the tiles and he slipped in his mad rush to reach the source of the cry, but he recovered his balance by slamming against the wall. Hurtling through the door, snatching aside the torn curtain, he saw Panhsj fighting off two men dressed as Talon's former opponent had been. Panhsj's left side was covered in blood and Talon could see that it was Panhsj's own.

He took in the situation at a glance. Khalidah was lying on the floor, blood on her neck and a knife that she had carried to defend herself lying near her hand. Talon wondered if she were dead, but there was no time to think of that. He noted that the children were huddled in a corner and that Kazim had a knife with him.

"Suleiman! They are trying to kill Panhsj!" Kazim squeaked unnecessarily.

Talon slipped in behind one of the attackers, just as that man realized that they were not alone. Talon's blade almost beheaded him but he was incredibly fast and blocked it just in time. There was a sharp rasp of steel and sparks flew as the swords met, then he slipped under the blade and shouted, "This is not our fight any more!"

He parried another blow from Talon, and then they locked swords. They came face to face and Talon stared into the dark eyes of his opponent.

As they strained against one another Talon grated out, "What are the Ismaili doing here?"

His opponent's eyes widened with surprise. "Who are you?"

"I am *Fidai*," Talon grunted, and started to use his greater strength to gain the upper hand; but the man, with a rapid twist that almost caught Talon off guard, dropped to one knee and tried to cut Talon's legs off with a savage swipe that Talon barely avoided by leaping high. He managed to slash down onto the man and to inflict a deep cut to the man's right side that made the man gasp and stagger back. But he still had the speed and strength to dive out of the door and vanish into the night.

Talon did not follow; his concern was for Khalidah, and Panhsj. The other assassin, seeing this new threat and hearing his companion call out, ever so briefly paused as he looked for an escape route past Talon. But then Panhsj charged. His blade hammered down the defense of the assassin and cut deeply into his shoulder. The man cried out and fell to his knees, blood gushing out of the huge wound Panhsj had inflicted.

"Don't kill him! Don't kill him!" Talon shouted at Panhsj, whose face was contorted into an expression of fanatical blood lust. He barely heard Talon. He stopped, his sword raised high for the kill; he towered over the man who now slowly toppled over.

"Watch for a knife, Panhsj. Stop his bleeding; we have to know who they are," Talon said.

He turned around searching to see if there were any other attackers in the room and then he went to Khalidah. He slowly turned her over and looked. Despite the blood, he could only find a small, dark bruise that was rapidly swelling on her right temple that also trickled blood. She groaned and opened her eyes. Her eyes tried to focus and then, seeing Talon, she gave a start and tried to sit up. Without ceremony, Talon picked her up and carried her to her sleeping platform and laid her down.

"Do not talk, you have been hurt," he whispered. "Kazim and Jasmine, attend to your mother."

The children, wide-eyed and frightened, did as they were told while he returned to the fallen man and checked to see if he was alive. Searching the man Talon produced a knife and tossed it away so that it fell against the wall. Panhsj knelt nearby, holding his arm, which was bleeding from a slash.

"Who are these people?" he gasped.

"From what I can tell they are Ismaili—you know them as Batinas or Hashishini—but why they are here I do not know," Talon grunted.

He tied the wounded man's arms behind him and then tore another strip of cloth from his robes and bound up the freely bleeding wound in the now semiconscious man's shoulder.

Talon removed the cloth covering from the face of the assassin and slapped him hard. The man, or rather, the teenage boy, for that is what he was, opened his eyes groggily and then focused on Talon and Panhsj.

"Kill me now," he pleaded in a whisper.

"You will be granted that wish, I promise you," Talon replied grimly. "But first you will answer a question or two."

The youth looked at him with hate-filled eyes and said nothing.

There was a loud commotion in the corridor and then several men burst into the room, led by Malek.

"What is happening?" he shouted. Then he saw the scene in the middle of the room. He held his men back. They peered over his shoulder at the chaos but were arrested by what happened next.

Talon smacked his hand onto the wound, making the boy arch his back and utter a shriek. The wound bled freely again.

"Answer some questions and you may go on your way," Talon said, through clenched teeth.

Twice more he struck the youth, each time with the promise that he would kill him following the answered questions.

On the third time the youth seemed to realize that there was no mercy to be found here. He shook his head and muttered, "We came to kill the boy."

"Who sent you?" Talon raised his hand as the youth hesitated.

"A man called Al Muntaqim, no other name. He is following us with his men, by ship...he will be here in the morning." The youth was very pale now, his forehead beaded in sweat.

"Are you Ismaili? If so, from where?"

"Sinan ...Rashid." The youth's eyes glazed over and his body tensed for a few seconds then relaxed. His eyes stared sightlessly past Talon's shoulder, then he fell over onto his side.

# Chapter 23

# Flight

Under the cover of darkness Talon stared in the direction of the quay where the dark silhouette of a ship was tied up; he could make out that its bow was facing upstream. It was a sizeable war galley, long and low in the water, larger than he had expected. Malek had told him it might be a Dromon. These were large and fast two-masted galleys that had been copied from the Byzantium navy.

This one, however, seemed to have an extra upper deck across the very back of the ship, beneath which he could make out what seemed to be a cabin space. He could see several men standing on this raised deck leaning on the rail and other men standing by the other rail, and he guessed they might be the steersmen. There were dim lanterns hanging here and there along its rail; they provided poor light to see by. Standing behind him and peering over his shoulder were Panhsj and Max. They too were trying to make out the activity on the boat; unfortunately for them, the men on the ship were clearly wide awake.

Every dark shadow that was scattered across the quay hid one of Panhsj's men, who had silently moved into place. They waited for the command to attack.

At Fayoum, earlier on, the chaos resulting from the panic and disruption of the assault by the Hashishini had finally been brought under control by Malek. The fire which had threatened to engulf the entire house had been beaten out, although it had caused extensive damage. They had dealt with the dead in Muslim way, but because of the urgency of their situation only hasty prayers were muttered over the corpses as they were interred in the garden.

A sense of fearful urgency had permeated everywhere and everyone. They now knew the intentions of the enemy, but he still did not have a name or a face.

The one assassin who had escaped from Talon had not been found, which was worrisome, but now everyone was alert and no one went about the compound alone.

Khalidah had recovered from the blow to her head and wore a linen bandage under her scarf. She had been dazed but aware, and the children, who were surprisingly calm, had tended to her with great care. They had been most supportive despite their fears. All the same, Talon noticed that Jasmine had a small fit of shivers in her mother's arms, and Kazim put his arms around Panhsj while Talon was binding up his friend's arm. "You will live, my friend, but we must get a physician to sew it up soon. For now we will bind it up well," Talon told Panhsj, who nodded with a grim smile, then patted the young boy on the head.

"It is good. Do not be afraid, young master. We will win this war," he said for the benefit of Kazim, who was on the verge of tears.

They discovered the dead sentries in the corner of the walled area, right at the back of the compound, their throats slit. This explained the manner of entry, but it did not answer the question of the identity of the person or people who had sent the assassins. They still did not have enough information about the man known as Al Muntaqim. That was obviously not his proper name but no one could think of whom it might be. It had been a shaken group who discussed the nature of the danger they now faced.

They had been forced to reassess their position and what they needed to do next.

Talon and Max were adamant that they should leave as soon as they could. Both had been in a siege before, and neither wanted to face the kind of odds that they knew were on their way to destroy them. An idea occurred to Talon during the discussion, but he was hesitant to put it forward. Eventually he decided that it was worth talking about.

"Why do we not take their ship which is still moored at Beneade and sail off in that?"

There was utter silence while everyone in the room stared at him as though he had just lost his mind. But there was another surprise to come. Khaldun, who had joined them in the room, his frail frame seated on a cushion, had heard and with a chuckle he weighed in on his side.

"We have not enough animals to transport us safely out of trouble and no time to escape into the desert, where we would be easily overtaken. Suleiman might be right! Although he sounds mad, there is a ship and we should at least see if we can take it. Then we have a means of transport," he said with raised eyebrows as though to say, "Has anyone a better idea?"

"How do you propose to take the boat?" Max asked skeptically. The question was on everyone's mind.

"I intend to walk onto the boat and take it off them...with your help," Talon replied with a tense grin.

"You know that if this mad plan of yours works, we cannot go north as we will run straight into Al Muntaqim. You told me the assassin said there were two galleys coming," Panhsj said slowly.

"You are right. I had forgotten that," Talon muttered.

"If we go south there are places where Lord Abbas was known and respected. We could ask for shelter there." Malek looked at Khalidah for guidance.

"You are right, he has...there are relatives of mine in the city of Aswan. There is a cousin of my Grandmother's side of the family who might be disposed to protect me," Khalidah said, a little doubtfully.

"How many of us are there?" Talon asked.

"There are about forty men and women and children altogether," Malek said automatically.

"How many soldiers from that number do we have?" Max asked.

"Twenty, as of the last count, but we lost some tonight," Malek said.

"A large boat could take us all. How large would the crew of this ship be?" Talon asked.

It was a question that hung in the air, but it was as though everyone had decided at the same time that this was the only course of action, and they had to make it happen or die in the attempt.

Hurried preparations had followed to leave within the hour. Some of the servants, particularly the women, wailed and wrung their hands at the thought of abandoning most of their possessions to looters, but Khalidah took firm charge and told the majority of the servants to go back to their houses in the villages and lie low until she came back. Allah willing, it would not be long. This left her with a smaller group of single girls and one old woman who elected to stay with her and take her chances.

"The land needs people to till it and maintain it. Whoever is coming might destroy the house and the compound, but they will see no value in destroying crops that they will want for their own. They might even spare the house," she told the weeping servants who were leaving to rejoin their villages.

She did not add that she was sick with fear for them, but she hoped that they would be spared, if only to work in the fields. Talon doubted Al Muntaqim would spare the house. When angry and frustrated, men were destructive. An hour after midnight they had abandoned the house and compound. The parting had been painful; no one was sure they would ever see the servants or the buildings again.

The plan was for Malek to provide a diversion and make the enemy think a much larger party had fled into the desert by taking some men and heading west, skirting the lake Birket el Querun to the south, then riding over the low but steep hills of the Wadi Moih. Malek took this role upon himself because he had men with him from this region that knew the desert like the back of their hands and could find the most obscure paths over the surrounding hills, even in the dark.

"We will leave a clear trail for Al Muntaqim to follow, but gradually we will cover our tracks more carefully, and then hopefully we will disappear," he told them.

"I would like to come with you, Malek," Max volunteered.

Malek shook his head, but smiled. "Allah's blessings be upon you, my friend. It will be easier for me and my men to go alone. Besides, I will feel better if the three of you are there to protect my Lady and the children."

Max bowed his head, accepting the fact unwillingly, but Panhsj gripped his good arm. "Malek is right, Max. I have heard of your prowess in battle and we might well find ourselves in the middle of a bad fight for the boat. He is going to play the fox, while we have to be the wolves tonight."

* * * * *

"They are still waiting for the killers to come back," Panhsj whispered in Talon's ear.

The three stood not far from the sad bundle of rags that had formerly been one of the syce boys who had volunteered as scout and now lay inert on the open ground. They now knew the reason they had not been warned. They could not move the body without being noticed, so it still lay in the middle of the dirt road.

"You are right," Talon whispered, "and I must show myself and pretend that I am the only one of the three that made it back." His heart was beating fast, for he had no idea if the men on the galley were aware of the turn of events. He was sure they would have sailed had they known.

Panhsj stared at him with a blank look. Talon felt he had to spell it out.

"One got away, remember? But I wounded him, badly. I do not think he has made it back or the boat would be gone, and it is time for me to move lest he get here first."

"Go with Allah. We will be right behind you," Panhsj said.

"Make sure our friend does not arrive while I am walking to the boat," Talon whispered back, his mouth dry.

He moved out of the shadows and began to limp towards the quay. The cloth on his leg was covered in someone else's blood. He reached the quay and began to stagger along the crude wooden planks, moving in and out of the large bales of flax and other debris that cluttered the wooden platform. He was within thirty feet of the ship before anyone noticed him and gave a shout. A heavyset man with a bald head leaned over the side of the galley and called out to him. The man was standing almost level with the planks of the quay. It would be easy for Talon to step down a short pace and be on the center deck of the boat. He kept his face concealed from view but he grunted as though in pain and staggered towards where the man stood looking at him.

"Were you successful?" the man asked in a loud voice.

Talon grunted and nodded and kept coming, he held his leg, which looked as though the cloth was saturated with his own blood.

He was by now abreast of the large man, who raised his lamp to get a better look at him. There was a sharp intake of breath. "You are wounded. Where are the others?" the man said in a loud voice, offering him a helping hand as he stood at the cut away part of the boat's side, where the gangway rested.

"Dead," Talon grunted in a muffled voice.

He limped across the board and almost fell into the man's thick arms. The man gave an exclamation of surprise which turned to a gasp of agony as Talon's slim knife drove into his chest. The man fell back, holding his chest with both hands and stared down at himself in shock, then slowly toppled backwards with a crash onto the deck.

At this moment the quay became alive with men brandishing swords and spears who seemed to appear from nowhere. They screamed like devils as they charged across the remaining feet of the quay towards the side of the ship. Panhsj and Max led the charge. Both were yelling and waving their swords ferociously over their heads. Panhsj, carrying a small round shield, his sword held high, leapt across the gunwale of the boat to land right in the middle of the confused group of crewmen who were still staring in disbelief at their leader who lay dying at their feet.

Panhsj and Max dispatched three of the crew within seconds. The others were quick to throw up their arms, screaming for mercy, dropping their weapons. It was over very quickly, much to the disappointment of the Fayoum men who now swarmed over the upper deck of the ship, disarming the remaining sailors and hustling them towards the back of the ship where Talon and Max now waited, leaning on the rail.

"Who is your captain?" Talon asked.

The men pointed in silence at the heavyset man dead in the waist of the ship.

Panhsj, who had emerged from the large rear cabin, climbed the stairs to join them. "It is safe to bring my Lady and the children," he said, and waved his arm holding the horn lamp slowly back and forth looking towards the darkness surrounding the fort.

"We must hurry,' Talon urged. "We need to be gone by dawn and that is only an hour away." Already there was a grey light in the east and objects were becoming visible that had been undistinguishable moments ago.

A small group of armed men hurried along the quay escorting Khalidah, the children, and helping Khaldun along, followed closely by the servants carrying huge bundles on their backs.

They were hustled aboard and taken straight into the cabin. Max supervised the casting off and had the ship pushed out into the river using long oars. Panhsj addressed the crew members still clustered uneasily in the waist.

"You will work for us or I shall throw you to the crocodiles, just as we are going to do with your former captain!" he threatened. They knew he meant it.

"We wish to go south, so hurry and get to your duties," he ordered.

The terrified crew needed no further persuasion and jumped to get the furled sails down from the long booms that were suspended from the two masts; next they steered the drifting boat out into the middle of the river.

A loud murmur was heard from below decks and Talon realized that it must come from the slaves who rowed the ship. He heard the crack of a whip and his suspicions were confirmed; a drum started beating a rhythm in the depths of the vessel as oars began to rise and fall. Soon the slim craft was moving swiftly out into the river and the bank faded into the darkness.

At Panhsj's command they headed directly out towards the other side of the river. He did not want any curious people to see which direction they would finally take. They could see lights from torches moving towards the quay as the inhabitants came to investigate the disturbance, but by this time they were well away from any danger from the shore.

"Remember what will happen to you if there is any treachery," Panhsj called down at the crew. His words were punctuated by splashes as the dead were dumped unceremoniously overboard.

After a while, when there was nothing to be seen of the river bank or the torches flickering near Beneade, he ordered the fearful steersmen to turn the ship upstream. The sailors hastily attended to the sails, hauling them around to catch the wind. They flapped, then bellied full and began to drive the boat silently up river. The oars rose and fell in unison to the soft beating of the drum. The creaking of the wood locks and splashing of oars, coupled with the hiss of water under the bow, were the only sounds from the ship as they sped south.

* * * * *

Al Muntaqim stood at the rear of the galley staring moodily at the river bank passing by and reflected upon the turn of fate that had driven him from Cairo. The return of the messenger whom he had dispatched to the sultan with the information about Abbas had forced him to think carefully about his future. The man had been close to death with the wound he had sustained while fleeing the cavalry, but he had, to his credit, managed to elude them and make his way unobserved to the palace.

It had been fortunate that he had done so, because Al Muntaqim had been making preparations to meet the division of men that were on their way from Alexandria. He had had to abandon the idea of going to meet them and go ahead with his coup. There was no time left; they could not be in Cairo in time to thwart the sultan and his army, not when he was racing back aware of a plot. He had sent a messenger to order them to return to barracks and to await his orders. They had only known that Bahir had called upon them, as he, Al Muntaqim, had been careful to conceal his own identity within the plot.

While he had no evidence that he might have been implicated, he did not want to find himself in a dungeon having to explain his way out of trouble. He preferred to have at least some distance between himself and the sultan, should their plot have been discovered. The messenger had died rather suddenly after his report had been made.

He had taken a small retinue and quietly headed for the port, where he always maintained a galley ready to go. This was one of three he possessed that from time to time preyed upon shipping in the seaways between Cyprus and North Africa. It had become a good source of revenue that did not have to be accounted for and provided more rowers for his galleys as the worn out slaves died off. One of the others was by now docked at Beneade, while the third was still in the middle sea looking for easy targets upon which to pounce.

This time he would be sailing south. He wanted to take care of some business before he either disappeared or returned to the sultan with a good story.

The Poet was on his own, having fled to Alexandria with the intention of taking ship to Al Andalusia where he hoped to vanish. Al Muntaqim would have liked to have silenced him but there had not been time. He knew the sultan could move very swiftly when he had a mind to, so he had hastened to leave the city, feeling a sense of relief when he saw its distant citadel and minarets receding into the darkness behind the swiftly moving galley.

The thump of the galley drum, the calls of the sailors and the creak of oars in their locks drew his attention back to the boat in which he was now traveling. He wrinkled his nose at the stench that wafted back with the slight change of wind from the waist of the boat. Years of soldiering and sailing had never accustomed him to the sheer filth and rot that came from the area where the slave rowers sat chained to their seats, laboring in the suffocating heat.

Two ragged and starved men to each oar, they moved with machine-like precision, back and forth, the oars rising and falling in perfect unison to the beat of the goat skin drum being pounded by another slave who sat near the main mast. An overseer with a long whip ensured that the slaves did not falter. The sail was set to catch the wind so that the combination of the two means of propulsion made the slim, predatory boat appear to fly up river, leaving feluccas and other cargo boats quickly in its wake as it sped towards its destination. It had now been almost a week since the disappearance of the woman and her children and the execution of Bahir. But during that week Al Muntaqim had been busy.

He had finally made contact with the Hashishini, and not before time, either, he told himself. Their message had been: "We will work with you to kill the sultan. He is an abomination and should be sent to his maker for judgment, but if there is other work, then you shall pay in gold."

Al Muntaqim could afford to wait. If he could not confront the sultan directly, then he would allow the assassins to do the work and then assume power for himself in the ensuing chaos that would result. The man's brothers and nephews would be too busy squabbling over the spoils to notice a well-organized coup taking place right under their noses.

He had warily approached the place where the killer sect had told him to meet them in a remote corner of the city. Once seated facing these slim, hard men, their faces almost completely covered except for their dark, watchful eyes, Al Muntaqim, who was afraid of very little, had a moment of doubt. His body guards would be no match for these people if there were treachery in the air, he reflected. No one offered tea or coffee.

He was used to issuing orders and having them obeyed by men who were for the most part subservient and often groveling. These men, almost indistinguishable from one another in their form of dress, clearly did not feel they needed to treat him with respect.

He wanted only two things and was pleased that one of them came free.

"I will support you in your endeavor regarding the sultan, as we agree with one another as to the objective. However, I will pay for another piece of work that will not tax your skills overmuch, and you can tell your master I shall pay well."

The leader had nodded his head and indicated with a short lift of the chin that Al Muntaqim should continue.

"You are aware, are you not, of the death of the Lord Bahir?"

There was a pause. "We are."

"Does it not strike you as strange that it should come so soon after the death of the Lord Abbas?"

No one spoke.

"I thought it might be because he had crossed your master," Al Muntaqim probed.

There was hesitation but then the leader spoke. "We had no business with Lord Bahir...or with the Lord Abbas."

Al Muntaqim sat back placing his hands on his knees to think about this.

"Do you know who might have done this monstrous thing to Lord Bahir?"

"It was not the work of an ordinary man...if what we hear is true. We thought it might be one of our people, but now we are sure it was not. It could have been the Persians; we cannot rule that out."

"I do not understand why it should be them," Al Muntaqim reflected. "Bahir was not one to get involved with the Persians; I think I would have known if he had been."

The leader of the group of men seated in front of him shifted impatiently.

"What is it you need from us that is so urgent?" he demanded.

"I want you to go to a place called the Fayoum and take care of the family of Emir Abbas for me," was the reply.

There was a long silence as the three men looked at him.

"All of the family?"

"In particular the boy; the women can be spared. Take care of any of the bodyguards you encounter. I shall be sailing there within a few days to arrive right behind you. You may take whatever you want and you may kill whomsoever else you wish, but do it at night and do not attract attention to yourselves. Get out as soon as you can, as I wish to look like a savior, and it would not be good to be seen with you."

"This will be expensive."

"How much is expensive?"

"Twenty thousand dinars."

"That is too much by half!"

At a sign from the leader the group began to rise.

"All right, in Allah's good name, sit down. I will give you fifteen and I shall provide you with one of my galleys to get you there speedily."

The leader of the group slowly sat down again and nodded coldly. He muttered something to one of the men with him, who got up and left. Al Muntaqim tensed, watching for any treachery, but the man came back a minute later with some tiny cups and some tea. They sealed the agreement with a sip of bitter tea from the not so clean cups and talked about the location of the estate buildings and the layout of the compound.

The leader of the group had demanded at least half of the gold before the work and had agreed, after much haggling, to get the remainder after proof had been provided that they had completed the mission. Al Muntaqim wanted to see the boy's head and his hands. They discussed the manner of the delivery once the work had been carried out.

* * * * *

At this moment, sooner than he had intended, Al Muntaqim found himself heading for the Fayoum. He expected to find the place in complete disarray after the assassins had paid their visit, which should have occurred by now. He would come in and take charge under the pretext that the Lady Khalidah needed a good strong friend to run things. Then he would make his move and assume complete control. The thought of the riches of Fayoum falling into his hands made him smile.

The first disturbing thing he noted when the village of Beneade came in sight was the absence of the galley he had sent the night before. He wondered if they had passed in the night, and if it was now anchored in the water ways of the river by the city of Cairo waiting for his orders. He had no doubt that the assassins would have completed their mission. It would have been unthinkable for them not to have succeeded

His ship docked just as the sun rose above the eastern horizon, amid a lot of noise and excitement on shore. He walked onto the pier and waited for his horses to be unloaded from the waist of the ship. He was puzzled by the crowd of people gathered around the primitive fort on the main bank near the cluster of huts and small houses that comprised the village. Finally his men and their horses were off-loaded, whereupon they rode towards the fort and then turned in the direction of the estate at Fayoum. Passing the people gathered around the fort, Al Muntaqim paused and had one of his men ask what was going on.

He was informed that there had been a tremendous commotion during the night and just afterwards the ship that had docked at the port had left. There was shouting and sounds of fighting, according to one of the men, but no sign of violence other than the body of one of the young syce from the estate of Lord Abbas lying with his throat cut in the middle of the road.

Al Muntaqim dug spurs into his horse and galloped off. He swore bitterly and galloped furiously down the road, followed by his puzzled men. His mind was racing with questions as they arrived upon their sweating horses to find that the compound of the estate was deserted. The gates were hanging half open and there was no sign of any guards. They entered warily, but it soon became clear that there was no one to greet them.

Al Muntaqim was livid with rage. He drove his horse into the empty compound and contemplated the blackened and damaged main house, the litter of baggage lying haphazardly around with other debris. The stables were empty of horses. Other than a dog lurking in a corner, chewing on a bone, there was no one to greet them; it was clear there had been a hurried departure.

He was interrupted from his raging thoughts by one of his men who hesitantly rode up and asked to speak.

Al Muntaqim would have preferred to beat the man senseless for not getting off his horse and prostrating himself before him, but it was one of his better soldiers so he grunted sour acknowledgement. The man pointed back towards the gate and said. "My lord, they left overland; they have not been able to conceal their movements. It is a large party with baggage, we can follow them! They are heading into the desert to hide. *Insha'Allah* we can catch them before evening."

Al Muntaqim did not wait; he turned his horse, gave swift commands and galloped out of the compound. "Find out if there are others still in this area!" he shouted, as he left with the bulk of his men.

# Chapter 24

# Galley Slaves

Malek did not stop his horse to look back along the trail, but as he traveled he stood in the stirrups to better turn around and stare behind him. He did this for the hundredth time, wondering when he would see any signs of pursuit. He had set a hard pace, but still one that conserved the horses. They had many more miles to ride. The sun was now well past its zenith, and everyone was suffering. The mid-summer heat burned them up and sapped the strength of both the horses and men.

This many miles to the west of the green banks of the Nile the desert was an empty wasteland of stones and rugged low escarpments that could hinder the way for those who did not know its paths. Fortunately his men, having lived in this region all their lives, knew it well.

They had negotiated the southern hills leading out of the wadi Moerh situated at the south of the Moeris basin during the night. They had ridden along the ancient canals at the far western end of the lake, and then made a two hundred foot climb to skirt the Kasa Kerdoun Mountain, with only the stars and a thin waxing moon in the eastern sky to illuminate their way. As they were cresting the top of the low but steep hills, Malek looked back at the shining waters of Lake Birket el Qarun. He hoped he would return one day, but there was no time to dwell upon these thoughts now. He called out to his men in a low voice, pointing to the west.

They plunged into the desert heading due west. They would eventually change direction then head south and again return towards the east to the deserted village along the river-way where they hoped to meet the ship. Malek muttered a prayer for the family and his companions' safety. He would not know until the very last yard whether they had accomplished their goal or not. If they had failed, then without doubt they were either dead or captured and he had gone on a fruitless journey. He didn't want to contemplate the possibility that Kazim would be executed and the Lady Khalidah forced into a life of virtual slavery along with her daughter Jasmine.

He thought about Suleiman and Max. What strange men Allah had thrown across his path. He was glad that they were still with them, and that the Lord Abbas had not killed them when his anger had been fierce. Suleiman was strange, without a doubt. Very strange, but he had proven to be a strong ally when they needed him, as had Max.

His attention was directed back to the route they were taking as the men said it was time to turn south. He knew they had ridden a good twenty miles into the stony wastelands. He turned one last time to look back into the haze to check the back trail and blinked.

Far in the distance was a small plume of dust. He called over to one of the soldiers.

"Hassan, look! What is that?" he asked, hoping for the answer he got, but he felt a trickle of fear at the same time.

"They have found our trail, *Oustez.*"

* * * * *

The galley that carried the family of Abbas and his followers anchored near the west bank of the great river. Jutting out of the bank was a squat pier of crude pilings and planks of wood that had once provided a stage for moving large stones onto a boat in mooring. Malek had mentioned that long ago this had been a place where local quarried stones were transported down river to the city of Cairo and even Alexandria; but in recent years the pier had fallen into disrepair for lack of upkeep, as the quarries were no longer needed. The village clinging to the embankment was in ruins and deserted.

Talon looked doubtfully at the rickety pier and wondered how the horses would fare on these loose boards when it came time to load them. His attention was drawn away by a sudden splash. He looked round to see two of the crew about to dump the body of one of the rowers overboard. The man had died of exhaustion and starvation. Talon was not surprised; they were skeletons down there performing an insane kind of dance to the rhythm of the drum. They sat where they were chained, and died there when used up. In this humid heat they died faster.

He decided to go and have a look for himself and see who these people were. He stepped down the hatchway and almost gagged at the heat and the stink that hit him like a physical blow. He found that he was facing four rows of men who were chained in pairs to one bench on either side of the center deck. He could not see the ones at the back who were hidden in the gloom of the closed deck. The only air that came into the space was from a small grating near each mast. He noted that if only the hatches at either end were opened it would create a welcoming draft.

He found himself staring at the human wrecks that faced him. Blue eyes and black eyes stared at him from under huge beards or tattooed faces of Nubians and men from even further south into Africa. Black men and white; they served the same drum. Their faces could not be read in this light and most lowered their eyes, unwilling to be caught showing any sign of defiance. Talon stood rooted to the deck in shock. He noticed one rower, who had once been a large man and was now a shadow of himself, who was staring at him with a fixed look that showed no fear.

He looked back for a moment into light blue eyes that were not afraid of him. For some reason, Talon nodded and then turned and climbed the stairs. He joined Max on the back deck which was situated over the cabin where Khalidah had taken refuge with the children and her servants from the blazing heat. Khaldun had joined them. This was midsummer and Malek had said it was the time of year for the Nile to rise above its banks. Indeed, he could see that the current seemed to have increased its speed and the waters had a different color.

Max looked at him with concern. "You look as though you have seen a ghost."

"I have, Max. The men down below, they are like ghosts, and many are of our kind," Talon replied.

He turned to Max with a desperate expression, "Max, we have to do something about those men. There are Christians among them. And the others...they too deserve better than what they are getting from this crew."

Max stared at him hard. "Are you saying we should release them? What would we do with them once they are released? How would we manage this boat without them? What if they run away?"

"Let me think." Talon turned away and contemplated the faded vegetation on the banks of the river. Soon the inundation would turn it back to bright green, if Khaldun was to be believed. He turned his mind to the problem of the rowers.

"Max, we could offer the slaves a way out. Yes, that is it. Max, I have it!" he exclaimed, grasping his friend by the arm; Max winced. "Ah, forgive me, I had forgotten," Talon was instantly contrite.

"No matter, T...Suleiman. What is on your mind?"

"My Lady gave me my freedom. I may leave now at any time, but I have told her I will not leave, at least not until I know she and the children are safe. This boat is our way to freedom, don't you see? The men rowing this boat are mostly Christians who have probably been captured in battle, or at sea. Remember the fight we went through?"

Max nodded. "But will Malek and her Ladyship agree?" He asked, his tone skeptical.

"They will agree that I can go...but you? Well...you are still a slave, Max; I might have to leave you behind," Talon grinned mischievously at his friend, who pretended to look deeply hurt.

"What if we promise these men their freedom, on condition that they fight and row for us before we grant them freedom?"

"You will have much convincing to do, not only Malek but Panhsj, and the other men, I suspect," Max said with his usual common sense coming to the fore.

Indeed it was not easy. Talon first went below with one of the crew and pointed out the man who had stared at him. The crew unshackled the man and dragged him into the harsh light of day to where Talon stood waiting. Panhsj and Max sauntered over and watched.

Talon spoke French to the man who was kneeling in front of him. "You may stand," he said, and motioned the crew away. They left the man to get up, and he held himself proudly, staring directly at them. The crewmen muttered among themselves, but did as they were told. Talon motioned some of the men from the estate to keep an eye on the surly crewmen, which they did willingly enough. There was no love lost between them.

The creature in front of him was starved and filthy, his beard was long and matted; doubtless it was full of lice. There were sores over his body, which stank. He wore only a loin cloth that was as filthy as everything else about him. His face was lined with weariness and exhaustion, but he was defiant all the same. He waited in silence, his eyes staring straight at Talon.

"Do you understand me?" Talon asked.

The man cleared his throat, as though unused to speaking and said, in accented French, "I understand you."

"Where are you from and how did you come to be here on this boat?"

"I am from the land known as England. I am a Norman," the man said, pride in his voice. "Our ship was overwhelmed by these pirates in the central sea. They came as a pack like sea wolves, and killed most of us, but I and some of my companions were taken prisoner."

"What is your name?"

"Henry of Wellford."

"My name is Suleiman; it is good we have met, Henry. Here is what I ask," Talon said. "I need your help to take this ship to the Kingdom of Jerusalem, but before we do that, we have to help some people regain what is theirs. Do you understand?"

Henry gaped at him.

It took some time, with the help of food and drink, to assist Henry to understand that he might be free again. Realization slowly began to dawn as he concentrated on what Talon and Max were telling him.

"I understand that we need to continue to row this ship for a while longer, but when we get to our destination we will be freed, and that you want to take us with you to the Kingdom of Jerusalem," he said, a bemused expression on his face. "Dear God, if this is true then it is a miracle!" he exclaimed.

"We need to know which ones of the men below will stay with us if we release their chains today and who will simply dive overboard at the first opportunity," Max said.

"I know most of them. There are other Normans; we were all sailors, but ill chance threw us into this hell. I have been on board for two months and I can tell you that if you promise to feed us and you release us, I will be able to persuade the larger part to stay. I cannot speak for the Saracens or the strange black men who we have with us. There are about ten of those heathens."

"Some may be criminals. But the black men might be from the same region as Panhsj. Let us ask him what he thinks," Talon said to Max.

"Who are you? Who in the name of the Holy Mother are you people?" Henry asked, staring at them.

"At this time, the less you know the better, Henry. Put your trust in God and us, for we intend to see you free," Max told him.

"The crew of this ship will become a problem sooner or later," Talon observed.

"If you will give me a sword, I will take care of that problem for you, Sir," Henry volunteered.

Max grinned. "A long stay at the oars has not dampened your ardor for a fight, I see," he commented dryly.

Talon left Max and Henry talking by the mast and returned to the back of the ship to find Panhsj. Panhsj looked past his shoulder.

"So you speak to a slave and give him food; why am I no longer surprised at whatever you do, Suleiman?" he asked.

"My friend, I think we might have a small army to go with our other men," Talon said calmly.

"Pshaw! That scarecrow could not even lift a sword in his own defense," Panhsj scoffed.

"But they can row, and if we feed them, well... they might," Talon said.

He spent the next hour persuading Panhsj that there was more to be had from the rowers. "The crew will not only betray us at the first opportunity, but will probably stab us in the back if we get into a fight."

"You are right; they are a danger to us while free," Panhsj mused.

"The men at the oars can not only row, but with some food and care, they might be able to aid our cause rather than hinder it. That one is a sailor, Panhsj, which is more than you or I," Talon said, pointing at Henry.

Panhsj nodded reluctantly. "I shall go below and see for myself if there are any people from my country, and then we shall see."

He came back onto the rear deck a little while later, in a thoughtful mood.

"There is only one from my region and he is not from the same tribe, but we communicated well enough. There are about ten men with him who would serve. The rest, well, I don't know, Suleiman. We are taking a big chance with the lives of my Lady and my lord Kazim by doing this."

"My friend, Allah is on our side. I suggest that later, when Malek is with us, we subdue the crew and replace them with some of the men below who can sail a boat, and then we do not have to worry about the crewmen any more. The rest of the men down there will take care of that."

Panhsj chuckled; his tattoos writhed as he grinned. "Your cunning is becoming legend, Suleiman. For now, put the man back with the others and we will release them when we get to our destination."

Talon agreed with this and persuaded Henry to return to the filth he had lived in for months with the promise of release as soon as they had their passengers on board and had reached their destination, which was Aswan. Talon hoped that he could keep his promise.

# Chapter 25

# Al Muntaqim

Al Muntaqim was still raging when he and his riders finally arrived back at the estate of the Fayoum. They were exhausted from their three days' ride into an empty desert and the temper of their master was terrifying. No one could understand how a large party of men, women and animals could so completely disappear into the desert wastelands west of the Fayoum. Al Muntaqim was inclined to take his anger out upon his own people when frustrated, so the men gave him a wide berth.

It was fortunate that he had not burned the buildings to the ground, Al Muntaqim reflected, or he would have had to go and rest on his Dromon tied up at the pier at Beneade. Poor comfort indeed, he thought, as he examined the courtyard and the half burned remains of the main house. Despite the fire damage, this would do nicely for his short stay.

A pleasant surprise awaited him when he dismounted. The leader of the men who had been left behind came forward, while two of the other men dragged a woman with them. She was young and looked terrified, protesting feebly. The men threw her at his feet in the dust, where she remained, her head down.

"Who is this?" He asked reaching down and raising her head up by the chin.

"She was trying to escape when we arrived. She had some cloth with her that she claimed was hers. I think she is a thief, my lord," his man said with a smirk.

Indeed, the woman was young and pretty, Al Muntaqim thought, as he looked down on the tear-stained face of the girl.

"You know what they do with thieves don't you? Tell me who you are and no harm shall come to you," he said quietly, but there was no mistaking the menace in his voice.

Anyess was shaking with fear. She knew she should not have come back to the compound, but the thought of the precious, richly colored cloth lying about in the deserted estate had obsessed her. She had felt a degree of resentment as well, thinking she had been deserted to fend for herself with her family.

Her mother had begged her not to go, and had her father been alive, she would have had to stay, but she stubbornly insisted that it would be safe. Finally her brother had agreed to come with her, and it was while the two of them were in the house that the strangers had arrived in the maidan.

Her brother had called to her in desperation to come with him and leave when he heard the sound of horses, but it was too late, and she had been trapped in the house while he managed to run away.

It did not take long for the looting men to find her hidden in a chest of linen. They had hauled her out and laughed at her stricken face and then taunted her while they passed her around from one to the other. They pawed at her, their hunger showing in their wolfish grins as they leered at her. They had not done more than that, as the leader had seen the opportunity to find favor with his Lord. He had used the flat of his sword on those who disagreed with him, even cut one who would not listen, and warned them off with the threat of their Lord's wrath if they disobeyed him.

So now she was half lying on the ground in front of Al Muntaqim, and he was asking the question again. This time he seized her by the hair and forced her head back, making her look up at him. "Who are you and what are you doing here?" he demanded.

"I...I am a servant, my lord. My name is Anyess, please do not harm me!" she cried.

"Tell me where your mistress is, and I shall be kind. Do not, and I shall have you turned over to my men, who have not seen a woman for many days." He laughed at her fearful expression.

Anyess thought about this, but she did not have much time, as Al Muntaqim shook her head, making her gasp with pain. She blurted out what she knew, but what she knew was wrong. She thought her mistress had gone to Alexandria; there had been a plan to either go by land or even by river.

Al Muntaqim left the compound more or less as he had found it, as he intended to come back. There was no point in destroying a place he now owned. He had been enraged to learn upon arrival at the port of Beneade that his other ship was possibly in the possession of the Lady Khalidah, and had most probably sailed north. How he had missed it on his way upriver puzzled him, but it was missing nevertheless and the people of Beneade seemed to think there had been a fight for the ship just before it disappeared. The thought that his ship might have been stolen by this woman Khalidah only added to his fury.

Thinking about the options open to Lady Khalidah, Al Muntaqim decided that she would probably sail to Alexandria where her father lived, and therefore set out with the intent to visit the city and find out. His mood was optimistic, for he had had a pleasant enough night with the girl, whom he had later turned over to his men for sport.

The body of Anyess was found by her brother later in the day after the visitors had gone. He cried bitterly over her corpse and then went to find his mother so that they could give her a decent burial.

* * * * *

Lord Al Muntaqim was admitted to the house of Emir Al Hakim ibn Hudhafah Ghassan, father of Lady Khalidah. After the elaborate greetings had been completed and the two were seated comfortably on a priceless carpet with richly woven cushions scattered all about the floor, coffee had been served and Al Muntaqim made welcome. The old man said carefully, "We are not always as honored as this, my lord."

"It is not often that I have ill news to bring, my lord," Al Muntaqim returned. There was no sign of the lady Khalidah, or the children, at the palace, at least not that he could tell. "You may recall, my lord, that terrible accident that befell Lord Abbas followed by the looting of his palace?"

Al Hakim sighed and said, "I recall it as though yesterday. I have not stopped mourning my son Abbas and weep for my daughter every day. I pray to Allah the Almighty that he will be kind to the soul of my son," he intoned.

"I too, I pray for my comrade in arms every day at prayers," Al Muntaqim said piously and added in a contrived tone, "My lord, it is about this that I have come to you for help."

"Speak, and I will do what I can to assist you. What is it?" Al Hakim's voice was suddenly strong.

"Your daughter has disappeared, my lord. No one knows where she is, and the sultan, may Allah protect him, is very concerned. He is asking all of us to try and find out what has happened to her and her family. It was my task to come and see you." The old man looked stunned. "What do you mean, in Allah's name? My daughter has disappeared? How could this be so? Is she not at the estates of Fayoum?"

Al Muntaqim looked puzzled. "My messengers tell me that she is no longer in the Fayoum. I have come to you to ask if she might be here. There is much concern for her safety and health by the friends of Lord Abbas."

"But she would surely have surely gone to Fayoum. She spent the happiest years of her marriage there. I cannot think where else in the world she might have gone!" the old man exclaimed in an agitated manner.

"Have you not had a message from her, perhaps?" Al Muntaqim enquired politely.

"Indeed I have not, and that is a puzzle too. I am sure she would have written once she arrived in the Fayoum. She would want to reassure me that she was in good health, and the children."

They talked at length about the situation and of their puzzlement, and finally Al Muntaqim took his leave.

* * * * *

Later, when Al Muntaqim returned to the house he owned in Alexandria and had calmed down, he thought about the situation. He had heard that the Poet Umarah was gone to Al Andalusia by ship and was inclined to do the same himself. He had no idea as to whether the sultan knew of his involvement or not. His spies had told him that the sultan had arrived with his cavalry demanding to see the poet, to be told that man had gone. This left the sultan with no one to link Al Muntaqim to the plot, but all the same his absence had been noted. He needed to go back and present himself to the sultan and make his excuses. It was a risk but well worth taking, as the stakes were very high and Al Muntaqim was not lacking in courage.

He was in a deep black anger over the disappearance of the elusive Lady Khalidah. How could a mere woman seem to be so resourceful, he wondered. He was still determined to find her. She and her son represented the last possible link between him and the conspiracy, and would provide, willingly or unwillingly, the property he coveted. Calling two servants to him he said, "You will scour the country for any trace of Lady Khalidah and her son. If she is gone to another country, I want to know. If she is still here in Egypt, I want to know immediately. I am going back to Cairo."

* * * * *

Deep in the heart of the big Souk of Cairo, just off one of the busy narrow streets, three men eased their way cautiously into a second floor room. Their swords were held at the ready as they crept into the filthy, almost bare room. The leader quickly took in the pallet in one corner and the inert body lying on it.

He moved swiftly over to the bed and knelt next to it to see if there was any sign of life left in the man. He wrinkled his nose at the stink of oncoming death and listened. Then he waved away the flies that were crawling over the blood-caked wound in the man's side. There were maggots and encrusted blood and puss in the area of the wound, which stank of rot. He glanced around, taking in the bloody rags thrown on the floor nearby, also covered in flies, the discarded sword, and the small bags in one corner. The newcomer shook the man, who groaned, then opened his eyes blearily to see who had woken him from his stupor. There did not seem to be much time left for him. He was the assassin who had escaped from Fayoum and now lay dying in this filthy rat-infested room in the back of the Souk.

"Water! Give me water..." he croaked.

The leader of the men gestured to another to fetch some. The man hastened into a small attached room and dipped a beaker into a large clay jar of water. They silently helped the sick man, whose parched throat and lips were so dry he could barely swallow.

"What happened, Yusuf? Why are you here wounded, and where are the others?" the leader of the new arrivals demanded in a curt manner.

"They...they are dead. We were told to go to Fayoum on behalf of the man called Al Muntaqim. It was for gold, and the Master allowed it as the fee was good," Yusuf whispered.

"We are here to collect the gold but...you say the others are dead? Were you not successful?"

"No. There is one there who knows our ways. He killed Hassan, and then wounded me. I have never fought one so skilled before. Someone called him Suleiman, and he told me he was a *Fidai*. He told me in Farsi, as though to warn me. He looked right into my eyes and told me," Yusuf gasped, falling back exhausted onto the filthy pallet.

"What happened to Mahmud?" demanded one of the men leaning over him, wrinkling his nose at the smell of death on their comrade.

"I do not know, but I am sure he is dead too. He was so quick... this man Suleiman. He has green eyes like a Frans," Yusuf said in a weak voice, his eyes closed and his face twisted in pain. They stared at one another in astonishment. They had not expected this, and Yusuf was going fast.

Soon after, the three young men, dressed in identical loose cotton pants, short boots with wide shirts held with a brownish red waist band, took the gold that they found hidden in the room. Leaving the body of Yusuf in the room, they slipped out as silently as they had come. Their weapons were concealed on their persons, but people in the crowded streets still gave them a wide berth as they looked purposeful and menacing. They had a long and dangerous journey to make to the far north of the county of Tripoli near to Syria. They needed to get a message to the Master and deliver what gold Al Muntaqim had given in payment.

* * * * *

Sultan Salah Ed Din Ayyubi was seated on a magnificent throne surrounded by his secretaries and several of his senior officers. The furnishings of the room were in keeping with the high office held by Salah Ed Din, having once been the trappings of royalty for his predecessors the Fatimid Sultans, now long gone.

The sultan did not approve of fine furnishings, nor did he use the title of Sultan for himself, preferring more the austere life of a soldier. But from time to time he needed to remind people what office he held. This was one of those occasions.

The curtains and carpets were the finest that could be found in the entire Islamic world, having been brought by the fleets of merchant ships that once plied the middle sea. Now the sea was owned by others, and the merchants used camel trains instead.

The last business of the day concerned his commander, Lord Kemosiri ibn Jibade, sometimes known as Al Muntaqim. The sultan was angry, but with his usual manner he was prepared to hear his officer out before passing judgment.

Lord Kemosiri was on his knees in front of the throne, looking up at the sultan with a contrite expression on his hard, lean features.

"My lord, all blessings be upon you this day. I know I am guilty of leaving my post. But it was to attend to the funeral of my uncle Mohammed ibn Faris Fawaz, who died suddenly of the river fever several days ago in Alexandria. There was no one else to take care of the proceedings because my nephew, as you know, has recently died. It broke the old man's heart, as he had practically adopted him as a son, and I was the only one who could assist in the honoring of the dead.

"I deeply regret my absence, but my lord, I did leave Lord Bahir in charge and no thought crossed my mind that there might be a terrible tragedy about to take place in my absence. As God is my witness, my lord, I would never have left, not even for my uncle, had I known what was about to transpire. This I only discovered when I returned last night. I came immediately to you today."

"While I respect the need to bury the dead correctly, it was because you were not here to control things that I had to leave my work in the Negev to come back. I heard there was treachery in Cairo and that the poet and several others were involved in instigating a rebellion against me. Did you know nothing of this either, Kemosiri?" the sultan demanded.

"My lord, I have heard rumors, and they point...ah, my lord, they pointed at Lord Abbas. My lord, I wept when I contemplated this, as I could not believe it myself when Bahir told me of it."

"Lord Bahir told you of what?" The sultan was leaning forward, and there was a murmur of interest from those who stood nearby.

"My lord, what I have is for your ears alone. I beg you to give me a hearing on this."

The sultan waved away everyone who was near, and when the room was empty of courtiers and only guards remained, he bade Kemosiri to come closer and be seated on a stool near to him.

"Speak, but I am already unhappy with what I think you are about to say."

Kemosiri lowered his voice. "My lord, I have it on good information that Lord Abbas was a member of the group of men who were going to take advantage of your absence and capture the citadel."

"How could he possibly do that while he was lying in bed with a broken back?" the sultan exclaimed. He gave a small, incredulous laugh.

"My lord Bahir and Abbas have not liked one another for a long time, it is true, and I can assure you that Bahir had to work hard to convince me too. I have always admired Abbas and not Bahir, whom I considered a much lesser man. Alas, however, there was proof, because the poet Umarah went to visit the house of Abbas often and we know he too is involved in some kind of plot to harm you. Now both men are dead, murdered by who knows whom, and where is the poet today, my lord? We should ask him."

"He is not in Cairo, and cannot be found," the Sultan said. There was annoyance in his voice.

Kemosiri almost smiled. This was going better than he had anticipated. He had known he would be in trouble for abandoning Cairo while the sultan was away, but so far there had been no indication that the sultan suspected him in anything. If he had, he knew he would not be sitting here now.

"That does not explain the battle I heard of in the house of Abbas, the fire and the subsequent death of him and many of his family," the Sultan remarked dryly.

"The story I was told, my lord, is that Bahir, ever the impetuous, went there to confront the Lord Abbas, but was met with spears and swords instead. He barely got out of there with his life and lost many men. The fire must have occurred later, because of a fallen lamp, perhaps? But Bahir withdrew and then sent a messenger to me to explain what had happened. I was very angry and replied that he should not have done this and that we should wait for your orders."

"I received your messenger, but he disappeared when I needed to talk to him," The Sultan said. "Bring the boy here to me," he called. "You should know that a man came to me in the Negev from the house of Lord Abbas, but his story does not seem to match up with that of Bahir's."

It took some time, but the ever hospitable Sultan offered Kemosiri tea and they were deep into a discussion about the successes of Turin Shah in Yemen, when the guards brought a young man, more a boy, into the chamber. The boy prostrated himself immediately in front of the sultan who said, "Stand up, Haytham. I want you to recount your story to my noble friend Lord Kemosiri."

The unsuspecting boy told them how he had escaped from the compound during the attack, but then he had returned and been captured by men who he did not know. A servant of Abbas named Suleiman had saved him and told him to ride to the sultan and tell him of the tragedy and about the involvement of the Poet.

The Sultan thanked him and bade him go. The boy looked curiously at Kemosiri but said nothing, then bowed very low and left in the company of the guards.

The sultan looked at Kemosiri. "So you see, there is a problem with what he is telling me and what I am hearing from you, and also what we heard from Bahir. I do not understand it Kemosiri ... do you have an explanation?"

Kemosiri had been sweating for a few minutes. He did not recognize the boy, but the boy might well have recognized him. Apparently he had not, and Kemosiri breathed a little easier.

The sultan continued in a thoughtful manner, "Why was Bahir killed in the manner he was? I hear it was gruesome; who in Allah's name would do this?"

"Alas, the death of Bahir points back to the house of Abbas, my Liege. It was also suggested that the Hashashini were involved."

"The Hashishini! What has Sinan and his unpleasant retainers got to do with any of this?"

"They hate you, my lord, and all of us. Remember they are Ismaili. It would not be hard for someone in the Abbas family to pay them to come and do what they did to Bahir. Perhaps they are more deeply involved than we think. Despite everything, the house of Abbas was once loyal to the Fatimid family." He paused briefly. "My lord, what was done to Bahir was terrible in the eyes of Allah. I mourn him, as I do my friend Abbas. How it could have come to this, God only knows, but if I think on it I have to ask myself this question," Kemosiri said with an anguished expression on his face. "If Abbas was innocent of the charges that are being discussed, why has the Lady Khalidah not come to you to ask for protection?"

The Sultan sat back in his chair, a thoughtful look on his face. "You are right. No one knows where she is at this time. The house of Abbas is apparently destroyed, but she is supposed to have survived; however, there is no sign of her or her children. Is she gone from Cairo?"

"I believe it to be the case, my lord. But I do know she is not in Alexandria because I have just come from there. Had she been there I am sure I would have known about it."

"Then where could she be? Perhaps you are right, Kemosiri. Why did she not come to me and ask for succor immediately if she had been innocent? That would have been the right thing to do. This whole thing is very confusing, but there are almost no witnesses to the truth. You were gone; Abbas is dead, and now so is Bahir. Not only that, the poet seems to have run off."

He sat back, his features bore a look of acute frustration and he pulled at his short beard.

"While I have a very hard time imagining my loyal servant Abbas plotting against me, I find it very strange that his family has seemingly gone into hiding. That points to guilt of some kind."

Kemosiri allowed himself an inaudible sigh of relief. There had been beads of sweat on his forehead, but now he felt that he was more in control of the situation.

"Rumor has it that the lady Khalidah, and the family, might have gone to Lord Abbas's estates in the Fayoum, my lord."

"Then I shall send messengers to order her to come back to Cairo so that we can hear her story. The son—is his name Kazim? —stands to inherit, but it must be done with my approval and only if the name of Abbas is cleared."

"My lord, I beg your forgiveness for having left my post, but I truly felt that for a few days at least it would be safe to do so. I shall atone for my neglect in whatever manner you should see fit. I beg firstly that I might serve you, and be charged with finding the poet and the family of Abbas, to bring them back to you for judgment and explanation, at the very least."

The sultan looked at him speculatively. "Yes, you have caused me much trouble, as I am certain that had you been here none of this could have happened and I would not have had to come back in a rush to deal with the aftermath. Allah alone knows what the truth is in this ugly matter, but I shall be lenient in your case, as I need good commanders." He looked straight into Kemosiri's eyes and said, "I want you to find the poet and bring him to me for justice, and the family of Abbas is to be found and brought before me. I wish to hear their side of this strange story."

Kemosiri bowed very low. "May Allah protect you forever, my lord. I am your humble servant, always."

He bowed his way out of the chamber, and rode back to his palace in a thoughtful but satisfied mood.

Upon his return, Kemosiri summoned Akhom, the former bodyguard of Bahir.

When the burly guard arrived, he bowed low, placing his hand over his heart.

"Allah's blessings, my lord. You summoned me?"

"I did, Akhom. You are to take the galley that has just arrived from the Middle sea and sail it to Al Andalusia."

"That is very far, Lord. May I ask the reason for this journey?"

"You are to find the Poet Umarah and bring him back to me. No one is to know he is your prisoner. You bring him into my presence, in chains if need be, and to none other. Do I make myself clear?"

"I fully understand, Lord. I am your servant in all things."

"Be sure that you do not fail me, as you failed your former master, Akhom," Kemosiri said icily.

Akhom bowed low, beads of sweat forming on his brow.

"You will also verify that the Lady Khalidah and her son are not in Al Andalusia at the same time. Should they be, you will kill the son, secretly, and bring the lady back to me."

"It shall be as you command, Lord."

# Chapter 26

# Aswan

Talon stood with Panhsj and Max on the upper deck of the dromon galley, waiting anxiously for Malek to appear on the bank with his men. It was sweltering in the burning sun. There was almost no breeze to alleviate the stink rising from the oar deck, coupled with the smell of hot tar and caulk from the ships timbers. The odors were heavy. Time appeared to have stopped. The whole ship was stunned by the heat of the day. Men lay about in inert bundles snatching any shade they could find.

Of the Lady Khalidah there had not been much evidence. Talon was aware that her head was still very sore and that she wanted to rest. It must be stifling in the cabin, he thought, even with the window shutters opened to allow what little cool air lifted from the river to flow through the small space. This reminded him of the plight of the rowers and he ordered the hatches to be opened at both ends of the rowing deck to allow air to circulate through the lower deck; yet another man had died and was carelessly thrown overboard to drift down stream, food for the crocodiles.

It was late in the day with sun almost below the top of the river banks, throwing the few palm trees into sharp relief, when a man on a horse appeared at the top of the bank and looked down at them. With the sun directly behind him it was hard to see if the horseman was one of the men who accompanied Malek or someone less welcome. Everyone became very tense as they watched him. But then there was a distant shout and Malek himself cantered over the rise, followed by his group of men.

They began to descend the steep bank towards the pier in a flurry of sand; there they dismounted and began the difficult business of urging their mounts along the surface of the pier. It took almost an hour of frantic activity to walk the horses aboard. After giving orders for them to be given water and washed down, Malek strode to the back deck and told them of their adventures. The boat, now full of the newcomers with their horses loaded and tied, pushed off and headed into the middle of the river; again the monotonous sound of the drum accompanied the rise and fall of the oars.

"Allah be praised, but I am glad to see you, Malek." Panhsj spoke for all three of them after they embraced.

"No more than I am to see you! Allah protected us this day. They are a long way behind us so I think we evaded them, *Insha'Allah!*" Malek said with a grin. There was a strip of dust in a wide band across his temples, eyes and nose.

"Did you see them?" Max asked eagerly.

"We caught a far glimpse of them just as we were about to turn south, Max, but they were hours behind us so we don't know who was with the group. My guess is that Al Muntaqim, whomsoever he is, is still wondering which direction we finally took." He laughed, but it was clear he was very tired.

"You and the men must rest," Talon said. "We have food, but you must find yourself a place to sleep wherever you can. This boat is overcrowded with people and the cabin is where my Lady is staying."

Malek nodded. "I want to hear about the capture of this boat when I am rested. Allah be praised, you have no idea how worried I have been. Praise be to Allah that we were both successful." He turned and strode down to the main deck to join his men, who were already seated on the planks telling of their adventures to the others, who in turn told their own story of how they had captured the ship with no casualties.

"We have to tell him of your crazed plan tomorrow, Suleiman," Panhsj said.

"We need to inform my Lady soon as well. But tonight we have to be alert, because I do not trust the crew. Someone of us will have to stay awake with at least one or two others," Talon said.

"I shall talk to them," Panhsj said, an ominous tone in his voice. "They will heed me."

Max and Talon chuckled at that.

The night was long, but the water cooled the air and it was not as arduous as during the day. Talon took a late watch and was informed all was well by Max as he relieved him on the after deck. "The crew seem to be quiet, Suleiman. Our men are watching them with the promise of the crocodiles for anyone who does not behave," Max told him and went down to the main deck to sleep.

The boat sailed up the river at a fair speed with both the huge lateen sails stretched taut before the night breeze. The oarsmen had ceased their work long ago and all was quiet below. The only men awake were the guards posted by Panhsj, the steersmen, and himself. Talon guessed that this type of sail, because of its triangular shape, could catch the wind from several quarters, which made it useful on a river such as this.

He wondered what the next day would bring. Staring at the crescent moon that now lit up the sky, blotting out the stars in its vicinity, he wandered again when he might ever see Rav'an again. He had spent almost a year here in Egypt, which made it nearly two since he had been taken away from her. His heart was heavy as he contemplated a world without either Rav'an or Reza in it. He muttered a prayer for them in the vain hope that it might be heard.

He had wanted to go down and talk to Henry, but realized that the men below were doubtless in an exhausted sleep which he should not disturb. He tramped around the rear deck restlessly and looked back down river, looking for signs of pursuit; there were none. He wondered for the hundredth time who Al Muntaqim might really be. Something nagged at his memory, but he could not bring it forth to examine it. He heard a tiny sound behind him and spun around, his sword almost out of its sheath, to find himself staring at Khalidah. She had reached the top stair of the ladder leading to the deck upon which he was standing.

She flinched but he snapped his sword back and bowed very low with his hand on his heart. Khalidah recovered her composure and advanced towards him, her slippers making very little noise as she approached.

"Peace be with you, my Lady," Talon said, straightening up.

"Peace be with you too, Suleiman. You are guarding us once more, I see."

"My Lady, I hope you have recovered from your injury?" he asked politely. Even though she was veiled she was a lovely ethereal vision in the moonlight. It was good she hid behind cloth, as the boat was filled with men, and not all of them friendly. The guards had noticed her. He glared at the steersmen, who turned their curious eyes away to stare studiously forward.

She touched the side of her head tentatively with her fingers, allowing her fine cotton veil to shift. Although he could see little of her face, her fine features were drawn with fatigue.

"I shall recover, with Allah's help. Khaldun is exhausted and asleep, as are the children, but I could not sleep, so I came out. I hope I am not disturbing you?"

Talon gave her a smile. "My Lady, this is your ship and I am honored to be in your presence."

She spoke in a low voice, "I hear Malek came aboard and that we are a complete family again. That is good, as I was worried about him, although I should not have been. He is a very resourceful man and his people know the desert better than anyone."

"He is indeed, my Lady, Allah be praised. We are all happy that he made it without incident, and just as importantly, we can hope that the enemy does not know where we are."

It was clear she wanted to stay, so Talon gestured towards the back rail furthest away from the steersmen. They leaned on the rail to watch the pale glimmer of the wake below. Talon made sure he was not too close. There was silence between them for a long moment until then she spoke again.

"We go to Aswan where my husband fought the Nubians not so long ago; I wonder what it will be like there."

"Panhsj can tell us, can he not, my Lady?"

"Perhaps he can, but I have a relative who is a distant cousin living there within the city of Aswan. I doubt if Panhsj has met him."

"Do you know him, this relative, my Lady?"

"I only know that he was a man of letters, like my father, and that he was also a mathematician and astrologer who shunned the big cities, preferring to live in remote places rather than the center of society, such as Cairo. Khaldun will certainly like him."

"These men are usually kind, and with Allah's guidance he will give you shelter, I am sure of it, my Lady."

"It is in Allah's hands, Suleiman." Then she changed the subject.

"When you leave us, where will you go, Suleiman?"

Talon hesitated, then finally he answered, "I have an unfinished journey to complete, my Lady. It must be when we have made sure that you are safe in Aswan."

"You will go back to your family?"

"No, my Lady."

"Then for what? Where will you go?"

Talon was silent for so long that she took it to mean he had not heard.

"Did you not hear me, Suleiman? Or will you not answer my question?"

"I...I go to search for my companions. I do not know whether they are dead or alive."

"Men lose companions all the time but they don't..." she stopped. Her head turned towards him and he thought he saw surprise in her eyes.

"Suleiman, is it a woman you seek?"

Talon just nodded.

She sighed and said softly, "You love this woman? Yes, you must. Where will you go to find her?"

"I have to go deep into Persia just to know if she is even alive, my Lady."

"But that is so far away. You would do this?"

Unexpectedly her hand came out and her fingers touched his that were gripping the rail for the briefest of moments. Her touch was so light he was almost unsure that she had, but his pulse began to beat harder than before.

"It is very well known to all of us that you are a man of many secrets, Suleiman. I too know this, but I am privileged that you have shared this secret with me. I shall say a prayer to Allah that she is safe."

"Thank you, my Lady. That is kind of you."

"I shall bid you goodnight, Suleiman. Peace be with you."

She smiled then and left him with a bemused expression on his face as he bowed to her retreating back.

"Peace be with you, my Lady."

The next morning the wind picked up enough for them not to need the rowers; and Malek, who had taken command, ordered the rowers to rest and to be fed. The sour crew under the supervision of his men went around with water and the daily gruel.

Panhsj had already revealed Talon's plan to Malek, who called him and Max over to discuss the situation. He was quite put out by the whole plan but was prepared to listen to Talon's interpretation before he vetoed it. He also wanted to discuss it with Khalidah, preferably at the same time, so they trouped into the rear cabin. There, after the usual greetings, they were bade to sit, and Talon told them all what was on his mind.

He knew that he would get only one chance to make his case. Even though Panhsj was half way convinced, Talon realized that Panhsj would do what Malek decided, for he was still subservient to him. Talon used all his powers of persuasion, pointing out that by making the slaves their crewmen, with the promise of food and a future chance to go to the Holy Land, they would have their loyalty. They certainly would stand more chance if it came to a fight with an enemy who far outnumbered them. The original crew was untrustworthy, and if any one of them managed to escape and find their way back to Al Muntaqim, they were in mortal danger.

Gradually Malek and Khalidah began to see the sense of his argument, and finally, after numerous questions, she asked, "How do you know these slaves, these rowers, won't cut our throats and take the ship off, once we free them, Suleiman?"

Talon thought about his answer. "Because I will give them my word that I shall help them get to the kingdom of Jerusalem, and I will make them swear by their God that they will work with us until that time. My Lady, we have to give them something to hope for, or they will surely be useless when we need them."

Everyone was silent for a long moment as they digested this.

Khaldun glanced at Talon then turned his look upon Malek, who was still somewhat skeptical.

"My Lady, Suleiman by all accounts has never led us false, although he knows how to lie like an Armenian merchant. Look at the story he told us about Alexandria!" Everyone laughed at this, and even Talon had to smile ruefully, while Khalidah put a hand over her mouth. The children began to giggle, and the tension was broken. Out of the corner of his eye, Talon observed Khaldun's beard jumping up and down as the old man shook with laughter, and he knew his proposition was going to be accepted.

"How then does my Aba feel about all of this?" Khalidah enquired of Khaldun.

"I support the idea, and for this reason," Khaldun said, composing himself. "Suleiman has told us a good tale in the past but he has never willingly allowed harm to any of us. He has not stated such, but it is clear to me we have little choice but to find men in any place we can. We have only twenty who can fight, other than your warriors sitting here. While we might find men where we are going in Aswan, it is not very likely. The rowers number some forty men, of whom a few are too sick to do much, but the rest will at least double our numbers. If we can find time to get their health back, these men who have pulled oars for months will be able to fight. If it is Allah's will, then we should use what resources we have at our disposal, my Lady."

"The man we talked to yesterday is a fighter for certain," Max pointed out.

"Then we must decide when and where we do this thing," Malek said firmly, with an enquiring look at Khalidah, who nodded her assent.

"Suleiman, you talk to that man and tell him to promise before his God that he will work for us until we are sure we are safe in Aswan, or elsewhere, we will free him and his companions. Before Allah, I, in turn, will promise that; but we will have to make sure that no one in Cairo ever hears of it, or they will construe it as treason!"

It was a sobering thought.

They sailed all day enduring the blazing sun and watching the fast flowing water change color as they proceeded up stream. At one point Malek came to the front of the ship to join Talon and Max, who were staring down at the dark brown color of the river.

"It's rising, the Nile is rising. We shall have to be careful because it brings with it much that is dangerous to a ship such as ours."

"What do you mean, Malek?" Max asked.

"The water brings with it trees and huge islands of reeds that can engulf a ship, such as that over there."

He pointed to a long green strip of reeds, about two hundred yards long, off their port bow moving with the flow of the water.

"That is a papyrus island and has to be avoided because if we are caught in its fronds we will not be able to pull the boat free and it could drag us for miles, possibly driving us onto the bank. Men would have to get onto the rushes to cut us free. It can be dangerous, as there are crocodiles," he said, and gave a sardonic laugh at their fearful expressions.

"This means that we have to anchor at night, or we will not see these hazards before it is too late," Talon remarked.

"You are right," Malek said. "We can anchor near the banks and wait till dawn."

"I suggest we find a bank full of those loathsome creatures and point it out to our friends of the crew. If they want to leave, then it is their choice, but only God will protect them after that," Max said with a laugh.

Malek looked at Max. "By Allah, but I think you are a cruel man, Max!" he said, but his cold grin belied his statement.

The ship dropped anchor that evening and soon it was tugging gently at its tether ropes while the people on the boat ate a sparse evening meal of dates and dried bread. Talon wondered when they would eat another meal similar to those he so enjoyed back at Fayoum.

They forced the crewmen to unlock the prisoners one by one. Henry was the first to be brought up, still tethered, where he was confronted, not by Talon, who stood back, but by Malek.

"Tell him, Suleiman, that I am unhappy with this arrangement, but that my word is my life, and I shall promise him his freedom in your charge if he will serve my Lady until it is time for you to leave us." Malek pointed to a sandy bank of the river where the long shapes of the river crocodiles lay and added, "If there is any attempt by any of your men to harm us, or betray us, we shall give you to those creatures."

Henry understood the message without Talon having to explain much. He drew himself up and faced Malek proudly. "I am a noble in my country, and although I hate all of your people, I shall give my word before my God, that I will not attempt to escape; and indeed, I shall serve you and that man, until it is time," he said with a chin movement towards Talon.

Malek nodded, and Henry was free. He gave a little bow and then looked bemused.

Malek then ordered his men to arrest the members of the crew and hold them, including the steersmen. The frightened men, having seen the gesturing towards the fearsome crocodiles, cried out in terror, thinking that might be their fate. They protested vehemently that they would work for Malek faithfully.

"You shall, you shall, all in Allah's good time," he promised them.

More men were released, and those who came from the western countries who knew Henry were more than prepared to work with him. They were stunned by this sudden turn of events in favor of their lives, and many dropped to their knees and thanked God for their release.

They were told that they might still have to row, but that they would not be prisoners. They were set to work cleaning up the lower decks as quickly as possible to make it a better place, for they could not all stay on the top deck. They set to with a will.

The remaining men, of whom there were about fifteen, were brought before Panhsj and Malek to be examined. Five were rejected immediately by Malek, as he knew a criminal when he saw one. These were sent back down below amid screams of abuse and hate. The other ten were turned over to Panhsj, who took them to the bow and spent an hour talking to them.

From his vantage point on the after deck Talon had the feeling these men would work for Panhsj when the time came. After making sure that things were going well, Malek ordered the former crew to be sent below. They protested loudly and plaintively as they were set down and chained to the seats of their former prisoners. There was laud jeering from the now freed prisoners as they watched it happen, but Talon impatiently raised his hand for silence.

"You are freed to work for us, but you do not have your freedom as yet," he chided them in French. He pointed to Malek.

"This man, called Malek, is the chief here, and if he decides that you have to go back down there, I cannot do anything about it, so keep your mouths shut. This man is called Max," he said, pointing to Max, who was standing nearby. "You will obey him at all times, do you understand?"

The ragged group of scarecrows became hushed. But they understood, and nodded in silence, although their exuberance was not stilled for long. Several offered their services as sailors, and Henry agreed to be their spokesman.

Malek's fighting men observed the whole thing with stoic wariness. He had explained the situation to them, but they gave the released prisoners a wide berth all the same, fingering their weapons and remaining watchful.

The journey to Aswan lasted another three days, and when finally they sighted the Island of the Elephant everyone was relieved that they were about to get off the overcrowded ship. The Norsemen who had volunteered to steer the ship called to Malek for directions and he pointed to the small harbor off the western bank. The other sailors, under the skillful direction of Henry, now hauled the sails round and the ship glided towards its berth.

# Chapter 27

# Sultan's Command

Three months later Talon and Max rode their horses at a comfortable pace across the dry, rock strewn desert towards the group of buildings clustered on a mound near to the great river. They reined in at the gate and waited for the guards to open it. A large hawk sat on Talon's right wrist, gripping the thick leather glove in its sharp claws. Most of its speckled white head was hidden by a leather hood and there were still blood stains on its chest feathers and claws from its recent victims.

The two had taken a ride late that afternoon, as much to talk in private as to hunt. They had hunted well and their bounty would be handed off to the cooks. The bird of prey belonged to the Emir, Khalidah's uncle. He had suggested that Talon take his birds out, once he recognized that Talon had a way with the hawks. He explained that he was too old to go out very often, and the birds did not get enough exercise. In truth, the old man preferred to spend long hours with Khaldun in his extensive library, where the two of them would recollect the old times and study the new arts of algebra and optics that had come from Persia. They had fallen into this pattern of life from the moment their ship had landed at Aswan and they had asked for asylum; an easily formed habit it was for two men of intellect.

Talon accepted the task of taking the birds to stretch their wings with gratitude, and now he and Max made it a routine to go off into the desert to hunt and talk about the time they might finally leave. Today had been no different. They had ridden for some miles to where a stand of trees grew around a small wadi and here they dismounted and squatted in the shade to examine their options for the hundredth time. Talon was impatient to leave, but Max pointed out they had unfinished business to complete.

"You know well there are other people who mean the Lady Khalidah and Kazim harm, Talon. Until we know who they are, it would be foolhardy and disloyal to leave just yet. All we would be doing is putting them at risk, and this time, Al Muntaqim, whoever he is, could be waiting."

"You are right as ever, Max, but we have been here in Aswan for months now. That makes it more than a year since we left Albi, and still we cannot go to the Kingdom of Jerusalem. I feel trapped."

"Ha, Talon, be patient, that time will come," Max said in a comforting tone.

There had been trickles of news from the north, most of it brought by the merchants and drovers passing through who stopped at the modest souk in Aswan and enquired about the situation further south. They needed information, and as often as not, it was dangerous for them to continue. These men were on their way to the savannahs and jungles far to the south, where the great elephants with two long teeth grazed. They made the dangerous journey to barter not only for the gold that was mined by the black men but also the tusks that the black men harvested at great peril from the huge beasts. The merchants who lived to return would bring back to Cairo or Alexandria rich bounty to sell to the eager craftsmen to convert into great works of art for the rich.

Malek had his spies listening in the souk, but he went himself with Panhsj and Talon from time to time to hear the merchants relate the latest skirmish with the Frans, or with some other Arab city like Aleppo. It was common knowledge that the hungry Sultan Salah Ed Din furthered his gains in the north. One consistent rumor they brought with them was the bewildering disappearance of the entire family of Emir Abbas.

This rumor was the subject of the discussion again today.

"If the news is correct, and the sultan is still looking for my Lady, then perhaps we could leave for Jerusalem and my Lady should go to him for safety," Max ventured.

"But Max, that brings us back full circle. We still do not know who it is that is trying to kill Kazim. It is about the Fayoum, I am sure. Malek told me it is one of the richest regions in all of Egypt, and whoever possesses it is one of the wealthiest and thus most powerful men in the country. Although you might never have suspected it, Lord Abbas was very, very rich, even though he was not one for showing off his wealth," Talon said. "I wish we could take the fight to them instead of being prisoners here!" he exclaimed.

Max grinned at Talon's glum expression. "It is not like you to be so down-hearted, Talon."

"You are right Max, we are sitting here waiting for something to happen, but we do not know what; and worse, we do not know when."

They rode into the Emir's palace compound just as the sun was setting across the western desert. As they walked the horses through the gates, they noticed a small detachment of men waiting on horses by the stables, and Talon sensed that the situation was about to change.

"Perhaps we are about to find out the when," he whispered to Max as they dismounted. The stable boy came to take their horses.

At that moment, Panhsj came striding towards them. "Greetings, my friends. Where have you been? Everyone is looking for you. We have to go before the Emir at once. My Lady wishes that all be present."

Max and Talon hurried after him, and they were greeted by an impatient Malek, who had been pacing outside the main hall. He nodded tersely and led the way into the house and down the cool corridor to the main audience chamber. There they bowed deeply and waited for the old emir to notice them and to indicate that they should be seated.

As this had occurred many times since their arrival, Talon did not feel any particular excitement, but he did notice that there was a stranger in the room. The man looked as though he had come from the governor's palace. His clothes were too fine for him to be one of the impoverished Emir's retainers.

Talon smiled at the children and Khaldun, who were seated off to the right of the emir. Talon's eyes roved over the usual servants and guards, then came to rest on the figure of Khalidah, who was seated to the left of the old man, and he found she was watching him. He bowed from the waist in acknowledgement, but by now the emir was talking.

"I have a letter from no less a person than the Sultan Salah Ed Din himself," he began in his reedy voice. "He offers me blessing and peace, but he also asks if I might know the whereabouts of the Lady Khalidah." He paused, almost for effect.

If he was expecting a reaction he was not disappointed. It was clear that the Lady Khalidah knew the contents, but only she did. The rest of the audience was now shifting in surprise at the news.

"My lord, how could he have known my Lady was here...?" Malek began.

"Allah knows. But it was only a matter of time, Malek," the old man said.

"However, this now places me in a difficult position. I cannot deny what is evident to others than ourselves. As it was, before, unless I was asked, I did not have to offer the information, but now..." His old eyes glanced at the man standing off to the left near the window.

"We must leave at once and find another place," Khalidah spoke up, and her voice carried clearly across the room.

"There is more to this letter, my Lady Khalidah, that I did not mention to you before," the old man said, almost reluctantly.

"My lord?" she asked, turning her head to stare at him.

"It also asks that, should you be a guest of mine, I am to provide an escort that will take you directly back to Cairo to be presented before him."

There was an astonished silence, and then Panhsj was on his feet. His sword almost drawn, he moved towards the man by the window menacingly.

Talon came to his feet, as did Max and Malek, but the emir said sharply, "Sit down, all of you. This man is merely the messenger, and he comes from the governor's palace here in Aswan, not from Cairo. The letter was sent to his care, but it is addressed to me."

They subsided, leaving the messenger looking apprehensive. The men before him were indeed menacing.

"You must understand that if the sultan has written a letter like this, then he has some idea that the lady Khalidah is here, or could be here. Now that I have a letter in my hand, I have no recourse but to provide an escort and must ensure that she arrives in safety before the sultan," the old man said firmly.

"So this is it," Malek said almost to himself. "We are commanded to take the lady Khalidah back to where her life, and that of her son, will be in danger once more, but now at the command of the sultan himself!"

The debate about how they would manage a safe return went on till the sun was well set.

* * * * *

They sailed soon after dawn, three days later. The horses, as usual, were reluctant to travel in the ship, so the soldiers and crewmen had to coax them aboard. It took longer than anticipated to guide them along the wooden pier and down into the waist of the ship, where they were tied to a long rail that ran down the middle between the masts.

The main party, consisting of lady Khalidah, the children, and the womenfolk, were escorted onto the ship and hurried into the cabin at the back of the ship. Talon was at the side of the ship when Khalidah came aboard, but other than a warm glance at him she said nothing. She did take his proffered hand for support, giving it a small squeeze as she came across the side. She led the children below into the cabin, closely followed by the women servants. The ever-protective Malek posted guards at the doorway.

The rest of the men at arms who would comprise the main fighting unit tramped aboard, leading some chained prisoners. These former crewmen were escorted below and secured to their benches amid much wailing and loud protestations.

Malek was taking no chances. He had spent much time talking to Panhsj and Talon about their experiences in Cairo, trying to gauge his enemy, and he wanted to ensure that his men were ready, their bows strung and spears prepared for attack from land or water.

Aside from the selected crewmen who now worked with Henry, the remaining freedmen went below and manned the oars. The difference was that other than the few men who were the former crew, they were not shackled to their benches and had weapons to hand should they need them. Despite all the scrubbing and cleaning of the middle deck, some of the odor still lingered. Now, however, the men were well rested and had lost much of their former emaciated look.

It was time to cast off. Talon looked back towards the shore and waved at Khaldun, who stood with the Emir on the top of the high bank above them, watching the activity on the ship as it pulled away. Khaldun had decided to stay in Aswan with the Emir. They had much in common, and the old man had asked him to remain, saying he was lonely and needed a friend to share the books of his extensive library. Lady Khalidah had urged Khaldun to do so, saying that the future was very uncertain and that she would feel better if he was safely in the Emir's protection. Talon had agreed, but he still felt a keen sense of loss as he looked up at the old man. He wondered if he would ever see him again. Their parting had been emotional; Khaldun had looked into Talon's eyes and said, "I know not what fate has in store for you, my Suleiman, but remember we are always here as your friends. Allah protect you."

Talon could only nod in silence and had embraced the old man hard. "I shall pray that Allah will protect you, Hajji. I shall miss you sorely." He turned away, pretending not to see the tears running down Khaldun's old cheeks.

The two old men waved back and stood watching as the ship was rowed out into mid-stream, whereupon Henry, who was now the unofficial captain of the boat, called for the oars to be shipped and the two sails to be set by his new crew. The men ran willingly to do his bidding, and before long the sleek vessel of war was being driven swiftly downstream with a wind almost on its tail. No one remarked that the ship was now being crewed by a mixed group of blonde, blue-eyed men from the Northern lands and black men from the deep south of the country.

The two old men standing on the top of the bank receded quickly into the distance, and Talon turned his attention to the activity on the vessel. Malek and Panhsj were on the high rear deck talking quietly together, leaving him space, while Max was up at the front with some of the soldiers keeping a sharp eye open for any sign of danger. They were sailing into an unknown situation and everyone was tense.

His thoughts went back to Aswan and their existence there. He had continued to enjoy working with the children because it also ensured that he kept his own mind sharp. He realized that he was sounding less like an elder brother to them, more of an uncle perhaps, and with that came the realization again that well over a year had passed since he had left the country of Langue d'Oc.

While in Aswan, Khaldun had often joined him by an old fountain in the gardens of the Emir and they had talked of many things. He would miss the old man's wisdom. Khaldun had talked about the country of Al Andalusia, with its fabulous cities of Cordova and Toledo. Talon resolved to go there one day. It would be within reach of the country of the Langue d'Oc, on the other side of the mountains called the Pyrenees. He might even be able to see his parents again one day. His thoughts wheeled through an arc and settled on the distant city of Isfahan. For some reason he felt that if Rav'an were alive she would find her way back to that city. Her relationship with Fariba was that of the younger sister she had never had. He sighed; his journey was taking far longer than he had thought it would to get back to the kingdom of Jerusalem, but perhaps this time they were finally on their way.

Two days later, around mid-day, Malek and others of his men began to recognize landmarks. Everyone became more alert. He sent word down to Lady Khalidah, warning her that they were nearing the landing of Beneade, that this was possibly the most dangerous point and to stay with her children below.

Malek's men, with bows at the ready, manned the sides of the ship. Kazim, who had been ordered below to join the women, flatly refused, claiming that he was now a man and could not be humiliated by being forced to do so. He was allowed to stay. Malek looked helplessly at Panhsj, who promptly volunteered to guard the boy.

"I shall guard him with my life, Malek. My lord, you must stay by me at all times," he admonished the excited boy, who nodded his head vigorously and then brandished his long dagger in the air. Panhsj found him the smallest shield on the boat and then pronounced him a warrior. The boy almost burst with pride.

"You are my guard, Panhsj, I will fight alongside you!" he squeaked in his excitement. Max and Talon were hard put to suppress their grins of appreciation at the boy's behavior. But both kept their faces solemn when they bowed to him respectfully.

Malek, with one fierce look at them, ignored the boy from that moment onward, standing close to Henry, with whom he had developed a kind of rapport. "Hold it in the middle of the river, Frans," he ordered.

Henry, who could understand some basic words, nodded and made a small adjustment. But Malek was not done yet. He called to Talon.

"Suleiman, do you see that large felucca ahead of us?" He pointed to a large boat that was sailing to the fore of them. Talon nodded.

"I want to sail on its right side and remain next to it as we pass Beneade. Can you explain this to the Frans?"

Talon pointed out the slow moving felucca to Henry and explained what was needed.

Henry laughed and laid his forefinger alongside his nose as he looked at Malek with renewed respect.

"That is a wily man, Suleiman."

"Indeed, I think he is, Henry, but hurry, we might need the cover soon."

Henry hastened to instruct the steersmen; he shouted commands to the crew, who ran to do his bidding. In a short time they were almost alongside the felucca and the crew of that ship stared in surprise at the heavily armed galley as it kept pace with them, almost within oar's distance. They shouted some questions, but the men in the waist of the galley shrugged and said nothing. This seemed to unnerve the crew of the felucca, who kept away from the side of their ship as they continued downriver. Malek and his companions ignored them and stared ahead, intent on the left hand side of the river.

They soon saw the small buildings and the silhouette of the fort of Beneade appear to their left. Everyone focused on the cluster of ships anchored near the town and alongside the quay. The entire ship was silent as they watched the receding river bank for any signs of danger.

"Allah willing, if there is anyone there watching for us, they will not see us until we are well past," Malek said in a low tone.

Talon agreed with Malek. The precaution was a good idea, especially as they did not know their enemy.

Then they saw a long, sleek form of a galley similar to theirs. It was moored to the pier, but even at this distance they could see intense activity on and around the ship. Men seemed to be running along the pier to jump aboard even as others were casting off. Soon they could see the oars rising and falling in the water as the ship was backed out. Its two sails fell untidily but were hauled in rapidly and bellied as the ship almost spun on its keel to face downstream and follow them.

The men on the afterdeck stared apprehensively at the ship as it glided into midstream behind them. They had already left Beneade far behind, but it was as though they were moving slowly compared to the galley now giving chase.

"At least they did not see us as we were approaching, so perhaps we still have a chance," Panhsj muttered.

"It was a good ruse," Talon said. "It might have given us enough time. We shall have to see, *Insha'Allah*. It is still a day's journey to the city."

His heart was beating hard as he contemplated a battle to come.

Malek turned and shouted to the men in the waist. "Get the rowers back into place! We must reach Cairo before they catch us."

Men ran below to the too familiar and hated places where they had lived and where comrades had died before. This time, however, it was willingly, as they faced certain death if captured by this hunter now in hot pursuit. The oars were pushed out and the monotonous drum beat began. Men rocked forward and then dropped the oars in the water and heaved themselves back in one well practiced swaying motion.

Talon and Max went down into the waist of the ship; they first checked on the restless horses and ensured that they were well secured. Talon glanced across the river to the eastern side. The banks of the great river here were not as high as those in the Aswan area, being dressed with dense thickets of papyrus and cane and having little inlets that had brown beaches. The log-like forms of the crocodiles could be seen basking in the sun; little white specs that Bilal had told him were birds that picked their teeth hopped about their inert forms.

Ahead of them he could see one particularly large island of thick weeds that had been left behind by the floods of the last month. It had drifted onto the side of the eastern bank and was now caught up by the tangled roots and the shallow bank. In places it was flat and almost at the same level as the water, while in others it was thick with reeds that stood higher than a man; but Talon now knew from what Malek had told him that, while it was a tight cluster of weeds floating as would an island, it was treacherous for anyone to try to walk across. They approached it cautiously, Henry helping the other steersmen to guide the ship well away from its dangerous tangle of roots.

Then one of the men standing on the starboard side of the boat in the bows shouted in alarm and pointed downstream. They stared towards where he was pointing. Half a mile ahead of them, a long sleek shape, driven by many oars, was sliding out from behind the cover of the weed island. Sure enough, it was another galley which was pulling out into midstream and was in the process of turning to point up stream. It was identical to the one behind.

The clearest thing Talon noticed was the long bronze plated ram attached to the bows that gleamed briefly in the sunlight. Its menacing point left a small bow wave as it dug into the swift moving waters of the river. The oars of that ship were moving up and down very fast as it maneuvered into position ahead of them to block their way down stream.

There was a collective murmur of apprehension from the men on the ship.

"We are trapped; they must have been waiting for us," Malek said in a tense voice to the others nearby, but then he strode forward and looked down upon the men.

"Silence!" he bellowed at the agitated, chattering men. "Hear me now. We must fight! Every man should make his peace with Allah and then prepare to fight. We will prevail if you listen to your commanders and put your faith in Allah."

"Suleiman, please inform our Lady of the situation. I intend to ram past that ship. Perhaps we can slide around it and make our escape; we have the current in our favor. *Insha'Allah* we will succeed." But he did not sound very hopeful. Talon could see sweat on Malek's brow below his pointed helmet as he considered the situation they now faced.

Talon ducked below the low beam and moved into the dim light of the rear cabin. It was stuffy here in the sparsely furnished cabin that was the width of the ship. He bowed low to Khalidah, who was standing facing him. Her women were in another compartment of the cabin. She indicated the ship that could be seen in the rear windows.

"We are hunted again, Suleiman?"

"My Lady, there are two ships, one ahead and one behind. Someone knew we would be coming this way and was waiting for us. There is danger, but we hope to break though and continue to the city."

"Are you sure they are our enemies?" she asked reasonably.

"No, my Lady, but it is not likely that the sultan would try to ambush us with two galleys in this manner. I think it is Al Muntaqim and his men."

There was silence for a moment, broken by a small whimper of fear from Jasmine, who tried to stifle it with her scarf, covering her mouth. Khalidah knelt by her daughter and put her arms around her.

"Be brave, my little one. Allah will protect us as he has in the past. Malek, Panhsj and Suleiman will not allow us to be taken." She looked up at him, directly into his eyes, and he saw certainty, but also he saw how she mustered her courage for the sake of this child by the defiance forming on her features.

"We are going to fight our way through, my Lady. You are safer here than on the deck. There will be guards for your protection," Talon said firmly.

She nodded with calm acceptance of the situation. "Protect my son for me, Suleiman."

"We shall, my Lady. Panhsj is with him every minute." He bowed his way out and walked back up on deck.

## Chapter 28

# Battle on the Nile

Malek held a hurried conference with the others.

"We must somehow drive past that ship in front of us. We dare not become entangled, so I want to try to destroy it by ramming it, but we will have to be very quick. Suleiman, will 'Enry be able to guide this ship to accomplish this?"

"Why don't we just try to shatter the oars of one side and avoid being rammed ourselves?" Max asked.

"It may come to that, Max," Malek said grimly. "But how do we keep our own from going the same way?"

"I can stand at the opening and just as we are about to strike them, we can haul in our oars on that side. There will be very little time, but it is worth a try," Max said, his tone anxious.

"The ship is drawing near!" Panhsj gestured urgently.

Indeed they were moving on a rapid collision course. Talon cast a hasty look behind him and saw that despite the exertions of their rowers, the other ship was now only several hundred yards behind them and appeared to be gaining. When he again faced forward he could see that the impact was imminent. He felt a familiar tightening in his chest and stomach.

"I shall go and warn the rowers!" Max called as he ran down the ladders to the rowers' deck, where he bellowed at the sweating, straining men.

"Listen, when I shout, you must pull in your oars on this side of the ship." He pointed to his left. "And be ready to come on deck to fight if needs be!" he yelled into the gloom.

Men called back they understood, and Max braced himself for the collision. Talon watched the scene unfold from the upper deck, while Max in turn watched for the signal.

"Watch me!" Malek shouted. Max waved his hand in acknowledgement.

Malek raised his right hand in the air, ready to drop it when they were committed. The ships raced towards one another, both bronze rams aimed directly at the other, and as they did, men on both sides raised their bows and began to shoot arrows at their opponents. Some arrows struck with a thud into the wood nearby. Kazim gave a yelp of surprise, but then recovered his dignity and edged closer to Panhsj, who towered over him protectively.

Watching the sleek vessel hurling towards them was unnerving, for there was every chance that one or both ships would drive their bronze rams so deep into the other's bows they could not extricate themselves, and then they would both sink.

Almost in slow motion the moment arrived. They were nearly bow to bow when Malek dropped his arm and Max screamed at the men inside the oars deck. Henry and the steersmen on deck hauled on the steering oar, and their ship glided away from a direct collision. The men below decks frantically hauled in their oars, assisting one another, since they were not chained to their seats any more. The oars came in just in time, but the other ship was not so lucky. Both ships lurched and there was a rending crash. The sharp bows of their own galley sliced through the oars of the enemy ship. A loud, repetitive crashing and splintering sound tore at the air. Parts of oars were thrown up to splash alongside or even fly over their own deck, forcing men on both sides to duck out of the way.

As the sharp prow of their vessel cut through the oars of the enemy boat, the screams of the men being mangled below on its oar deck could be heard. Kazim flinched, but Panhsj patted him on the shoulder and said, "Be strong, little master, this is how war is fought. Keep your shield high, as they will shoot arrows at us now."

The boy gulped and lifted his small metal shield to cover his chest and stayed close to the huge man, whose own large shield would have covered them both. There was no time to heed the screams of the pitiable slaves, as more immediate concerns were upon them. Grapples were flung and the men on the other ship continued to shoot arrows at them. Talon's men returned with their own barrage of arrows, and he joined in. A man perched on the front of the ship with a sword in hand, ready to jump aboard, fell backwards—pierced through his chest by one of Talon's well aimed arrows. Others fell with screams, but they were replaced by more howling men who clustered in groups waiting for the ships to close so they could jump across.

Henry and his steersmen hauled with all their might on the steering oar to guide the ship away, but their efforts were hampered by their reduced motion from the sails alone. They were driving through the last of the oars, leaving a shattered chaos in their wake, and that is when Henry saw his opportunity.

"Max! Oars, we must have oars!" he yelled over the increasing din of the men.

Max heard him and yelled at the men below push their oars out again. The oars began to reemerge as the men hastened to do his bidding.

As their ship slid by the other, the archers on the top deck fired arrows at one another from a distance of only twenty feet, and men died on both sides. Talon aimed and loosed arrow after arrow, aiming for the crew of the ship who were trying to restore some kind of order on the top deck, when several men at the rear of the ship caught his attention.

They had a metal pot on the deck and one man was about to dip an arrow into it. With a chill Talon realized what it meant: he had used this same tactic when attacked by the corsair in the Middle sea on his way to France. This time he could not retaliate; they had no fire on board, but the enemy did. He ran towards the front of the ship, dodging past men who were screaming abuse at the enemy and shooting arrows as fast as they could. He noted with approval that his men were firing accurately and their skill was showing results, but their own men were dying too. He had little time to waste.

He jumped onto a grating, looking for his man again, and saw that he was just about to reach for his bow, now with a flaming arrow in his hand. With one swift motion, Talon drew and fired. His arrow sped across the short gap to drive through the neck of his victim. The man threw up his arms and fell over backwards onto the metal pot. He tumbled onto his side and, in doing so, tossed the contents of the pot across their own deck.

The embers flew into the cordage nearby and spread across the planks. The men scattered in panic, leaving the embers unattended. Several did return and tried to gather up the smoldering wood and put it back into the pot, but Talon killed two of them before they realized that they were a target and the rest ran off to find cover.

Most of the men on the enemy ship had no idea that they faced grave danger until it was almost too late. Then they smelled the dreaded stink of burning tar smoke. There was a yell of panic and any thoughts of the attack faded in the face of their new adversary as they made haste to deal with the fire spreading on their deck.

Malek called to Max to tell the men below to start rowing fast. They rowed for their lives; oars bit into the water and the ship seemed to jerk forward; but some of the ropes were still attached to the two ships, hindering their escape. Men leapt forward to cut them free. Some were struck by arrows, but others took their places and hacked at the ropes with their swords until they were finally free. Their motion increased rapidly, leaving the other ship almost still in the water: its sails held it against the current; but the crewmen, who had been decimated by the archers from Malek's ship, were now preoccupied with extinguishing the fire. The stricken boat began to turn slowly and drift sideways, its sails started to flap, and smoke poured from the after-deck.

Talon saw they were now free to move out of immediate danger but this was to be short lived; their short delay had been enough to allow the second to close on them.

To everyone's astonishment, Khalidah climbed up to the aft deck and called out, pointing. Her veil had gone and she had a strange expression on her face.

"Look!" she shouted.

Malek and Panhsj spun around; Kazim was almost knocked over by Panhsj as he whirled about.

"It is Kemosiri ibn Jibade! How could it be? He is come to help us, praise be to God!"

Malek stared at the man who was standing high on the rear deck of the ship that was bearing down upon them. Panhsj stared too, but neither of them seemed to think they were being saved. Everything about the man on the ship descending upon them spoke of danger.

"God protect us, but I do not think so, my Lady," Malek said in a low tone.

The man whom Khalidah had called Kemosiri was watching them, and even at this distance they could see a look of triumph on his face. He was dressed in rich clothing under a very fine suit of chain and he wore a lose turban on his head wrapped over a well-fitted helmet. His sword was drawn. He casually saluted, but then turned and shouted some orders at the men clustered around him.

A shower of arrows was loosed from the waist of his ship straight into them. Each man dove behind the thick wooden rear of the ship. Malek drove a stunned looking Khalidah down with him as the arrows thudded into the wood next to them. One of the steering men fell with a surprised look on his face right in front of Khalidah, who shrank back with a cry of alarm.

Talon rushed onto the deck in time to see the ship bearing down upon them. He stopped abruptly, pointed and yelled, "That is the man! That is the man who was with Bahir! He is Al Muntaqim!"

He rushed to Khalidah and grasped her by the arm.

"My Lady, what are you doing here?"

Khalidah stared at the other ship as though she had seen a snake. "You said he is Al Muntaqim, Suleiman? How do you know this?" she gasped.

"Because I was in Bahir's house when he and the poet were talking together, but there was this other man who they kept calling Al Muntaqim, my Lady. It is that man, I have no doubt of it." He pointed again at the man on the ship. "There is no time, hurry!" They were drawing closer. "You must go below. Now!"

They had no time to react. The enemy ship commanded by Kemosiri was descending upon them at a great speed, and they were only just getting under way again. It was too late.

The sharp prow of Kemosiri's galley struck the rear end of their ship. There was a splintering crash and the entire hull shuddered as the ram from the other ship drove into their rear; the prow had smashed through the rear panel of their vessel and buried itself deep into their own. The shock of the collision brought them all to their knees. Kazim was tossed onto the deck; Panhsj seized him and pushed him to the front rail, too concerned to do more than snap at the boy to stay there. Before the crashing and splintering sounds had stopped, men were leaping across the gap and attempting to climb onto their deck.

Khalidah gasped, "Jasmine!"

Talon hastily pushed her towards the steps and without looking to see if she had gone, turned and slashed down on the arm of a large bearded man with bad acne scars who was about to climb onto the deck. He fell back with a shriek, his arm spouting blood. But other yelling and screaming intruders had managed to make it to the deck. A vicious fight broke out as Malek, Talon and Panhsj fought them, screaming into their faces as they stabbed and slashed at the boarders.

Then there was another shudder; at a shouted command from Kemosiri's galley, its oars reversed and began rising and falling very fast, so that the ship drew back and extracted its ram from their ship with another splintering crash. It began to move forward again to close on their starboard side with the clear intent of boarding them.

Talon could see the man called Kemosiri calmly giving orders and the crew running to obey. There were not as many men on this ship as had been on the other, but easily enough to overwhelm them if they came aboard in one mob, which was obviously their intent.

Talon could not use his bow, as the men on the deck were swinging wildly at one another and it would have been fatal to pause and try to get off an arrow. Malek and Panhsj fought like tigers alongside him, and the survivors of the first wave were overcome and killed. It became chillingly clear to Talon that Kemosiri did not value the lives of his men at all. Otherwise he would not have pulled away to leave them to the tender mercies of the defenders. There were bodies piled against the rail, and the deck was red and slippery with their blood.

The men paused to take stock. Malek had taken a nick and Panhsj was cut on the forearm, as was Talon. Mail could take a sword slash but it left a bruise, while sharp knives could penetrate and kill. Fortunately, other than two of their own men dead and one wounded, they had survived. Henry gripped a sword that was bloodied. He had defended the steersmen fiercely during the melee. There was no time to lose, as Kemosiri's vessel was now moving alongside and had knocked some of their own oars aside in the process. Talon realized that Max must have seen what was about to happen and had again ordered their oars to be brought in.

Leaving Henry and Panhsj on the after deck to defend Kazim, and a couple of men to help guard the steersmen, Malek and Talon rushed down the steps to join their own men, who were now grouped on the starboard side either shooting arrows as the new attackers or brandishing spears threateningly and howling battle cries.

Grapples flew through the air to land with thuds on deck or to grab at the sides. Men hacked furiously with their blades at the ropes that held them, but more came. The enemy followed in a screaming rush. Talon felt this would surely overwhelm them, there seemed to be so many. Men flew across the gap clutching ropes, or charged recklessly across the remaining space between the ships, to hack and kill as soon as they landed.

Kemosiri was in the van and immediately began to demonstrate his skill with the sword as he dismembered three men in as few seconds. Men shrank away from him as he led a charge towards the rear. Talon found himself being pushed back towards the wall of the cabin by a mob of shrieking, bearded men who bayed like wolves scenting the kill. He and the men with him fought savagely, giving and taking no quarter, but they could not hold back the mob of Kemosiri's men, who scented blood and pressed in on them, thrusting and hacking at them with spears and swords. His sword arm began to tire and his shield arm felt bruised from all the strikes he had fended off. More than one spear went under his guard to strike his mail shirt in bruising thrusts, but none had penetrated as yet.

He noticed with growing alarm that in this close quarter fight they were losing men faster than the enemy, who were steadily gaining on them. Pushed hard against the wall he could not see what was going on, and he lost sight of Kemosiri for a moment. In spite of the din of clashing steel and the shrieks of wounded and dying men, he heard the sound of swords striking above him and despaired. He blocked a savage spear thrust to his stomach and with a yell stabbed his sword into the throat of his attacker.

"They are on the rear deck, Malek, we cannot hold them!" he shouted to Malek, who was fighting nearby.

Malek hacked down on a man in front of him, cutting deep into the shoulder. The man screamed and fell, his wound spouting blood. Malek glanced at Talon.

"Then God has deserted us, my friend, so we shall die here. I did not wish to see it end this way," he gasped, blood running down his face from a small wound.

Talon looked around for Max, fearing that he might have gone down, but he was right next to him, his arm pumping furiously like a piston, stabbing at the enemy who crowded in on them; men fell whenever his sword reached.

Then they heard a blood-chilling roar from behind their attackers that turned all heads. From the deep end of the oar deck boiled a wild assortment of yelling men who brandished axes, swords and other hastily obtained weapons. They charged into the rear of the struggling body of men at the base of the rear deck and set about slaughtering the invaders. Axes and swords rose and fell as the berserk rowers attacked the enemy fighters from the rear.

Kemosiri's men were caught utterly by surprise and began to fall away as the newcomers' attack took immediate effect. Some of the enemy began to see they were trapped between the two forces and tried to get back onto their own boat. They scrambled over the side of the ship, but many were chased and hacked down by the men from the lower deck. A black man, screaming incoherently and stabbing at anything in his path, drove through the remnants of the invaders and very nearly plunged his spear into Talon, who managed to jump out of the way with a yell of surprise. The man's spear drove into the wall with a thud. Talon tapped him on the shoulder and Malek laughed, helped pull the spear out, and then pointed the man at the other ship.

"There, go and kill them, my friend. They are the ones you want."

The wild-eyed man rushed off screaming a battle cry to join in the slaughter of the luckless ones from the Kemosiri's ship.

Talon turned and ran up the steps to the after deck. He was afraid of what he would find. Henry was still on his feet, although he was bloody, and some of it was his own. His chest heaving he raised his hand and pointed to the other side of the deck. One of the steersmen was dead while another was streaming blood from a wide gash in his arm, but he still stood by the steering oar. On the side opposite Henry was a small group of men still fighting, but the boarders had clearly had lost heart and were now trying to get away. Several jumped overboard.

Panting for breath, Talon glanced around. The two ships had become locked together, and while their crews engaged in fighting they had drifted downstream and were now being pushed by the current against the mass of fibrous vegetation on the reed island. They were in no danger but neither were they going anywhere. He noticed some of the enemy soldiers were trying to flee across the green island of reeds.

He looked for Panhsj and saw him lying in the corner. A pool of blood surrounded him. With his heart in his mouth, Talon pulled him over onto his back. To his immense relief, he saw Panhsj was breathing, but he had a nasty cut across his chest. He had also taken a blow to the head which had knocked him unconscious.

Talon had no time to do anything for his friend. He looked for Kazim but could not see him the deck.

"Where is the boy, Henry?" he called.

Henry pointed at the other ship. "They took him," he bellowed.

Talon's eyes flicked feverishly to the ship still entangled alongside. There was no sign of Kazim. Then he saw two men clambering over the far side, clearly with the intent to escape across the floating island to the shore. One of the men held the struggling Kazim. Evidently the boy was testing his patience. The man slapped Kazim hard. Talon watched the two men began to make their way across the matted surface, half carrying a now dazed looking Kazim. They were heading for the tall reeds that were only a few dozen yards away. Once there, they would be completely invisible to the rest of the fighters and could escape unnoticed in their own time.

Talon seized his bow and, holding it high, sprinted across the deck. He took a step onto the side rail and made a flying leap into the air, his arms wind-milling wildly as he flew. It was a long jump that could have landed him in the water, where he might have drowned under the weight of his chain mail. As it was, he just managed to land on the soft edge of the island with a great splash. He felt the surface give and he flung himself forward to sprawl on the matted surface, relieved that he had not gone through it into the river. Wet and muddy but still in possession of his bow, he ran after the two men and Kazim. When he caught up with them they were almost at the wall of tall reeds.

"Stop, Al Muntaqim, or Kemosiri, I don't care who you are," he shouted. "You will stop or I shall put an arrow in your evil back!"

The men froze and then turned to face him. Talon was confronted by the man who had caused the death of Khalidah's husband, and many others. He also recognized the heavy person of Akhom.

"So I was right," Talon said. He held his bow taut with an arrow notched in place.

"You are the friend of Bahir, and you, you scum, are his former servant." He nodded at Akhom, who glowered back.

Akhom held Kazim in front of him as he would a hostage. The boy was still dazed from the hard slap he had just received, but he recognized Talon.

"Suleiman, help me!" he screamed.

"Cut his throat if this man does anything!" Kemosiri shouted, staring hard at Talon.

It looked as though he was going to make a try for Talon, thinking he had him neutralized because of the boy.

"Why are you hunting this family?" Talon called out

"Because Abbas, the fool, betrayed his own. The Sultan is a usurper. The throne rightfully belongs to the family of Shawar of the Fatima, from whose family I am descended, and so is his family. The sultan and his uncle are heretics and should be sent to answer for their sins to God. Besides, the Fayoum is the biggest prize in Egypt. Now that the boy's father is dead, why would I not take it for myself?"

"Did you bribe the eunuch to use that snake?"

"He was easily bribed and greedy for gold."

"It served him nothing in the end. Bilal cut his head off."

"I had wondered about that, but the fire started so suddenly I could not tell if he survived or not. No matter; he served his purpose."

"You were a trusted friend of my Lady Khalidah and her children!"

"Sad and true, but the Lady can still be my wife, once I have rid myself of you and the boy."

"I killed Bahir, so why do you think you can kill me?"

There was a pause as Kemosiri stared at Talon. "So it was you," he breathed. "Now it makes more sense. I thought it was the Hashashini from the north, but they denied it."

"Suleiman, don't let them take me away!" Kazim cried, interrupting them.

"So you are Suleiman. You have made a nuisance of yourself on more than one occasion," Kemosiri snarled.

"Do you intend to kill the boy?" Talon wanted to test the man.

Kazim, who had been listening with wide eyes, gasped at these words.

"I will in time," Kemosiri said in a casual manner. "But he is a useful bargaining piece for now."

Talon marveled at the cold-blooded way in which he discussed the death of the boy in front of him.

Talon noticed the reeds behind the two men shift at their base and wondered if anyone else might be nearby. He had seen some of the men from the ship fleeing into the cane brakes as they tried to escape the fury of their pursuers.

Then they heard a scream. It came from only a short distance to their right. Involuntarily every eye went in that direction. From out of the tall papyrus reeds a man ran, yelling and pointing behind him, while more screams came from the forest of papyrus and cane, which now tossed furiously thirty yards away. There was a shriek and then the cane movement subsided. The first man stumbled off, still yelling, towards the ships.

Talon recovered quicker than Akhom, who failed to use the boy as a shield. An arrow sped towards the man and the boy. It buried itself deep in Akhom's upper thigh. The man gasped with pain and collapsed onto the wet matting clutching at his wound. He dropped Kazim, who fell on hands and knees and then scrambled hurriedly over the soft thatch towards Talon. Kemosiri snatched at him as he darted by, but missed.

Kemosiri snarled a curse and lurched forward, but he did not watch where he placed his foot. It went deep into a hole in the matted weeds. He sank up to his right knee and was struggling to extract himself when something dark charged out of the cane and seized him by his lower left leg in its massive jaws. Kemosiri turned to see what had grasped him so hard and then he screamed; it was a high, desperate scream of pure terror that froze Talon where he stood. He gaped, almost paralyzed with fear.

He watched as Kemosiri try to escape the jaws of the huge crocodile, but it had a firm grip on his leg. The beast reared back, dragging Kemosiri with it. Then it stopped and, lifting its jaws, slightly opened and then clamped down harder. Kemosiri flailed frantically at the snout of the ferocious animal with his sword to no avail, and then the reptile did something that caused Talon to gasp in horror. It began to roll over and over. This drove Kemosiri onto his face and then onto his back several times. He was covered in mud. He had lost his turban, exposing his shaved head. He lost his sword and beat feebly at the nose that was close to his groin with his fists. Then he arched back in agony as the beast crunched down on his leg and crushed the bone; his eyes stood out white in his mud-covered face. The veins on his neck raised and his mouth was opened wide in silent agony.

"Help me, in the name of God! No! No! Aaaaaah!" he shrieked, staring back at Talon. His voice choked off as the creature shook his whole body from side to side.

Sickened at the sight, and badly shaken, Talon recovered enough to put Kazim, who was clinging to him and crying with fear, off to the side. He rushed to try and save his enemy, but he was far too late. A scream of warning from Kazim told him that another animal had arrived. It too attacked the still living Kemosiri, who had now lost his leg and was seized by his second assailant around his midsection. It was too late to do anything to stop the monsters as they fought over the body. Escape was urgent before the fearsome creatures turned their attention to them,

Before their eyes and with incredible speed Kemosiri was dismembered by the two crocodiles, each being ten or more feet long. Massive jaws snapping, their tails lashing and bodies heaving, they fought over the remains of what had once been a man. Talon glanced at Akhom who was trying to crawl away, drooling with terror.

"Kazim, run for the ship and do not stop for anything. Run, and mind your step!" he shouted to the boy who was transfixed by the horror he was witnessing. Talon had to shake him hard to wake him up and pushed him to make him go. Then the boy ran on wings of terror as though fleeing something from hell.

Talon strode over to Akhom and said, "If you do anything I shall push you into their jaws, otherwise, you may live to tell about this plot."

"Take me with you. In Allah's name, please take me with you, I beg of you!" the man babbled.

Taking advantage of the crocodiles' preoccupation with their victim, Talon hastened to help Akhom to his feet. They staggered off towards the ships. Other men were emerging from the brakes and fleeing the island back to the ships. The terrors they were encountering on the island far outweighed the fate that awaited them as prisoners.

Talon kept glancing back at the two crocodiles fearfully; they terrified him. He became even more concerned when one of them, looked around, noticed their clumsy flight and began to follow them. He could not believe how quickly it could move on the shaking surface. They had only twenty yards to go to the side of the ship, but the uneven and treacherous surface of the matting beneath their feet impeded their progress. The creature gained on them. Talon was on the verge of dropping Akhom to face his attacker when he heard a shout, and other men ran past him, yelling at the creature and warding it off with spears.

It hissed its anger through its gaping, bloody jaws which displayed two sets of jagged teeth, still holding fragments of flesh and bone. With loud shouts and prods from their spears, the men held it off while Talon was assisted over the side of the ship.

"Tie him, he is my prisoner," he gasped, pointing at Akhom.

Akhom was seized, and despite his cries of pain, was securely bound before anyone bothered to pull out the arrow.

Talon stared back over the side at the men still holding back the hissing, jaw-snapping brute. Its tail lashing with anger, the crocodile was slowly driven away and must have decided that there were easier pickings elsewhere. It lumbered slowly back towards the papyrus and cane forest.

Talon slid down to sit on the deck, resting his head against the side of the ship with his eyes closed and gasping for breath, his arms hugging his knees. He felt a surge of relief at having escaped the jaws of the river monsters, but he shuddered involuntarily as he relived the ghastly death he had just witnessed. Max scrambled over the side nearby and hastened to Talon's side. "What happened, Suleiman, are you hurt? What in God's name happened out there?" Max asked as be bent over Talon.

Max was joined by Panhsj, who appeared groggy and had a rag tied around his head and another wide bandage across his bare chest.

"Panhsj, Allah be praised, you live!" Talon cried.

"Allah be praised indeed, Suleiman. I am alive despite their efforts to kill me." The big man gave a lopsided grin. Malek was calling and waving to them from their own ship. Talon noticed Khalidah standing beside him.

Both men helped him to his feet. "Come Panhsj, Max, I have to tell her. Where is Kazim?"

"He came over the side of the ship like a terrified monkey and ran into her cabin as though he was pursued by demons," Panhsj said. "He is down in the cabin."

"I am not surprised, Panhsj. You will have to comfort him. Those...those monsters ate Al Muntaqim, the man you know as Kemosiri, right before our very eyes."

Talon described the events that had taken place on the reed island.

Khalidah gasped with horror. The men wore shocked expressions.

"I did not know his proper name until just now, only the name others gave him. He was supposed to be a friend of the family, and still he betrayed you, my Lady," Talon said.

"It was Kemosiri? He it was who betrayed my husband? I am glad that Allah finally decided to punish him," she said in a cold voice. "It was him all along. He tried to dispossess my family and kill my son. This death was fitting."

"We must keep that man, Akhom, alive, Malek," Talon advised. "He is the only one who knows everything about a plot to kill the sultan. You can use him to clear my Lady of any suspicion."

"We will do so, Suleiman, have no fear. But we found a man in chains inside the cabin of Kemosiri's ship, my Lady. I do not know what to do about him. He claims to be a poet and an unjustly held prisoner."

Talon's ears pricked up. "A poet you say? What is his name?"

The man in question was being escorted out of the cabin and now stood in front of them.

"My Lady, sirs," said the poet Umarah ibn Ali al-Hakami, "Allah be praised for his mercy. Thank you for saving my life. That monster Kemosiri was going to kill me, I am sure of it."

Talon laughed.

# Chapter 29

# Farewell

The decision to turn around and moor at Beneade was made by Malek. They could not possibly continue down river in their present condition. His men were exhausted, there were many badly wounded among them who needed urgent attention, and the safety of the Fayoum beckoned.

He was also determined not to abandon their own damaged ship, as it would make a valuable asset if they could repair it. They could, albeit with much effort, haul the crippled ship back to the port and hope to carry out repairs. It was also important to place the prisoners in safe keeping under the watchful eyes of the men of the fort.

The remaining enemy galley from downstream had managed to put out the fire on board and had approached cautiously to observe the situation. When it became evident that their leader was defeated, it turned on its own length and fled downstream. Malek shrugged as he watched it disappear into the haze of the river.

"Let them go. We cannot catch them now," he said. "They will become pirates, and one day they will be brought to justice."

The men set about transferring as much cargo and wounded as possible to the captured ship, but they could not move the horses. They were in a pitiable state. Several were dead, many arrows protruding from their bodies, while others were wounded. They heaved the dead horses overboard. For a few very long minutes the men on the ships watched with horrified fascination at the gristly sight of the crocodiles savagely tearing at the carcasses in the shallow waters around the ships. The water turned red and frothed with blood.

The Franks worked to make a thick cable from whatever spare rope could be found which they linked between the ships. It was exhausting work and took a long time to complete, by which time it was late afternoon.

It was a battered pair of ships that finally made it to the pier of Beneade. A crowd of curious people were gathered to watch them arrive. Tired men jumped onto the wooden planks and made the ships fast. Then the laborious process of unloading the remaining horses and the wounded took place.

Once this exhausting task was completed, Malek went below to bring Khalidah on deck with Jasmine. They were joined by a very subdued Kazim.

Talon hoped the boy would get over the awful shock he had been subjected to. He himself was not sure how long the dreadful images would remain with him. He talked about it with Panhsj, who told him, "You might be surprised to hear, Suleiman, but when a child is as young as he, they often do better than older boys or men."

Talon had nodded. He understood better than Panhsj knew.

Khalidah looked back at the ship as she stepped onto the pier, then her eyes found him and she paused for a moment. She raised her hand in a small salute, a tired smile on her lips, before following Malek to the waiting horses. Talon told Malek that he and Max would stay with the ships for the time being and work with Henry to tidy up the ruin left behind from the battle.

"You will have enough to do at the estate without worrying about the ships, Malek. We will take care of everything, do not worry. Henry and Max know what they are doing."

Malek agreed. He wanted to have the family safely installed in their estate, if indeed it still existed, and as soon as he could. The ships were an added responsibility he was glad to hand over. Still, he looked at Talon for a long, speculative moment. "I will see you soon, my young friend. Look after things for me. Peace be with you."

"Peace be with you, Malek."

Promising to follow as soon as possible, Talon and Max watched them leave with the larger part of the soldiers as an escort. The poet went with them, bound and under the watchful eyes of two of Malek's best men. The man looked fearful and subdued; he knew his fate was close to being sealed. Kazim waved back at them as he rode proudly alongside Panhsj, who was keeping a sharp eye open for any hint of danger. They did not know how they would find the estate or what unwelcome guests might be there.

Talon, Max and Henry held a brief conference as they chewed on some bread and dried goat's meat, leftovers from the trip north, and tried to work out what they had to do.

"We now have two crews of rowers, one group free and one still slaves, but they are my people; I went below and had a look at them," Henry remarked as he chewed a mouthful of bread.

"You know, Suleiman, we could simply leave now and no one could stop us. They cannot sail the ship we came north in, it is dangerously full of water, even now. We could transfer our crew to the one we captured and leave."

"Talon will not do that to these people," Max said.

"You called him, Talon, I heard you, just now!" Henry said, surprised.

"Yes, he is called Talon, and he is a Frank like you and me, but while we are here he is Suleiman, Henry. We will explain one day." Max said in a low voice.

"No matter, Max," Talon said. "Henry, keep calling me Suleiman for the moment. It is better. You are right; we have an opportunity to leave and Malek knows this as well as we. But...I respect that man a great deal, and after all we have been through with him and his brother, I simply cannot leave, no matter how much I want to, and Max will tell you how much."

"Henry, before God, I see these people in a different light after what we have been through together. We owe it to Malek and the Lady to help them get to Al Qahirah and the safety of the Sultan's protection. Then we can leave. Isn't so, Talon?" Max said.

Talon nodded. "Lady Khalidah still has to present herself to the Sultan and explain her side of the story, Henry. We can help with that, so it is important that we see them safely to Al Qahirah.

"You both know about the poet and his involvement. He is our prisoner and will have to face torture and death. His testimony will exonerate the Lady Khalidah and ensure that her lands are not confiscated. Kazim will have his inheritance. I want that for the sake of Abbas, who was a good man...even if he did throw me and Max into prison." He gave a wry grin at the memory.

"Will that man, Malek, keep his word and allow us our freedom?" Henry asked nervously.

Max chuckled. "That is the main reason we must not desert them yet. Be sure of one thing, Henry, Malek will keep his word," he said, clapping Henry on his thin shoulders. "Now we must make the other ship clean, and release the men chained below. Henry, come with me, and you, Talon, take some rest. I don't think you are over that scare with the crocodiles yet." He gave a theatrical shudder. "My God, but that must have been horrible."

"He was a terrible man, but even he deserved a better death than that," Talon agreed, shaking his head.

Henry went across the deck to the other ship with Max and they disappeared down the hatch. The sound of shouts and cheers from the slaves who had been informed of their freedom came back to Talon as he stood on the aft deck of their ship watching the sun set behind the low hills that defined the Fayoum.

He was tired. The fighting and stress of the battle and the macabre death of the man who had haunted them for so long had left him drained. He had sustained superficial wounds in the fighting—his chain mail had deflected much of the effects of cutting weapons—but he felt bruised all over. He thought of the gentle hands of the girl Aicelina in his father's house, who had put soothing balm on his bruises after a terrible battle for survival. He wondered if he would ever have someone do this for him again.

They had to plan their next move. They were still not sure whether all their enemies were dead or captured. His thoughts went to the city of Al Qahirah and he began to wonder how they could slip by the sultan's ships and get out to sea. He needed to talk to Malek about that. There was no doubt that Malek would allow them to go, but they could not implicate him in the escape or Malek's head would fall. Talon ruminated on this as it was getting dark; he yawned and turned to go below to sleep: he felt he would sleep like the dead, oblivious of the bustle and movement on both ships that would go on deep into the night.

He was about to enter the cabin when he heard a voice calling from the pier. Men called out and a young voice responded, followed by the patter of running feet on the planks of the pier. The next moment a figure ran into the lamplight, his light turban waving behind him. Talon gasped, it was Haytham. Talon strode to the side of the ship and embraced the boy as he almost threw himself at him. They held onto each other in a tight embrace.

"I thought you were dead!" Talon said, stepping back and holding the laughing boy at arm's length.

"Peace be with you, Suleiman, but I thought you were all dead! Allah be praised, it is not so. I could not believe my eyes when I saw Malek and the lady Khalidah. They told me you were here!"

"Is all well at the estate?"

"All is well, which is why I am here. My Lady and the children are safe and my...my lord Malek bid me to tell you to come in the morning, he wishes to talk and plan."

Thoughts of sleep disappeared. Talon looked at Haytham with delight.

"There is much to tell on both sides, Haytham. We will drink tea and talk. I need to know that you reached the sultan."

"I did, Suleiman! I was almost dead and so was *Rakhsh*."

"Ah, *Rakhsh*, is he well?"

"He is well, and I have brought him to you, Suleiman. He is a wonderful animal." Haytham sounded so wistful that Talon laughed.

"Haytham, know this, he is yours."

Haytham gasped and stared at him as though he could not believe he had heard this.

Talon laughed again and said to the boy, "I give him to you, but...there is one condition."

"What...what is that, Suleiman?" the boy asked apprehensively.

"That you cherish him."

Tears ran down Haytham's cheeks. He reached for Talon's hand and whispered. "Suleiman, may Allah be kind to you. You *know* I love that horse. I have slept in his stables these long months while I did not know where you were."

Talon cleared his throat. "We must talk no more of it. You have to tell me about your adventures, and especially what the Sultan did once you told him of our troubles."

Max joined them later for a happy reunion and the three, fatigue temporarily forgotten, talked of all that had happened.

Talon was most interested in the time when Haytham had been asked to attend the sultan with the man called Al Muntaqim present. He made the boy describe the man very carefully and only then did he turn to Max and say, "It is one and the same man. It was Kemosiri, alias Al Muntaqim, now I am sure. I feel that my Lady is safe. Other than the poet, who will tell of the full plot, there is no one else we need to fear. For the sultan, that might be another matter."

Max sipped his tea and nodded. "This makes it easier for us to leave."

"You are leaving us, Suleiman?" Haytham asked.

"We have talked to Malek, and that is why, I suspect, he wants us to come and see him in the morning. We agreed that only when my Lady was safe, Max and I would leave," Talon said.

"But why? Who will lead the chogan team now? Bahir and my master are gone, may God be kind to their souls, and you are the only one left," Haytham said, his mouth turned down with his distress.

Max and Talon laughed. It seemed to be such an incongruous thing to discuss, given their recent perils, but Talon understood. The boy was desperate to return to a normal life after the disruption they had experienced.

"Haytham, you will lead the future teams on behalf of my lord Kazim, and one day he will assume the role; but you must be a good teacher so that he learns from the best," he said in a solemn tone.

"I shall not disgrace you, Suleiman, of that you can be sure," the boy said earnestly.

They went to bed with the night well advanced and the stars a blaze of light in the great black canopy above. The workers had gone to sleep in various parts of the ships, while sentries spoke to one another in low tones. Talon stumbled to bed and fell into an exhausted sleep.

*****

It took a week of hard work to repair the galley and make ready to sail south to the great city of Al Qahirah. Malek's plan was simple: they would sail in two ships; once there, the Lady Khalidah would be escorted to the palace of the Sultan for her audience by Malek, Panhsj and the soldiers. Talon, Max and the Franks, who had by now been released, would take one galley and 'escape' into the Middle Sea.

"I shall be sorry to see you and Max go, Suleiman," Malek told Talon one day as they were watching the repairs going on all around them. "You have helped us many times. I pray that Allah will guide you and that peace will go with you."

"I sometimes wonder what Allah has in mind for me, Malek. I will miss you, the children and the Lady Khalidah. She is a woman of great courage and determination. I too pray that Allah will protect her and allow my lord Kazim to become the master of his rightful domains," Talon responded.

Malek smiled at Talon's words, then said, business-like, "It should seem that you overpower my men and steal a ship. You should take all the Franks with you, otherwise I suspect that 'Enry will take them anyway, and I do not want a battle on the wharfs of Al Qahirah harbor."

Talon grinned at Malek. "You are a wise man, Malek. I shall miss your council. Perhaps we should ensure that we leave at night?"

"You need to know something. There is a city called Damietta along the river further north of Al Qahirah, almost at the entrance to the sea. It is the entrance to the main Nile channel from the Middle Sea and it is your only way out. Although there are other passages to the Middle Sea they are very treacherous, with sand banks and debris that come and go with the summer flood. This is the only stretch of river between Al Qahirah and the sea that is kept open at all times by sultan's order, for the sake of commerce. However, you must also deal with the chain."

"What chain is this, Malek?" Talon asked, his heart sinking.

"There the people of Damiate have placed a huge chain across the river where they have narrowed it. Those people exact a toll from ships coming into the river to go to Al Qahirah. The chain is also to prevent invader fleets from gaining access to the river. The

Frans tried to come up the river past Damiate some six years ago. The chain helped to contain them and the sultan defeated them. He decided to reinforce the towers so that now they are almost impregnable. You will need to use all your cunning to get by. I fear that it is raised at night to prevent pirates from sailing in under cover of darkness."

Talon thanked him and went off, deep in thought at yet another obstacle to their freedom. If they were caught they were right back where they had started more than a year ago. He didn't tell the other Franks what he had heard. That would have to come later. It was a daunting prospect to think they might still be trapped in Egypt, despite everything they had been through. This left him worried.

His contact with the Lady Khalidah and the children had lessened. He spent his time with Max and Henry to repair the crippled ship and prepare for their journey. He did not think it wise to tarry at the estate.

He was reluctant to go there more than he had to and knew it was from a sense of guilt. The temptation to stay and live out his life here in the Fayoum was strong. Images of the lake and the vast fields of crops and the quiet of the region haunted him. It would be a calm, pleasant life and he could probably be almost as a member of the family. The thought of pressing Max to depart with the Franks and leave him behind crossed his mind more than once.

Max and Henry at first attempted to draw him out of his thoughts, but then they left him to work it out. He had to face his future and there were hard choices to be made; it did not improve his mood.

The day they planned to sail finally dawned. Talon stood on the deck of the ship that would take Khalidah and the children north to Al Qahirah, while Max and Henry waited on the other ship. Almost before the sun had risen, Malek, with a strong escort of soldiers, brought Khalidah and the children with him to the harbor and they were helped on board.

They cast off and rowed into the middle of the great river followed by the second galley now being rowed by freed men. They soon hauled in the oars and set sail with a good wind behind them. It took all day for them to sail north, but by evening they saw the tall spires of the city mosques in the distance. As the miles shortened to their destination, the number of the sailing boats increased and soon the water appeared to have white crests on it from the traffic of the small boats plying to and fro.

Talon had been summoned to the cabin by Khalidah during the trip. Dreading the encounter, he slowly made his way towards the rear of the ship, nodded to Malek on the top deck, and entered the cabin, pushing aside the light curtains across the door.

Khalidah stood alone in the middle of the cabin, waiting. The boat rocked a little as it sped down the river but other than the slight creaking of the wood and the murmur of voices above, it was quiet.

"You asked to see me, my Lady?" Talon said with a low bow.

She lifted her head and stared at him.

"It is time and you must leave us?" It was more of a statement than a question.

"Yes...I must leave you, my Lady, but hear me first. This I have to tell you."

She nodded in silence, and he continued.

"The sultan is still in grave danger, both from the Assassins from the region north of the Fran Kingdom, where they are governed by the man known as Sinan Rashid Ed Din, and for all I know from the Master, the Agha Khan from Persia himself. The sultan must protect himself. These people seek his death."

"How do you know these things?" she asked.

"Because I am one of them."

She gasped and placed a hand on her heart. He made to step forward, afraid she might fall. "All this time? You are one of them?" She whispered, fear in her voice.

"I did not come as one, although Khaldun somehow knew what I am, even though I did not tell him. But now I have to tell you. I was captured by the assassins of Persia. I am what I am because of them, but now we are mortal enemies, at least with Sinan, because of what I have done to protect you."

She had been veiled when he came in but now she let her veil drop and he saw that her eyes were red rimmed and she looked exhausted. It was clear she had been crying.

"My Lady, what is it?" he asked with concern.

"Do you not understand what it is that ails me, Suleiman? I do not care what they made you. I care what you are now," she said. There was a tremor in her voice that cut to his soul.

"My Lady," he whispered. "It cannot be...it cannot be." He could not go on, his words caught in his throat.

She came into his arms then and he held her as though to crush her.

"Do you have to leave me? Do you not wish to live here? What will persuade you to stay?" She groaned into his shoulder.

There were tears in his eyes now. "You know how much I wish to stay! But you know too, I have to leave...I...I cannot stay for many reasons, but I leave a part of my heart with you, my Lady."

"You take all of my heart with you, Suleiman! It is so cruel that Allah should have done this to me just when I have regained most of what I thought I had lost. I mourn the loss of my husband, but I shall be lost when you leave."

"You have regained your honor and your family rights, my Lady. Your son, for whom you have fought, will one day be a great lord and you will find peace in that. I am a commoner and cannot take the place of your husband," he said, trying to keep the tremor out of his voice.

"I would that you could... Ah, Suleiman, what am I to do?" she whispered as tears flowed.

"We both know it cannot be," he said, "as it is one thing to be the tutor of your son but quite another to be your lover and his step-father. I cannot do that to him nor be the cause of the trouble that it would bring to you," Talon said into her hair. He breathed her clean scent and wondered what he was doing holding this beautiful, noble lady in his arms. He released her and stood back trying desperately to control his emotions. He needed to leave the cabin without giving away anything to those outside.

She too stood back and replaced her veil. It was a resigned gesture and seemed final.

"Then that is as Allah wishes it. I cannot stop what is ordained. I bid you farewell. Suleiman, please leave me now. I must prepare for my audience with the Sultan." She turned away as though a sleep walker.

Talon hesitated, but then collected himself and whispered, "I shall not forget you, my Lady. I pray Allah will protect you and your children for all time. Peace be with you, Khalidah."

"Peace be with you, Suleiman, and go with my love," she whispered as he left.

* * * * *

They docked in the bustling port of Al Qahirah just as the sun was beginning to set. The sultan, alerted of their late arrival, had offered to give Lady Khalidah hospitality and an audience the following morning. Malek was in a hurry to disembark, as they still had a mile or so to travel to the palace of the sultan and, as he told Talon, he did not want the added worry of trouble in the darkening streets of this crowded city full of cutthroats.

As the ship came closer to the piers they said their farewells, and Malek and Panhsj had tears in their eyes. They embraced Talon. He too felt strong emotions flood over him and he embraced them back equally hard.

"Allah protect you. Go in peace," they said to one another.

"We have been comrades in battle and we have won. Now we shall sorely miss you, my friend," Panhsj grunted. His face was twisted into a ferocious expression as he tried to control his emotions. Talon embraced him and slapped him on his back hard and tried to keep from weeping.

It was even worse to say good bye to the children, who both came running into Talon's arms. He stood holding them tight to him. They wept and begged him to stay. They did not know how he was to leave, simply that he would not be accompanying them to the city and this would be the last time they would see him.

He finally released them and gently wiped the tears from Jasmine's cheeks with his thumb.

"I go because I have no choice, my princess," he said softly. "Had I a choice, I would stay. Look after your mother and learn much, my Jasmine. I shall miss you."

She nodded in mute acknowledgement. "Allah go with you, Suleiman." She cried and ran back into the cabin to join her mother. Khalidah had not emerged.

Kazim stood in front of Talon, his feet planted apart, trying to hold back his tears and behave like a man. He was aware that Panhsj was nearby, although that man was staring into the distance pretending not to notice.

"I shall...I shall miss you, Suleiman. Will you write to me one day and tell me where you have gone?" he asked in a low voice.

Talon reached for the boy and held him close. "Indeed I shall do that, my Prince. Allah protect you and may he guide you in all things. Listen to Panhsj and Malek, for they are good men and will help you become a great lord, and always protect and respect your mother and your sister. Peace be with you."

"Peace be with you, and Allah protect, Suleiman," the boy said in a muffled voice.

*Wake! For the Sun behind yon Eastern height*
*Has chased the Session of the Stars from Night;*
*And, to the field of Heav'n ascending, strikes*
*The Sultan's Turret with a shaft of light.*
*— Omar Khayyam*

# Chapter 30

# Towers of Damietta

Talon was rowed across the water to the other galley where he was greeted by a somber Max. "It is often hard to say goodbye," he said briefly, pretending not to notice Talon's strained face as he helped him onto the deck. Talon nodded in mute agreement, then turned to Henry.

"Malek said we must wait until they have gone into town and then come close to their ship and take with us the Franks and other North men rowing for him. The black men will stay with Panhsj. Malek said he would find replacements for his rowers easily enough when he needs them."

"Of that I have no doubt," Max said in a dry tone. "There are slaves enough on the wharfs."

They watched as Khalidah and her party went to shore and disappeared into the warren of streets. Once it was dark, Henry called hushed orders to the rowers and eased their galley alongside the other. The three guards remaining on Malek's galley who had not been alerted to this maneuver watched curiously as the two ships bumped against one another. They did not suspect anything when Talon and Max came aboard with a few other men. They were overpowered without injury and placed in the rear cabin, trussed up and gagged. The men waiting below hurried up and clambered over the side onto the other ship. This was done quietly, with little notice. Even so, a curious official called over from the quayside asking if everything was alright, and what were they doing?

"We are transferring slaves," Talon called back. "Nothing to worry about. Go in peace."

"Peace be with you too," he replied and went on with his night vigil.

They pushed off into the darkness and silently rowed the galley back into the middle of the river. There was a light mist on the water that they found useful to disguise their passage past the great watch towers that guarded the city walls overlooking the river. No one called from the other galleys anchored in the harbor as they slipped past, nor were there alarms. They set sail and moved cautiously downstream.

Talon held a quiet conference with Henry and Max. There were two other men with them.

"This man is Guy," Henry said, indicating the larger form in the dark with his thumb, "and this is Nigel. They were with me when we were captured."

Talon and Max grunted greetings. It was time to tell them of the perilous run to come.

They were dismayed by the news. "Why did we not know of this before?" Henry exclaimed.

"Would it have made any difference?" Max asked, sounding mildly irritated. He slapped his thigh. "There are endless difficulties with this country," he growled to no one in particular.

"Malek told me of this to warn us. We are now fugitives again, and if those crew men get free, pursuit will be sooner rather than later. Our problem is to get past the towers and well out to sea before anyone knows we are running," Talon said.

"How far do we have to go before we come to this Damietta place?" Nigel asked.

"It is almost at the entrance of the great river and a good six hours sailing, perhaps more."

"Then we will be there in the dawn hours. That might be good. The sentries are always sleepy at that time and less alert," Guy said.

"Lord protect us, but we know neither the river features, nor what to expect around any corner. It could take us all night, so we might well be there in daylight. Is there no other route?" Henry asked. He slapped his arms around his chest in an agitated manner.

"Malek said the river was very dangerous along any other avenue, although there are many. If we get stuck on a sandbank in the dark, we are lost. He said we would be well advised to stay on the main river and try to slip through Damietta, rather than risk an alternative route. There are pirates in the side streams."

"We are more than a match for pirates with this many men on board," Guy said scornfully and waved his hand about at the crowded decks full of armed men.

"It is not the pirates we have to fear, Guy," Talon said patiently, "but the sultan's navy who also patrol these streams looking for the pirates. How do you think they would react if they came upon us stuck in the mud somewhere?" he demanded.

There was a long silence as the men considered this.

Henry sighed. "You have not led us amiss before, Suleiman or is it now Talon? We will do as you bid and try for the open sea through Damietta. God protect us. I had thought our troubles were behind us and we could just sail away."

"It is Talon de Gilles, and I had hoped for the same, Henry, but it is not to be. Yes, we must make haste, even in the dark. Time is not on our side."

The long ship glided silently downstream, close to the middle of the river. Lookouts in the bows on both sides called low warnings if they saw anything that looked like an obstacle. Most of these were other boats that were doing the same as they: driving down the middle of the river hoping to avoid sandbanks and other small islands that surfaced from the deep water. When they came too close to another boat they remained silent, even when others called across the water to them. Their size and deadly shape and the silence of the men aboard might have seemed menacing to others on the river that night, because the calls were few.

* * * * *

It was many hours later that Henry estimated they might be close to Damietta. "I can smell the salt. Even below decks I could always tell when we were coming to the sea," he claimed in a low voice.

"Then you would know the place, would you not, having passed it before?" Max asked without thinking.

"Max, none of us knows, because we were below decks and rowing for our lives. We did not see anything. I cannot help."

Max looked chastened. "By God, I am sorry, Henry, I did not think."

"No matter, but we must be careful now. We should not charge into a trap that might be awaiting us."

Henry stayed at the steering oar while Max and Talon went forward to join the lookouts at the bows of the fast moving vessel and stared into the darkness ahead. After about half an hour Max whispered, "I see a light in the distance, Talon."

They saw the light, but whether it was a beacon, or many lights, they could not tell at this distance. They glided forward, now drifting on the current of the river, as the sails had been furled on the orders of Henry. It became clear that they were about to reach a large port.

Henry, without being told, ordered the oars to be shipped out and the crew to row in reverse in order to slow the ship's passage downriver, until they knew what they might be facing. Talon and Max were still peering into the gloom at the lights, which seemed to come from not only the water level, but also from high above to either side of the river.

"There! There are the towers," Talon whispered. "Dear God, but they are huge. We must stop and find out how to get past them."

"How will we know if the chain you talked about is up or down?" Max asked.

"We might not know until too late, Max. We must stop before we are seen and plan what to do next, now that we can see the towers."

"Why don't we just sail down the middle of the river and break through the chain?" Guy asked as he came to join them.

"Malek told me that it was strong enough to stop a much larger ship than ours," Talon said. "We cannot afford to be stopped. We are a target for anything they might have to toss at us. Look, they have forced the river to narrow very much at this point so they can hit us with arrows, if they wish. It is only two hundred paces wide."

They all stared at the dark shapes of the towers, massive in the dim light.

"Then what do you suggest, Talon?" Max asked.

"Perhaps we can go over land and disable the system that hauls it up and down?"

"That sounds like madness," Max muttered. "But I do not have a better idea."

Henry had already reacted when he heard the relayed message from Talon. He ordered the ship to move closer to the shore where he ordered the anchor dropped; it fell noiselessly into the swiftly moving water.

"I wish I could use an anchor at our rear but we do not have one," He told Talon as the ship turned on its rope and snubbed against its line, facing back up the way it had come.

There was a small boat in the waist of the ship that was heaved over the side and dropped into the water. Talon climbed down into it, followed by Guy and Nigel, who had volunteered to join him. Max had wanted to come along too, but Talon told him, "I need you here to keep an eye on things for me. Henry will be fine, but if something happens to me, I want you to have a chance to get back to Jerusalem. Stay alert. We will surely be in a hurry when the time comes to leave."

Max agreed reluctantly. He had wanted Talon to take a small force of men with him, but Talon told him that silence was what he needed, not a lot of men getting lost in the dark and fighting with shadows. Max waved them off as they rowed out. It was not as dark as it had been a half an hour earlier. They made good progress down river, hugging the flat, reed-filled banks on their way towards the tall towers. Talon looked apprehensively at the dark shoreline, remembering the crocodiles lurking on the sands. He prayed that none of them lived here, or if they did that they were not hungry enough to want to attack a small boat. He did hear a splash and he shivered. The images of the last incident were still vivid in his mind.

The tower on their side of the river became more distinct in the dim light. It was illuminated by many lamps on two main levels. The enormous structure was both wide and tall and gave the appearance of being a single wide tower about thirty feet tall and almost as wide, with another tower on top, of a smaller diameter, that was about twenty feet tall. The whole construction loomed high, even though they were some distance away. Both towers dominated the entire area of the port at the narrowest part of the river.

Guy held them close to the bank, ready to pull in at a moment's notice. They were in deep shadows, well shielded from the tower, but it worried Talon that there was so much light at the top. He saw what seemed to be wooden frames perched on the very top and one situated on the lower tower. It was difficult to make out what they were, but he suspected they were catapults.

Talon knew that if someone discovered them and challenged them they had no recourse but to pull out into the middle of the river and take their chances. On shore they would be easily taken. He whispered to Guy, "Pull in there. I think I see a small inlet that will hide us when we get out."

Guy dipped his oars in deep and pulled hard the last few yards for the shoreline. They slipped silently into the reeds and grounded in the mud. Talon had his hand on Nigel's shoulder.

"Wait; look for anything long and dark. I do not want to step into the jaws of a crocodile," he whispered.

Nigel nodded in silence. No sound greeted them, other than the incessant croaking of frogs and the light soughing of the wind that rustled the reeds. They peered into the darkness trying to sense danger of any kind. Talon's eyes had adjusted to the dark and he could see the lighter color of a narrow trail leading onto the main bank. He hefted his bow and, taking a deep, silent breath, stepped gingerly into the ankle deep water and moved forward to stand on dry land. He stood listening for a long moment, and then motioned Nigel to join him. Guy, as formerly agreed, stayed with the boat.

It was time to go. Moving quietly and with every sense alert, they breasted the bank and found themselves on a pathway. It was a track that ran along the top of a causeway and linked to the mainland further east. Glancing about, Talon remembered what Malek had said, that the river had been deliberately narrowed at this point to facilitate the cable and the guard towers.

The tower was only a hundred yards away, and despite the illumination of several flaming torches, it was eerily quiet. Talon and Nigel moved slowly along the causeway, keeping within the shadows cast by the canes and tall papyrus growing along the banks, looking for any sign of activity, but they could see none.

Coming closer, still keeping to the dark shadows, Talon's attention was drawn to a shape protruding from the tower's wall at about the height of three men. He realized that he was looking at a huge cable that he assumed might be supporting the chain. He peered out at the river and noticed small crests of turbulence that followed a line across the water towards the other tower. The chain was there, just beneath the surface.

They were now within twenty yards of the silent tower and still no alarm. He stared hard up at the battlements to see if there was anyone who might see them, but it seemed deserted. He decided that they needed to get right under the walls so that the casual observer would not see them if he glanced outwards.

Indicating the wall of the tower, Talon pointed and then led the way, feeling horribly exposed from above. They made the rough stone walls in a silent rush, and then paused to listen. Other than the monotonous singing of the frogs and the light rustle of the cane there was no other sound to cause them alarm.

Talon's nose twitched; there was an unpleasant smell emanating from the tower. It was rancid and pungent. Nigel theatrically held his nose as he looked at Talon. It was time to investigate. Indicating that Nigel should keep his distance but to follow him, Talon slipped like a shadow around to the water side of the tower and stopped. There was a man sitting on the bank night-fishing.

Talon faded into a darker patch of shadow against the wall motionless for some long moments. Nigel too vanished into a dark shadow. The man seemed totally oblivious of their presence, even whistling tunelessly as he held his rod over the water and waited for a fish to take his bait. Praying that Nigel would stay where he was, Talon slid forward until he was just behind the man, who must have sensed something because he began to turn his head. He never knew what had been there.

Easing the unconscious man down onto his back Talon dragged the body into deep shadow. As he looked up at the huge frame that supported the cable, Nigel joined him. He could see that he would have to climb onto this if he wanted to cut the cable that was almost as thick as his waist. He wondered how many strokes it would take to cut it with a sword. It might have to be both of them at the same time, and for sure the alarm would be raised.

He looked down at the unconscious man. Perhaps they could get into the tower and work the mechanism. How had the man come out? Then he noticed the small doorway set deep in the wall. Gaining entrance was easy, the door was unlocked, and opened with only a slight creak from its hinges.

Talon eased himself into the semi-darkness of the tower, half expecting to bump into someone on the other side, but there was no one. Nigel slipped in behind him and stopped to stare upwards. Talon decided that the men on guard were bored with their duty and had become lax. There were several oil lamps in niches in the stone walls half way up the wooden stairs that led to a trap in the ceiling above. It provided enough light to show him the complicated array of wood levers, huge barrels, and cogs that he assumed were part of the hauling machinery.

He tried to understand how it worked and then saw what appeared to be a massive wedge that locked everything into place. The huge coil of the cable lay like an enormous snake on the floor nearby. Where it exited through a wide slit in the wall of the tower it was held taut by a solid barrel of wood resembling a turning mechanism. This was locked in place. There was an enormous wheel that the cable was wrapped around, and some of it lay on the floor in untidy coils. He realized the rancid smell was the stink of animal grease from the mechanism that hauled the chain up and down.

Talon could see that it was a clever device. It would only take a few men to turn the winch system and bring a massive chain up from the river bed to stop a fleeing ship. One end even fed out the back of the tower to some unknown destination which he assumed might be for horses to haul upon should they be needed.

Glancing up to see if there was any activity above, Talon motioned Nigel to come with him and climbed the stairs until they were on a small platform that ran alongside the cable winch. The cable was pinched at this point between two great rollers which were locked into place. It seemed that he might be able to release the cable fairly easily, but how to make sure the men above could not get it back up before their ship made it through the gap?

He looked around trying to decide what to do. Nigel must have thought about fire at the same time, because he pointed silently at the rubbish on the floor below. There was much wood in the space around the base of the structure and some bundles of rags and other rubbish. There were even large barrels of the noisome smelling grease against the curve of the wall. The guards were not too particular about their place of duty, it seemed. The place was full of old bits of rubbish and even animal bones were discarded on the floor.

They hastened to pile as much as they could on the steps above them that led to the mechanism and then Talon retrieved the oil lamps. He made sure he had two places for fire, one on the steps and the other right under the greasy wood structure where flame would have a good chance of catching. He wanted enough time to elapse, allowing for their return and for his ship to sail through. After that it did not matter.

The last lamp was ready to go out by this time and Nigel was almost unable to light his fires, but then the flames took and soon a merry blaze started in two places. It was time to see if he had understood what needed to be done to release the cable. Talon pulled hard on one huge lever to see what would happen.

The events that followed took him by surprise. The action lifted a huge pawl of wood and wedged it in place. There was a whipping sound and then the shriek of spinning wood as the weight of the huge chain outside asserted itself. Both men ducked in fright as the cable whipped out of the opening towards the river. It was only because they had shrunk into a crevice in the thick wall of the tower that the writhing cable did not decapitate both men on its way past. As it was, it smashed part of the stairway before everything crashed to a halt.

The silence was stunning for a couple of moments before they heard panicked shouts from above and the smoke of the fires made them aware that they were also in danger. Clearly this was not the right way to release the cable, but it had proved effective enough.

Talon and Nigel jumped the last couple of steps to the floor just as the hatchway above opened and men yelled down at the lower tower. They shouted in panic at the sight of the flames, which had now taken hold in earnest on the steps. They were hesitant to come down in the face of the roaring fire. Talon loosed a couple of arrows directly up at the gap and was rewarded with a yell of surprise and pain and the hatch was slammed down.

It was time to leave. They ran out of the building and pounded off down the track towards the rowing boat without looking back. More shouts ensued, as men, now wide awake and peering downwards, noticed them running away. Several arrows thumped into the mud to hasten their departure but neither was hit. They arrived breathless at the reed-filled bank to find the boat waiting and piled into it in an untidy heap. "Row!" Nigel croaked.

"What happened? I heard a big noise and then a huge splash; the whole cable seemed to fall into the water," Guy asked them. They sat gasping for air while Guy pulled hard on the oars.

"It is a wondrous mechanical device which can be easily moved. A marvelous thing I have never seen the like of before. But now we should have a little time before they can repair it," Talon said, grinning. He was panting with the excitement and the short sprint.

Nigel seized one of the oars from Guy, joining him on the bench, and they rowed furiously back towards the ship. It took well over half an hour to do so, every minute begrudged by Talon who exhorted them to pull harder. He imagined the men in the tower braving the flames to haul the chain back up from the bottom of the river.

Soon the ship appeared and they scrambled aboard, abandoning the row boat to the river. Henry had already ordered the anchor to be hauled in. Their ship turned slowly in the current until it was facing downstream and then, with shouts and calls, the sails were raised and they manned the oars. The ship gave a jerk that they felt along its entire frame and then began to race downstream. Talon noted with apprehension that dawn was arriving fast and they would be easily seen from the towers.

"Row for your lives, or we will not see the Holy Land!" Henry bellowed.

"How did you do it, Talon?" he demanded. "We heard nothing, nothing at all until something ripped the air and we heard a huge splash in the distance."

Max grinned at Talon and slapped him on the back. "We have to get past the towers before the explanations. Look, we are almost there."

Indeed their course was bringing them to the point where they would soon be between the great towers that were now very close. Looking to the right everyone exclaimed. Even in this uncertain light they could see in the tower. Smoke poured out of its openings. By now the alarm had been raised on the other tower, where men were running about and pointing at the ship that sped towards the narrow gap.

A few arrows fell into the water, but not close enough to harm anyone. There was wild cheering from the men on deck, followed by shouts and yells from those still rowing below as they realized that they were through and might at last be free of danger and imprisonment. Max and Henry were pounding Talon on the back and laughing with excitement.

They all heard a distant thump from the far tower. Seconds later a huge column of water appeared twenty yards behind them. There was another muffled thump from the other side of the river and another column of water rose high into the air on the starboard side. They stared at the spouts in astonishment and then alarm.

"Dear God, but they are hurling stones at us!" Max yelled. "Pull for your lives! We are far from being out of danger yet."

They stared towards the distant tower that had suddenly become a menace. They heard again a thump in the distance and this time saw a huge stone flying through the air towards them. This one was well aimed. It crashed into the ship just forward of the afterdeck and scoured its way in a spray of flying splinters across the planks to smash out the other side. The whole ship shuddered and rocked before continuing on its way. Two men had disappeared in a welter of blood and splinters and two more were left shrieking in agony, their limbs shattered.

A stunned Talon picked himself off the deck where he had been thrown by the impact of the stone and found himself gaping at the utter destruction the stone had wrought. Men were scrambling to their feet looking dazed, but the screams of the wounded made them turn to the urgency at hand and attend to them. Another stone struck between the masts. This one crashed through the planks of the deck to plunge into the rower's deck, leaving a gaping, jagged hole near the starboard side of the ship. If it had struck more to the center, it would have sunk them.

The ship heeled to the right at the blow and men were thrown against one another on the deck. Shrieks of agony and fear that chilled his blood came from below deck. Talon forced himself to run down to the main deck and then down the hatchway to the oar deck.

What greeted him there stopped him in his tracks. In the darkness of the deck where the rock had struck there was carnage. The missile had wrought devastation among the rowers. Men were scrambling about, trying to get the dead moved and the oars replaced. Wounded were lying nearby with limbs missing and their lifeblood pumping out, or lying inert, their bodies crushed by the passage of the rock.

His stomach went tight. "My God, but we cannot take much of this! They will sink us with these missiles," he said, and as though to emphasize his thoughts there was another huge crash and the deck above caved in. He ducked and dove to his left onto the laps of two rowers, but this time the deck held. The ship rolled over from the shock then rocked back to center. Talon peered up at the deck, but although the planks were cracked and broken inwards the stone had not come through. The rock had bounced off the stout deck and then gone through the railings to splash into the sea. There were men scattered all over the place where they had been thrown by the shock of the missile.

He heard Henry roar at the crew to tighten the sails and then another roar from Guy from his bench as he encouraged the other rowers to keep working. Men heaved, gasping for air, their teeth bared with the effort and sweat pouring off them in the closed area of the oar deck. There was panic in their eyes as they realized that they were far from safely out of danger.

Talon scrambled to his feet. The screams of the wounded reverberated in his head. Someone brought a lamp and accompanied Talon as he made his way to the area where the first rock had entered. It was still wedged against the side of the hull where it had come to rest. It was about four times the size of a man's head, almost round and covered in gore. After staring at it for a second he pulled himself together and helped get the four wounded men laid out on the central walkway where he concentrated on binding their wounds with rags to stop the bleeding.

Men moaned as they were roughly manhandled by their comrades. They had to be moved out of the way to be treated. The two dead men were left where they were until they could be dealt with. Max peered down through the hole, his eyes searching. "We are out of danger for the moment; their missiles are falling well short now, God be praised. Talon where are you? Are you there?"

"I am here Max, what is going on up there?"

"We are safely past the towers, thank the Lord. We must sail out to sea a few miles yet. Then we will know for sure that we are out of their reach."

No one had any breath to cheer. The horror of the stones had been a sobering experience.

Talon returned above deck to be greeted by a relieved Max and Henry. He stared at the damage to the deck and the sides.

"The Good Lord be praised, we were very lucky, Talon," Henry said. "If the other tower had been working all its catapults, we would have had a worse time of it."

"I wondered what those frames were on the top," Talon remarked. "Now I know. Thank God we got clear. Those stones make terrible missiles."

"Now you can tell us all, how you managed to get the chain dropped. God be praised, we are heading for the Holy Land," Max said, sounding very relieved.

An hour later the swell of the sea greeted the galley and it began to pitch. Small waves slapped the bows and sent up a light spray that wet their faces. Henry ordered the rowers to stop. They had a good wind behind them. They sped out of the delta, meeting the sun coming up over the eastern horizon. The water changed from muddy brown to light blue and then deep green. It was time to look after their wounded and to say prayers for the dead and for their deliverance.

Talon's memories of the last time he had been to sea came back in a rush and he began to feel slightly queasy as the ship began to rise and fall with a mild twisting motion as they moved into the swell of the Mediterranean. He looked back at the low coastline with mixed feelings as he stood in the waist of the ship.

# Chapter 31

# Acre

That morning, Salah Ed Din, Sultan of all Egypt, and now Yemen, was seated upon the throne he disliked so much, observing the person who was standing in front of him with keen interest. Khalidah, richly dressed and well veiled, had come to her feet at his command and stood with Kazim and Jasmine next to her, awaiting his pleasure.

"You are well met, my Lady Khalidah," Salah Ed Din said. "Welcome to my palace. I have often thought of you and the tragic circumstances that befell you. My sorrow is as yours over the loss of your fine husband, Abbas. We grieved at his injury in the chogan match and we were devastated to hear of his death later. I have searched far and wide for you to find out how to help, but you had disappeared from the earth."

"The people who destroyed my husband are now dead, my lord. I fled because you were not here in Al Qahirah for me to appeal to for protection and I feared for my life and that of my children if we remained. Now I seek only to prove my innocence from any false charges brought against me by those same men," Khalidah said boldly. She lifted her head and looked straight at the Sultan, who gazed back at her in surprise.

"I have been made aware of some accusations, my Lady, but there appear to be no witnesses to substantiate them. At this time, I do not think they are valid."

"My lord, although they were false, the accusations were still made. If it pleases you, I have a person who can explain not only the murder of my husband but also the plot to kill you."

There was a gasp from those nearest to the sultan and he himself stared at her in surprise.

Khalidah turned and motioned Malek and Panhsj to come forward. They advanced towards the throne, dragging another man between them. The two men went on one knee before the sultan, but they hung onto the arms of their trembling prisoner, whom they dragged down with them.

"Umarah ibn Ali, al-Hakami, it is you?" The sultan said; his tone was incredulous.

"My lord I ..." he got no further.

With icy scorn in her tone Khalidah interrupted him. "You can be sure, my lord, that this groveling filth will confess to everything. His leader, Kemosiri ibn Jibade, who hatched the plot, died in the jaws of a crocodile. A fitting death, I think, for the foul play started against my husband at the game of chogan. Not having achieved their treacherous aim they murdered him in his own bed."

"Murdered? So that is what happened? I remember there was a man who took care of your husband on the field and then sent the messenger to me while I was in the desert. What was his name again?"

"His name was Suleiman, my lord, and he did save me and my children. Had it not been for that man and my loyal servants here with me, these people would have destroyed us completely. This is the last "witness" that I know about, other than Akhom, who is now in one of your dungeons." She gestured to the prostrate poet.

"What has happened to this...Suleiman? I would thank him," said the Sultan.

"My lord, he is gone, back to where he came from, but I confess that I do not know where that is. He is not from our country, my lord. However, before he left he asked me to pass a message of warning to you."

The sultan's eyes narrowed at this apparent effrontery. He did not like being threatened by anyone. "A warning. How so?"

"My lord, it is not as you think, but it is in earnest and for your own safety. He told me that the Assassins are part of the plot that was meant to dispose of you and might still be. He said that you should know that those who work for Sinan Rashid Ed Din, the school's teacher, have not finished and will try again to harm you."

In the dead silence that ensued the men around the sultan closed in on him as though to protect him.

"How could he know this?" Salah Ed Din demanded after some long moments, while he scrutinized her face.

"Because he told me he was trained in Persia by these same people and he knows them well."

She glanced at Malek and Panhsj still kneeling nearby. They were gaping up at her in astonishment.

"I have heard from my people that he stole a ship of mine and has disappeared," Khalidah said with a deliberate look at Malek and Panhsj.

"He did what?" the sultan exclaimed.

But Khalidah said, "He is not your enemy, nor is he mine, my lord, because he helped me in every way by destroying my...and your enemies, including Lord Bahir, who was also complicit. My lord, he said you must take steps to protect yourself, but he cannot help you or my family further. I am therefore here to throw myself and my children upon your kindness and mercy." Khalidah knelt again before the sultan.

"Then this is the same man who broke through the chain at Damietta at dawn this morning with a galley, it was yours!

"The sky between Damietta and Al Qahirah was filled with messenger pigeons today. The commander of the towers sent a flock of them, he was so agitated, telling of a galley full of hundreds of pirates that attacked one of his towers, killing many of his guards, then cut through the chain and escaped into the Middle Sea. This man is bold indeed, but I shall just have to investigate the facts for myself."

Khalidah said nothing, although she seriously doubted the story. Malek and Panhsj looked their disbelief ,which amused her. They, like she, suspected an entirely different version.

The sultan stood up and then stepped down from the throne to stand in front of her. His head was turned to the poet and, with narrowed eyes, "Take this...thing out of my sight and record everything he confesses," he snapped at the vizier nearby, pointing to the poet, who began to whimper and tremble.

The vizier gestured to guards and they rushed to do his bidding, ignoring the cries and pleas of the poet, whose wails stopped abruptly as he was hauled out of the room. The sultan turned his attention back to Khalidah, who still knelt before him. He held out his hand to her.

"Please rise, my Lady. As Allah is my witness, you are under my protection henceforth. Your husband's estates and property are yours and your son will grow up under my protection, to become the Lord of all his father once held. This I promise."

* * * * *

The tired and ragged men on the fleeing galley were jolted out of their sense of relief when a lookout posted on the forward mast shouted that he could see ships exiting the estuary behind them. Talon ran up the steps to join Henry and Max as they stared back to where they had left the river mouth. His heart beat faster. The unmistakable triangular sails of two war ships were visible racing out of the delta in hot pursuit.

The seaman in Henry took over. "Man the oars! We are being chased! Everyone to an oar!" he roared.

"We have a three day sail to Acre, and with God's help and a following wind we can stay ahead of them," he said to Talon and Max, trying to sound confident, but he looked nervous.

Initially the two ships appeared to be gaining on them, so that they could soon see the oars rising and falling rapidly and small figures on their decks.

Max looked at Henry with apprehension on his face. "They have sent their hounds after us, Henry. Can we outrun them?"

"They only have one sail each, and while they might be smaller and lighter we have two and our oars, and a longer hull. The wind is good, right behind us. With God's help we will lose them. I shall maintain this course, but tonight I shall turn north east," Henry said.

Talon watched the sleek, deadly hulls of their pursuers racing after them. Their sharp bows drove through the waves, sending spray high off to either side. They reminded Talon of hounds who have the scent of their prey in their noses and would follow relentlessly.

"We might be able to fight them off, but it would be far better if we can just outrun them," he said to Max, who nodded, his expression grim.

Henry began to shout orders to tighten the sails and exhorted the men below to row for their lives, as they were not free yet. The rowers needed little persuasion; the tempo of the oars increased rapidly and their ship surged forward.

The minutes stretched into long hours as all that day Henry kept their ship well ahead of the following galleys. He relieved the men below at regular intervals, having almost two full crews, which made a great difference, and gradually the distance between them and their pursuers lengthened. The men below rowed until some of them collapsed from exhaustion and then others took their places.

The men on the upper deck stood watching the distant ships, tense with anxiety. As darkness fell, Henry calmly continued on his course until it was nearly midnight, then he ordered the steersmen to shift to a northeasterly course. Despite their exhaustion no one could sleep, and they all prayed he would be successful in eluding their pursuers.

The next morning, tired and red-eyed men examined the western horizon from end to end but could not find the other ships that had dogged them all through the first day. They were gone. The weary rowers slept at their oars, too tired to find other places to rest.

"You lost them, Henry, God be praised," Max said with relief.

Two days later, a lookout on the forward mast head shouted that he could see land. The galley had a good wind behind and drove its sharp prow through a choppy sea. It sent occasional sprays of water high into the air to wet the faces of the eager men on deck. Henry, who had demonstrated his seamanship to perfection, peered forward from his position near to the steersmen.

"This might be the land just to the south of Acre. We are nearly there, praise be to God."

The battered ship had weathered the seas well. Two of the wounded had died, but Talon was trying to keep the others alive until they could be taken ashore and given into the dubious care of the Christian physicians.

Several hours later they could see land from the deck and Henry turned the ship to sail northward, keeping parallel with the distant coastline. Before long he steered them closer to the land, and they saw clusters of buildings surrounded by a great wall that marked a city of some substance. Sailing out of the heavily fortified harbor opening was a galley, not unlike theirs, but with only one sail. It headed straight for them. The men cheered wildly at the sight of it and were still waving or praying on their knees when the speedy galley drew to within a hundred paces of them, tacked about almost within its own length and began to sail parallel with them. A man clad in chain mail with the unmistakable red cross of the Templars embroidered on the left side of his surcoat climbed into the rigging of the ship and waved at them.

"Who are you and where from?" he shouted.

Max looked at Talon and asked, "Shall I answer them, Talon?"

Talon nodded agreement. Max leaned out from the side of the ship and shouted.

"Max Bauersdorf, Sergeant of Templars, with released prisoners from Egypt. Guide us in to port."

The official on the other boat gave a surprised exclamation. He waved to them as dozens of the ragged men on this strange ship waved and shouted joyfully back at him. He stepped down from the side and his ship and sped ahead to escort them into the bustling port of Acre.

Men were openly sobbing as they stared at the longed-for Holy Land which had been denied them for so long. Talon leaned on the rail next to Max. He contemplated in silence the place he had left bound in chains over two long years ago.

* * * * *

In a city called Isfahan, many weeks ride away to the East, a rider dismounted and handed his lathered horse off to a syce who ran up to take the reins. He walked slowly, with a very slight limp, into the wide gardens of a fine house, heading for a particular

402

place in the garden where he knew he would find the person he was seeking.

"Peace be with you, my dear friend. I am glad you are back."

"God protect you, Khanom."

"You must take refreshment and then we can talk. What is the news from the North?"

"There is no news but...there is something."

"Tell me before you go what is this...something?"

"Everyone is talking about an incident in Egypt, months ago now, where there was a plot against the Sultan Salah Ed Din that was thwarted. The people who belong to Sinan say there is a man named Suleiman, but who looks like a Frans. They say he is very skilled in our arts and not only killed most of them who were involved in the conspiracy, but then stole a ship full of Frans and sailed away; they know not to where. Our people in Persia laugh, because Sinan is not liked by them and he is very angry at being thwarted, but they laugh behind their hands when they say it. It is a great mystery."

The woman put her hand to her mouth, her gray eyes wide with surprise in a lovely face that had gone a little pale. "Reza, please do not tease me!"

"I would never tease you, my Lady Rav'an, at least not about this." His teeth gleamed white in his dark face as he smiled. "It is surely strange news and it is being spoken about by everyone in the North."

"Do you think that ...perhaps it might be?"

"God alone knows. I cannot be sure, my Lady. It is curious nonetheless; I too am wondering."

"We must tell Fariba! Come and join us when you have bathed and are refreshed. There seems to be much to talk about."


# The End

# About the Author
—
## James Boschert

James Boschert grew up in the then colony of Malaya in the early fifties. He learned first hand about terrorism while there as the Communist insurgency was in full swing. His school was burnt down and the family, while traveling, narrowly survived an ambush, saved by a Gurkha patrol, which drove off the insurgents.

He went on to join the British army serving in remote places like Borneo and Oman. Later he spent five years in Iran before the revolution, where he played polo with the Iranian Army, developed a passion for the remote Assassin castles found in the high mountains to the north, and learned to understand and speak the Farsi language.

Escaping Iran during the revolution, he went on to become an engineer and now lives in Arizona on a small ranch with his family and animals.

# ASSASSINS OF ALAMUT
## BY
## JAMES BOSCHERT

*An Epic Novel of Persia and Palestine in the Time of the Crusades*

*The Assassins of Alamut* is a riveting tale, painted on the vast canvas of life in Palestine and Persia during the 12th century.

On one hand, it's a tale of the crusades—as told from the Islamic side—where Shi'a and Sunni are as intent on killing Ismaili Muslims as crusaders. In self-defense, the Ismailis develop an elite band of highly trained killers called Hashshashin whose missions are launched from their mountain fortress of Alamut.

But it's also the story of a French boy, Talon, captured and forced into the alien world of the assassins. Forbidden love for a princess is intertwined with sinister plots and self-sacrifice, as the hero and his two companions discover treachery and then attempt to evade the ruthless assassins of Alamut who are sent to hunt them down.

It's a sweeping saga that takes you over vast snow-covered mountains, through the frozen wastes of the winter plateau, and into the fabulous cites of Hamadan, Isfahan, and the Kingdom of Jerusalem.

"A brilliant first novel, worthy of Bernard Cornwell at his best."—Tom Grundner

PENMORE PRESS
www.penmorepress.com

Historical fiction and nonfiction
Paperback available for order on line
and as Ebook with all major distributers

# GREEK FIRE
## BY
## JAMES BOSCHERT

In the fourth book of Talon, James Boschert delivers fast-paced adventures, packed with violent confrontations and intrepid heroes up against hard odds.

Imprisoned for brawling in Acre, a coastal city in the Kingdom of Jerusalem, Talon and his longtime friend Max are freed by an old mentor from the Order of the Templars and offered a new mission in the fabled city of Constantinople. There Talon makes new friendships, but winning the Emperor's favor obligates him to follow Manuel to war in a willful expedition to free Byzantine lands from the Seljuk Turks. And beneath the pageantry of the great city, seditious plans are being fomented by disaffected aristocrats who have made a reckless deal to sell the one weapon the Byzantine Empire has to defend itself, *Greek fire*, to an implacable enemy bent upon the Empire's destruction.

Talon and Max find themselves sailing into perilous battles, and in the labyrinthine back streets of Constantinople Talon must outwit his own kind - assassins - in the pay of a treacherous alliance.

PENMORE PRESS
www.penmorepress.com

Historical fiction and nonfiction
Paperback available for order on line
and as Ebook with all major distributers

# A Falcon Flies

by

## James Boschert

Talon has returned to Acre, the Crusader port, a rich man after more than a yea
in Byzantium. But riches bring enemies, and Talon's past is about to catch u
with him: accusations of witchcraft have followed him from Languedo
Everything is changed, however, when Talon travels to a small fort with Sir Gu
de Veres, his Templar mentor, and learns stunning news about Rav'an.

Before he can act, the kingdom of Baldwin IV is threatened by none other tha
the Sultan of Egypt, Salah Ed Din, who is bringing a vast army through Sinai t
retake Jerusalem from the Christians. Talon must take part in the ferocious batt
at Montgisard before he can set out to rejoin Rav'an and honor his promise mad
six years ago.

The 'Assassins of Rashid Ed Din, the 'Old Man of the Mountain', have targete
Talon for death for obstructed their plans once too often. He is forced to take
circuitous route through the loneliest reaches of the southern deserts on his wa
to Persia to avoid them, but even so he faces betrayal, imprisonment, and th
threat of execution.

His sole objective is to find Rav'an, but she is not where he had expected her t
be.

**PENMORE PRESS**
www.penmorepress.com

Historical fiction and nonfiction
Paperback available for order on line
and as Ebook with all major distributers

# Force 12 in German Bight

by

## James Boschert

Considering that oil and gas have been flowing from under the North Sea for the best part of half a century, it is perhaps surprising that more writers have not taken the uncompromising conditions that are experienced in this area – which extends from the north of Scotland to the coasts of Norway and Germany – for the setting of a novel. James Boschert's latest redresses the balance.

The book takes its title from the name of an area regularly referred to in the legendary BBC Shipping Forecast and one which experiences some of the worst weather conditions around the British Isles. It is a fast-paced story which smacks of authenticity in every line. A world of hard men, hard liquor, hard drugs and cold-blooded murder. The reality of the setting and the characters, ex-military men from both sides of the Atlantic, crooked wheeler-dealers, and Danish detectives, male and female, are all in on the action.

This is not story telling akin to a latter day Bulldog Drummond, or even a James Bond, but simply a snortingly good yarn which will jangle the nerve ends, fill your nose with the smell of salt and diesel oil, your ears with the deafening sound of machinery aboard a monster pipe-dredging ship and, above all, make you remember never to underestimate the power of the sea.

'Roger Paine, former Commander, Royal Navy'.

PENMORE PRESS
www.penmorepress.com

Historical fiction and nonfiction
Paperback available for order on line
and as Ebook with all major distributers